# SISTERS OF THE RESISTANCE

JINA BACARR

Boldwood

First published in Great Britain in 2024 by Boldwood Books Ltd.



Cover Design by Colin Thomas

Cover Photography: Colin Thomas and Alamy



A CIP catalogue record for this book is available from the British Library.

Paperback ISBN 978-1-83751-521-9

Large Print ISBN 978-1-83751-520-2

Hardback ISBN 978-1-83751-519-6

Ebook ISBN 978-1-83751-522-6

Kindle ISBN 978-1-83751-523-3

Audio CD ISBN 978-1-83751-514-1

MP3 CD ISBN 978-1-83751-515-8

Digital audio download ISBN 978-1-83751-516-5

Boldwood Books Ltd
23 Bowerdean Street
London SW6 3TN
www.boldwoodbooks.com

*To every woman who has suffered at the hands of an invader.*
*We prayed it would never happen again.*
*But it did...*

# INTRODUCTION

When I set out to write about two sisters faced with the horror of sexual assault during wartime, I wasn't sure how readers would react. Would the story be off-putting? Too real? Not real enough? I breathed a sigh of relief when you wrote in your reviews about the impact the story had on you, that it was a story that needed to be told. The feedback I received was amazing.

Thank you to all of you who wanted a sequel to *Sisters at War*. I pick up the story of the Beaufort Sisters in wartime Paris where we left off, at the Hôtel Drouot auction house on May 8, 1942. Don't worry if you're unfamiliar with the story; I've sprinkled in backstory so you can jump right in. I've also enhanced the reunion scene with the two sisters that appears at the end of *Sisters at War*.

Again, I must add a word of caution.

In this novel, *Sisters of the Resistance*, I have written a story some readers may find disturbing, a story of sexual assault against women, mostly ignored by history but more timely than ever. I pray you will come along with me as we continue on our journey.

You're in for a bumpy ride.

Jina Bacarr, 2024

# PROLOGUE

## PARIS, MAY 8, 1942

*Ève*

It's rather odd what I remember about that hot August day less than two years ago, when I witnessed my sister Justine being assaulted by an SS officer. Major Saxe-Müllenheim. I record his name here so you may remember it because when this war is over, I swear he will pay for what he did to her. *I swear it.*

For now, I carry on, working with the Resistance, committing acts of sabotage against the Nazis that this twenty-year-old girl never dreamed she was capable of... Sneaking into railyards and setting fuses, blowing up locomotives, writing political tracts and printing leaflets to rally protests against the occupiers, and begging others to join the fight.

But on that summer afternoon there was no resistance, no printed words of defiance against the invaders. Just a busy bee buzzing in my ear while I gathered herbs in the garden for my science experiments, the subtle scent of sweet basil tickling my nose. Humming, I fussed with the pink velvet ribbon Justine had given me to tie back my long hair, while my brain barely registered the sound of black hobnailed boots stomping on the polished floor, like a drumroll announcing what was to come.

The SS major grabbed me first and threatened to assault me before my brave Justine came to my rescue, her blue eyes blazing and her spirit on fire. But coward that I am, I didn't fight hard enough to save my sister when he took her instead.

Which is why every day I relive the horror of that afternoon, when I retreat into the purple shadows here in the library at Maison des Ombres Bleues. The House of Blue Shadows. The *grand maison* is named for the deep blue shadows that flood the library every day at twilight like a pool of mystical magic.

My refuge.

We, Justine and I, call it Maison Bleue, a three-story mansion. *Très* French in its décor, but with a swash of Imperial Russia apparent in its appointments, thanks to its mistress, Madame Ekaterina de Giocomte, a woman with exquisite taste and a flair for the dramatic, all accompanied by the chirps of her two lovebirds in a golden cage.

Like dining on a cloud from another time.

Ever since I was a little girl, I've gone to the library to think, let its shadows wrap me in an invisible cloak where I could dream, be whatever I wanted to be. I was a girl so innocent then, my heart filled with sentiment, and I'd smile over how Justine loved to tease me about my obsession with counting the petals on a daisy, my mind as hungry as the soil to absorb knowledge…

'Someday you'll find your prince, Ève.'

'It's not a prince I'm wishing for, dear sister. I'm thinking how fragile life is, like a daisy, that it can lose its petals to a brisk wind or under the heel of a shoe smashing it to the ground.'

'What are you talking about?' she asked, curious.

'How fate plays a role in our lives.'

'Fate? Surely we can steer our own destiny.'

'Can we, Justine?' I'd raise a brow, pull off a petal. 'Who knows?'

I didn't find out how right I was until the war came and the Nazi major invaded our home, intent on looting precious works of art. He'd walked in through the front portal without knocking as if he were the master of the house.

*Damn Nazi had no right*, I'd said, but that didn't stop him from poking his nose into the library. Tossing admiring grunts at the art hanging on the walls. Asking me questions.

'Jews live here, *n'est-ce pas*?'

How had he known?

'Monsieur and Madame de Giocomte. Yes?'

I'd nodded. 'I work for Monsieur and Madame,' I'd told him. 'French philanthropists and members of the elite Parisian bourgeoisie.'

'So you're not Jewish?'

'No.'

He'd taken a step closer, as if noticing me for the first time. His direct gaze gave me goose bumps, like when a certain biology professor at school had asked me to stay after class to explain my experiment: growing mold on a Petri dish. He'd spent the entire time putting his hand on my knee, not listening to a word I'd said.

I suspected—in that moment—that this SS officer possessed the same dirty mind.

He'd continued. '*Gut*. I shall commandeer the paintings of the de Giocomtes for safekeeping... In the name of the Reich, of course.'

*Really?* I'd looked at this invader, disbelieving. He was lying, had to be. I couldn't believe the Nazis would have the nerve to steal these magnificent works of art from the de Giocomtes. I had no idea then that Himmler had stuck his woodpecker's beak into the Paris art world. Later I discovered that he had ordered the SS to loot art. At the time all I knew was that the invasion of Maison Bleue by this SS major was an insult to the de Giocomtes... and what did being Jewish have to do with *anything*?

I didn't know then that being Jewish was *everything*.

The Führer himself had given the SS the power to confiscate Jewish property, and that included these exquisite paintings at Maison Bleue.

I'd stood there, indignant and unwilling to accept that fact, thinking he couldn't be serious about his threat. 'The de Giocomtes are influential and prominent members of the French Jewish community and are not to be trifled with,' I'd said. I was of the mind they'd have his rank knocked down for his arrogance. In my naiveté, I believed they had that much power, not only because of their financial holdings, but also their elite ranking in the Paris art world as avid collectors of works with a noble provenance. Again, life under the Occupation hadn't sunk in yet. There would be no comeuppance for this SS officer's outrageous behavior. I soon discovered in this new Nazi world order, no one dared to say 'no'.

And that included me.

I should have kept my mouth shut and ignored the German staring at the walls of art, pacing up and down the library, nodding his approval like a royal minister, except one who wore a double lightning bolt insignia on his uniform. Even then, I'd sensed here was a man obsessed with what he couldn't have, his hunger to possess beautiful things for the sheer hedonistic pleasure. And like all Nazis, the major considered himself superior to anyone and took what he wanted without asking. I'd jerked my head around when I heard the pounding of more boots on the Italian marble floor. More German soldiers; in fact, a two-man crew, going in and out quickly, carrying the artwork out to the waiting truck covered with a tarpaulin.

Or was there another reason?

Yes. He'd wanted the paintings for himself. When I'd protested the art theft, he'd then grabbed me, *touched* me. His black-gloved hands knowing no boundaries. With his Aryan smugness, he slammed me up against the library wall, rubbing his chest against my breasts, and pushed against my thin print dress. It was ugly. Degrading.

*Why me?*

I'm plain, I'd thought. The girl nobody notices. The girl lost in her books and science experiments at the Sorbonne laboratories, back when they were still open. Not feminine and curvy like my sister Justine.

I never expected this Nazi monster to invade our home and claim *me* along with the de Giocomtes' art collection. Including the painting of Justine and me, officially known as *The Beaufort Sisters*, but to us—always *The Daisy Sisters*, because the avant-garde female artist had painted us awash in bright yellow daisies. A poster-sized painting that made me feel warm inside every time I gazed at it hanging on the satin-embossed wall at Maison Bleue.

I'd smelled my own ripe fear rising from my sweaty armpits when I defied the SS officer. He mumbled I too was a spoil of war and his for the taking, along with the art hanging on the walls of the *grande maison*. The house is a glorious place near Rue Monceau, on a street so tiny it has no name. A beautiful garden and greenhouse provide outdoor calm and serenity, but inside the mansion beats the heart of Maison Bleue. The character of the home hung on those walls, glorious Old Masters and flamboyant, lovely Impressionists. I swear the house wailed and moaned when the major ordered the German soldiers to rip down the paintings and confiscate the artwork collected for years by Monsieur and Madame de Giocomte.

*Who could stop them?* We were alone in the house. The de Giocomtes had left for Deauville, the servants gone... Cook and the two maids, Lucie and Albertine. Maman had been at work upstairs on her sewing machine. She's a seamstress for Madame and adores her. No one was there to prevent the Boche major from carrying out his nefarious deed.

No one... but me.

I'd stood my ground, refusing to cower before him, but that hadn't stopped him. He had no qualms about groping me with his black-gloved fingers, the fine leather crackling when he ran his hand over the bare skin between my thighs.

I'd squeezed my eyes tight. Bit down on my lip. I knew what he intended. Wanted. I just couldn't form the word on my lips.

*Rape.*

*No. I won't give in to him,* I'd thought. *I'll fight him... Kick him. Whatever vile thing he tries to do to me, he'll get no crying, no pleading from me—*

But I hadn't counted on my sister Justine jumping into the scene... defending me.

*'Let her go, monsieur,' she cried out.*

*The major laughed. 'Who are you?'*

*Her hand to her throat, her eyes wide, Justine stepped forward. 'I repeat, monsieur,' she said, gritting her teeth. 'Take your hands off my sister.'*

*'Your sister?' His voice deepened, his interest piqued.*

*'Yes. She's impulsive and didn't mean to offend you.'*

*'I'll let her go,' he gloated, 'if you trade places with her.'*

*'Monsieur!' Shocked, she clutched the doll she was holding to her chest, a nineteenth-century lady doll she used to design Madame's gowns.*

*'It's your choice, mademoiselle. I intend to have one of you.' He looked from Justine to me. 'Or both.'*

*Justine raised her chin, her steel-blue eyes defiant. 'You wouldn't dare, monsieur.'*

*'Wouldn't I?'*

I'll never get that scene out of my head when the SS officer grabbed Justine. It haunts me. To think that for her courage, my wonderful sister was kidnapped. Her dress in tatters.

Her pride stripped away. Her virginity shattered like a lovely, painted vase.

*A vase that can only be broken once.*

The arrogant Nazi tore the doll from her hand and smashed it to the floor. Its open glass eyes staring at me, accusing me.

*It should have been you, Ève.*

Yes, it *should* have been me. *Not Justine.*

Golden, honey-blonde, my sister was a living, breathing symbol of Parisian womanhood, her femininity so appealing to the debauched Nazi, he groaned out loud when he saw her. Panting like a tiger hot for a mate, the SS officer pushed me aside like a day-old croissant, then went after Justine. He couldn't leave her alone, his hunger so acute to taste the forbidden fruit of his conquest, running his hands up and down her slender body while she'd flinched and I'd watched, helpless.

Justine had yelled for me to '*Run, go!*'

I'd shrieked. '*No!*'

I couldn't leave her. I had to do something, but what? My plea to stop meant nothing to the Nazi. He'd have no one but her.

Justine had held her silence, pushing back against the SS major when he'd ripped her dress open down the front, then fondled her breasts. And he didn't stop. The horror on her face was like watching a beautiful Jumeau doll set on fire... then melt before me into a puddle of humiliation.

He'd laughed, the raw lust in his eyes forewarning what he had in store for her. Justine then looked over at me, her eyes begging me not to do anything that would get us and Maman shot.

Without missing a beat, he'd then forced Justine into his Mercedes touring motorcar with the tiny swastika flag flying on the hood, the vehicle scattering gravel as it sped away down the private driveway, taking my sister, shivering and trying to keep her torn dress closed, the Nazi snorting and panting with delight, congratulating himself. He'd scored not only the paintings from the wealthy Jewish family, but the beautiful blonde as well.

*Justine. Taken.*

I never saw her again.

* * *

Now back in the library, I shake my head in denial still. How could he have taken her from me? From Maman. From Maison Bleue, the home we'd known since we were little girls. I can't say how I survived that day, but I did. I went on to university and focused on my studies. I was a first-year student at the Sorbonne and as content as a bluebird flying free when my nose was in a Petri dish. Then the Nazis poked their noses into our lives and closed the school, so I joined an Underground network to fight the Boches. But I knew deep down in my heart I'd never let go of the mystery of what happened to my sister. I did everything in my power to bring her home. I reported Justine missing and the sexual assault to the French police. They ignored me, insisting an SS officer would never commit such an act. *She's dead*, they'd told me, then tossed my inquiry into a dustbin.

Afterward, I grieved for her, cried for her, and blamed myself for what happened when the heel of the black hobnail boot crushed my world.

Those memories remain still, stuck in the back of my mind like a ghostly hum that never stopped. Reminding me, taunting me.

I tried to push them deep down in my soul to assuage my guilt though, and instead vowed to go on, keeping her memory safe and warm in a special place in my heart.

Until today at Hôtel Drouot.

When my dead sister came out of the shadows.

Very much alive.

And working for the Boches.

# 1

## PARIS, MAY 8, 1942

*Ève*

For two years, *two years*, confusion and outrage had swirled in my brain, believing the sister I adored had died at the hands of the SS. Sexually assaulted before my eyes. Kidnapped. Then she disappeared. Until this woman shows up at the Hôtel Drouot insisting she's my sister Justine. Peering through a thin blue veil, she looks smug and indignant when she corners me in the main auction house in Paris.

Wearing an outrageous hat.

It's dramatic, shaped like a blue oyster with a choker of pearls dangling from the high crown, with a long veil shimmering with shiny sequins trailing down her back. Her hair is dyed platinum blonde, and she reeks of 'collabo', in a teal silk suit woven as fine as mist. Her eyes sparkling but cold. Blue ice.

*Mais oui*, it *is* Justine.

I can't believe it. My sister so elegant and clever, moving with grace among the crowd of greedy art patrons and stiff Nazi officers, smiling in her most charming manner and cloaked with a supreme confidence, like her feet aren't touching the ground. As if she belongs here. With *them... Les Boches.*

It's obvious, *n'est-ce pas*? Justine sold her soul to the Nazis.

I can't believe she aligned herself with the enemy for a new hat. No fear, no embarrassment... Just a coolness about her that made me think she was carved from smooth white marble while I burn inside. Yes, I speak with anger and pain laced with dark humor. But shock does that to you, turns your cold grief into a hot ball of fire. Makes you fight back against this new truth because the old truth was something you'd learned to live with. To accept.

Not this chic Nazi collaborator.

I know I'm judging her by her stylish clothes and that over-the-top hat, but you must understand I can't even mend my worn-out shoes because the Germans shipped all the leather back to the *Vaterland.*

I go numb. Seeing Justine involved in God-only-knows-what dirty Nazi business is a kick to my heart, and if I don't find some ridiculous notion like that hat... *something* I can grab on to to explain her shameless behavior, I shall go mad.

How in the name of our dearest *maman* did it come to this?

This insane afternoon at the Hôtel Drouot came about when I saw the notice in the *Gazette* that the stolen painting, *The Beaufort Sisters,* was up for viewing this afternoon. The painting, along with others looted from the de Giocomtes' private collection, isn't going on the auction block today, but it is scheduled to be shipped to Nice for an upcoming special auction at the Hôtel Savoy.

I was so anxious to see it again, I didn't care if I have to put up with snooty art dealers and a maddening melee of bargain hunters eager to get in on the 'deals'. I can't remember a day when I didn't look at that painting and give thanks for our *maman*'s ingenuity when we were little girls to find us a home with Madame de Giocomte. The elegant woman thinks of us as the granddaughters she never had, her kindness giving us a wonderful life in a fashionable district of Paris.

I'd often stare at the beautiful painting of Justine and me, back when we were young girls filled with romance and dreams. I was fourteen in 1936 when I'd sat for the famous female artist with my sister, then sixteen. She depicted us in masterful brush-strokes wrapped up in a field of daisies. Brilliant yellows and silky-white petals so lifelike, you'd swear you could smell the scent of fresh flowers and feel the breeze amongst the swaying stalks, blowing onto your cheeks.

I'm here to steal back *The Daisy Sisters.*

Which is why I'm armed with a Luger I'd taken off a Nazi guard when I'd blown up a German depot with a homemade bomb some weeks before. My specialty. I can put together a fuse and a charge, dynamite and a stick of phosphorus and set the Nazis flying on their backsides in record time. I've become quite the saboteur since the war began and I'm proud of it. I put my studies in chemistry to good use, lying on my belly in the dirt setting up an explosive on a railroad track. I swear I can reach up to the sky where freedom still shines and grab a burning star to set off the fuse.

I'm damn good at what I do.

And I've never been caught.

I don't intend to get caught today, so I'd hidden the pistol in my jacket pocket and plopped Maman's old black hat with its droopy feather on my head to look respectable. No one would guess I'm armed. The Luger might come in handy if I have to bluff my way out of a dangerous situation. I've never handled a German-made gun before. All we resisters usually have are old weapons left over from the Great War, ones that Michal secured from a pawnshop on Rue Saint-Jacques. He never said where he got the bullets, but I suspect the shop is a front for another Resistance cell.

Ah, yes, Michal.

I take a moment to ponder my girlish fascination with this man.

My female urges swell into a rolling wave when I think about him. A man I barely understand, though I want to badly. *Polish guerrilla fighter*, he says. But I know there's more to his story. He's too knowledgeable about Nazi strategy in warfare to be a regular soldier, and how he handles himself in hand-to-hand combat shows a man of experience. His ability to lead, give commands. And his overwhelming charm. Suave, tough, and smart. A man I've fallen for against my will. Whenever he looks at me, brushes up against my arm, or grabs my hand when we run for our lives from a German patrol, I don't want to let him go. He makes me laugh when I want to cry... And he has made me cry when he's thrown himself into danger to protect me. I protest that I can take care of myself, but it's so wonderful to have a man like him in my life, even if he doesn't see me as a woman with feelings and needs.

I'm his partner and we share everything—the risks, the responsibilities—everything... except a bed. Nothing more.

I have tried to keep it that way, have fought against my attraction to him. Not least because I've always thought of myself as not being good-looking enough to attract a man who drips masculinity, a man brave enough to escape from the Nazis in war-torn Warsaw, a man whose heart and soul is committed to freedom. Why would such a man want to crawl into bed with a tall, lanky girl with dynamite powder smudged on her face? But Michal has got under my skin, in the most marvelous way, with his wit and courage... and how he looks at me. With respect. And every once in a while, the war ceases to exist, when his eyes light up with a sparkle I feel is just for me, when I let down my waist-length hair and I feel pretty, *really* pretty. Of course, Michal would never approve of my crazy scheme to steal back the painting of Justine and me. He'd tell me it was too risky. I wouldn't have listened to him. How could I? He'd never understand the insatiable need I have to get back something from my old life *before* the war, something to make me feel normal again.

My plan was simple: blend in with the crowd and then hide and wait for closing time so I can take back what the Nazis took from us. Remove it from the frame, roll it up and stash it in my empty satchel. It should have worked. It *would* have worked but—

The dream shattered when Justine showed up.

I'm still reeling from seeing her dolled-up like she stepped out of La Mode, though most Parisians can't even get a decent pair of shoes. The Hôtel Drouot is the *last* place I expected to find my sister milling around with art patrons and anxious investors wrapped up in greed and desperation. It made me nauseous to see the bidders clutching their programs and circling like vultures, intent on buying up *objets d'art* looted from French Jews. How can she live with herself? It makes me sick to my stomach. The auction house smells of ripe Gallic sweat and Nazi arrogance, an unlikely duo coming together under one roof, loud and outbidding each other.

Justine must have *known* I'd show up to see the painting along with the art stolen from the de Giocomtes.

The painting meant the world to me because it was all I thought I had left of my sister.

Now I'm not so sure it matters. I'd taken a seat in Hall 1 on the first floor when Justine caught my eye. I barely recognized her. I thought I was seeing things. I blamed it on too many missions working with Michal sabotaging Nazi trains going east, my brain rattled by loud explosions, my nostrils filled with the smell of chemicals and dust.

But no, the ghost of my sister is real.

I studied this woman I'd thought dead, staring at me, anxious, wetting her lips, alternating with her looking at me with coy glances then at the Gestapo man in the black trench coat sitting in the corner working a crossword puzzle, his head down. He looked familiar. *Am I crazy?* I'd thought. I swear I saw him at the American Hospital of Paris with a blonde when I rushed Michal there after he was shot by a German patrol. I thought then the woman resembled my sister; now I *know* it was her.

Next, she sets the stage, why she tricked me into showing up here today.

The question is, *do I take the bait?*

Justine makes a bid of 70,000 francs for a Corot painting expected to fetch nearly a million francs, waits for a higher bid, then floats towards the exit of the hall, like she caught the tail of a breeze.

*What's her game?*

The Justine I have seen today is no longer that young idealist I knew, a portrait of sweet maidenhood. She's changed. Her eyes are piercing, her lips redder and fuller, her confidence snooty and self-absorbed, as if she swallowed a magic potion that turned her into an evil queen. She's working for the Boches, otherwise she'd have come home to Maison Bleue, *n'est-ce pas*?

She turns as she leaves and smiles at me, her big blue eyes bidding me to follow her.

*Follow her?* I hesitate.

I suspect a trap, but I can't help myself; the temptation to speak to her, hear her voice, ask her *why* she betrayed France, betrayed *me*, is too great. A glance at her rear view reveals her shapely curves, sexy, her elegant figure no doubt pleasing to the Nazi hierarchy. I shake my head. I can't understand *why* she'd collaborate with the Nazis after that SS major sexually assaulted her.

Every day I tell myself it should have been me.

I can't let her get away without an explanation. How can I resist? Heart pounding, I race after her, my mind confused. I can't understand how, *why*, she let me think she was dead. Swaying her hips, she lures me to the dingy, low-ceilinged basement of the five-story art auction house. I hear her precious voice, for the first time in two years, but she's boasting that while *I'm* groveling for food with a ration card, *she's* designing hats for German wives in a fancy milliner's shop on Rue de Rivoli. The House of Péroline.

*Hats?*

It turns my stomach. Fawning over the enemy, while Frenchwomen starve. Then she has the nerve to make fun of *my* hat.

Maman's hat.

Droopy and sad, its gray-blue feather poking me in the eye, the poor thing is all tuckered out from bucking the fierce Teutonic winds blowing through the city. Frazzled and done. Like me. My heart tugs when Justine criticizes the battered black *chapeau* sitting atop my head. She *knows* it was Maman's and how much it means to me because she was wearing that hat the day we first met Madame de Giocomte, which made it more hurtful—that she'd denigrate our dearest mother like she was a troublesome servant.

I stutter, my emotions so intense I feel lightheaded. Dealing with Justine's betrayal is a shock that has me knotted up so tight inside I can't let go of the pistol clutched in my hand, my fingers numb, cramped. I lost all feeling in my body seeing her strutting like a smug Nazi princess, every wonderful memory we had as sisters growing up at Maison Bleue flashing before me. Two little girls dipping their fingers into Cook's soft confectionary sugar when her back was turned and licking them clean, then munching on almond cream-filled croissants crunchy with pecans so sweet our teeth hurt. Our every whisper and giggle, intimate as only sisters can be.

What happened to *us*? Our hopes, our dreams. *Our sisterly bond?*

God, I ache down to my bones, all the worry and pain and grieving I've done over losing Justine popping like a blister when she steps back into my world like this. My attention is no longer on her silly hat. I purse my lips and look her straight in the eye. Her pretty face glows with a mannequin-like sheen on her pink skin like she's not real. I wonder for a moment if she is... for she makes no move to come closer.

*Is she happy to see me? Will she hug me?*

*Kiss me on each cheek?*

No.

My sister declares war on me.

# 2

## PARIS, MAY 8, 1942

*Ève*

*The basement of the Hôtel Drouot*

'You must leave Paris, Ève, for your own good.'

I stand rooted to the spot like a duck with its big, webbed feet stuck in the mud, listening to Justine's open declaration of war. War between *us*. Her pouty expression clearly stating there isn't room in the city for *two* Beaufort Sisters.

*Non? Let the battle begin.*

'You know I'd never leave Maman and *she*'d never leave Madame de Giocomte.' I lift my chin. 'The two of them are still grieving.'

Justine rolls her eyes. 'Over what? Did Maman run out of wool for her dear POWs?'

Our *maman* hasn't stopped knitting socks for French POWs since the Armistice.

'No,' I say flatly. 'It's Monsieur de Giocomte. He's—he's not with us anymore.'

For a moment, I see fear splash in her eyes, turning them a

dark blue, then it's gone. 'What are you talking about? Monsieur was in excellent health.'

'Don't pretend you don't know.'

'Know what?' Her eyelids flutter. *Is she acting?*

'The French police arrested Monsieur de Giocomte last December, along with seven hundred other Jewish men and deported him on a train east.' My shoulders slump, deep worry for this good man making it difficult for me to finish. 'We have no idea where he is, if he's even still alive.'

'That's *impossible*,' she says in a huff. 'Damn! The major *promised* me the de Giocomtes would be safe. Not that I care. They *are* Jewish. But I don't want to see Maman living on the pavements and coming to me for handouts.'

'The major is a liar,' I shoot back.

She doesn't answer me. By her silence, she agrees. Which gives me a chance to make my plea to get her back.

'He *raped* you, Justine. What spell has he cast over you?'

'You wouldn't understand. You don't see anything else besides your silly experiments.'

I groan. *Another insult.*

'*Please*, I beg you, join us and we'll fight the Boches side by side. Sisters belong together.'

'I can't, Ève. It's—it's too dangerous. For me... for you.' She adjusts her veil. 'Even if you *are* my sister, I can't keep protecting you if you insist on participating in insurrection against the Reich.'

*What?* Strange words I never thought I'd hear from my own sister.

'I don't understand you, Justine,' I admit. 'Why do you stay with that German pig?'

Her eyes widen. 'I'd watch your tongue, Ève. The major is a

distinguished SS officer. With everything he's done for me, I have no choice.'

'We *all* have a choice, dear sister.'

Again silence, then: 'I don't, nor do I wish one. Besides'—she grins big—'I rather enjoy the privileges that go along with being the major's girl. New leather shoes, a pretty apartment, lunch at the Ritz.' She smacks her lips. 'They serve the most delicious steak tartare.'

*Damn*, she's frustrating me. Justine doesn't like raw beef. I'm done. I can't hold in how I feel, no matter how awful it sounds. 'You're a coward, Justine, letting Maman and me believe you were dead when all along you've been cavorting with the Boches.'

'I call it acceptance. I do what I must to survive, Ève, and you'd be wise to do the same.' Her tone is harsh, pushy. This isn't the sister I know. 'Now, *go!* Or I won't be responsible for what happens to you. Or Maman. Is that clear?'

*Did she really say that?*

I stand there, my mouth open, still holding on to that damn satchel even if my plan is foiled. I oozed with frustration a moment ago, but it's nothing compared to the sinking feeling that sucks the energy out of me. When I'm around Justine, I feel ordinary because she's so pretty and I'm not, and, well, I can live with that, but she never made me feel unwanted. And that breaks me into a million pieces. My big feet feel like they're stuck in quicksand and it's pulling me down. The sad part is, I don't try to free myself. Why bother? I've just lost the happiest part of my life and the ending to this story hurts me.

Then Justine goes on a rant, insisting I should *thank* her for warning me to leave Paris. 'I'm taking a great chance, Ève, arranging this meeting.'

I take in a slow breath. 'Why bother if you're going to humiliate me?'

She pushes the veil behind her ear, but she won't look at me. 'Because, dear sister, you're an embarrassment to me and it has to stop. *Now*.'

*Prissy, isn't she?*

'Oh, and you sleeping with the enemy *isn't* an embarrassment?' I shoot back.

She works her jaw and takes a moment before she blurts out, '*Mon Dieu*, Ève, don't you know what you're doing with your silly student demonstrations? Hanging out with radicals and Communists. Your stupidity put you on a Gestapo list.'

'Oh, God… How can you be sure?'

'Herr Geller, the Gestapo man you saw working the crossword puzzle, told me.'

*So she knows I'm working with the Underground. How?*

I have to think. Fast. *Deny everything*, I hear Michal telling me. As if he's done this before. How did he escape from the Nazis? Is that why he's so seasoned? His advice works for now, then what? Somehow, Justine unraveled my secret life with the Resistance and hit me hard with her accusation like cotton threads snapped when pulled taut. Who told her? Have we a traitor in our network?

'Our *maman* is also on the list,' she adds with a smirk, to shock me.

I freeze. Maman on a Gestapo list? She *is* joking?

She isn't. She repeats it to me, her voice so cold and devoid of emotion, her face frozen with a perpetual smile you know isn't real. Like when the Nazis pretend to be your 'friend'. Justine doesn't even *try* to be my sister. She's mean, stuffy, and smug.

Seeing what she's become, I hang my head in shame then lower my eyes so she can't see the wetness on my cheeks. With those words, she erases me from her life as easily as ripping off a satin hatband. Our close sisterly bond torn apart with each sharp word she hisses at me through her teeth.

But there's something else, I can feel it as only a sister can. Festering so deep in her heart her cheeks flame from keeping it in. Something she's desperate to share, but can't. I know my sister, know the signs when she's biting at the bit. A soft tear smearing the rouge on her cheek. A look of longing at Maman's hat. A tenderness in her voice she can't hide.

Justine is keeping a secret.

What? Why? What could mean so much to her that she wouldn't risk coming home to Maison Bleue, to Maman, to Madame de Giocomte? I can't accept that she'd stay with a man so cruel, so heartless.

Unless...

Oh...

Did she—

When I look at her closer, I see her breasts are fuller, her cheeks high with deep circles visible under her eyes. But she also appears wiser, like she observes the world through a different lens, where her life no longer revolves around silken threads cut on the bias, but something so precious she's willing to risk everything.

*Why didn't I see it before? What kind of sister am I?*

*Justine has a child.*

She doesn't say it, but the softness in her eyes, the catch in her voice, the haunting breath that escapes her lips tell me what I need to know. The birth of her baby is a cord she can't ever cut. No matter her feelings for him, it ties her to the Nazi bastard who raped her. Perhaps he convinced her that *his* sin makes *her* a collaborator. It's not true, of course. But I know my sister. Justine was only ever a creator, a weaver of dreams, always in color, not black and white, because she sees life in bold reds, calming blues, and sensational yellows.

Which means she'll do *anything* to keep her world and her baby's from turning beetle-green—the color of Nazi uniforms—even if it means staying with the major, in spite of his monstrous act. To keep her child safe.

I let go with a lonely sigh. I understand. Well, almost.

My mouth droops and I can't will my lips into a smile. The guilt overwhelming me keeps me silent while I process the ache growing inside me. My heart weeps for *le bébé*, I'm filled with concern for her and her child. How can I blame Justine?

*What would I have done?*

I'm afraid to answer that so I don't. For now, I wish I could cradle my niece or nephew in my arms and comfort them, let them know they have family who loves them. For how could I blame an innocent child for the mother's sin of collaboration?

Even if she *is* my sister.

Justine stares at me, says nothing, but I've never seen such frustration in her at keeping quiet. I know I'm right about the child. My sister was never very good at keeping anything from me. Doesn't she trust me to keep her secret? That hurts the most. No, I can't let her go. I convince myself I can save her. I take a step to reach out to her.

'Justine, *please*, listen to me—'

Her eyes narrow. 'I have to go. *Adieu*, my little sister.'

'No, *you can't*, I won't let you.'

'You can't stop me, Ève.'

'No?' I slide my hand into my jacket pocket and wrap the cold metal of the German service revolver in my palm. *She can't show up and then run off without an explanation.* Hint there's more going on with her than she's willing to share. *I won't let her*. I owe it to Maman, to Madame de Giocomte who took us in and gave us a home. I was eight and Justine was ten and we lived in the slums in the north of Paris with Maman after Papa met the wrong end of a dagger in a street fight. I can't live with seeing their hearts broken if they find out Justine is a collaborator. They never need know, if I can just change her mind and bring her home.

'You're not leaving, Justine.'

Before I can grasp the consequences of my foolish action, I draw the pistol from my pocket, my finger tightening on the trigger, hoping to scare some sense into my sister. I'd never hurt her, and why I've done that—a moment of panic, I imagine—I don't know. As if a stolen Luger is the answer.

'You haven't got the guts to shoot me, Ève.'

'Don't I?' comes my choking response. 'You're a collaborator, Justine, and—'

*They shoot traitors* races through my mind, but I can't say it out loud.

My hand shakes with a sharp fear I never expected, that I hold such power in that hand. I've never fired a pistol before, never had to, and now I'm pointing it at my sister?

Am I crazy?

'It's over, Ève. That silly part of our girlhood, *The Daisy Sisters,* is no more. A dream, a fantasy... gone. *Poof!*' She mimics pulling apart a make-believe flower with her gloved fingers. Her eyes narrow, destroying my girlhood memory when she'd listen to my meanderings and didn't make fun of me. 'And what's a daisy without its petals?'

Swishing her veil over her shoulder, she turns on her heel and walks away, but not before she looks over her shoulder, pouts her lips and sways her body in an arrogant manner before she pushes a pile of old dishes off a nearby table. *Crash!* Flying off the table, landing on the basement floor so hard, the dishes explode into pieces, sending a cloud of white, chalky dust into the air.

Choking, I drop the satchel and go after her but I don't get far. The silly feather from Maman's hat keeps getting into my face. Then I hear a scuffle somewhere up ahead. Justine? Did someone attack her? Where is she? There's no light in the basement corridor.

*Damn*, I can't see clearly.

I lurch forward in my platform heels, banging my knee against an old armoire and stumbling over the pile of dishes broken into so many pieces I trip over my own feet and stupidly squeeze the trigger and—

The burst of gunfire shatters what's left of the dishes, sending shards flying everywhere and knocking the breath out of me. The kickback lands me on my backside. I fired one shot into the darkness.

*One shot.*

*Did I hurt her?*

No... Maybe... I didn't hear her cry out... Oh, I don't know.

I scramble to my feet, brush off sharp pieces of china, praying I don't cut myself. I *have* to find my sister. Help her. My heart pounds madly, fear striking me when a *second* shot echoes in my ears.

And this time I *do* hear a woman scream.

*Justine.*

*Oh... my... God... Is she dead?*

# 3

## PARIS, MAY 8, 1942

*Justine*
*Moments before, at the Hôtel Drouot*

*My sister Ève hates me.*

With the memory of the shocked look on her face piercing my heart, I walk quickly in my blue linen pumps through the maze of hallways to the auction house basement, knowing I'd wanted to speak to her, but desperate to escape her glaring eye. My ploy worked. I saw Ève, talked to her, but our reunion had disappointed me. Why am I surprised? I acted horribly, both harsh and hurtful, like rubbing lye soap on red chapped hands and peeling away the skin... Like I had peeled away the happy years we spent growing up in Maison Bleue. We didn't embrace, didn't laugh or tease each other. It was so sad.

Why? Because I'm 'the major's girl'.

A moniker I pretend to wear proudly around the SS officer. Everyone in Nazi society knows I'm the good little French girl who laughs at their dirty jokes and revels in the privileges I enjoy at the expense of my countrymen and women.

And now Ève knows it, too.

I shiver, my hands shaking. Oh, I was horrible to her. I didn't recognize the words coming out of my mouth, foul and hateful, praising the Nazi regime. Yes, I lied to her. I had to. I'm no collaborator, but I stood there like a condemned saint and took my punishment. I didn't flinch, didn't show emotion. If anything, I arched a brow as arrogantly as I could muster and let her race through her tirade and accuse me of working for the Nazis. Yes, I let her believe I'd stoop that low. I did what I must to save her. Maman. Madame de Giocomte. And Ninette, my little girl. I never dreamed Ève would pull a gun on me, so I ran, my new shoes so tight they pinch my toes—

*Crack!*

*Oh, God, is that a pistol I heard firing?* Did Ève shoot at me?

Does she hate me that much?

Of course she does. I'd hate me, too, this blonde soubrette spouting the rhetoric of a collaborator with the grooming of a pampered poodle. At that moment, my feet turn leaden and I can barely continue my way up to the ground floor from the basement in the Hôtel Drouot. I never should have been foolish enough to believe I'd come away from my rendezvous leaving Ève unscathed. The reality that I've destroyed our relationship hits me hard. I have no sister now. I remember when she was who I would turn to for a warm hug or shed a tear with when I needed it. And oh, do I pine for it. I tried to reach her if only in my imagination, but how do you embrace air?

But I must protect my life, and my own war work. Because the truth is that I walk my own Maginot line between two worlds in this horrible war, living a double life working for the Allies *and* spying for the Germans.

It goes like this: I feed the major disinformation I get from my Allied handler Arsène to the Nazis, while reporting to *him* the Nazi gossip I hear in the House of Péroline, the hat shop where I work on Rue de Rivoli. I also eavesdrop on conversations when the major introduces me as his French companion at the Hôtel Ritz or Bal Tabarin cabaret.

Especially General von Klum, who has been a surprising bee in my bonnet since I took on this job. He's quite smitten with me and I use that to my advantage. I can't imagine what my sister would say if she saw me flirting with the enemy, but I've gained the confidence of the congenial general with the bushy brows who sniffs and snorts and noses around me like a lovesick puppy. He's loose with his cognac *and* his tongue, never believing a pretty woman, especially a Frenchwoman, has brains. I keep promising him more than a kiss on the cheek.

It never happens.

If he wasn't a Nazi, I'd almost feel sorry for the frustrated general—he can't get anywhere with me, but he assures me that he has no problem making moves on the Eastern Front.

'We'll be in Stalingrad by Christmas, mademoiselle,' he whispered to me not long ago as I leaned over to fix the strap on my high heel sandal, showing him ample cleavage. Tradecraft. He wet his lips and put his hand on my knee then boasted German troops were on the move for a series of offensives, including their intention to launch a massive attack to the south and southeast.

'Why would you want to leave Paris for the cold, Russian winter?' I teased him.

'Why, mademoiselle,' he said, squeezing my knee, 'oil fields.'

'Oh,' I said, giggling, encouraging him to tell me more about their plans to seize the oil fields of the Caucasus and cripple the Soviet war effort. Seems the Nazis are running out of the black gold. What surprised me is that, for a flicker of an instant, I saw doubt in the general's eyes. Frustrated and a bit tipsy, he blurted out that German troops aren't used to the bitter, frigid cold of Russia. How many men will be lost? What if they don't have enough oil... Will the fight be for naught?

An unusual statement I won't forget straight from the lips of a Nazi general.

I never felt more certain in that moment I was doing worthwhile work. For France. The Allies. Arsène tells me that the intelligence I glean from him proves very useful to London.

I'd never tell Ève even if we *were* speaking since my work is top secret. In the back of my mind, I want to share with her like we used to do. I was a fool to think this war would be over by now and she'd never find out I hobnobbed with the Nazi higher-ups.

Now that hope is gone. I didn't want to believe it, but isn't Ève shoving the cold barrel of a Luger in my face proof enough? If I ever doubted the Gestapo man's warning that Ève is in the Resistance, I don't anymore. Do I dare imagine she took the pistol from a dead Nazi? I have to smile. My bookish little sister has more guts than I imagined. Which makes her more of a danger to me. More so now that Ève knows what I've become.

The major's mistress.

It's all a dangerous game I play to keep my child safe, *ma chère* Ninette, barely a year old. The major has tried more than once to take her from me, but so far I've succeeded in foiling his plans. Still, I live in constant fear of losing my baby to his outrageous plan of sending her to a home for children born of liaisons with SS men. I stumble over excuses every time he brings it up, then die a thousand deaths when he sneaks up on me and rubs the back of my neck with his long, gloved fingers, his way of signaling he wants sex.

A cold, precise act.

No emotion from him, numbness from me. I find no pleasure

in his touch. I learned to push down the disgust I feel when he kisses my bare shoulder, with lips that never burn with passion for anything but taking what isn't his.

That doesn't mean I don't cry into my pillow at night, wishing for another man's touch, his strong arms holding me. Breathless with desire, I hug myself tight, then run my cool fingers up and down my arms, pretending I'm not alone and the wonderful man I dream about is teasing me with his touch.

Arsène. My double agent spy handler.

Strong, bold... and handsome.

When I feel daring, I slide my hands over my ribcage and down to my thighs. My body aches with a need that evokes an emotion I never expected: that I *can* feel pleasure. Then it ends and the shivers come again, for the man who I long for but who can never be mine. He knows my secret, but he has a job to do and that doesn't include giving comfort to a woman like me. A Nazi mistress.

Arsène is a British agent, though he's never admitted it outright. I've never seen his true self either, because he is always in disguise... whether in a brothel as an old soldier, or in church when he dons a priest's black robes and hears my 'confession'. I've even seen him as a German soldier and a handsome, debonair waiter at Bal Tabarin.

Yet I've learned to look under the disguise and more than once I've taken in the powerfully masculine aura of the man and 'seen' what my eyes don't. A strong soldier of the night who can be mysterious and grave one minute, then playful the next, especially with Ninette. She adores him and recognizes him, no matter what cloak he wears. I think she has a sixth sense. She inhales him, like me. There's a scent about him that's warm and adventurous, exotic yet comforting. A man I sense can face down any danger with his broad smile and fierce dark eyes, but he also has great heart. I think too often about him holding me tight in his arms, my breasts squeezed against his broad chest. And yes, I've thought about kissing him.

His lips brushing against mine, his hands tight around my waist.

Then, shocked by my brazenness, I disband that idea.

*Impossible.* A sinner like me has no right to wish for a man's embrace. Two years after the major raped me and I still feel guilty. Feeling that it was *my* fault because I didn't resist hard enough. Yes, I know such resistance often results in a woman's death at the hand of her abuser, but will I ever get over it?

I wonder.

'It's a thread in the fabric of your life,' Arsène says, insisting I *will* learn to stop punishing myself. How can I? The Vichy government blames us women for the defeat of France, that because we fought for freedoms denied to us before the Nazis took over, because we entered the workforce, it's *our* fault we didn't produce enough babies. So many husbands and lovers died in the Great War, the birthrate declined. *You neglected your duty*, they say, *to bear children.*

Which makes me wonder what the Vichy government would say about me having a child for the occupier. Would they cheer me? Or stone me? The thought makes me queasy. More disturbing to my psyche is, what will happen to women like me after the war is over? I can't believe the Allies won't win, but when I defend my actions, will angry Parisians believe me? That I was a double agent? What I did, *why* I did it? Give me a chance to prove it? I pray so...

Winning the war is what counts, not me.

I stifle a tear. I do worry about Ninette. A deep sadness drenches me. If only Ève knew about my child. She'd adore my little girl. I almost told her, *almost*, but I stopped at the last second. I can't ever tell her lest she hate my child, too. Oh, the insufferable pain that Nazi has caused me. I *try* to go on each day, do what I must to survive, bide my time until the day I can speak up after we oust the Boches from Paris. Then I will toss away my shame and stand publicly and testify against Major Saxe-Müllenheim, declare in a clear voice what he did to me and others like me. Innocent women whose only crime was catching his eye. I can't believe he won't be accused of war crimes, and I'll be first in line to speak the truth about him. Yes, I seek revenge, but first we have to win this war... which is why I had to make Ève believe I work for the Nazis.

Now she's so angry with me, it makes me shudder.

Isn't that what I wanted though? Isn't that the only way to keep her and Maman and Madame de Giocomte safe? To keep the Gestapo away from them, until I can work out a plan with Arsène to get them out of Paris?

God help me.

How I miss my dear sister.

I can't get my old life with Ève out of my mind. Before the Nazis occupied Paris in June 1940, each day was a glorious adventure of art and scrumptious food and dreams as magical as a rainbow. Even when the sun didn't shine after a rainy day, Ève and I believed in that rainbow. It was in our hearts, nurtured not only by our wise *maman*, but Madame de Giocomte. She made us her family, listened to us, helped Ève with admittance to the Sorbonne and championed my designs with her lady friends as if they came from the best couture house in Paris.

We thought the ride would never end.

Were we really so innocent back then?

We lived in a grand house near Parc Monceau where our *maman* is a seamstress for the wealthy Jewish banker, Monsieur Itzhak de Giocomte, and his exquisite, Russian-born wife Ekaterina, a prominent cello player. Madame de Giocomte insisted we were safe there. Why not? The de Giocomte family enjoyed the position of valued members of the community, she was quick to say, having settled in France over two hundred years ago from Venice, bringing with them a fortune in jewels. I disagreed. We heard what happened to Jews in Germany and Poland and I feared the de Giocomtes would be targets. I wanted to rally against the Nazis, but how?

No one had a clue.

And no one saw what was coming... That the Nazis are beasts and show no respect toward women, even their own. The major told me how young girls in Germany are chosen for their Aryan purity to breed with the SS. Imagine, he has this wild idea about opening such a home for girls here in France. It won't happen, it can't, but I know that was on his mind the day he invaded our home. I shall never forget seeing Ève in the clutches of the major, trying to act grown-up, brave, but she was just a child. Barely eighteen.

The debauched SS officer snorted and smacked his lips with one thing on his mind.

Rape.

I *couldn't* let that happen to her.

So I went with that monster, this man who delights in taunting me with brash threats about taking my child Ninette away from me to be raised by a good German family. Does any woman of violent rape ever refer to a baby born from that moment as 'our' child? I know I can't. I can deal with the major, but for now my job is to keep Ève from getting herself killed, because I know my sister; she's not giving up the fight.

If she doesn't lie low, she'll end up in the hands of the infamous Gestapo man.

Pudgy, round-faced with eyesight as sharp as a bullet. And just as deadly.

Herr Avicus Geller.

The man is obsessed with carrying out the law. And routing out Resistance fighters. He keeps a list of suspects and checks them off one by one, or so the major told me. He first suspected Ève when she was seen hanging around the Musée de l'Homme, Museum of Mankind, before they arrested the leaders of the network last year. He hasn't let up since, putting her name on his list. It's a game to him and in his mind, if there's even the *slightest* chance she's connected to the Underground, he pursues it with vigor. He became determined to prove it when he saw Ève at the American Hospital of Paris under dubious circumstances when he escorted me back to my apartment after I fainted at the Bal Tabarin. My sister had accompanied a man with a gunshot wound and in Herr Geller's mind, that tags him as a Resistance fighter. Now he's consumed not only with making my life miserable, but also Ève's. I sense a deep hurt in him that turned this Gestapo man's heart blacker than the devil's arse. It's nothing he said —he reveals no information about his personal life—it's the intense stare he throws out when he plays his hand, catching you in his web. A macabre pleasure shining in his eyes watching you squirm. I wouldn't be surprised if he trapped rats when he was a boy and chopped off their tails and watched them run around in circles. He's cruel, calculating... and greedy. He's blinded by the strictness of the law and sees nothing but black and white.

Like the crossword puzzles he obsessively completes.

Determination to stay free of his clutches scorches the bottoms of my feet. I rush up the stairs two at a time, determined to elude not only my sister, but also the Gestapo man. Knowing he's capable of humiliating me is more than I can bear. Of course, he knows I'm Justine Beaufort and my sister is Ève Beaufort, but when he's angry with me, Herr Geller resorts to calling me Rachelle D'Artois. A moniker bestowed upon me by the major, a sophisticated detail the SS man finds amusing when he introduces me to his 'circle' of Nazi officers.

Which reminds me.

I can't forget when I heard Herr Geller discussing with the major what happens to female prisoners detained at Gestapo headquarters on Rue des Saussaies. I'm not blind to his lack of subtlety; no doubt the major encourages him. He speaks loudly so I overhear him, how women suffer hard blows on their lower back and buttocks until they're covered with black bruises, how their most intimate places are abused in a manner so cruel I put my hands over my ears because I couldn't bear to hear any more.

*I hate him.* This buzzard who picks at its prey, not with sharp talons but words that wound deep, so deep I clench my gut tight and I can't breathe. He reminds me often of my place in this chess game, how the Nazis dominate the royal pieces while the rest of us are pawns and totally dispensable. In their eyes, Frenchwomen are nothing but fluff, rouge, and silk stockings. No wonder I find it hard to keep my temper when Herr Geller turns up at inopportune moments.

Like today at Hôtel Drouot. I evaded his scrutiny when he was busy working that silly puzzle and I induced Ève to follow me. That doesn't mean he didn't get wind of my scheme. I have no doubt he's looking for me. It's not *if* but *when* he tracks me down. He never makes a move, unless he's two steps ahead of his prey.

I wipe the sweat off the back of my neck with my long veil. When he finds me, he'll torment me with his threats. A game he plays. So far I'm winning, but what if my luck runs out? I'll end up in solitary confinement at La Santé prison where—if I'm convicted of being what the Nazis call a 'dangerous criminal'—I might be guillotined.

In public view.

I shiver, the horror of that making me tremble when—

I hear a *second* shot fired.

*Ève.*

I cry out and fall to my knees, panic rooting me to the spot, my heart pounding so hard, I struggle to get to my feet. God help me, is *she* the target of a Nazi rifle? I'm going back to find my sister. If anything happens to her, I'd be to blame. I won't be able to live with myself. This whole fiasco was supposed to keep her safe, not harm her.

I grab onto a door handle to get to my feet, not easy in these damn high heels. I jump at every noise, a hard knot forming in my stomach. I imagine rodents crawling through the cellar of the auction house, and wonder if the two-legged rat in a black trench coat cornered my sister and shot her.

I head back down to the basement, determined to find Ève, preparing a new story to make her understand. I'll tell her about the baby... my sweet Ninette... But not that I'm a double agent. No, I can't do that. Still, I *can* make her understand my predicament and then everything will be all right. She might still hate me, but the most important thing is we'll be sisters again, and I want that more than anything.

Which is why I race into the darkness, stumbling in my tight blue heels, anxious to make my plea to Ève, my emotions pumped up with adrenaline, my eyes shining with excitement—

When I run smack into Herr Geller.

Waving his crossword puzzle in my face like a mad hatter.

I wonder what rabbit hole I fell down when the scurrilous Gestapo man says, 'Have you a word for "traitor" beginning with "s", Mademoiselle D'Artois?'

# 4

## PARIS, MAY 8, 1942

*Ève*

Crazy thoughts go through your mind when you're on the run.

Like, why didn't I tell Maman I loved her this morning? Kiss her on the cheek and hug her.

Things I take for granted, but it keeps me from focusing on the terrifying fear racing through me that I'll end up hanging from the end of a meat hook in a Gestapo torture chamber. Oh, my God, those poor souls. Michal told me such a place exists beneath the Eiffel Tower. *How does he know this? Was he held there?* I suspect there's more to his story than he lets on.

Head down, I snake through a narrow alley. Think, *think*. I can't. I'm torn apart inside, every word Justine said to me, every gesture from this woman who claimed to be my sister, embedded in my soul. I can't believe she'd willingly align herself with the Nazis after the SS major raped her.

*Because she hasn't the guts to fight the Boches?*

No, *no*, I don't believe it. It sours my stomach to say that. That is *not* Justine. Yet I can't deny she's changed, and in an excruciating way, I'm learning to understand that even the bravest woman can break under the assault of a man's ugly deed. I feel deep inside me she's so ashamed of what the Nazi did to her, she's suffering guilt that she survived and believes she's bound to him. It's not true, of course, but how can I make her see that?

I can't.

She's lost to me a *second* time.

I keep telling myself I shouldn't have panicked and run off, I should have gone back to look for my sister, but what choice did I have? The gunshots fired echoed throughout the ground floor in the Hôtel Drouot, creating chaos when someone yelled out a woman was shot and giving me time to push through the Rue Rossini exit *moments* before German soldiers, with bayonets drawn, would have stopped me for questioning.

I pull Maman's hat down over my eyes. I have to keep going, remain free. With Monsieur de Giocomte deported to what we now believe is Poland, Maman and Madame depend upon me. I keep up a normal pace so I don't attract attention from passers-by. Justine warned me that a Gestapo man is after me and, if there's one thing I've learned as a saboteur, it's that I don't want to draw attention to myself. I can imagine Michal's voice telling me to dump the hat, but I have that sentimental attachment to it I can't break, especially now, that what started that day for us when Maman wore that hat is gone. Justine isn't coming home to Maison Bleue.

People walk briskly with their collars up and shoulders stooped, keeping their heads down, precious baguettes held close to their chests. Traffic on the boulevard consists of German army trucks, a horse and cart with a bewildered farmer holding the reins, desperate to steer away from a German soldier screeching around the corner on a motorcycle. I step under an arched doorway, keeping out of sight, when the reckless motorcyclist clips a girl riding on her bicycle. She tips over and lands on her rear. He splats her with dirty water from a big puddle and then races on, but not before she attracts the attention of two other Nazi officers in a passing touring car. Grinning, they slow down for a better view, but they don't stop to help her. Instead, the leering officers twist their heads to see up the girl's skirt.

'*Sales Boches*... Dirty Boches,' the girl yells, then gets back on her bicycle and peddles away before the officers lose their smiles.

I take advantage of the moment and sneak out of my hiding spot, walking fast, eager to disappear in the endless zigzag of small cobblestone streets and narrow alleys, crouching in doorways and clutching the Luger under my jacket close to my chest, ready to defend myself. Heart pounding, my hand moist and still wrapped around the pistol, I've lost all feeling in my fingers from gripping it so tight. I doubt I could fire it anyway. It's more than cramped muscles making me numb. In spite of Justine's betrayal, I'll never forgive myself if I've hurt my sister with my stupidity.

*Don't jump to conclusions. They said a woman was shot, not that she was dead.*

I *want* to believe Justine is alive. My sister is no pushover; she's made from strong fibers like fine leather, smooth and fine.

Looking over my shoulder, I cover several blocks going north from the Hôtel des Ventes toward Rue Damrémont in Montmartre. I'm headed to the apartment where Remi, the leader of our cell, hangs his beret on a knife embedded in an oak door. The man is a street fighter and operates on both sides of the law, but even he can't secure enough weapons. Our cell has a small cache of pistols but it's not enough. I'll turn the Luger over to him and report what happened, then ask Michal to check with his informants about Justine.

I keep going, my head on a swivel. *Always suspect you're being followed*, Michal drummed into my head. *Plan, think, concentrate on what I taught you and you'll outwit them.*

Not easy. Everyone's paranoid these days about being tailed and arrested by the *Brigades spéciales*. Everyone knows the plain-clothes French police sneak around like sewer rats sniffing for 'domestic terrorists', *résistants* to sink their teeth into, to torture. I heard they aren't shy about shoving a girl's head into a bucket of freezing ice-water—or worse—to get names.

I shiver. I will *never* give up my friends. Michal, Remi, Iris, Claude, even Coralie with her flirty smile aimed toward Michal. It's unthinkable. Though I do wonder if Coralie worked her magic on Michal, acting sweet and innocent to get the courier jobs leaving tracts and leaflets in lockers at the train station, or acting as a decoy because in his words, 'She knows her place.' I don't trust her, but the others do since she does her part. We're members of the Jade network and risk our lives to free France. We didn't know each other before the war, but a hatred of the occupiers unites us. No one disputes the Underground didn't happen overnight. How could it? We were still in shock that France surrendered so quickly after the German forces bypassed the Maginot Line in May 1940. Tanks and troops advanced to the coast and the French Army suffered a major defeat. The news came swiftly, hotly, in our ears that French troops had abandoned the city and the next day the Nazis rolled into Paris with their tanks. Nazis on horses. Marching bands down the Champs-Élysées.

'How did this happen?' we asked. There was no fighting in the streets. Paris was declared an 'open city', and Justine and I stood on the balcony on the second floor of Maison Bleue, gawking at the purple-blue sky hovering over the city at twilight, holding hands tight and declaring our loyalty to France, taking pride in being Parisiennes and vowing they couldn't take that away from us. The next morning, workers removed the sandbags on the boulevards. Cabarets reopened and dancers kicked their legs high. Hitler entered the city, posed in front of the Eiffel Tower for the newsreels, and then left.

And *voilà*, the Nazis settled in and occupied Paris.

*Now what?*

We tiptoed through the days, *weeks* that followed like frightened, barefoot children hugging each other, speaking in whispers while the high-pitched whistle of Nazi soldiers patrolling the boulevards sent chills through us. We didn't know whether to laugh or cry when the black and white billboards went up in German with Gothic script. Then we had to put up with German soldiers drinking beer in our favorite cafés and sitting in our chairs. Watching them, tapping our fingers on round marble tabletops, we waited and waited.

'We'll get used to it, *n'est-ce pas*?'

Others had a different opinion.

'Well, they kept the Communists out of Paris, that's something.'

'Let's wait and see.'

Then the occupiers became part of our daily lives. Tall, athletic young officers with clear eyes. Royal-looking, handsome. It was quite disturbing. Who were these men acting like blonde gods? This was *not* what anyone expected. Where were the warlike demons waging war on the innocents? Oh, they were there, hiding underneath their snappy uniforms. Tipping their caps and clicking their heels, the Nazi soldier was always polite, smiling. Giving up their seats on the Métro to elderly ladies with gnarled fingers praying the rosary for better days. Distributing food to the poor on Rue des Rosiers, alongside Madame de Giocomte muttering under her breath, 'It won't last. You'll see.'

She didn't back down. Even the Boches couldn't put a damper on her charity work. For years she's supported those in need, and most recently, newly arrived Jewish refugees from Russia living on Rue de Vaucouleurs in the Belleville section. Madame de Giocomte identifies with their plight and threw her heart into a new charity to help them. Her eyes deepen to a purple hue like the shadows at Maison Bleue when she speaks about how important nourishing food is to survival for these people. And how she won't let them down. She and Maman hand out baskets of leftovers from the *grande maison* to the hungry every week.

And so it went, the people of Paris convincing ourselves that since the Nazis acted 'civil', we believed their pied piper promise that life would go on as before in the City of Light.

It did. For a while.

But Madame was right. It didn't last.

Things happened. *Bad things.*

Shop windows of Jewish businesses smashed. Apartments requisitioned to billet Nazi officers. Their owners tossed out into the street. Then came rationing. No petrol.

I could go on, every day bringing some new restriction and making us hate the Boches more and more, especially what they were doing to French Jews. They could no longer teach at the Sorbonne; they had to register as Jews at the local police station. Why, they couldn't even buy flowers! The Nazis took away their rights to distance them from French society, to dehumanize them as a people. That hit us hard. The de Giocomtes have treated us like family since the day Justine saved Madame's big, floppy hat from an angry swan in Saint-John's Pond. Even now it makes me smile... Two little girls dolled up in Maman's handiwork made from scraps of silk and organza. A seamstress so deft of hand and eye, she wove magical dresses out of silk scraps to save us from a life in the slums north of Paris. A day we strutted like *petites* princesses in the Bois de Boulogne and attracted the kindness of a wealthy madame who came to our rescue. Madame de Giocomte hired Maman that afternoon and brought us to live at Maison Bleue.

Even after the Germans occupied Paris, the glorious mansion stood stately and untouched. We had no idea then what devious Nazi plan was already at work to loot art and deprive French Jews like the de Giocomtes of the legacy on canvas they worked so hard to build. We took each day as it came and somehow we survived. We ignored the red banners and flags with black and white swastikas hanging from the hotels and state buildings. We kept our heads down, our noses clean, and our hearts beating in a perpetual rhythm of hope that others felt as we did, that somehow we'd connect with them and join the fight and drive the occupiers out of Paris. We changed road signs, gave wrong directions to German soldiers. Meanwhile, we observed. Looked for signs of resistance from others... Sly glances, whispers here and there. But nothing happened.

Until it did.

My senses reeled like a spinning top out of control, its tricolors blurring into madness on that day I lost Justine to the Nazi major. The day he stole her girlhood. And mine. What he did to Justine tore me apart emotionally. I'll never forget how my sister stood up for me, sacrificing herself so I could be free. I was barely eighteen, she was twenty; my big sister looking out for me.

And then this... this greater *betrayal* when the major stole her soul with his gifts and promises of a good life while others starve, how he plucked the goodness out of her heart, and the sister I love never stood a chance to get it back. There before me stood no daughter of France. She was gone, too. I shall never forget what just happened today at the Hôtel Drouot when I confronted her. She didn't apologize for collaborating with the Boches; she almost seemed proud of it. Then why did she warn me? Does she still have sisterly feelings for me?

If so, *why does she stay with the Nazi major?*

I blow out a big breath. The damn feather on Maman's hat is a nuisance. It keeps poking me in the eye, as if she's berating me for my rashness.

*Go back, Ève. Bring her home,* I imagine Maman's voice begging me. *She's your sister. Do something.*

*I tried, Maman. She won't come. She prefers her Nazi friends.*

No, I can't tell her that. Maman lives in her own world, back in a time when the streets of Paris glistened after a Maytime shower, leaving behind water droplets like perfect pearls, the lovely scent of herbs and roses in the garden making me feel so alive.

I breathe in that memory despite the sharp smell of decay in the alley giving me a headache. I find courage in remembering those days, now but a whisper in my ears. It was a glorious time before the Germans occupied Paris, the memory filling me with a rush of emotion that gives me strength.

I have a job to do.

A job Maman doesn't approve of.

I fight the Boches the only way I know how. As a denizen of the night. I use my science skills to destroy the Nazis, but Maman would never approve of me joining the Resistance. Remi, the head of our network, didn't either. *Women don't belong in a man's war*, I heard him say so many times, but I proved my worth with my bomb-making skills. I'm known as impulsive, cocky—Michal will attest to that—but always loyal to France and to our cause. I'm not the same girl I was before the Occupation.

But then, apparently neither is my sister.

Imagine what Maman would say about Justine becoming a Nazi's mistress? I don't have the heart to tell her or Madame de Giocomte, fearing Maman will never recover and Madame will regret the day she saved us from the slums.

Worse yet, I have no way of knowing if Justine was hurt when I heard the second shot ring out. I wouldn't be surprised if that secret policeman in the black trench coat pulled the trigger. I've heard how the Gestapo turn on informants and collaborators once they outlive their usefulness. I pray my sister survives.

I can't turn my back on her. I can't give up hoping she'll join us.

Heart pounding, I slow down my pace, look for a safe place to rest, get my bearings. I can't panic. Michal says that's when you make mistakes, the Nazis find you, and you're on your way to 84 Avenue Foch for interrogation. I won't let that happen to me. I avoid the grand boulevards, keep to the narrow streets. The neighborhood changes. German soldiers look at me in a way they don't try to hide. I'm walking in Montmartre, the section of Paris where the Nazis don't play by the rules. Dark alleyways, houses with no electricity, no running water. I pass by a boy about nine working a communal pump to fill a bucket, his eyes watching me, waiting to see what I do.

I clutch the pistol tight in my pocket, keeping it out of sight so I don't frighten him when—

A German soldier turns the corner, whistling, but he doesn't see me. I put my finger to my lips and the boy nods. Most likely, he's witnessed the unthinkable here when a Nazi takes what he wants, his young mind scarred but his courage strong. He motions for me to go down a narrow passageway behind a high wall, a closed-off area filled with broken furniture and sundry junk, the smell of rot and mold and fresh urine creating a stench so strong, I gag. I can't turn back. I race down the alleyway until I find a courtyard covered with trash and dead leaves where I can hide, then I hear—

A loud screeching assaults my ears, fever pitch, primitive.

*A cat?*

Crying out like it's being skinned alive. The loud squeal unhinges me. German soldiers looking for sport? I wouldn't be surprised. The two-faced Boches aren't allowed to smoke on the boulevards by order of the High Command, but behind closed doors I know what cruelty they're capable of. I can't stop the bile filling my throat, fearful of them catching me. I slump down on the stoop of a shop closed up tight with long wooden boards criss-crossed on the door and the word *Juif*, Jew, scrawled in jagged red painted letters. The German soldiers won't bother patrolling here and the smell should keep away the Gestapo man, though I suspect he's used to the disagreeable odor.

*Like begets like.*

My nails catch the peeling paint on the shutters as I try to unlock them, seek refuge inside the abandoned shop until the danger has passed. Can't. They're nailed shut.

I close my eyes and clear my mind, grabbing a breath before I set out once again on the streets, praying twilight will be my friend. I can't stop. Got to keep going, find a hiding place before the Gestapo man tracks me down. No doubt my dutiful sister gave him a description of me after I fired off a wild round at her. *Black hat with a feather. Brown corduroy jacket. Print dress. A stolen Luger she brandishes about like she knows how to use it. She doesn't.*

Yes, I fear my own sister sold me out to the Nazis for a new hat.

I walk quickly past a cabaret barely holding it together with a two-girl peep show and a besotted accordion player gargling a saucy tune. *Keep going.* More pubs, laughing, drunken squeals. I block them out, sort through my options—go home, hide, run, leave Paris... No, I can't. I'd never abandon Maman and Madame. And Michal. That man wraps me up in a sunny glow every time he smiles at me. Of course, I keep my distance. Falling in love during wartime is too unpredictable. I like my life organized. Like my lab. Vials and Petri dishes lined up like soldiers, my notes written in blue ink on square notepads. Clean and neat.

I veer off onto another dimly lit side street. I have spent so much time lamenting my conversation with Justine, I've ignored the signals the atmosphere has changed. I steer clear of stray cats and drunken Germans whooping it up on wine since the clubs ran out of beer, but I ignore loud footsteps pounding the cobblestones behind me, the scraping and moaning and yowling of a more dangerous feline.

Until it's too late.

* * *

'Get off my street, whore!'

A female smelling strongly of patchouli and another ripe odor jumps on my back, screeching, her sharp nails catching on my jacket. Grunting, I hold my breath to escape the stink and push her off me. For one shattering moment, I fear I'm about to lose everything when she grabs me around the neck. And then I don't; even though she's choking me, I don't lose my wits. I'm no stranger to her tactics. I've shoved the heel of my boot into the groin of more than one Boche.

*'Ye-ow!'* I cry out with courage fueling my outburst when I jab the woman in the ribs hard with my elbows, loosening her hands around my neck, then I stomp on her right foot with my plat-

form heel. She goes down on the ground, groaning and rolling up into a ball. I whirl around, but before I can take off down the narrow alleyway, she grabs me around the ankle and I hit the uneven cobblestones hard, the breath knocked out of me. Only by luck does the pistol in my pocket not go off.

Now that the streetwalker has me where she wants me—secured by her surprisingly strong fist—she lets me have an earful.

'I ain't seen you before, mademoiselle,' she huffs and puffs. 'What's the likes of you doing here?'

She coughs, wheezing and spitting up green phlegm.

I take advantage of her weak moment and yank my foot free, then struggle to my feet. 'I'm not what you think I am. I'm a student at the Sorbonne.'

'*Ha!* You expect me to believe you? You're just like the others. You think you can move in on my territory when your belly starts growling, and steal my johns with your smooth skin and white teeth?'

*Breathe in... breathe out.*

I should be amused by her accusation, but I'm not. I've got to talk her down, then get out of here. 'I don't want any trouble, mademoiselle—'

'Francine. The Boches call me Francie.' She smooths down her hair streaked the color of a pomegranate, adjusts her wrinkled dress, her black brassiere straps showing, choker around her neck. 'I bet you fancy a Nazi lover to give you silk stockings while your boyfriend sits in a POW camp. Not on my watch. I'll show you what happens to girls like you.'

She pulls out a steel hook from a leather sheath strapped to her thigh. It makes a whooshing sound when she waves it around in a circle. I've never felt my heart pounding so hard.

'Listen, Francie,' I begin, backing away, 'I have no intention of intruding on your business, but I understand how you feel. Servicing the German occupiers would make any girl's life miserable.'

Even as the words come out of my mouth, I regret them. Harsh, if true. She's a threat to me, but I feel for her, too. Imagine gritting your teeth when men push their tobacco-stained fingers between your legs, sniffing, probing because you're hungry, homeless.

Isn't that also rape?

How can I judge her when I nearly suffered the same fate at the hands of the SS? Am I any better than she is?

*No*, Madame de Giocomte would say, reminding me that war unites women in ways that social class never will, that we're in this fight together to save our men, our families... save France.

'So you think you're too good to give it up,' Francie says, coughing, 'while girls like me lie on our backs to survive?'

'No, I didn't mean that.' I try to take back what I said, but she's nose-to-nose with me, pointing that hook in my face. The stink of her dirty breath makes me nauseous.

'I *hate* letting them Nazis touch me,' she insists, 'but a girl's got to eat.'

She coughs, sniffles. And are those tears forming in her eyes? *An ally, perhaps?*

'We have that in common, mademoiselle.' I sidestep her, but she grabs me by the shoulders and presses her hook against my cheek.

'I pulled in twenty thousand francs in three days when the Nazis first occupied Paris. Then their prissy generals decided we're not clean enough for their precious soldier boys, and *poof*! The pickings ain't so good these days.'

Before I can stop her, she goes on a rant, eager to share with me her life story before she... *what*? Cuts off the tip of my nose?

So I listen to how she was born under a windmill in the old Meudon white chalk quarry south of Paris, and how she started turning tricks at thirteen when her *maman* tossed her out because the woman's new boyfriend fancied *her* instead. How she's been working this block ever since and—

'If you think I'm going to let a skin-and-bones tart like you take over *my* beat, you're mistaken, mademoiselle.'

'I'll just be on my way,' I begin, eager to diffuse the situation, then she lifts Maman's hat off my head with her hook and plops it on her own. So much for her being an ally.

She's a thief.

'Give it back!' I yell.

'It's *mine* now.' She laughs. 'Your *chapeau* with its sassy feather will do nicely for my afternoon stroll in the garden of the Moulin Rouge, flirting with them Nazis while lining up my next meal.'

I should run, get out of here, but I let sentiment rule my head. *'Give it back!'*

'Beat it. *Va-t-en*, get out of here!'

'Not without my hat—'

I try to grab it, but she slaps me across the face so hard, she splits my lower lip. She raises her hook to finish the job and I duck. My mind goes numb. No one ever hit me before, no German soldier came close, and for the first time I choke on blood in my mouth. It's then I realize I'm not invincible and I'm not brave, just lucky. Except for scrapes and bruises, I never tasted a coppery sting on my tongue during a mission. It puts a different spin on my predicament, not just with this woman, but with the Gestapo man. And the threat of his unbearable torture is more real to me and scares the hell out of me.

*What if I break? Give up my comrades?*

I can't, *I won't*, but I'm seeing a side of myself I don't like, that

I'm vulnerable to physical pain, a screaming gaping hole in my psyche I've never dealt with, giving me insight into understanding what Justine experienced, why *she* broke. But that doesn't excuse my sister's terse words earlier. Still—

*I want to forgive you, Justine, get you away from the major... Why won't you let me?*

It's all coming together, why Justine risked meeting me, why she hasn't given up on me, why she ran so she doesn't have to explain her unspeakable ordeal, the great pain when the major raped her. God knows what she endured during childbirth, but knowing my sister, she embraced that baby with a mother's deep love. She always wanted children of her own, designing infant gowns and sweaters for Madame's charity for the Jewish refugees, saying it was 'good practice' for her own baby.

God, I *must* find her.

I wipe the blood off my face with the back of my hand. First, I have to deal with this jealous woman as fierce as an alley cat in heat. I raise my hand to hit her back, but she lurches at me with the sleek speed of a fox. I use her impulsive move against her and sidestep her, letting her fly past me. She whirls around like a can-can dancer and heads back in my direction. Cursing, she raises the hook, aiming to get close enough to rip open my cheek. I stick out my wooden-soled shoe and trip her, and she stumbles and drops the steel hook.

I kick it out of the way. 'My hat, mademoiselle.'

'No. It's mine now.'

'Not for long.' I grab onto the pistol hidden in my jacket pocket to frighten her and get the hell out of here. Before I can yank the weapon out of my pocket, a black police van screeches to a halt at the end of the narrow alleyway, blocking the exit. Black curtains cover the windows. Ominous looking. Two uniformed French policemen jump out, armed with long billy clubs.

'Now look what you done,' Francie yells. 'It's a raid!'

'What?' I ask.

'The police, mademoiselle. When them flics show up, it's because they have orders from the Nazis to round up us girls and check us for the pox.'

I see the cold fear squeezing her eyes into pinpoints. *She's terrified.* An instinctive fear cuts through me I can't shake.

'The pox?' I repeat.

'What's with you, girlie? Oh, your type don't get it, I suppose.'

'No... I-I haven't.'

'You will if you hang around here long enough.' She laughs. 'The German High Command thinks cracking down on street prostitutes will "cure" what ails their soldiers.' She shakes her head. 'Not them oversexed prigs.'

'But why target you?'

'The Germans have strict rules about soldiers frequenting only Nazi-approved brothels.' She scoffs. 'They split their trousers at the thought of them hooking up with us girls on the streets who are barely eking out a living.'

'Why?' I ask, curious.

'It's the Boches' obsession with hygiene,' she insists, then spits on her dirty fingers to clean them.

Whatever's going on, I'm not hanging around for a grilling by a pot-faced police officer or a bug-eyed German doctor eyeballing me where it's none of his business. I take off in the opposite direction, but a French policeman in a flowing cape takes two long strides toward me. I don't get far in my platform heels. He grabs me by my upper arm, squeezing it hard.

'Not so fast, mademoiselle.'

'*Let me go*,' I cry out, desperate to get free, but the pain in my arm is as sharp as a knife cutting into a vein. 'I'm *not* a whore.'

'That's what they all say.' He laughs, then releases me and pushes me toward the black police van. 'Get on with you... or I'll toss your sorry arse into a cold, damp cell in Saint Lazare.'

'No, I'm innocent. I won't go with you.'

I cross my arms over my chest, protecting my pride. I have to. I have a great fear if I get into that van, I'll never see Maman or Justine again.

# 5

## PARIS, MAY 8, 1942

### *Justine*

'I asked you a question, Mademoiselle D'Artois. I need a word beginning with "s" for "traitor".'

Herr Geller growls, standing squarely in the doorway leading downstairs in the Hôtel Drouot, his bulk as well as his ugly snarl cutting off my escape. I swear his face glows red and hot, a sweaty sheen making it shine. He's stewing like a lobster in a pot, angry with me for pulling that stunt earlier and eluding him.

'Let me pass, monsieur.'

*Keep calm, don't feed his anger.*

'Not until I get your answer.' His growl is deeper, guttural.

'I owe you *nothing*, Herr Geller.'

'That's where you're wrong, mademoiselle.' His upper lip wiggles. 'We are, as you French say, "in bed together".'

I raise a brow. 'Since when did the Gestapo engage in pillow talk?'

'A minor deviation, mademoiselle. I assure you it won't

happen again.' He narrows his eyes. 'You and I have important business to discuss.'

'Oh?' My lips pale. I bite back my fear of him and turn away.

'No more hide-and-seek.' Herr Geller blows his hot breath on the back of my neck. 'The word for traitor I'm looking for is S-I-S-T-E-R. *Where is she?*'

'Ève?' I shrug my shoulders. 'I have no idea.'

*Did he see us together?*

Could be. He's aware *The Daisy Sisters* was showcased here in the Hôtel Drouot before making its way to Nice for a special auction at the Hôtel Savoy.

'I *could* post a sentry outside the de Giocomte residence until your sister shows up, mademoiselle, but I find these dissidents often waste my valuable time *not* giving up information, not to mention it can get messy.'

'Why pick on me to do your dirty work?' I ask.

'I'm not a man to take chances, but you intrigue me. You put on a good show for the major, but you're a beautiful woman who didn't willingly join the Party and that makes your loyalty weak in my eyes.'

'You're testing me.'

He shrugs. 'Yes. I'm asking you again. I want to know where your sister goes, who she meets, names, addresses, journals, lists. I'm giving you the opportunity to show your complete loyalty to the Party by giving up whatever information you have about her activities.'

'I *swear* to you I don't know where she goes or who she meets. I haven't seen her since that day the major raped me.'

'You're lying.' Herr Geller brings the conversation back to where he wants it. On Ève. 'She followed you here to the basement. What did you two talk about?'

'I came here alone... to see the painting of us. Nothing more.' God help me if the Gestapo man overheard me warning Ève, but I was desperate. When I found out the major intended to showcase the painting to lure Ève here, I took advantage of the moment to confront my sister and warn her. I'll never forget the hurt in Ève's eyes when she looked at the canvas depicting two sisters deeply entwined in each other's lives, whatever our differences.

Now that bond is broken.

What a terrible shame she must have felt when she discovered the sister she loved was no more. Yet how brave Ève was to show up here, knowing she was watched, observed, though I'd hoped to spare her that.

I know I failed her when the Gestapo man spews his hatred toward me.

'I know you spoke to your sister, but she escaped in spite of my attempt to stop her.'

He points his service revolver at me as proof, making no attempt to hide the smeared blood on his hand. I take a step back, his blatant display of violence upsetting my psyche. Was my sister also a victim of a violent assault?

*I remember the second shot I heard.*

*Ève.*

*Oh, God, my little sister. She can't be dead or he wouldn't be interrogating me. She must be alive, but did he wound her? Will I ever know?*

'It was *you* who fired the shot I heard,' I accuse him.

'Most unfortunate. A snoopy auction employee waved her cleaning mop at me.' He snickers. 'My weapon discharged.'

*Ève's not hurt... thank God, but what about the cleaning woman he shot?*

*Another victim caught in his snare.*

My pulse races, but I strive to keep calm. 'You were aiming at me.'

'If I were, mademoiselle, I wouldn't have missed.' He shoots me a piercing look. Reluctantly, he lowers his Luger. 'I need you alive. Your relationship with the major could be very useful to me in the future.'

'And the woman you shot?'

'She'll live.'

Flat. No remorse. The man has no soul.

He wipes his gun clean with a fine linen handkerchief, taking his time, knowing I heard the shouts and the German soldiers rounding up the art patrons and dealers, the loud whispers that a woman had been shot. *Killed...* someone said. Thank God they were wrong. I kept out of sight here in the basement to escape the scrutiny of the French police arriving on the scene, trying to keep order while Nazi soldiers herded everyone together with the butts of their rifles and then pointing their bayonets at them.

It was maddening.

But not as maddening as Herr Geller's complacent attitude toward the poor soul he shot. A strange thought enters my brain, that the Gestapo man is incapable of feeling emotion toward women. *Did his mother beat him? A girl refuse him?* I can't imagine him filled with passion for anything but Nazi law.

'I'll ask you one last time, mademoiselle. *Where is your sister?*'

'Why are you so interested in Ève? She's just a silly schoolgirl poking her nose where she shouldn't.'

'True, mademoiselle, but it's the job of the Gestapo to cast our net wide with informants. I believe she can lead us to an important Polish military officer who escaped us in Warsaw. A man cunning and clever... and attractive to women.'

'Ève?' I laugh. 'She'd run faster than a scared rabbit if a man even looked at her.'

'Someone gave her that pistol, mademoiselle, most likely a guerrilla fighter. And when I get my hands on her, I intend to find out where he is no matter what methods I must employ, even if she *is* your sister.'

I feign innocence with a pouty red smile. 'I told you, I don't know where she is.'

'The Gestapo is no fool, mademoiselle. Don't lie to me.'

'I wouldn't think of it, monsieur. I know what's at stake.'

I glare at him. I don't back down and neither does he. Unspoken between us but always there is the threat the major made to take my little girl Ninette away from me. Herr Geller knows how deep my love for my child is, the most beautiful and intimate relationship of my life, and how I'm not ashamed to speak about her, though it pains me to do so in front of the secret policeman. For here before me is the most unpredictable devil in the shape of a man. A Gestapo man capable of cruelty that goes beyond physical pain. How he can dissolve your strength into a puddle of mush if you let him. It's amazing how strong my fear of him is. Like drowning at sea... floundering around, gulping in seawater. Alone.

'I suggest you tell me what you know,' he insists, 'so we can get on with the business of routing out these *résistants*. Again, I need names, mademoiselle, names that your sister can provide.'

'Ève knows nothing, monsieur.'

'Ah, so you admit to seeing her. You disappoint me, mademoiselle. You failed the test. I shall be keeping a closer eye on you.'

I bite my lip. The damage is done.

'You think you're so clever, monsieur.'

'I am.' He smirks. 'Now since you admit to seeing her, what was she wearing? Hat, coat, dress?'

'I don't remember. Is it my fault the little bitch pulled a gun on me and I had to run?'

That *really* hurt to call out my sister, but if I'm to keep up my act, I have to toughen up.

'We have ways of jogging your memory.'

He squeezes my arm tight, and the pain is excruciating. A dizziness invades my head and a sudden nausea hits me. He's referring to beatings, penetration. Stripped down and forced to undergo not only the suffering associated with torture, but also the humiliation. Because we're women, we become sex slaves.

He keeps twisting my arm. I have to say *something* before I pass out.

'No hat,' I blurt out. 'Camel coat, brown shoes.'

He laughs. 'Your sister wore a black hat with a feather, brown corduroy jacket, and a print dress. Next time, think twice before lying to the Gestapo or you *will* end up on Avenue Foch.' He grumbles. 'I don't take kindly to wasting my time when I could be hunting Jews.'

He lets me go but I refuse to let him see me uncomfortable. I turn my back to him—yes, I dare to do so—and close my eyes tight so he can't see the pain he inflicted on me. It's not the first time I suffered at the hands of a Nazi. I can't push aside the day I was raped, when the major tossed the vintage doll I used to design sample gowns for Madame de Giocomte across the library, smashing it on the parquet floor. It had been a special gift from Madame, but in that moment it became a symbol to me.

*Never to let a man break me again.*

I wanted desperately to believe I'd survive the major's sexual assault, and I did, but I never dreamed a man *more* evil existed. A creature like this Herr Geller who delights in a ritual he calls 'rounding up Jews'.

'Why can't you leave those poor people alone?' I cry out, my voice cracking. 'They've done you no harm.'

'I have my orders, mademoiselle. We'll soon be implementing a new law so the Gestapo can easily identify Jews too. They'll be required to wear the yellow Star of David on their clothing.'

I gasp. 'Then the rumor *is* true.'

He smirks. 'Yes. It's part of the Führer's Final Solution.'

My mood darkens.

*What is this 'Final Solution' he's hinting at?*

I feel my cheeks flush. I can't help it. It's frightening to think anyone wearing a yellow star can be shot on a Nazi whim. Even more frightening to me is how it will affect Madame de Giocomte. She escaped to France from Russia years ago for a new life, after the murder of her first husband. A second chance at love with an amazing Frenchman had given her a life she'd never dreamed of. But then to lose him, and next her dignity, feels like too much.

And poor Maman.

I imagine her protesting loudly when she's ordered to sew a yellow star on Madame's lovely coats and sweaters. She's so proud of her handiwork for Madame and will hate to see it blemished with this ridiculous Nazi law.

'You shouldn't listen to rumors, mademoiselle,' Herr Geller continues. 'They can get you into trouble.'

'Even when the information comes from General von Klum?' I snap back. I remember the conversation well because I noticed a melancholy about the general. He wasn't as flirtatious. Instead he shared with me not only the latest Nazi propaganda, but his intimate thoughts, including his doubts about Hitler's push into Russia. I was quite surprised by his openness.

Herr Geller snorts. 'Even generals aren't safe from the Gestapo.'

'I doubt if the general will be pleased to know he's not above suspicion.'

'No one is above suspicion, mademoiselle, *especially* you.'

He eyes me with a long look at my breasts, revealing more of himself than he ever has with that one look. Was I wrong about him? Does he feel a physical attraction to me? That he's more interested in toying with me for his own amusement? A sexual game without the sex? *His lust for something he can't have?*

'I believe, Herr Geller,' I say, pressing my point, 'my position as the major's girl buys me a pass from you.' I smile with a little mischief in me. 'I won't be taking you up on entertaining me at Gestapo Headquarters.'

'You won't always enjoy the protection of Major Saxe-Müllenheim.' He grins. 'The major has forgotten his duty, something he's wont to do when it comes to a beautiful woman. The day will come when he *shall* pay, I promise you.' His dark eyes take on a yellowish glimmer, like witch's teeth glowing under a devil's moon. 'Then we'll see if you defy my orders.'

I shiver. He *hates* the SS officer.

At first, I thought it was because Herr Geller will do anything to uphold the law (he has a macabre moral compass that never points north), often decrying the fact that the major steals paintings that should go to—I can't believe I'm saying this—the *Führermuseum* in Linz. Now I'm certain there's also a personal connection to the major hidden under layers of Nazi protocol nearly impossible to unravel.

That doesn't mean I won't stop trying.

'You flatter yourself, Herr Geller. The major is as calculating as you are precise with your crossword puzzles.'

The Gestapo man snorts his agreement.

'I'm a patient man, mademoiselle. I have found in dealing with you French that a beautiful woman hides her sins well.' He grunts. 'And *you*, mademoiselle, hide *many* sins.'

The man is relentless but he knows when to let go, that he'll get nothing more out of me though I have no doubt he'll be watching me. He wishes me a good afternoon, then gives me a quick Hitler salute before turning on his heel. I raise my hand weakly to return the salute. I have to keep up the act, but I don't have to do it with vigor. Still, I worry. Whatever Herr Geller is up to, I can only guess. What worries me is he has a vague description of Ève. She's not safe from him. I have no doubt he'll be watching Maison Bleue. If only I could get a message to her, but how?

I put Herr Geller to the back of my mind as there is another problem for me. We agreed the major would wait for me outside the Hôtel Drouot, where I expect he's stewing in his Mercedes motorcar, perturbed by the commotion going on in and around the hotel and anxious to leave. He wouldn't soil his gloves or his reputation getting caught up in the melee. Most likely, he's fuming in the backseat, muttering angry epithets, wondering why I'm taking so long to carry out my mission. He had ordered me to convince my sister to bring me into her Resistance network so I can report back to him with names. I never had any intention of carrying out his orders; my only thought was to warn Ève. I did. But at what cost? Still, the major will be furious when he discovers Herr Geller intercepted me for his own interrogation, but even the major must bow to the wishes of the Gestapo.

No one stops me when I head upstairs to the ground floor and leave through the Rue Drouot exit, the crowd thinning and the excitement over for now. I brace myself for the major's probing questions, his lip curling when I tell him I couldn't convince Ève to reveal anything, then no doubt his hands sliding under my skirt as he reminds me that personal failure is *not* acceptable in the New Order. I can't tell him I didn't see her, sadly. Herr Geller would be eager to catch me in a lie and he'd use it against me.

A cool shiver races up and down my spine.

I was wrong.

The major is waiting for me, but he isn't in his car, and he isn't alone.

I see him cavorting with a young woman so thin her movements are like faint whispers as she walks into the late afternoon sunlight, her hair brownish-amber, her lipstick a brutal red. She's young, no more than eighteen, but she's trying to look older with the deep lip color. She's wearing a tomato-hued dress cut on the bias and buttoned up the front and accented with a high white collar and cuffs. Dark stockings. A white hat with a small brim, white gloves. The quality of the silk, the innovative design discreetly telling me she's wearing couture. The girl is either a model or a member of the Parisian crème de la crème. He must have introduced himself at a nearby café and then sweet-talked her into leaving with him.

He's forgotten all about me.

I'm stuck without a ride. The last time he left me to walk home alone, I got blisters on my feet. I head toward the motorcar. I'm not in the mood for this after dealing with Ève *and* the Gestapo. I intend to tell the major in a genteel but firm voice that Herr Geller interrogated me about Ève and we should talk when—

I see the girl shake her head 'no' back and forth and try to pull away from him. He won't let her go. Oh dear, I recognize that icy blue anger shooting from his eyes, his pressed lips. He hates being told no. I pull back into the shadows of the five-story auction house so he can't see me. I don't have a good feeling about this. I know how the major lets his ego override his reason. How can I forget how he was the time I insisted he wait for me to come to his bed until *after* I had breastfed Ninette? He watched me doing the most natural thing *une mère* can do for her baby with a jealous scowl on his face, then headed out to the *One-Two-Two* bordello, for uniformed German officers only, to satisfy his urges instead. My fears are realized when the major forces the pretty girl toward his waiting motorcar, holding her by the elbow, her mouth twisting up in a macabre way, her eyes big and frightened.

*What did he promise her? Silk stockings? Chocolate? An apartment on the Right Bank? Did she see through him and change her mind?*

Too late. The die is cast. She's caught in his trap.

I stop, my heart pounding. I know I should turn on my heel and walk away and leave him to his dirty SS business. I can't. An unforgiving memory in me shrouded in pain and humiliation intensifies and roots me to the spot when I see him shove her into the Mercedes. I must do *something* to stop him, to help that girl and save her from him. But then I see him climb in after her and slam the door behind him so hard the shiny metal buckles and turns liquid in the sun, and he draws the curtains shut so no one can see inside.

I can see it though. In my mind.

I know what comes next. His grabby hands finding his pleasure by ripping open the bodice of her dress rather than unbuttoning it, then lifting her skirt high above her waist and snapping her garters so they smack against the soft skin of her thighs like the sting of a wasp. Then squeezing her breasts and digging his fingers into her flesh till she begs him to stop. Her underwear ripped and then—

I hear a muffled cry. Then another.

Yes, it's happening again. Another rape.

But this time I'm a witness.

*I won't let him ruin another girl.*

I walk with a grand purpose up to the Nazi vehicle, ignoring that disgusting little swastika flag on the hood flapping in the breeze, ready to yank the door open and act shocked and indignant like a jealous lover when I see them huddled together. Yes, he'll spew epithets at me in German, but I'm depending on the fact he needs me to spy for him at the hat shop, the House of Péroline, where I work, to avoid any reprisal more dire than that. I listen to the careless gossip of Frenchwomen for news about the whereabouts of Jewish citizens not eager to comply with the compulsory registration laws, or others who have gone into hiding or left Paris. Then my hope is he'll push the girl out of the motorcar with her hat askew and eyes wet from weeping, but it'll all be over before he was able to sexually assault her. Then we'll drive away and pretend nothing happened.

I don't count on the loyalty—and German strict adherence to obeying orders—of his driver. The young soldier bolts out of the vehicle when he sees me approach, then stands at attention, pulling his sidearm out of his holster and pointing it at me. He shoots me a fierce look that says he's duty bound to keep me away. I don't move. It's obvious if I try to interfere, he won't hesitate to fire his weapon.

Wound me, even kill me.

I've never felt more useless.

Like rainwater dripping on the wilted petals of a rose until they fall off and float away on a puddle. Nothing I can do will save it. I can only stand here. And observe.

I can't get inside, and it's killing me.

I watch the motorcar shake, the curtains covering the

passenger windows flutter, the girl's muffled cries that go silent when I imagine he puts his gloved hand over her mouth. Then more shaking in a syncopated, grinding rhythm you become familiar with when you lie under him in the dark and count the painful minutes until it's over. The soft skin between your legs red from him rubbing, raw and painful. I shall never forget him reaching a climax with his SS officer's cap still perched upon his head.

Then he's finished. The deed accomplished. No word of comfort. No holding your hand, stroking your cheek; *nothing*.

I'd prayed he'd had his fill of conquests, that his passion to remain in Paris to work directly under Hans Posse, Hitler's 'art curator', would quell his libido and need for female conquests. *Why should it?* He faces no restriction of his salacious activities from his superiors, no reprimand. Even the Gestapo sees no clear path to stopping him. He's an SS officer. 'A god, and should be treated as such by all Frenchwomen,' the major likes to boast. Which means his modus operandi hasn't changed since he attacked *me*.

Then raped me.

In the back of the *same* Mercedes motorcar.

# 6

## PARIS, MAY 8, 1942

*Ève*

*Take me to Saint-Lazare? But I'm not a whore.*

Can't the policeman see that?

I wear no makeup, no black net stockings or fancy pink lace garters. No ruffles on my dress. No scarlet paint on my cheeks. I wear a cotton print dress, brown corduroy jacket, clogs with wooden soles. Not the usual froufrou favored by a streetwalker, but these days many housewives have taken to the pavements to survive. To eat. See that their children eat, have milk so they don't starve and develop rickets, their bones softening from no milk and no sunshine because they're in hiding to escape the Boches. Is this why Justine stays with the major?

To feed her child?

Of course, I've never had a man of my own, or children. I doubt I ever will. What man wants a female who gets excited over moldy vegetables and fruit?

Sarcastic, yes. Because I'm angry. I've gone on countless dangerous missions sabotaging the German war machine, and here I get picked up by the French police for soliciting. I can hear Michal whispering in my ear, 'Don't panic, Ève. You'll get out of this. You always do.'

I smile. He's that way, seeing the best in me. He's always warning me to be careful, that a young woman like me—he guessed I'm a virgin; I didn't tell him—is vulnerable and a prize for the sport of German soldiers.

I shudder. My teeth chatter. The stories I've heard about Nazi brutality shatter my confidence. Beatings. Broken bones, burned flesh. How could I have been so stupid to strike out on my own? Even more stupid, my identity card is hidden deep in my skirt pocket. So far, the policeman hasn't asked for identification since he assumes I'm a streetwalker and not worth his time. But what if this policeman has sticky fingers and searches me? What if he *did* see a Gestapo alert for Ève Beaufort? *Suspect last seen wearing a brown corduroy jacket and black hat with a feather. Armed and dangerous.* No more deluding myself.

I'm in a serious situation.

I clear my throat. For the first time in my life, my good grades in school and curious nose in a book aren't going to save me. I have no choice but to make my case to this cocky policeman who must think I'm dumb if I believe his threat to take me to Saint Lazare. The women's prison shuttered up tight years ago. Or is he joking because he knows where we *are* going and it's no better than a rat-infested, vermin prison?

'*Please*, monsieur, I'm not a *fille de joie,* I'm a student at the Sorbonne.'

'And I'm Marshal Pétain.' He laughs, referring to the Nazi-appointed French general and leader of Vichy France.

I try to find another tactic, like flirting, which I'm terrible at, before he pushes me into the black police van when—

I hear the woman with the pomegranate-colored hair also

protesting her innocence to the second policeman dragging her over to the van.

Francie.

She pulls away from him. He puts his hands up in disgust and mutters under his breath, 'These whores aren't worth the time.' He shrugs his shoulders and strolls over to the van at the end of the alley, lights up a cigarette no doubt procured from the black market, then jumps into the driver's seat to hide the deed.

Leaving his partner to finish the arrest.

Wearing Maman's hat, Francie is determined that *won't* happen.

She pulls down the brim at an angle and wets her lips. The effect is comical, her attempt at sophistication reminding me of a street mutt pretending it's a poodle.

'You can't take me in, monsieur,' Francie insists. 'I'm respectable, not like this *fille*.'

'*She* attacked *me*, monsieur,' I plead.

'Did not. *She* stole my hat *and* my jacket.' She pulls hard on my sleeve.

'Get your hands *off* me,' I protest. 'You're tearing my jacket.'

'I'll tear the hair out of your head if you don't give me back what's mine.'

My mouth drops open. I can't believe this woman. 'Not if I rip yours out first by its dark roots.'

'I dare you.' She spits at me.

I turn to the policeman watching us with amusement. 'Arrest her, monsieur!' I yell.

'And miss the show?' He folds his arms across his chest and grins. 'Go ahead, tear each other apart and save me the trouble of bringing you both in.'

He sweeps his glance over the girl, lingering over her ample bosom emphasized by her cleavage. His eyes widen, then he makes a crude gesture with his hands. The girl laughs, then pulls a fast move on me I never saw coming.

'*Ai... eee!*' she yells, grabbing my long hair flowing down to my waist and twisting it around her fist. *Damn, that hurts.* 'Give me my jacket, mademoiselle,' she insists, pulling my head back. 'Then I'll be on my way and *you* can enjoy an evening at the police station polishing the captain's boots.'

I can imagine what *that* means.

'I will not.' I struggle to free myself from her grip, my scalp on fire, my arms bruised, muscles sore, grunting and groaning until I gain the advantage and twist around and clip her on the jaw. Michal always says I have a good left hook and takes credit for teaching me. She flies backward and lands smack on the pavement.

'Enough, you two,' the policeman orders. 'Get up, whore.'

Recovering quickly, Francie makes cooing 'ooh la la' noises while wiggling her bottom in his face.

While I rub my aching knuckles.

'Give her the jacket, mademoiselle,' the policeman orders me. The girl hasn't stopped gyrating her backside at him, leaving him with a big grin and a sweaty face.

'No, monsieur, I won't do it.'

*I can't.*

What if the French police find the stolen German pistol? They'll claim it belongs to the streetwalker since she claimed the jacket is hers. The girl is mean and greedy, but she's innocent. It won't matter. They'll confiscate the handgun and sell it on the black market, then send Francie to Cherche-Midi prison where she'll conveniently disappear, to hide their dirty deed. The last thing they want is the Wehrmacht snooping into their activities.

'Yes, you will, mademoiselle or... *ah...*'

*Is that a groan I hear?*

'Or what, monsieur?' I ask, not believing I'm caught up in a situation becoming more dangerous by the second.

'Or *mon ami*, the captain,' Francie butts in, her voice breathy, 'will take it from you.'

Now I *am* in a mess. If he searches me and finds the pistol, I *will* go to prison. There must be another way. I need a plan. Yes, of course. Remove the pistol, then give her the jacket and make a run for it and pray the policeman is more interested in indulging in a sexual game with the streetwalker than going after me.

I heave out a loud sigh. 'You win.'

'*Bon,* mademoiselle. Hurry up.'

The policeman pulls at Francie's skirt, reaching underneath and grabbing at the thin cotton slip that separates him from getting what he wants and intends to get. This lonely policeman who spends day after day rounding up ladies of the night, stashing them into a black police van, following orders from the snooty officers of the Wehrmacht but *never* pleasing himself, succumbs to the basest of human needs. *Why should the brass have all the fun?* I imagine him saying.

Francie rubs her body against him, whispering in his ear and making him groan.

This girl knows all the tricks.

Leaving me out in the cold.

She continues her game, raking her eyes over me in triumph… from my long, messy hair to the tips of my shoes. I turn my back as if I'm embarrassed by their blatant sexual display and remove the pistol from my jacket, then stuff it into my skirt pocket.

Two bullets left in the chamber. I shudder. I pray I never have to fire it again.

I admit a pang of guilt hangs over me. If she's arrested, there's a good chance the Gestapo will question her since she's wearing

Maman's hat. True, a lot of girls wear black hats with feathers, but Francie has a big mouth and who knows what the secret police will trick her into admitting once they start interrogating her. I don't want to make trouble for her, but if she doesn't have the pistol on her, they'll believe her story that she was lying. If they bring Justine in to identify 'her sister Ève', she'll tell them they've got the wrong girl.

The real question is: will Justine be happy or sad that it's *not* me?

'Here, take the jacket.' I rip it off and toss it to her. She smiles big, believing she's won.

'I'd take the dress, too, mademoiselle,' she bullies me, 'but it's so drab and ugly I'd never attract a man wearing that.'

I'm not listening to her insults when Francie puts on the jacket and parades in front of the policeman then lands a big kiss on his mouth. I'm already halfway down the alleyway.

I turn right, then jump over a low stone ledge and make my way through a dark passageway that leads to the boulevard, counting my blessings. I'm shaking so much, I nearly trip over my own feet.

Another escape.

It's unreal to me how often this keeps happening. Since joining the Resistance, I've been shot at, nearly blown up by a bomb that went off too soon, hidden in an empty beer barrel that smelled so bad I gagged, and jumped off a moving railcar. But I've never come this close to being arrested.

Because of a streetwalker named Francie who never got a break in life.

In another time, our paths would never have crossed. I'd never be in a situation where I held a woman's life in my hands. I pray I made the right decision to let her take over being 'me' and hope Justine will be relieved I'm not in Gestapo hands. In spite of her sins, I believe the young girl born Francine under a windmill is a victim like so many women.

I head south toward the ninth arrondissement where the foul stench of spent lives turns into a heady rose scent where even during the Occupation, the flowers bloom, if not as tall as before but surviving. I have a more pressing situation to deal with. My plans have changed. Instead of heading for Iris's apartment on Rue Damrémont to hide out, I'm going back to Maison Bleue, Maman will wonder where I've been. She knows I saw the notice about *The Daisy Sisters* in the *Gazette*, but she doesn't know I'm here. Yes, it's dangerous. The Gestapo is on high alert, dragging in anyone remotely fitting my description, and if they make Justine identify me and she says the girl isn't me, the German secret police will come snooping around the estate looking for me. I've got to warn Maman and Madame de Giocomte. Get them new identity papers and convince them they must leave Paris.

Which means I have a new mission.

And it begins with a pair of scissors.

# 7

## PARIS, MAY 8, 1942

*Justine*

I'm shaking like a naked fool when I head for the hat shop where I work, the House of Péroline on Rue de Rivoli. An exquisite pearl in the Paris shopping district, where I'm pleased to say our *chapeaux* outsell the hat departments of Aux Trois Quartiers and the Galleries Lafayette combined. A lovely aura of femininity abides in the shop where a woman, whether she's French or a German auxiliary worker, feels pampered and confident. Yes, we cater to everyone. We have to. We're on the list of 'Nazi friendly' shops. I'm not thrilled about that, but I find listening to the German girls' gossip provides me with intelligence I can pass on to Arsène. I'm surprised how loose these Fräuleins are with their tongues. For example, I've picked up enough German to recognize something's amiss with the head of the German Security Police.

Reinhard Heydrich.

I've heard stories about his brutal treatment of Jews which set my nerves rattling when he was here in Paris. Gossip is he wants to run Paris like he did Czechoslovakia, and the whispers among the German office workers was that a girl there ought to keep her eyes lowered and her skirts long, to avoid attracting his attention. Or she could end up in his lair of deviant sexual activities. God help France if he's posted here. I pray he stays in his own backyard.

Meanwhile, I'll continue to sell dreams and hope in the House of Péroline. The Fräuleins who wander into the shop are young, vulnerable, hailing from small German towns and thrilled to work in Paris. I tell them this is a place where a girl can fantasize about what *she* wants to be, not what the Party tells her she *should* be, and she can make that fantasy come true with a new hat.

A hat I designed.

Today that fantasy lies like a cold stone pressing down on my heart. The pain won't go away. I'm tapped out, my energy depleted. I don't believe my own spiel. How can I when I can't forget the ugly image of the major pushing that poor girl into his motorcar? It will haunt me for a long time. I *must* find out what happened to her, if she *was* raped by the major, and tell her she's not alone. That I'm here for her. But can I help her forget?

No, you never forget.

Last week I was chatting with Madame Péroline over a cup of the bitter root brew we call coffee about that August day in 1940 when the major sexually assaulted me. I don't remember why it came up, but it does every once in a while when the shop is slow and we both get maudlin, her over her husband and son in a POW camp, and me wondering how I survived these past two years without losing my mind.

Then I saw Ninette playing with her rag doll. My little girl hugged the bright blue button-eyed doll she calls 'Maman', for she's fascinated by *my* blue eyes, as she rocked back and forth with a smile on her face. Madame Péroline asked me if Ninette helps me forget. *No*, I told her. You never forget. And that other women have also been hurt by the major and other Nazis like him.

I won't give up seeking justice for them.

It's a task that takes a toll on me. Yes, a *physical* toll. I am still surprised how my body changes when I talk about the rape: my voice goes higher, I get shaky inside. Then my cheeks flush hot and I feel embarrassed and wonder why I ever told anyone. Why didn't I keep it to myself? Does Madame Péroline see me differently now? The last thing I want is for her to feel sorry for me.

I want her to see me as a survivor... not a victim.

I clamp my legs together without realizing I'm doing it. An automatic reflex, I imagine. The sudden sharp ache in my groin doesn't surprise me. I'm still not over my trauma of feeling violated, but this time the pain I can only describe as cut glass isn't for me. It's for that girl. My heart pounds, imagining the fear and self-loathing she must be going through. Facing an unknown future because of this Nazi, a man who holds her life in his dirty hands. I should have known he'd let his ego out of his trousers and strike again.

Another victim. Another heartache.

I *swear* I will make it up to this girl for what the major did to her. Yet I wonder, do I dare pray he will no longer seek *my* bed?

*How can I even say that?*

Guilt floods through me. I hate myself. I'm ashamed. Am I turning into one of 'them'? Thinking only of my own gain?

*Or am I just human for wanting the sexual humiliation to end?*

My emotional musings have led me to pay no attention to where my feet are taking me and I wander past the hat shop. I spin around, but I'm shaking so badly my own hat tilts to one side and nearly falls off my head. I grab it tight. I need to regroup, go back to my cozy apartment on Rue des Martyrs after I pick up Ninette.

I lift my chin, wet my lips, inhale then breathe out to compose myself, not show Madame Péroline my fears. She's a good soul and she put her life on the line for me. For Ninette. Madame Péroline spoils her terribly, but I know she's safe here. We clashed at first when the major shoved me in front of her like a prisoner on parole, insisting she give me a job in the name of the Reich, but the lively milliner has become a good friend, watching over my little girl at odd hours, not giving up any information about me to the Gestapo when they interrogated her. Beat her.

She knows nothing about Justine Beaufort; only the identity given to me by the major, as Rachelle D'Artois, comes into play. I'm in too deep to tell her the truth.

I smooth down my powder blue suit, set my hat back on my head and rearrange my long veil over my shoulder before I buzz into the milliner's shop glowing in girly pink and soft pastels, a break for our customers trying to survive in a world at war. My world changes, too. My heart warms when I see my little girl waddling on her chubby legs, her arms outstretched when she spots me. Her blue eyes shine and I smile over that adorable way her lips curl when she says, 'Maman, Maman.'

The words catch in my throat every time I hear her call my name. Is there anything sweeter than the angel breath of your child's voice? Like pings on a harp. It touches your heart.

I take long strides to her, and my mood changes. I cringe when I see a figure hovering in the shadows like an unwelcome dinner guest. A guest in uniform. *What's the SS doing here?* I don't need this. I can hold my own with Herr Geller, but an eager by-the-book Nazi officer is as unpredictable as a frog with a belly full of bugs. He's here for a reason, and it can't be good.

My first thought is, has something happened to Ève?

Did the Gestapo man send him here to watch me break when I hear the news? Catch me at a weak moment, believing I know more than I'm telling? No, Herr Geller wouldn't miss the show. He'd want a front row seat.

What about Ninette? Is this SS man here on orders from the major to take her? I'm not taking any chances. Keeping my baby away from this Nazi is the only thing that matters to me.

Before I can pick my baby up in my arms, I hear—

'You are Rachelle d'Artois, mademoiselle?'

The indignant Nazi officer—a lieutenant—comes out of the shadows and leers at me.

'Yes.' I keep my voice steady.

'I've been waiting for you, mademoiselle.'

That worries me.

'Madame Péroline,' I say, attempting to prevent my voice from cracking, 'can you watch Ninette for me?'

I look over at the hat shop owner rubbing her fingers together, hesitating for a few seconds before grabbing Ninette. She cradles my little girl in her arms. The child frets, but Madame Péroline doesn't let her go. She knows I live in fear of the major taking my baby away from me. She waits for my signal. I motion for her to go to the back of the shop. She nods, ready to race out the rear entrance with Ninette if the situation turns ugly.

I take on a nonchalant attitude and pick up a bonnet off the shelf covered with fruit made from beeswax.

'May I ask *why*, monsieur?' I avoid eye contact with the Nazi, instead rearranging the waxy purple grapes, the musky, honeyed scent making my nose wiggle.

'I'm in need of your services, mademoiselle.'

*I don't like this. Does he mean sex?*

The major made it clear I'm to flirt with the SS officers, notably General von Klum, but not sleep with them.

'I beg your pardon, monsieur?' I feign innocence, though out of the corner of my eye I see him staring at my legs. I'm wearing sheer silk stockings, a rarity in Paris these days.

'It's for my... wife back in Germany, in Hamburg. She recently gave birth.' He smiles like a fox chomping on a rabbit's tail when he pulls out a photograph of a young girl with blonde braids, sad eyes, and a crooked smile. She can't be more than sixteen. I'm not surprised he stumbled over the word 'wife'. The major enjoys reminding me I'm a lucky girl, having been *chosen* to have a baby for an SS officer. This poor girl was likely recruited because she has light blonde hair and I suspect blue eyes.

Like me.

'She's very pretty... and so young.'

He runs his black-gloved finger over my cheekbone in a slow crawl to intimidate me. I shiver. I can't help it.

'It's an old photo taken when she attended a girls' boarding school in Luxembourg.'

I'm about to ask him, *When did she graduate? Yesterday?* But after dealing with Herr Geller, I know when to back down. That doesn't mean I like it.

'Ilse is a proud member of the Party,' he continues, 'and a good German mother.' He pushes out his chest with pride. 'She bore me a son. I wish to buy her a hat from Paris as a reward and I'd like *you* to pick one out.' He grins. 'She likes pink.'

*What young girl doesn't?*

After prodding him, the lieutenant admits the marriage was 'arranged', the latest scheme by the Nazi higher-ups to procure a future 'army' for Germany with young girls chosen for the privilege to bear the children of the elite SS.

I let out a deep sigh. *Isn't that also rape?*

I doubt the lieutenant sees it that way.

'It will be my pleasure to pick out our prettiest hat for your "wife",' I say with a rush of air escaping from my lungs. Still, I question his motives even if he's not the first German soldier to wander into the shop with a photo of a wife or sweetheart asking for help in choosing a hat, but something's off. He works his jaw, sniffs the air filled with a lavender scent, then wriggles his nose as if the full scale of femininity in a shop filled with lace and blooms and velvet ribbons is too much for his stoic SS mind to handle. Like he's outnumbered by an army of hats.

*Why did he choose this shop? Why today?*

My instinct proves me right when he takes me by the elbow and leads me away from the shop window. 'I also have a message for you from Major Saxe-Müllenheim.'

'Oh?' I knew he was up to something.

'Forget whatever you *think* you saw this afternoon near the Hôtel Drouot.'

'Don't you mean, what I *know* I saw?' I stare him down. 'The pretty brunette with the major?'

'Yes.'

'Doesn't he have the guts to tell me himself?' I cock an eyebrow.

'You dare to disobey a direct order, mademoiselle?'

'You can't order me to forget a woman forced into the back of a motorcar against her will.' I make my stand, say what's on my mind because if I don't, I'll burst. 'She isn't the first girl he's forced to satisfy him.'

He bristles.

'It's not your affair, Mademoiselle d'Artois. Is that clear?'

'What if she gets pregnant? Will you buy *her* a hat, too?'

He laughs. 'You French. You're nothing but trouble. You satisfy our needs, but you don't compare to our German women.

Virtuous, warm, caring mothers who tend to the hearth *and* their children.'

He nods toward the back room where Madame Péroline is hiding out with my little girl.

Inside I'm seething at his cold remarks about my maternal skills, but I control my temper. Pull back. Tradecraft, after all. I've already gotten his dander up with my outburst. I shouldn't have been so blunt. I try to walk it back. I smile and give him the full-on spiel expected of me, even if I want to throw up.

'I do what I must to fulfill my duties here in the shop, monsieur, even if it's at my own expense so German women can enjoy Parisian fashion.'

He smirks. 'Well said, mademoiselle. We Germans pride ourselves on our mental and physical strength. Something you French could learn from us.'

'Next you'll tell me food rationing is good for the figure,' I mutter under my breath.

'I admit, French girls *do* have a certain charm. Like you, mademoiselle.' He looks me up and down, enjoying the view. 'I see why the major finds you most attractive and chose you to have his child.'

I slam the bonnet with the waxy fruit down on the table, the phony grapes shaking loose. I regret it immediately when he glares at me, but I've never had to endure this kind of talk with another Nazi except General von Klum, who, even though he's wildly flirtatious, at least treats me with some respect. I can't let this Boche get away with his painful words.

'Is there even one decent man among you, Lieutenant, who *doesn't* condone this outrageous behavior of "choosing" women... *girls*, for sex and having babies?'

'In a word, mademoiselle, *no*. Every soldier in the Führer's army enjoys the privilege of leaving his calling card.'

*Did he really say that?*

I rage inside, his vile meaning making me sick. 'You *can't* believe that to be true. It's degrading to women.'

That did it. I went too far. He doesn't like being talked back to by a woman, especially a Frenchwoman, and he makes a threatening move toward me, then thinks better of it. 'I'd watch your step, mademoiselle.' He leans over and whispers in my ear, 'If I were you, I'd rather have me as a friend than an enemy.'

I squish my nails into the waxy grapes. 'Of course, monsieur. I regret if I caused you discomfort. You're right, the Nazis are our friends.'

My stomach turns. It *always* turns when I have to let them have the upper hand.

He dismisses my remark with a wave of his hand. '*Gut*. It's time you French know your place. *We* are the conquerors and you are subject to the Führer's wishes. And mine. I control your fate. You're most fortunate I have my orders to deliver the message to you and nothing more.' He whispers in my ear, 'I would enjoy watching you moan and squirm beneath me.'

*You and your dirty mind can go to hell.*

I want to say it out loud, but I don't. Instead, I force a smile when he puts out his gloved hand, palm up. 'The hat for my wife, mademoiselle, and I shall be on my way.'

I shove a frilly pink cloche hat at him with tiny rosebuds on the brim and a lace veil, then I charge him three times the listed price.

He pays it without flinching, then clicks his heels and gives me the Hitler salute. I'm careful to salute back, keep up the act.

Then he's gone.

Taking his Nazi arrogance with him.

# 8

## PARIS, MAY 8, 1942

### *Ève*

'Ève, *mon enfant*, why are you cutting off your beautiful hair?'

Maman goes into hysterics when she finds me upstairs in our room, Justine's and mine, at Maison Bleue, chopping off my long brown hair with her big, silver sewing scissors. *Snip, snip*. I feel my cheeks heating, my heart pounding in an awful rhythm that pulses loud in my ears.

*It took you years to grow your hair down to your waist.*

*Now you're cutting it off in five minutes?*

What choice do I have?

The Gestapo man is after me, not to mention the French police.

After my run-in with the streetwalker and the police, I'd made my way home sneaking through alleyways and slipping through an unlocked door in the back of an apartment and exiting out the front. I was fortunate not to encounter any Nazis, though I did wake up a crotchety concierge who assumed I was sneaking out of a man's room. She'd banged on his door and gave him an earful, giving me time to escape.

After that, I ran and ran until I reached Maison Bleue and let myself into the three-story mansion unnoticed by slipping through the trap door near the greenhouse. The wood is overgrown with dandelions, making it difficult to see, and leads down to the root cellar and into the kitchen through a hidden door. No one knows about the entrance except Cook and me. And Justine. Cook told us how Monsieur de Giocomte's great-great grandfather used the secret door to sneak his lover, a young Italian countess, into the *maison* without anyone seeing her.

Today, the hidden entrance saved me, allowing me to arrive in the house undetected. I have no idea if the Gestapo are on their way here.

To Maison Bleue.

I can't let them arrest me. I have things to do.

Like staying alive.

And getting Maman and Madame de Giocomte out of Paris.

Chopping off my hair is the first step.

I squeeze my eyes shut and *cut*. No mind I could miss with the scissors and slice off my finger. My emotions are running high... After all, this is my hair, the one thing about me that makes me feel pretty. Vivid memories of Maman brushing my long hair every night since I was a little girl hit me hard... Will she still love me?

*Stop being silly.*

To be honest, she'll get used to me having short hair, but my news about Justine will change her world. When Maman finds out I couldn't talk my sister into coming home, she'll be so upset she'll stop talking to *me*. Maman loves me, but Justine is her golden child. I don't mind. I've always understood I'm different than my sister, but I pray someday Maman will see that I shine golden in different ways.

And what about Michal? Will he *ever* see me as pretty with short, boyish hair?

I'll never forget the first time we met during a mission setting explosives on a train headed for Germany with ill-gotten goods. When my cap flew off and he saw my long hair come tumbling down, his eyes popped and for a moment I saw that look men give a girl when there's a spark... desire. Of course, he sloughed it off, but I thought we had something then.

Now I'll never know.

And where *is* Michal now? He comes and goes like spring rain, sprouting up like a wildflower when you least expect him. Last we spoke, his skin was drawn tight over his cheekbones with a new scar fixed on his chin. When I asked him where he got it, he mumbled something about a Nazi bayonet that got too close. He appeared downhearted with all the arrests of Resistance members, and the money to fund our network is nearly depleted, not to mention we have few weapons.

I have the feeling Michal made his way to Lyon in the Unoccupied Zone in the south to get more guns and ammo and gather intelligence. God, I miss him. I have no idea when he'll be back.

*If* he comes back.

*Michal would want you to do what you must to save yourself.*

That moment of truth hits me hard and sends me into action.

Off comes my hair in long bunches fluttering like the feathers of angels' wings through the air and landing on the tips of my platform heels. I don't stop. Can't. I swore I wouldn't cry and I'll not start now. I made up my mind to follow my instincts and disappear before the Gestapo rubber stamp me as a *résistant* marked for jail and torture.

'I *have* to cut off my hair, Maman, and take on a new identity.'

I brush off stray curls resting on my shoulder. 'I can no longer pretend you and Madame are safe at Maison Bleue. You're not.'

I chop off the hair closer to my ear.

*Careful. There. Left side done. Now for the right.*

'We *are* safe here, Ève.' Maman picks up bunches of my hair and holds it close to her breasts. I see her eyes get misty. The cut locks represent to her a time in our lives we'll never get back.

'You can't be sure, Maman. That's why you have to leave Paris.'

'No, we shall stay. Madame de Giocomte has sent word to a member of the Rothschild family in England requesting their help with the Vichy government,' she says, cutting me off with a deep fervor in her voice that reminds me Madame's influence is everywhere. 'She paid a bribe to a government official to send her letter through diplomatic circles.'

'How can you be sure they received it?' I ask.

'The Rothschilds are dedicated to upholding the cultural heritage of France. Surely they will intervene for Madame de Giocomte to keep Maison Bleue out of Nazi hands.'

'They can't help us, Maman.' I let go with a long sigh. 'We're on a Gestapo list.'

Her hand goes to her throat. 'It *can't* be true.'

'It is.'

'Who told you that?'

How can I tell her, *your own daughter*? Then watch her fall apart before my eyes? I'm at an impasse. If I tell her it was Justine, it will break her heart. It's important she stays strong, physically and mentally, while I arrange for their escape.

'I can't tell you, Maman. *Please* don't ask me again.'

I pick up a silver-plated hand mirror Madame gave to Justine. Maman hasn't moved a thing of Justine's except to wrap up her broken doll from that fateful August day in black velvet scraps and bury it in the bottom of a drawer. I didn't understand it at first and asked her, *Why keep it?* Then I realized it was her way of putting her lost daughter to rest and I never mentioned it again. Now I use my sister's mirror as a barrier between us to avoid her probing me for answers. I look into the glass, turn my head left then right to check my handiwork. Uneven, but it will do.

Maman has her own opinion. 'My God, Ève, you look like an upside-down teacup.'

I grin. 'I do, don't I?'

In spite of the grimness gripping my soul, a chuckle escapes my lips. My hair is wavy and thick... what's left of it. Running my fingers through my shorn hair, a heavy sigh escapes my lips. My chest is tight and I swear my heart is racing. I don't recognize myself except when I look at my eyes. Big and shining. I never realized how doll-like they are, like Justine's. And here I never believed her when she said we look like sisters. We did. Not now. Not with my crude haircut. A nostalgia for my long hair is already setting in, but if I don't change my appearance, we're all as good as dead.

Or worse.

Each day we hear more about the deportation of Jews to Drancy—a transit camp northeast of Paris used to transport Jews east. Madame de Giocomte isn't safe and Maman is on a Gestapo list. Remi, the leader of our cell, warned us that when he was picked up for being out after curfew, he overheard German soldiers gloating about Jews soon being forced to wear a yellow star on their clothing and anyone in sympathy with a Jewish person will be arrested and must wear a white armband with a yellow star with the words 'Friend of the Jews'. The camp is about an hour from the station where Monsieur de Giocomte boarded a train and was deported last December. I can imagine

Maman and Madame thinking if they're arrested they will just meet up with our beloved patriarch. They won't think the Germans will herd them onto a third-class compartment on a train with bars on the windows headed east. Not only Jews but political dissidents—girls, women like me working for the Resistance, typing up pamphlets and leaving them on seats in the Métro—are sent there. And French citizens, too. I found Cook in tears last week when she heard about a dear friend taken to prison for using leftover food to trade for shoes for her children.

Is there no end to this Nazi madness?

I'm not taking any chances.

Right now, I need men's trousers, a jacket. Maman could probably alter Monsieur's clothes for me quicker than it would take that Gestapo man to work his silly crossword puzzle. Then I'll make my way back to Montmartre, find Iris and ask her to get Maman and Madame new identity cards, then check with Remi's contacts about getting them out of France along the Comet Line—an escape route to the southwest dodging Nazi patrols and making the exhausting nighttime trek along an old smuggler's route over the mountains. First by train then a local guide, *passeur*, to escort them on their long journey by bicycle and then on foot over the Pyrenees to Spain, on to Gibraltar and finally to London. There Madame de Giocomte can make contact with the Rothschild family once again. I might never see them again, but they'll be safe.

'Please try to understand, I'm saving you and Madame from a vile Gestapo man who enjoys making arrests, including me.' I look directly at my dear *maman*, a woman filled with goodness who wouldn't hurt a living creature. 'And that includes getting to me by hurting you and Madame.'

She lays her hand across her chest. 'But why us, Ève?'

'The Gestapo found out I'm in the Resistance and the secret

police want me to give up names, *which I will never do.*' My emotions get the better of me and I bang the delicate vanity table with the hand mirror so hard it shakes. Frustration makes me blurt out, 'I can't believe my own sister sold me out to the Boches—'

'*Justine?*' Maman starts breathing so hard, she holds on to the bedpost to steady herself. Her face is ashen and her hands blessed with nimble fingers that never miss a stitch shake so badly, she can't stop. 'What's going on, Ève? *What aren't you telling me?*'

I'm done for.

Why can't I keep my mouth shut? Or did my subconscious blab it out because I know it's terribly wrong to keep such a precious secret from my dear *maman*? Even if the news that Justine is a Nazi collaborator tears her apart like it did me? Fear and fatigue broke down my defenses and there's no turning back. I *have* to tell her the truth about Justine.

My penance for keeping quiet is a bout of nausea that sends bile up my throat. I feel like I'm going to be sick when I blurt out: 'I saw Justine at the Hôtel Drouot, Maman... She's alive.'

'*Mais non*, it can't be true!' She clasps her hand over her mouth and sinks to the floor in a puddle of gray-blue cotton, her legs giving out. Shocked, yes, but there is joy seeping out of her like melted honey, because her little girl is alive.

'I couldn't believe it either,' I continue, 'but I saw her there wearing the most outrageous blue hat with shiny white pearls and the most ridiculous long veil.'

Maman smiles. 'Yes, that sounds like my Justine.'

I know what's she thinking, that since Justine was a little girl, she wanted to be a designer, see her work in the best couture houses not just in Paris but in New York, Lisbon, and London. Well, she's on her way to getting that wish, but at what cost?

I race through the events earlier, helping Maman to her feet while telling her how Justine made a brazen move to show herself during the bidding of a Corot painting knowing I'd follow her to the cellar of the auction house where I confronted her. The harsh words we exchanged, the heart-stopping moment I laid eyes again on *The Daisy Sisters* stolen by that arrogant SS officer and how my sister used it to lure me into her trap.

'*Trap?* What are you talking about, Ève?'

I explain how it all came to a terrible climax when she accused me of working for the Resistance, *to warn me*, she said. Or was it a clever ploy to cajole me to reveal my friends? Convince me to join her in helping the Nazis?

It sickens me.

'Your daughter, *my* sister,' I begin, choking on the words, 'the girl we love and cherish, isn't dead. But she's changed.'

'What do you mean, *changed*?'

'She's—she's not the same girl.'

'What is that supposed to mean?' Maman demands.

'Justine is working for the Nazis, Maman. She's involved in what they call *collaboration horizontale*.'

Maman slaps me. Hard. 'How *dare* you accuse your sister of such blasphemy.'

I touch my cheek, already turning hot. I feel pain blister my skin. Unlike when the prostitute hit me, this time the pain is also in my heart. I deserve it. I've broken my *maman*'s spirit, her faith, her trust in her daughter that's never wavered since the day the SS major kidnapped her.

'It's true, Maman. Justine sold me out. Put the Gestapo on my tail.'

'Your sister would *never* do such a thing.'

'How can you be so sure?' I beg her, wanting more than anything for my mother to give me hope that I'm wrong. What frightens me most is that if I'm right, my relationship with my sister is irrevocably broken. That hurts the most, making me search my heart and ask, *What was she thinking when she saw me? Did she feel a fraction of joy? Did she remember that we were once so close we shared every secret?*

'I feel it here, Ève... in my heart.' Maman crosses her hands over her chest and looks upward. 'Justine is a good girl. She loves France, loves us.' She squeezes her eyes shut, her words fervent and pious. 'My baby is alive and she'll be home soon. I know it.'

Folding her hands together, she murmurs prayers of thanks to God. It's as if she never heard me say that Justine is a collaborator. All that matters to her is hearing her child is alive. Do I dare tell Maman that I suspect she's a *grand-mère*? No, I must not. Then she'd never leave Paris. And what if I'm wrong? It would break her heart. If I'm right, I have no doubt Maman will embrace the baby as her own.

'I assure you, Ève, no matter what you saw today, Justine is no traitor to France.' Maman crosses herself. 'I'd bet on my life to prove it.'

'I wish I could agree, Maman, but you didn't see her as I did.'

She takes my hands in hers. 'Don't give up on your sister, Ève, for my sake.'

To please Maman, I nod my head, even though I don't believe Justine is innocent. No Parisienne has access to such expensive silk and pearls unless she's the mistress of a German officer.

I can't see how Justine would engage in such degrading antics willingly. Yet she was so insistent on me being an embarrassment to *her*. That hurt. Still, she *did* warn me. Do I dare believe Maman is right? I wish it were so, but I can't take that chance. I know how the Gestapo think. It's only a matter of time before I'm arrested. They won't take me in right away; they'll wait. Follow me. Men in black trench coats hissing at me like a snake popping up from a hole in the ground, watching me, waiting for me to make a mistake. But I have the advantage. They're looking for a girl, not a young man. That's why I'd decided to cut my hair. I wear men's clothes anyway, when Michal and I go on a mission to blow up a German depot or set explosives on train tracks.

After today, Ève Beaufort is no more.

I shall become a student named Luc Dumont, but I need a new identity card since the Nazis now require everyone over sixteen to carry one. Michal will help me. *Bon*, but I've yet to convince my *maman* she's in danger.

'I must get you and Madame out of Paris *now.*'

'I'm not leaving, Ève. Your sister will do the right thing. Come home to us. You'll see.'

I whistle through my teeth, frustrated at trying to make her understand Justine has no intention of doing 'the right thing', that she's found a new life with this Nazi major—God, how can she let him touch her?—or is it because having the fashion career she always wanted is more important to her than saving France?

*Saving us?*

'I begged Justine to join us in our fight to drive the Boches out of Paris, Maman, *begged her*, but she's—she's different. I didn't know her; *you* wouldn't know her. She's not your golden child anymore.'

'How can you say that about your own sister?' Maman's joy turns to disgust. She doesn't see clearly what Justine's betrayal means. I've got to get it through her head that whether Justine is dead or alive, the damage is done. I'd rather die than see her and Madame become prisoners of the secret police.

I repeat, 'We're on a Gestapo list, Maman—'

'I don't want to hear any more, Ève.'

'But you're in danger, Maman. *And* Madame. Surely you don't want anything to happen to her.'

I hear a woman clear her throat behind me.

'I'm not leaving Paris, Ève.' It is Madame de Giocomte.

I spin around. 'You must, Madame, *please* listen to me.'

She shakes her head. 'I intend to wait here at Maison Bleue for Monsieur de Giocomte to return.'

How much has she heard, I wonder? *Everything*, by the deep concern in her dark eyes glowing like black obsidian. A secret fire in their depths tells me her soul still burns with love for Monsieur de Giocomte.

'He's not coming back, Madame.'

'We don't know that, Ève. The Germans said it would be for only a little while.'

How well I remember that day when the French police showed up at 4 a.m. with the Gestapo and gave Madame fifteen minutes to pack a suitcase for her husband, who was already showing signs of forgetfulness and confusion. Then the day at the train station at Compiègne when the Nazis put him and hundreds of Jewish men on a train going east.

There's not been a word from him since that day.

But Madame hasn't given up hope.

To me, it seems the two women are acting in a play of their own making, one where they write the ending.

I can't play the dutiful daughter and granddaughter anymore.

'*Damn you two!*' I cry out. 'Don't you see what's happening? The Nazis are only just beginning with their plan to deport Jews. They're taking them to horrible places Michal calls "concentration camps". God only knows what happens there, but nobody comes back from them.'

'We're safe here, Ève.'

'You're *not* safe. I insist you both come with me, now!'

I see a change in Maman's and Madame's faces. The intelligence I have may be exaggerated, but if it's true, the Nazis are orchestrating a 'killing machine' that doesn't use bullets but the very air we breathe. Intelligence is scattered, but information leaked to an informant working for the German Resistance mentioned the SS have been given complete control over 'Zyklon-B', the brand name for hydrogen cyanide, a deadly pesticide invented in the twenties.

I was horrified.

Every chemist is familiar with the highly toxic compound because it's used to disinfect military barracks and ships, but I have yet to understand how the Nazis intend to use it to execute what Michal says they call the 'Final Solution'. The intelligence is very recent, he tells me, and mentions 'death camps'. After what he'd seen the Nazis do to Jews in Poland, he's worried it could happen here in France.

I change up my tactics.

'You have nothing to lose by coming with me now, Maman, Madame. If things quiet down, you can return here to Maison Bleue, and go on with your lives. I'm only asking you to leave for a while, so Michal and I can dig for more information, find out the Nazis' plans.'

Both Maman and Madame de Giocomte remain tight-lipped. They clasp hands, but I can't read what's going on in their minds. Several long minutes pass, then they whisper to each other, their faces solemn and their eyes misty. This Russian Jewish woman and our good-hearted French seamstress of a mother share a bond so special, nothing can separate them. Mother and daughter by choice. I'm more determined than ever to get them out of Paris, though I'll miss them with every inch of my being.

We truly are a family and here I am breaking up that bond. Again. First with Justine. And now with these two women who I adore.

Am I crazy? Or is it because I love them both so much I'll sacrifice having them close to me to save them?

Still, they remain silent.

The suspense is killing me.

'Maman, Madame de Giocomte, *please*, let me help you. It's too dangerous for you to stay here.'

I suffer through what seems like loud, endless ticking on an old mechanical clock while they huddle together, whispering back and forth, heated at times, but speaking so low I can't hear what they're saying.

Then the moment comes when Madame de Giocomte holds her head up high, her hand clasped with Maman's.

'We have made our decision, Ève.'

# 9

## PARIS, MAY 12, 1942

*Justine*

The streets of Paris were once magic roads to me that led to wonderful places. A lively café brimming with music and conversation. A boulangerie seducing passers-by with the heavenly smell of anise and almond and vanilla. The Louvre, filled with centuries of art. Aux Trois Quartiers department store, a fashion lover's paradise. The Bouquinistes, booksellers, along the Seine luring the curious to discover the joy of reading, stamp collecting.

Now the streets of Paris lead to nowhere I want to go.

I remain in my apartment when I'm not at the hat shop, sifting through old fashion magazines Madame Péroline has squirreled away for me, looking for inspiration for my hat designs—not easy since we lack materials like lace, taffeta ribbons, felt. Even rayon is hard to get, since what supply is on hand goes to a German factory to make artificial silk. I deal with it. It's important I keep my job at the milliner's. I have important work to do. For Arsène. And the Allies.

I report what I hear, pass misinformation to the Germans... and stay alive. I wish I could keep Ninette away from the everyday tension that grips me working as a double agent for the London war office. I feel like I'm being watched. I sense the long shadow of the black swastika passing over my apartment every day like a dark cloud. I've had no formal training as an operative, but I know in my bones *something* is wrong. Days have passed since the incident at the Hôtel Drouot and then afterward when I spied the major taking that girl into his motorcar to satisfy him. Knowing him as I do, I doubt the major had plans to kidnap the girl; rather it was a random encounter because he was bored waiting for me. Then, rather than grilling me himself, he sent the SS lieutenant to warn me to forget what I saw.

Since then, except for a few German auxiliary workers, it's quiet at the shop. Adding to my jumpy mood, the major hasn't visited me at my apartment on Rue des Martyrs. Even Herr Geller keeps his distance. I imagine he has someone far more important than me to harass.

Still, my mind replays that day over and over. I can't forget that girl.

Young. Round cheeks. Rounder hips.

She wore a fruity-red dress with a high white collar, button cuffs. Full skirt. Stylish hat. Dark stockings an older woman might wear with a rip up one side. Did she trip trying to elude the major?

The young girl reminded me of an apple fallen from a tree about to get quashed by hobnail boots.

I'm in a quandary about how to proceed. I know the major finds pleasure with other women, but this is the first time I've actually *seen* how he caught a pretty mademoiselle in his grip. Like I'm standing outside of myself and watching what happened to *me*.

Which is why I'm on a mission of mercy to save the woman's soul. Even if I *can't* change what that fiend did to her body, I feel a compelling passion to help her, if only to put my mind at rest and soothe my aching curiosity about the girl's welfare.

After dropping Ninette off with Madame Péroline, I head over to Chez Mimi. It's a decent walk along the boulevards, but I'd rather take alleyways and passages and not attract attention. My usual driver, a stiff-necked, young soldier who does the Nazi salute better than anyone I've seen, isn't on call today. Good. I'm on my own. I tell myself I'm doing the right thing, but I have mixed feelings about visiting the brothel. It's where the major dropped *me* off after he first attacked me in the back of his Mercedes motorcar. To recover, so he could make me a more permanent prize in his collection.

But it's also where I met Arsène.

In disguise as an old soldier.

Scraggly, gray wig under an old cap, tarnished medals tacked on a weather-worn navy pea-coat, his spine bent over, but he eyes as sharp as a sniper's scope. He's seen it all. How the major's girls before me spent weeks in the brothel for 'healing' before the SS officer finds work for them, like answering the telephone in a German-run military office where a French speaker is preferred, or smiling and taking tickets at the Soldaten Kino, a German soldiers-only cinema, or acting as a hostess in a restaurant in a Nazi-run bistro.

*Why find them jobs?* I asked.

Because they can't go home.

It's verboten.

I know. I tried. Lucie, a young maid at Maison Bleue, paid the price for my boldness when I contacted her and begged her to take a message to Maman and Ève that I was safe. The major ordered me to have no contact with *anyone*, but I know how my family worries about me. Soon after that morning, the Gestapo sent her to prison as a political dissident, a fancy word for a 'dispensable problem'.

I will never forgive myself. I'm hoping in some way to make up for my terrible mistake by helping this girl, but I can't be too careful. The brothel caters to Nazi SS officers.

I let myself in around the back at the service entrance and find Mimi smoking a cigarette in the parlor. Blowing smoke rings, her feet up, no customers, two girls playing gin rummy. It's a quiet afternoon here at Chez Mimi before the over-sexed Nazi officers invade the establishment. The madam and her working girls grab a little peace from the raucous Germans demanding beer and girls and song, providing the latter with loud, drunken bouts of German drinking songs. A half-filled bottle of brandy sits on the round table next to the velvet divan where the madam keeps the tip tray filled with *jetons*, tokens with the brothel name and address. The soldiers are fond of slipping them into their uniform pockets for souvenirs. She's a hard-nosed businesswoman, charging them in the end, but she treated me with kindness.

I've never forgotten that.

She's used to me dropping in, bringing her a new hat on occasion. A signal I need to see Arsène, but she doesn't know that.

I'm empty-handed today, raising her curiosity.

'What brings you here, mademoiselle?' She invites me to join her in a brandy. I decline. I need to have a clear head. I look around and notice she set up a tall, black lacquered screen *japonaise* with four panels inlayed with pearl in the corner. I hear whispering coming from behind the screen.

'It's a rather sensitive nature, madame. I don't know where to begin.'

'*Ah,* don't be shy, mademoiselle, no one will judge you if you came to confess your sins to the good priest, Father Armand.'

She nods toward the murmuring coming from behind the screen. I smile. Of course. Father Armand is no stranger to Chez Mimi. The priest from Sacré-Coeur makes the journey here from the cathedral to give spiritual help to any girl who needs it. It must be an agony for a girl to confess her sins, to then have no choice but to do it again to survive in this terrible war. But Father Armand understands. He's a man of God who helps the homeless, the addicted, prisoners in the deep depths of despair.

When I first came to the brothel he didn't judge me, but that was before I jumped headfirst into working for the Resistance against the Germans by appearing to be working with them. I wonder what he'll think of me now that he'll see me as a collaborator. The hardest part is enduring the sneers, especially those I saw on Ève's face. I've half a mind to confess my role-playing to the priest—that I'm working for the Allies—but I'd be putting Arsène in jeopardy, not to mention my little girl. So I must live with the looks of disdain.

I imagine Father Armand kissing the big cross he wears around his neck and praying for me, while I see nothing but contempt for me in his eyes. The truth is, I don't have the right to ask God for forgiveness until this war is over. I pray I will have done my part in ousting the Boches from Paris and any indiscretion, any mention of collaboration with the Nazis, will be wiped clean from my soul.

But today, I have a more urgent need.

'I'm looking for a girl the major brought here a few days ago.' I describe her to the madam... Brunette, round face.

'I remember her. Pretty. Big eyes that never stopped weeping.' Madame Mimi pauses, thinking. 'Scared, she was, and if my instincts are right, seeing how I've been hiring girls for this work for over twenty years, she was as innocent as a white lily before the major—' She clears her throat. 'She's gone, mademoiselle. Left of her own accord.'

That *does* surprise me. The major never let *me* out of his sight... or the Gestapo's.

The madam gives me 'that look', squinting her eyes, a signal I'll get nothing more from her, so I change tactics. 'Is Arsène here?'

Madame Mimi shrugs. 'Ah, that old soldier didn't show up yesterday *or* today. He's probably off on a drunken binge. Too many Nazi bigwigs harassing him, I gather. If I didn't know better, I'd swear he ran off with that girl, even if she was a Jew.'

I double blink. 'She was Jewish?'

Madame downs another whiskey. 'Surprised me, too. Not the major's usual type.'

She means he prefers Aryan-blondes.

It becomes clear to me what happened. The unfortunate mademoiselle was in the wrong place at the wrong time, her virtue taken in a moment of lust to assuage the major's needs. He raped her simply because he could.

*Damn Nazis.* Why does that disgust me so?

'How do you know she was Jewish?' I ask.

'She showed me the necklace the major ripped off her neck, a small Star of David hanging on the broken gold chain.'

My eyes widen. Of course that would send him into a rage, especially if he didn't know she was Jewish until *after* he'd taken his pleasure with her. I pace around in a circle, thinking. I'm more concerned than ever about the girl's welfare.

'Do you know where she went, Madame? I'd like to talk to her... help her if I can.'

Madame Mimi burps. Loudly. Then she's strangely quiet, knowing she let her penchant to chat go too far. She gulps down another whiskey. I press her again, another burp, then I hear the rustling of heavy robes behind me.

I see the priest emerging from behind the screen out of the corner of my eye, followed by a young prostitute walking behind him, then racing upstairs to say her penance. Or maybe to gulp down a brandy to get through tonight?

'She's dead, mademoiselle,' he says to me. 'May God keep her soul safe.'

*'Dead?'*

I never expected that. I pull back, his words piercing my flesh. It takes a moment for his shocking words to register in my mind. The major is an animal, *mais oui*, but from what I've seen, that doesn't allow him to straightforwardly kill a woman. He prefers to watch his conquests wither away like a lovely willow standing alone in an empty field, its roots drying up from loneliness.

'Yes, mademoiselle, the girl is dead.' Father Armand frowns.

'She *can't* be, Father. I don't believe you. You have no proof.'

The good father winces, mulling over my words in his mind, as if asking God for guidance.

*Should he risk speaking with me? A Nazi collaborator?*

I have my answer when he folds his hands in the voluminous folds of his priest's black robe, leans over and whispers in my ear, 'Come with me and I will prove it to you. I pray you have a clean handkerchief, mademoiselle.' The priest's eyes remain solemn, his nostrils quiver and his eyelids flutter. 'You'll need it.'

* * *

'Until the Year of our Lord 1907,' Father Armand begins in a monotone, as if he's delivering a eulogy, 'a small, square black building harboring souls blue and bloated stood here behind the

Cathedral of Notre-Dame. It was a theater of the absurd, the grotesque... the unwanted. Suicide victims.' He blesses himself. 'It was casually referred to as The Morgue.'

'The *Morgue*?' I shiver. Grisly thoughts invade my already depressed mood.

'Yes, mademoiselle. A place where death was put on display in its most naked state, where the public viewed victims of drownings and suicide, poor souls who sought the peaceful waters of the Seine for their final resting place.'

I watch the priest dart among the midday strollers nodding and blessing them with the sign of the cross. He leads me across the grassy mall behind the centuries-old cathedral, the great flying buttresses of Notre-Dame arcing like the prow of a ship over three hundred feet above my head, the elegant madame of Paris reaching toward a sky where the air is fresh and clean. I wonder how many church-goers look upward to grab a piece of heaven to survive another day of the Occupation.

'I thought that was only a scary bedtime story, monsieur.'

'No, mademoiselle, it was very real. The Doric Morgue attracted Parisians daily from dawn to dusk, a place where families searched for a missing loved one and could redeem the body for twenty francs. A fee paid to shield their loved one from lurid looks, the unfortunate victim laid on a cold slab in their natural state.' He clears his throat. 'As you can imagine, viewing young women became a debauched sideshow best left to the imagination.'

He bows his head, not wishing to elaborate.

'Why are you telling me this, Father?'

'When I passed by here early this morning, I saw the young mademoiselle in question.'

'I don't understand.'

'You will. Look.'

Confused, I glance around the square, then a long, slow shiver makes its way up and down my spine when I spy black marble slabs on wheels at the rear of the cathedral with several—

'—*Dead bodies,'* I whisper, covering my mouth with my handkerchief, the vomit stuck in my throat. The priest was right about the handkerchief; the smell is decaying and overpowering, like rotting fish. I can't believe what I'm seeing... Three women and two men laid out in a row as if they're sleeping. Bluish tinge coloring their skin and swollen flesh bursting through their tight, wrinkled clothing confirms what the priest said. They're—

'Suicide victims, mademoiselle, fished out of the Seine by anglers eager to make a few francs.' Father Armand gently but firmly leads me by the arm toward the bodies. 'Poor souls took their leave of the earth by drowning, but it's not always clear if they jumped into the river or were already dead when the deep waters claimed them.'

'How long has *this* exhibition been going on?'

'Not long. It's a new wrinkle to life under the occupiers that I pray will be eliminated. Till then, under orders from the Nazis, the police set up the bodies here for exhibition so relatives can claim them.'

'But why *here*, now?'

A look of disgust settles in the holy man's eyes like a cold chill. 'According to the gossip I hear after Mass, a Nazi officer with a macabre sense of humor resurrected the practice of displaying unidentified bodies for his own amusement.'

I nod. I'm not surprised; I've heard stories from the major about SS party games. Dehumanizing rituals to humiliate their conquests. I was shocked when he recounted a party he attended where a beautiful nude woman acted as 'a serving plate' for caviar and other delicacies to enhance the officers' taste buds.

*It makes me sick.*

But this—*this* is criminal.

Father Armand agrees. He says he has petitioned the head of the Abwehr at their headquarters in the Lutetia Hôtel to abolish the practice for hygienic reasons. Knowing the Nazi propensity toward cleanliness, I predict no more dead bodies will show up here.

'Is *this* the girl you were looking for, mademoiselle?'

The priest points to the female body at the end of the row.

I force myself to look at the girl, bloated and decomposed from floating in the Seine for days, smeared with the residue of the river filth and her own bodily fluids.

'Yes.'

She wears only a faded taffeta slip. A torn, thick cotton stocking hugs her right leg. Her shoes are missing, along with that necklace of the Star of David she apparently once wore. Her rich, dark hair clings to her head like cordoned rope. The sight of her face, swollen and distended, her once pretty features deformed into an ugly mask of bone and leathery skin, grabs me, pulling me down into depths of hell I didn't know existed. Till now. It's horrible and cruel. I swear the major will pay for this when the war is over.

*I swear it.*

*Did she commit suicide?* I wonder. She wouldn't be the first young woman to escape the violation of her body by the enemy by taking her own life, let her spirit soar. To be free. But I can't stop thinking about what Madame Mimi said when the major discovered the Star of David around the girl's neck, his fury unleashed. I look closer. Even after being in the water for days, dark, purple bruises, ligature marks around the girl's neck, are visible, as if she were choked to death.

In that moment, I have no doubt the pretty mademoiselle did *not* seek the solace of the Seine as her only way out.

She was murdered.

'This girl is no suicide, Father.'

He cocks a brow. 'Why do you say that, mademoiselle?'

'The bruises on her neck.'

'Why would someone kill her?'

'I thought I knew the major, that he had some decency left, but I was wrong. His standing in the SS would never survive *this*. After raping her, he wouldn't take the chance of her being pregnant with a Jewish child. *His* child.'

It makes sense. He'll do *anything* to keep Ninette, but that is because my little girl can pass for pure Aryan. Whereas my gut tells me he'd do anything to get rid of a baby that would, in the eyes of the Party, taint his bloodline.

Father Armand puts his arm around my shoulder to comfort me, says nothing but his eyes grow darker than the holy robe he wears. I sense he has something on his mind, something that becomes urgent when a Gestapo car screeches to a halt, ten, fifteen meters from where we're standing. The big, black Citroën with protruding headlights like two naked eyeballs never fails to send fear through me. The priest blesses himself, sending a quick prayer to God when the secret police show up.

Trouble.

'I must be on my way, mademoiselle,' he whispers, 'but not without conveying an urgent message to you.'

'A message? For *me*?'

He clears his throat. 'From a friend at the brothel.'

*Arsène.* He *knew* I'd show up looking for the girl after the SS lieutenant threatened me. But can I trust the priest? I have to.

'Yes?' I ask, breathless.

'Noon, mademoiselle, Tuesday, the Church of Saint-Pierre-de-Chaillot.'

Our usual rendezvous point.

'How do I know I can trust *you*?' I ask, keeping my eye on the Gestapo man huffing and puffing as he gets out of the black motorcar. 'That this isn't an elaborate Gestapo scheme?'

'You don't.' He lowers his eyes. 'But our informant passed on what happened at the hat shop with the young SS lieutenant.'

I pull back, thinking. 'No one saw what happened except Madame Péroline.'

His silence tells me Madame Péroline is also working for the Resistance. *Why didn't I see it before?* She looks out for me, for Ninette, but always plays the frazzled, flighty woman... To allay suspicion, of course. And she plays it well.

The priest continues with: 'The Gestapo is becoming bolder in their attempt to exert control over policing the city's residents. They're capable of accusing *anyone* guilty of resisting even without cause.' He pauses. 'Take great care, mademoiselle, in who you trust. Not everyone is what they seem... and others will surprise you.'

Before I determine if Father Armand is setting me up or telling the truth, the rotting smell of the dead is replaced by a different offensive odor. Herr Geller. Waddling like a walrus, he approaches me, his puffy cheeks bulging. He wastes no time in harassing me. In a rare moment, he removes his black Fedora and holds it to his chest in respect for the dead. I'm not surprised to observe he has a bald spot.

'Pretty girl, mademoiselle, *n'est-ce pas*?' He sighs over the girl's decomposing body. 'Even for a Jew.'

I can't let him get away with that. 'Why can't you let the dead lie in peace, Herr Geller?'

He smirks. 'Too bad she committed suicide.'

'Don't lie to me.' I point to the bruises on her neck. 'She was murdered.'

He snorts. 'You were warned, mademoiselle, to keep your nose out of what isn't your business. If you don't, you'll find yourself detained at Gestapo headquarters for an interrogation you *won't* find pleasant.' Then another surprise when he whips out a black cloche hat with a droopy feather from his trench coat pocket. 'Like the girl who wore this hat.'

*Maman's hat.*

He waves it so close to my face the feather tickles my nose.

'Ève... *my sister*,' I blurt out, panicky. 'What have you done with her?'

'I would be delighted to tell you that Mademoiselle Beaufort came forth with names and addresses of enemies of the Reich—'

'Ève wouldn't give up anyone.' *Even me.* 'I know her. She's strong... and loyal to France.'

He grits his teeth, works his jaw. I'm puzzled. I can see by his ruddy cheeks and squinty eyes he's fighting back words he finds distasteful. 'Your sister is also clever like you and eluded capture by the French police. We found a girl wearing this battered hat, but she turned out to be a common streetwalker. I have released her, since her job servicing our soldiers is vital to the war effort.'

I can't help but smile. That means Ève is free. *Thank God.*

'However, I'm a patient man,' he continues, tossing Maman's hat onto the cobblestones, 'and in my business, I have found I have more to gain by waiting for the most opportune moment to make my play. When I *do* arrest your sister, and I will, she won't be so lucky. I have the most fascinating, spiked object in my bag of tools that when introduced as a phallic symbol, it *makes* a woman speak.'

Horrified at what he's suggesting, I clench my fists tight. 'Why can't you leave her alone? Or is it because you love to torture *me* with your sick innuendos? Well, it won't work, monsieur. Ève is a thorn in my side, but I have no ties to her anymore, nor do I wish to. We're no longer sisters.'

Father Armand comes to my rescue before the secret policeman loses his patience and arrests me. His eyes hard and determined, he lays his hand upon my arm. 'Come, mademoiselle, we must do God's will and pray for the dead.'

But Herr Geller intends to have the last word. 'You make a good speech, mademoiselle,' he grumbles, 'but the game is far from over.'

'Go inside the cathedral, mademoiselle. *Quickly*,' urges the priest, pushing me along, but not before I grab Maman's hat from the stones and dust it off. Herr Geller doesn't follow us. Instead, he turns on his heel and heads hack to his ugly black motorcar.

Of course he does.

Neither the devil *nor* the Gestapo have permission to enter His house.

# 10

## PARIS JUNE 2, 1942

*Ève*

From the moment Maman and Madame de Giocomte utter a forceful and unanimous '*We're staying, we're not leaving Paris*', I have my work cut out. I won't put them in jeopardy because of my stupidity to confront my sister at the Hôtel Drouot, my girlish pride challenged by her refusal to come home. I'm determined to get them out of the city and safely to England.

No matter *what* I have to do.

Every day—three weeks and counting—I make my case to these two women about why they must leave, that Justine isn't coming back, and that they're in danger. They listen, I repeat, then they ignore what I said.

I'm getting nowhere.

So I keep trying, believing I can change their minds. Make them understand that even as women, they're not immune to the wrath of the Nazi war machine. Madame de Giocomte disagrees, citing that although Monsieur de Giocomte and other Jewish men were deported, the Boches wouldn't *dare* transport women to those wretched labor camps and, God forbid, children.

Unthinkable.

Why don't I believe that?

*Because* I live in a Jewish household. And, even if Madame de Giocomte ignores the talk that goes on between neighbors about impending roundups, I fear it's true. If there's one thing I've learned in this war, it's the importance of intelligence-gathering no matter the source, whether it's Cook overhearing chatter in a bread queue, or the maid Albertine browsing in a bookshop and discovering a Resistance pamphlet stuck between the pages of a novel, or Maman repeating the gossip she overhears when she and Madame visit the refugees on Rue des Rosiers. I *do* know Madame tried to get in touch with her sister-in-law, the baroness, her daughter and her four children. I have a fond memory of the eldest daughter Delphine and how she watched out for her little sisters. An innocent girl who I pray will escape harm during this terrible war. I remember how Maman fixed up Justine's old blue dress special for her with big, shiny buttons and a lace collar, and the girl's eyes glowed. Madame begged them to stay safe here, but the baroness left Maison Bleue in a huff months ago with her daughter and the girls. We heard they were living in the Jewish quarter—they registered their new address with the local police as the law requires—but the baroness refused to see Madame. Then we lost track of them. We pray they left and crossed the border into Switzerland.

They wouldn't be foolish enough to stay in Paris, *n'est-ce pas*?

Meanwhile, I'm not giving up convincing Madame de Giocomte to leave France.

Not a simple task. Living at Maison Bleue these days is like riding on a velocipede, pumping and pedaling as hard as I can on a manual bicycle carousel and going around in circles.

Adding to my frustration is the constant worry the secret police will show up and arrest me on a trumped-up charge. No hard evidence, simply on 'suspicion' of anti-Vichy government activities. I come and go through the hidden root cellar entrance in case anyone is watching the house after I observed a black Gestapo Citroën motorcar cruise by the *maison* on the private street. To intimidate me? Playing mind games? Most likely waiting for me to return.

But I've left Ève Beaufort behind.

*She's* wanted by the Gestapo.

Enter a new player in the fight.

Luc Dumont. A young medical student and the son of Maman's cousin from Marly-le-Roi outside Paris. I took the name from a character in a Sylvie Martone film who saves the intrepid heroine from a mean old duke. I have a new identity card with an official Nazi stamp courtesy of a printer Iris knows working for the Resistance. Remi and Iris know I'm on a Gestapo list, but I didn't tell them Justine is the source of that information —I couldn't bear to name my sister as a collaborator even if it's true.

I pursed my lips together trying to look tough when they took my photograph. Maman says I look like I'm about to sneeze. Madame says I look angry. Who isn't these days?

The identity card is damned near perfect with my name and information written in Gothic black script, but it's not foolproof. If I'm stopped on a train by German soldiers, it will pass them sniffing the ink or holding it up to the light. What are they looking for anyway? But if I'm detained by the French police or Gestapo and they search local police records, they won't find Monsieur Dumont registered. A young man without papers is suspect and most likely hiding a criminal record.

*Just another number for their quota*, they'll say, taking my freedom away.

Then I'll find myself at Drancy in a situation no female wants to be in. I shiver uncontrollably, guessing what they'd do to me. Rape, torture. I've heard it doesn't matter if you're French or Jewish. The Nazi doctrine has no place for anyone who doesn't adhere to the Aryan rules of perfection. And that includes race and religion. No one can live up to their standards, which I believe is an excuse the Nazis use to turn their noses up at anyone they don't like, including this 'Final Solution' I keep hearing about. I pray I won't have to endure that kind of scrutiny. Cutting my hair is the first step, then binding my breasts with long strips of muslin, filling in the arch of my brows with brown shoe polish, and then adding a pair of Madame's shoulder pads to Monsieur's brown jacket after Maman alters it for me. The physical is important, but the illusion isn't complete unless I work hard on making my identity as a man believable, taking long strides, swinging my arms, hunching my shoulders like I'm shy, wiping my nose with the back of my hand, learning how to smoke cigarette stubs. It's common to see young men jumping on the half-smoked cigarettes German soldiers toss on the pavements.

The only glitch is I'm as antsy as a snorting pig on market day.

I'm out of the fight and it's killing me.

Remi ordered me to lie low until the Gestapo tire of searching for me, so I hide out in Maison Bleue, ready to make a quick escape if I hear a knock on the door, getting into Cook's hair, sticking my fingers into her gooey bread dough and kneading it to work off nervous energy, then fussing with rearranging the books in the library, working on my experiments with what few natural ingredients I have, while I ponder when and *if* Michal is coming back to Paris. All the while, I pray I can talk these two women who mean everything to me into opening their eyes and seeing what danger they're in.

Today's not that day.

They ignore me. Again. Madame is busy listing the names of new Jewish refugees who need clothes and Maman is helping her, sewing odd buttons on torn sweaters and fixing hems on old dresses. So after a breakfast of stale bread, cooked carrots, and barley coffee as well as too many *'We're not leaving Paris'* moments from Maman and Madame to count, I pop on a brown tweed cap, pull the brim down over my eyes and take refuge in the backyard garden. The deep, rich foliage isn't visible from the street, giving me reason to spend time here, finding peace with my herbs. Rosemary and thyme. My basil, however, looks droopy and limp. I'll try replanting the roots, sing to it if I have to. The aroma is uplifting and sensual, adding an extra beat to my heart's rhythm that invigorates me and sets me to humming. Convincing myself I can bring the plant back to life.

Strange, when I was a student, I was filled with so much enthusiasm and great plans about how I was going to save lives, then the Nazis came. It's important I remember how I felt, not forget that girl with big plans once existed, that in spite of what they've done to keep us down, they can't break our spirit.

*I swear they won't.*

With renewed vigor, I get down on my knees and start digging up the basil from the garden bed when I hear—

'What is your business here, monsieur?'

I shiver at the sound of that low, sensual voice.

*Michal. He's back.*

I chuckle. He doesn't know it's me. *Hmm...* A sly, naughty thought spins around in my brain. Can I fool my Polish fighter with my new identity?

In a lighter moment during this horrific war, I decide to find out.

My heart races as I continue digging with a careful hand to uproot the basil plant, its spicy aroma with a hint of clove adding a pleasurable sensation to this unexpected encounter with the man I try so hard to forget but can't.

'I'm the new gardener. Madame de Giocomte hired me.'

'Madame would never hire a stranger,' he insists. 'Who are you... and don't lie to me or I'll turn your sorry arse over to the French police and let them deal with you.'

'Luc... Luc Dumont. Madame Beaufort is my mother's cousin.'

He circles me, trying to get a better look at my face, but when his eyes wander over my body, taking a longer look at my derrière up in the air than society allows, I tremble slightly.

'I have never heard her mention you when Madame allowed me to hide out in the coach house... *Luc.* How do I know you're not an informant?'

'Madame Beaufort will vouch for me.'

'And Ève?'

'She's—she's not here.'

His voice takes on a serious undertone. 'Where is she?'

'I don't know, monsieur.'

'Don't tell me she's been arrested?'

'No.'

He heaves out a sigh of relief. 'I'm surprised she *hasn't* gotten herself into trouble. She's the most difficult, thick-headed, stubborn woman I've ever met.'

This is *not* what I expected to hear. Tightening my gut, I get to my feet, dust off the moist dirt on my hands, my knees, while keeping my back to him. '*Really?* I'd say she's smart, independent and thinks for herself.'

'She's a nuisance... even if she is good to look at.'

*What's this?* I find his comment disturbing even if I feel a slight tremor of delight at hearing he finds me attractive. 'She's not a daisy planted in a pot.'

He grins. 'With her long hair blowing in the wind, she's as *pretty* as a daisy,' he emphasizes, 'but when she's angry, she can be as obstinate as a garden weed.'

'*A weed?* Surely you joke, monsieur?'

'Not in the slightest. She's the most frustrating woman I've ever met.' He makes his point with laughter in his voice. 'She refuses to obey my orders because her "gut tells her otherwise", she insists I listen to *her* ideas, then she gives me half a dozen reasons why *her* plan will work.'

'You find that amusing?'

He shrugs. 'What can I say? I'm stuck with her.'

'Oh, so you're stuck with—'

'*You*, Ève. I'm stuck with you.'

I make a face. 'What gave me away?'

'Your arse.'

'*Michal!*'

'When you spend numerous missions with a woman lying in the dirt, planting explosives on railway tracks, her body pressed up against yours, all warm and womanly, well, you get the idea.'

I lower my eyes, my cheeks tinting. 'You're very observant.'

'It's my job or I'd be dead by now.' He sucks in his breath then exhales loudly. 'And in spite of the sleepless nights you cause me, you're a damn good field agent.'

'You mean for a girl?' I tease him, remembering how at first he didn't want to work with me because of my sex.

'I mean you're a smart, courageous fighter, Ève. And that's the last compliment you'll get from me.' He frowns. 'Now will you please explain to me *why* you're dressed in Monsieur de Giocomte's old clothes and calling yourself Luc?'

* * *

My heart sings a happy tune on a summer afternoon sitting here with this man, who I never dreamed could see me as a woman, having identified me just as such. It's wonderful since he doesn't usually pay me much attention these days.

He's a man fighting his own demons.

More so since he received a letter from Warsaw smuggled into France via the Red Cross, news he won't talk about and I won't ask him. I fear he'd shut me out and I don't want to lose what we *do* have. So I say nothing. And we *both* lose.

Why is it men have this fear of sharing their pain?

Why can't he be more like Justine and I once were? Sharing everything. How I wish things were right between my sister and me, but that's a dead issue now that I've seen her, talked to her. I can't believe that woman I saw at the Hôtel Drouot is Justine. She's changed so, adapting that superior air all Nazis love to show off with their heel clicking and straight back bowing. Justine carries it off with her chin lifted and hip swinging walk.

I pick the leaves off my poor, limp basil, smelling them. Michal dips his head toward mine to smell them, too, and I get a whiff of motor oil and gunpowder, my heart racing when I explain to him what happened, choosing my words carefully.

'The Gestapo found out I'm working for the Resistance.'

Dead serious, he says, 'I know.'

'You do?'

'Remi told me.'

'You *knew* all along and you let me go on like a chatty gardener? You sod!'

He grins. 'You're quite convincing as a young man, Ève, except when you wiggle your—' He checks out my derrière, making me blush. 'Nose like a rabbit.'

I attempt to change the subject, turn the tables on him. 'Why are you back in Paris?'

'You.'

'Don't try to flatter me. There's another reason, surely? One with pigtails and bows and a flirty smile.'

He laughs. 'Don't tell me you're jealous of Coralie.'

'Me? Never.'

She's pretty but she's more interested in flirting than fighting the Boches. She's a wide-eyed girl a little older than me with pink cheeks and girlish curves. The boys flirt with her and she flirts back until Remi orders them to keep their minds on business. I'll never forget her acting as the lookout at the Musée de l'Homme. How she smiled and batted her eyes at Nazi soldiers carousing in the museum. There's no stopping her flirting, but I heard she found someone new to entice with her charms. Now I wonder.

I keep telling her the Nazis won't always be fooled by her using her schoolgirl innocence to talk her way out of scary situations and then she'll be in trouble. Deep trouble.

Michal raises his brows and twists his mouth in that smirk of his I can't deny is unnerving, as if the man has seen me naked. Then he turns serious. 'I need your help, Ève.'

'*My* help?'

'Yes, I received intelligence about a German weapons depot near Jonzac and—'

I nod. I know the area—a city in southwestern France in the Occupied Zone.

'—supplying guns and ammunition to Nazi land offensive troops in Normandy and along the Atlantic coast. I traveled down there to make contact with the local farmers hiding stolen weapons and ammunition, weapons the local Resistance fighters "borrow" from the Germans. I'm headed back there and...' He gives me that raised-brow look that emphasizes his dark, sexy eyes. 'This is a two-man job, Ève. I need a partner. You.'

'Me?'

'I can't think of anyone else I trust more with my life.'

'Me, too,' I whisper under my breath, but I'd die if he heard me.

'I won't lie to you, Ève,' he continues. 'It's a dangerous mission. There's no guarantee we'll make it back to Paris alive.'

'I see.'

'But if we do, the others—Remi, Iris, Claude... Coralie—will have a fighting chance against the Nazis with arms and ammo. We can save lives. Are you with me?'

I attempt a weak smile. How am I going to tell him about Justine? That I feel I can't leave until I get Maman and Madame de Giocomte safely out of Paris?

'I'll do anything to oust the Germans from France—'

He cuts me off with: 'I knew you wouldn't let me down...' He pauses, then gives me that stern, direct look I've come to know that means he's depending on me. 'Several Resistance fighters have infiltrated the French laborers working at the depot so we'll blend in as a married couple.'

*'Married?'* My eyes pop.

*How can I tell him I cut off my hair? That I... What was it Maman said? That I look like a teacup.*

'You're safe with me, Ève,' he says, trying to convince me. 'I promise.'

He takes my reluctance to mean something of a more intimate nature that both frightens and excites me.

*Nights alone with Michal in the same room... same bed? How can I say no?*

*I have to.*

'I can't do it, Michal,' I blurt out.

'Why not?' He doesn't look offended, merely puzzled.

With my hand shaking, I pull off my cap, exposing my short hair curling around my ears. 'I cut off my long hair.'

He grabs me by the shoulders. 'Is that what's bothering you?'

'I look funny.'

'You look beautiful.' He traces my high cheekbones with his fingers, thinking. 'This gives me an idea. We can both get jobs at the Nazi-run depot.'

'I can't leave Maman and Madame de Giocomte. They're in terrible danger.'

His eyes harden. 'Danger?'

'It's all my fault,' I admit. 'I went to the Hôtel Drouot to steal back *The Daisy Sisters* and I saw Justine. She's alive and working for the Boches.' I hold my head in my hands. 'I can't believe my own dear sister is a Nazi collaborator.'

There. I've said it. The words come gushing out of me, the disbelief and hurt coloring my voice with a despair I still haven't accepted. I don't know if I ever will.

'I thought your sister was dead.'

'So did I.'

I admit I disobeyed his orders and fell into her trap. How she warned me to stay away from her, that I'm an embarrassment to her, and that I'm on a Gestapo list of *résistants*. Maman, too.

'I have no doubt the Gestapo will arrest Maman *and* Madame de Giocomte and interrogate them about my whereabouts. I can't stand the thought of them in Nazi hands. I *must* get them out of Paris.'

'Leave that to me,' he insists. 'I'll make the arrangements to get them out of France. Your *maman* and Madame de Giocomte will take the train to Toulouse where my contact will meet them and transport them safely across the border to Spain.'

'Are you sure it will work?' I ask.

'We've been very successful in helping Allied airmen shot down by the Germans escape from Belgium and France. Your *maman* and Madame will be in good hands.'

I let go with a big sigh, relieved. But why did it have to come to this? Maman and Madame forced to leave their home. I gather up the torn-up basil in my hands, its strong scent forever in my mind, reminding me of the day it all began, the day I lost Justine.

No wonder it's given up the fight to grow here.

'I'd just come in from the garden the day my sister crossed paths with the SS major. Nothing's been the same since.' I dig a hole in the dirt and replant the limp herb. '*Nothing.*'

Michal puts his hands on my shoulders, a seriousness in his eyes drawing me into a place in his heart I've only glimpsed. 'Don't judge your sister too harshly, Ève. If she's anything like you, there's more to her story. Not everyone fights the Boches with guns and ammo.'

'What do you mean?'

'I knew a girl in Warsaw...' His eyes take on a distant glow that doesn't dim. I see the heartfelt reveal in the way his dark eyes turn a lonely brown. My heart tugs. He's rarely shared anything personal about himself. 'After she believed her fiancé was murdered by the Nazis, she used her pretty face to lure the enemy into a trap to avenge his death, not once but several times. She shot German soldiers. Then she was compromised by an informant and arrested by the SS.' He stops, pulling the words from the core of his being from a place so deep, I know he's never expressed his pain before. His eyes are misty, and this is the closest I've ever seen him to breaking down. I want to put my hand over his, but I don't. I don't want to break the spell. 'She died in Gestapo hands,' he says finally. 'From what I heard, she was the victim of unspeakable torture and rape.'

I keep silent. Waiting.

His face, rough and handsome with a two-day old stubble, is flushed with anger, but he can't—or won't—say any more. He's talking about himself and the girl he loved. Iris told me the story when I first joined the Jade network, making me promise never to say anything. I didn't. Now that Michal has told me himself, I know he trusts me. I don't know why that's so important to me, but it is. I love him even more.

Do I dare believe he could ever love *me*?

I wish I hadn't cut my hair, then I could go along with his plan, and at least pretend we were married, find pleasure in that and dream he's in love with me. Never have I needed to feel close to a man. Never have I *wanted* a man to take me to him as a woman and make me his. It's at this moment that I realize I will never love anyone else *but* him.

*Ève, you silly fool.*

# 11

## PARIS, JUNE 1942

*Justine*

God has no use for Nazis.

And neither do I. They harass Jews and anyone who doesn't agree with them, they steal our leather shoes, and deprive innocent children of fresh milk. Is there anything more inhumane?

And yes, He *will* punish them.

I keep that thought in my mind to give me strength as I push the pram with my sleeping baby inside along the grand boulevards, believing justice *will* prevail when this war is over and I will be part of that justice. For now, I'm headed toward the Church of Saint-Pierre-de-Chaillot seeking sanctuary.

And hopefully the answer to the question causing me sleepless nights: *where is Arsène*?

I haven't heard from him in weeks.

I note there are few people about on this late morning where I'm filled with questions and a sticky summer humidity that makes my crisp cotton dress stick to me. I reach the church and observe an old man sweeping the pavements with a broom, two shop girls chatting with each other, a French policeman whistling as he watches the girls stroll by, and a tall SS officer wearing dark glasses with his nose in a German guide of Paris. I turn away. I can't stand to look at the smiling Nazi soldier on the cover.

No honking taxis. They've all but disappeared since the Occupation began.

And no Arsène.

I sigh, my breath warm, my heart disappointed. He's made no contact with me except for the message via Father Armand. I cling to the hope he'll show himself when it's safe and we can catch up. Oh, how I yearn to embrace that normalcy I've grown accustomed to, having him to talk to about Ninette, showing him how big she's grown since the horror of the bombing in the Renault plant last March when I almost lost her. Or listening to Arsène read to Ninette from a children's book about a young deer roaming about in a grand forest with his friend Hare. He can't. The book is banned by the Nazis because the author is Jewish.

It's not only wrong, it's sad. Very sad.

Still, through all the hopelessness and fear and despair that's gripped me since the major first assaulted me, I've kept my faith in God. It's gotten me through the worst of the emotional stress, but the physical discomfort I suffered has its own issues. The soreness in the most delicate of places persisted for weeks. Even now, though the physician at the American Hospital of Paris assured me when I delivered Ninette I suffered no physical harm from the rape, it still feels like it isn't right. Then there had been the matter of the bruises on my legs, arms, wrists. How I wished I'd had Ève to help me heal with her exquisite knowledge of herbs and salves. I remember when she concocted a remedy for me in an amber glass filled with honey, lavender, and olive oil. I was fourteen and took a bad fall. I was all about designing petticoats back then with sassy full skirts for the dancers at the Moulin Rouge. To try out my design, I took to dancing the cancan on the marble bench in the garden but slipped on the morning dew covering the surface and scraped up my bare legs. Ève fixed me up with her salve, rubbing it on my legs with a gentle touch while poor Maman lamented about my 'boorish' behavior, saying no gentleman wanted a woman who showed off her legs.

I sigh.

Now SS officers gawk at my legs with no pretense of not enjoying the scenery when I cross them in a seductive manner. I hate it. Their leering glances make me feel dirty. I hide my uneasiness behind a pretty smile with my lips outlined in bright Corsican red, but it doesn't take away the case of nerves I get from all the attention. To my despair, I'm getting in deeper and deeper with the major's cohorts when he shows me off, not only at Bal Tabarin but also Maxim's and La Tour d'Argent. He complains when the officers attempt to seduce me… and if I sit in a corner nursing a brandy, he complains I'm not sociable.

I can't win.

I don't know how much longer I can go on with this double life. That's partly why I'm on my way to church, hoping Arsène shows up. I need someone to talk to, someone who understands the grueling toll this craziness takes on your body, your mind, to keep up the pretense you're something you're not. Each day, my fear of losing my real self becomes a bigger ache in the pit of my stomach, that I won't be able to wipe off that red-lipped smile, that my descent into this world of Nazi games and appeasing them will become my only existence and the girl I was will be gone forever.

I can't—*won't* let that happen.

So I wait for Arsène. Two weeks ago I came to the church on the day Father Armand gave me, eager and impatient to retrieve my sanity and connect with this man of incredible mental strength. He never appeared. I waited another week—nothing. Now I'm back.

On a Tuesday.

Twelve noon.

I grip the carriage handle tighter, the fine, smooth leather covering it screaming its pricey cost. I'd never indulge in silver buttons or plaid inlays, but the major likes to make a statement when I take Ninette for a stroll. A status symbol for a 'child of the Reich'. Yes, it's come to that. He uses that term more often than her name when he talks about Ninette. When I see the questioning looks I get from other mothers walking their babies, their hand-me-down, weather-beaten prams rife with cracks in the leather, I want to tell them I'm not what I seem. I'm not a kept Parisienne by choice. I'm a mother fighting for my child... and France.

Of course, I don't.

Like I keep my secret life from Ève.

I've made discreet inquiries about her through the ever-generous-with-information General von Klum, but she seems to have disappeared. Did she escape Paris and leave Maman and Madame de Giocomte here? I doubt it, which worries me. Another reason I must see Arsène, beg him to find out what he can about Ève and warn her without compromising me. My head begins to throb, the torment of my deceiving her not letting up. I've begged God for forgiveness for lying to my sister and bending the rules so many times I pray He looked the other way. I had no choice if I wanted to save those I love. Convince Him this sinner isn't totally at fault, that I have strong convictions that rely on the way of the heart rather than the mind. In times like these, it's all I have left to fight with.

I believed I was winning until this morning.

When an irrepressible evil took that hope from me.

*Who else?* Herr Geller.

I long suspected the devil wears a black trench coat with wide lapels that remind me of a Griffon vulture's wings. Today I'm certain of it. He surprised me earlier in the Bois de Boulogne when I was walking Ninette along the path under the oaks and chestnuts. He wasted no time telling me what was on his mind.

'I drove by the *maison* of Madame de Giocomte, mademoiselle.'

He fell into step beside me, vaulting out of his black hole on his hind legs, I imagine.

'Are the roses blooming?' I asked, tucking the silk quilt around my sleeping child. She looked so peaceful, her long lashes resting upon her chubby cheeks. A doll's face.

'My sources tell me your sister hasn't returned home. Where is she?'

'I have no idea, Herr Geller.'

'Why should I believe you?'

'Why would I contact her? And how would I find her if you can't? She took a shot at me, remember?' I cast an innocent eye in his direction. I didn't blink. Yes, I'm good at what I do, *very* good.

'I'm *missing* something.' He narrowed his eyes. 'A clue that eludes me, but I've been so damn busy.'

'Chasing rainbows?' I quipped in an attempt to keep the conversation light, but he ignored me. He had something on his mind.

'As it turns out, mademoiselle, your sister is no longer my priority,' he said, regarding me with an upturned look as a serpent would. 'I have orders from Berlin to assist in implementing the Führer's plans for the "Final Solution".'

*Final solution of what?* The name made me cringe, making me more curious than ever, but I said nothing to antagonize the secret policemen further and let him rant.

'It's most unfortunate,' he continued, 'that the untimely death of SS General Heydrich put us behind schedule—'

'The Butcher of Prague', they called him. Shot and wounded by a Czech resistance fighter in an elaborate plan rumored backed by London. The Nazi later died from his infected wounds.

'—leaving me little time to chase after a schoolgirl.'

'Yet you have all the time to harass me,' I protested. 'A fool's errand, monsieur. I have no interest in my sister's doings. She's dead to me.'

He shot me a nasty look meant to unhinge me. 'I *could* make additional discreet inquiries about your sister. Who knows? I may find a servant or neighbor willing to inform on her for a tidy sum.'

*The bastard.* He was testing me. Again. He has no idea where my sister is or he would have arrested her. Then again, neither do I. All I can hope is that Ève took my warning and left Paris.

'Ève never bothered with the servants, always flitting around with her silly experiments, doing what she wanted.' I shrugged my shoulders. 'If she's wandered off, they wouldn't even notice. I imagine they don't have time for anything these days but queuing up for bread.'

He chuckled. 'Well played, mademoiselle. I had no doubt you wouldn't give up your sister even if you knew where she was. You don't.' Then, in a more serious tone that sent shivers up my spine, he said, 'I'm warning you, watch your tongue. If you were anyone else, I'd have you shot for your insolence but fortunately for you, you're a valuable asset.'

I smiled, but I took his words of warning seriously. I can never forget he's the enemy and holds my life and my daughter's in his hands.

He tipped his Fedora. 'Good day, Mademoiselle D'Artois.' Then he turned and walked in the opposite direction.

'No Heil Hitler?' I called after him.

He turned around. 'You surprise me, mademoiselle, but you don't fool me. Heil Hitler.'

I raised my hand and mumbled the Nazi salute, but he was already out of earshot. I didn't know what just happened, but it made me more cautious than ever to maintain my cover.

* * *

Loneliness can make a woman do strange things. Like moaning with contentment when I fluff my blanket around me at night, pretending Arsène is holding me tight. Or taking a stroll past Madame Mimi's with Ninette sleeping in her pram, hoping he'll wave to me from the attic window. I'll never forget how Arsène saved me from despair when I thought about taking my life after the major brought me there. Or the loneliness digging so deep into my head I take a second look at the SS officer standing outside the Church of Saint-Pierre-de-Chaillot because he's tall and seems familiar. I feel his open stare boring into my back when I start up the steps, dragging the pram up to the landing. Eight steps. It's surprisingly lightweight. I do my best to ignore the Nazi wearing dark sunglasses that catch the dayglow. He's abandoned his tour book and approaches me, muttering in halting French to ask if I need help.

'*Non, merci.*' I turn my head, not daring to look at him. He gives me a funny feeling. He could be the young lieutenant who harassed me at Madame Péroline's hat shop set on me by that Gestapo watchdog, but I don't remember him being so tall. Or his wide shoulders.

Then who is he?

*You know who it is. Arsène.*

*Don't be crazy. He wouldn't be so brazen to masquerade as an SS officer. It's too dangerous.*

*Wouldn't he? When* hasn't *he surprised you?*

I bite my lip, thinking about the consequences if I approach him and the soldier *isn't* Arsène. Arrest, then a trip to Nazi headquarters and Herr Geller's infamous 'kitchen'. Besides, he said nothing to me to let me believe it *is* him.

I convince myself he's merely a lonely soldier.

I reach the top of the landing and push through the brick-red, double doors of the church with the pram. I debated all morning about bringing my little girl with me, making Ninette an innocent accomplice to my role as a pretend collaborator. However distasteful that is, I must keep up my cover and not raise suspicion with the major *or* the Gestapo.

Yet the sanctuary I've embraced here in the past as warm and holy seems cold and unfriendly today, as if a fallen archangel is lurking behind a holy statue just waiting for me to make a mistake. Meanwhile, Ninette is sleeping, smacking her lips and dreaming of... sweet cream, perhaps? *Bon.* For now I have quiet in my head—the gift of a sleeping child to her mother—so I can focus. When she wakes up, I want to show her the tall iridescent stained-glass windows and artful fresco scenes on the ceiling. She loves reds and blues and her eyes light up when I wrap her in bright, dyed lamb's wool, her lips moving with sounds only she understands. She looks at me and coos and squeals, and that makes me smile.

I'm so fascinated by this little world she's created, I become distracted and forget this isn't the time or place to enjoy these precious moments between mother and baby. I must be on alert at all times.

Like now.

I need my wits about me.

I do a quick surveillance inside the church. It's quiet; *too* quiet. Call it instinct, but something's amiss. Day in and day out, this House of God plays host to French mothers and grandmothers nearly every hour until curfew, kneeling, praying with their rosaries wrapped around their hands and whispering pleas to the Lord to bring their boys home or keep their daughters out of the enemy's reach.

Not today. The vestibule and pews are empty.

I push the pram off to the side, pretending to search for something under the blankets while I look everywhere for Arsène disguised as a tall, broad-shouldered priest in black robes wearing a clergyman's hat topped with a black pom. 'Father Paul', as he once pretended to be. Could he be in the crypt in the basement? I'm not keen on pushing the pram down the steps, so I wait. I have previously found him in the confessional waiting for me at the appointed time.

*Twelve noon.*

I check the exquisite Swiss wristwatch set with diamonds and sapphires the major insisted I wear—set to German time as ordered by the occupiers—so I'm never late for an appointment with him. How well I know the Teutonic obsession with precision. Like sex. He never varies the position or shows any interest in me as a woman. Merely a vessel for his needs.

I pray I may never have to endure that act with him again.

My watch reads five minutes past noon. I've seen no one go in or out of the confessional.

I take a chance.

'Time for Maman to confess to her sins, *ma petite*,' I whisper, taking my child out of the pram and holding her close to me as I open the creaking wooden door to the confessional. I imagine it squeaks so the priest knows someone has entered the box.

I settle in on the wooden seat as I've done numerous times, my heart racing, cheeks tinting at the thought of connecting again with Arsène even if I can't see him, touch him. I feel a strong need to hear his rich baritone coming through the grill.

Not today.

I jump back with a start when I hear: 'Bless you, child. Tell me what's on your mind today.'

The priest's voice—if he *is* a priest—is a coarse and raspy whisper. I squint, trying to see who's on the other side of the grill. I can't. I see nothing but the profile of a man with a short nose and sagging chin.

He is *not* Arsène.

*Is it a trap?*

Father Armand's words about not trusting anyone keep popping into my head.

'Bless me, Father, for I have sinned...'

*And forgive me for what I'm about to do.*

*Pardon, mon enfant, Maman needs to make her escape without arousing suspicion.*

I wince when I pinch her little bottom ever so slightly, but it's enough to wake her up. My little girl opens her eyes and even in the semi-darkness, her pupils are big and shiny and wrapped up in the pleasantness of her dreams. She is *not* happy. She frets and gives me a distressing stare. Crying, tearful. *Oh, is she angry with me.* I try to calm her down, but Ninette starts howling and fussing.

Perfect for my escape.

'I'm sorry, Father, my baby... she's—she's wet... I've got to tend to her.'

I leave the confessional before the priest can protest. I try to quiet her by putting her on my shoulder, then wrapping her up in the cream-colored silk blanket while whispering words of comfort. She calms down enough to give me a chance to look around. A new player has entered the scene. I see a short priest with a slight hunchback lighting votive candles with a long taper and peeking out of the corner of his eye in my direction. A silence that seems destined to outlive purgatory descends between us. I rearrange Ninette's blanket, undo it, and then do it again, all the while watching the priest.

When he lights the same three candles twice, my skin prickles. Then he knocks over an unlit votive candle with his wide sleeve and he stoops down to retrieve it.

I see the tips of black hobnail boots.

I freeze. It *is* a trap.

'*Ma chère* Ninette,' I whisper, my lips brushing her hot cheek. 'Hold on tight to Maman, we're going to play a little game. We're getting out of here before the bad man shows up.' I sigh. 'May God help us.'

She lets go with a howl. She *knows* who I mean. Herr Geller. I swear, even when she was in my womb, she'd kick and cause a ruckus whenever the Gestapo man was near.

Before I can think, or plan, I walk slowly to the holy water font at the church entrance holding Ninette close to my chest with one hand and pushing the pram with the other. The priest seems miffed when he sees me leaving. He nods his head and two men sneak out from behind the altar. No doubt they're *Brigades spéciales*, French plainclothes police sent by—

I smirk. *Who else?* The black seal in a shiny trench coat.

Herr Geller.

He's testing me, hoping to get something on me.

I rock my baby back and forth in my arms, blessing myself then her with holy water while keeping up a lively conversation with her.

'*Alors, mon enfant*,' I begin, kissing her forehead after anointing it. 'You and I are lucky today, the church is empty and our prayers will reach God *tout de suite*.'

I swear she smiles at me, and my heart tugs.

With my baby in my arms, I push the pram through the double portals of the church, knowing the priest and his henchmen are watching me, hoping I make a mistake.

I do. But it's not what anyone expected. Including me.

'*Ooh!*' I cry out, turning my ankle when I miss a step, my high heel catching on the edge of the limestone. I overestimated my ability to keep my eye on the priest *and* maneuver a baby in my arms and a pram at the same time. I wince with pain and with a grimace on my face, I let go of the baby carriage. It rattles down the stone steps then into the street, no traffic except a cart with a donkey. The animal *hee-haws*, the priest cursing when he races after me and—

Before he can catch up to me, an SS officer scoops me up in his arms.

'*Let me go, monsieur!*' I cry out, my heart pounding at finding myself and Ninette in his grasp. This can't be happening. *Anyone* but the SS.

'Hold on to your baby tight, mademoiselle. I won't drop you.'

'Monsieur, *I beg you*, put me down...'

'And leave you as bait for the Gestapo? *Never*, mademoiselle.'

Feeling panicked, shocked at his words, I hold my breath. There's something about that voice that makes me tremble. That sixth sense I've developed since I met Arsène is evident in this man. Dark glasses cover his eyes, his officer's cap pulled down low, but you just know that face is good-looking, strong. My heart soars. *Yes, it's him.* I was right. He's taken on the disguise of a Nazi soldier before to get me out of a dangerous situation, but then it was to make a fast getaway. Here he seems more relaxed, leisurely, and if I dare say it, he possesses that godlike aura SS officers like to project, like he's not only in charge, but he moves with the grace of a conqueror who knows no boundaries. Anything he wants is his.

Does that include me?

How did he pull this off? Does Arsène even speak German?

I know he learned French while he was stationed in Algiers with the Foreign Legion and he's familiar with certain dialects of the tribes of the Sahara, but he's English born.

So much I don't know about him, but I trust him with my life. And Ninette's.

'Arsène...' I whisper, then moan when he tightens his arms around me.

He smiles wide. 'Don't worry, mademoiselle, I will see you to safety and take you home,' he says in a loud voice for the benefit of the Nazi priest watching us, waiting. The plainclothesmen draw back, disappointed. And somewhere in the small crowd gathered on the pavements, I bet Herr Geller is watching.

For once, I'm not afraid of him.

Arsène carries me holding my child to a Mercedes motorcar. I cringe when I see the familiar vehicle, but I get over it. I have to. With great care, he helps me into the passenger seat. I see a big wicker basket in the backseat for Ninette. I smile. He thinks of everything. Then he hands the pram over to the old man with the broom I saw earlier, 'ordering' him to keep it safe in a nearby shop until I return to pick it up.

Where—*how*—did he commandeer an official Nazi car? My head is spinning with questions.

I ache to touch him, but for now I'm satisfied to hear his voice deep and resonant whispering in my ear, 'You and your baby are safe, Justine,' because in spite of the hated Nazi SS uniform he wears, I'm the happiest I've been in a long, long time.

My favorite man, my hero, is back in Paris.

* * *

'How did you know I wouldn't fall for that Nazi trick?' I ask.

We're parked on the Left Bank near an old bridge crossing over the Seine. The big, gray ugly motorcar with the tiny swastika flag on the hood passed through the narrow street with only centimeters to spare, like a caterpillar wiggling its way through a tunnel.

'I didn't, but—'

He removes his dark glasses while I study his face, clean shaven, dark hair. The man wears the SS uniform well. He possesses an arrogance that allows him to take chances. Confident but not off-putting. But his eyes aren't a cold Aryan blue. They're dark and filled with secrets.

The most handsome man I've ever seen.

Arsène.

'I believe in you, Justine,' he continues. 'I knew you'd act as if you were there for confession, then pull back when you didn't connect with "Father Paul".'

'And if I *had* believed you were behind the grill? What then?'

'The Boches expected you to "spill the beans", as the Americans say, tell them what you know.' A moment of silence, then: 'The secret police were waiting to arrest you.'

'Why me?'

'The Gestapo suspect the church is a rendezvous point for the Underground.' He laughs. 'So far they haven't caught anyone doing more than confess their sins, but the church is compromised. I had to come up with a new disguise.'

'Why didn't you tell me before I went into the church?' I run my fingers through Ninette's curly blonde hair. My little angel has no idea how well she played her part. I shall tell her when this war is over.

'I had to let the scene play out to remove any suspicion of you.' He grins. 'You were never in danger, *ma chère* Justine. I had two men posted nearby.'

I nod. That explains the 'old man' sweeping the pavement and the French 'policeman'. My dearest Arsène looks out for me, but what I love the most is when he puts his arm around my shoulders and squeezes me. Before I can stop myself, I nestle my head against his chest. Ninette snuggles up in my lap exhausted and goes back to sleep.

I'm wide awake.

The adrenalin pumping through me comes from hearing his heart beating loud and strong against my ear, not my escape. Before we took off, *my* heart stopped when I saw the Nazi priest and his cohort jump into a Gestapo black motorcar then follow us around the Eiffel Tower, then east toward Père Lachaise cemetery. Arsène drove around in circles until we lost them. Lucky for us, a Nazi motorcade clogged up the Rue de Rivoli with three touring motorcars holding a dignitary and his staff. 'Adolph Eichmann is in Paris,' Arsène tells me, 'with his henchman, Alois Brunner. They're here to discuss plans for deporting Jews.'

Names I'm not familiar with. *Should I be?*

I'm not thinking about that now. Somehow he knew the Gestapo was on to our meetings, and he let them play out their game, exonerating me when I didn't fall for their trick. I'm waiting to hear what Arsène has to say. I get pleasure hearing him speak, but I'm also curious about him. Will I finally get answers?

'I still can't believe you put on that SS uniform.'

'Men do strange things in war, Justine. Women, too. We have to think—*look* like the enemy.' He holds me tighter. 'I'd do anything to keep you and Ninette safe.'

'Even if it means masquerading as a Nazi?' My heart races, bad memories swirling in my head.

'Yes. It's not the first time.'

'But you're wearing the SS uniform.' I feel cold and numb. I can't hide the hurt in my eyes, my lower lip trembling.

'I anticipated the uniform would upset you, Justine, but this is the only way I can keep close to you without arousing suspicion.'

His voice makes me shiver, the heat of the day giving way to a pleasant chill that comes over me at odd moments, like when Ninette says a new word or laughs at my joke. A thrill. I feel that way now. This is the first time I've seen the resistance fighter without a disguise like a hat or phony beard. He's so handsome I can't stop looking at him. Strong nose, flirty dark eyes that sparkle when he smiles, sensuous mouth I could kiss forever.

If only...

I sigh. Wishful thinking, *n'est-ce pas*?

When I ask him where he's been, he admits what I suspected. A mission for the British Foreign Office. What intrigues me is, would such an assignment be handed to a field agent? Or is there more to Arsène's backstory than he lets on?

'The London office is in turmoil since the coup in North Africa failed to establish a pro-Allied government,' he says. 'My mission was to infiltrate the locals and bring back credible intelligence.' He hints he was in Libya with orders to go undercover to discover how deep Nazi involvement goes, while securing the latest news about Rommel and the Africa Corps reportedly trapped at a desert crossroads.

'The battle is ongoing and with the RAF disrupting German supply lines, the Allies are hopeful for a victory.'

I look at him for a long moment, studying the silver glimmer in his dark eyes like a shining star pointing the way to a clear road to victory. I have no doubt he's committed to believing we *will* win. My heart swells, his confidence warming me, his bravery amazing me, his manliness taunting me to go farther into his world of intrigue with him. I inhale him and it's wonderful.

I don't deserve this happiness.

As I sit close to him, safe and warm, I start fidgeting with my hands, grabbing the loose threads on Ninette's blanket. I have something pressing on my mind, something I have to talk to him about before I burst.

I take a deep breath, then: 'The major raped another girl.'

Simple, direct.

He nods. 'Father Armand told me you witnessed the abduction.'

'Yes, I saw him force her into his motorcar like he did to me and...' I choke on the words. 'We know what happened next. The pain, the humiliation, the defeat of a woman's innocence by this monster.'

'Don't beat yourself up, Justine. You couldn't have saved her.'

I turn to him, tied up inside with ropes forged in guilt. 'I should have tried harder, Arsène. I didn't. And she's gone.' I grit my teeth. 'I *swear* I will get justice for this girl and God knows how many others who suffered at the hands of the SS.'

He grabs me by the shoulders, his hands strong and his words comforting. 'You're a brave woman, Justine, but there are times when you must wait, plan, be patient. The day will come. But for now, *ma chérie...*' He gets out of the motorcar and opens the passenger door. 'What you need is a walk among the chestnuts to clear your head.'

'Ninette—'

'I'll carry her in the basket.' He extends his hand to me. 'Walk with me.'

I plant a warm kiss on my baby's forehead, then tuck her blanket tightly around her as she lies in the big wicker basket. Arsène draws the window curtains to keep out curious eyes though the street is deserted. Who would dare question an official Nazi motorcar parked here with that damned little swastika flag on the hood waving in the breeze?

Minutes tick by like heartbeats. We walk along the Seine, Arsène holding my hand and carrying my little girl in the basket in the other, the slow pace of the river giving me the solace I need. I want to believe there is no war, that I don't see the SS uniform Arsène wears, only a handsome cavalier who's there for me.

We stop under the bridge where the smell of chiffoniers lingers. Rag pickers long gone who made their home here, their fires to keep warm nothing but cold ashes, the sweat of their struggle to survive each day still hanging in the air. To me it's a heavenly place when Arsène sets down the basket with Ninette in a shadowy corner and puts his arms around me. Before I can ponder what this moment means—do I really want to?—if it will change anything between us, he kisses me. His mouth claiming mine, his lips parting and the taste of sweet wine hitting my tongue before he sucks the breath out of me with a long, loving, delicious kiss.

And I melt in his arms.

At last.

* * *

My joy is short-lived.

When we break the kiss, I get the strangest shiver that we're being watched. I can't shake it. It's dark under the bridge with a sole streetlamp casting an eerie glow. I grip Arsène's hand tight and when I spin around, looking for my baby—

The basket is empty.

Ninette is gone.

'*Oh, my God, no!* Where *is* she, Arsène? Who could have taken her? *Why?*' I'm panicking, the guilt flooding through me, the self-deprecation that I'm a bad mother hitting me hard because I stole a few moments alone with this man who means so much to me.

*More than my baby?*

Of course not. But I'm so hungry for love, some goodness in my life, I let down my guard.

And now I'm paying the price.

'Stay here, Justine.' His eyes dart everywhere, alert, probing. 'Whoever took her is playing games with us.'

'How can you be sure?'

'He left the empty basket, knowing how you'd react, the sudden fear and panic surging through you, the guilt racing in your mind and poisoning your happiness.'

I slow down. Arsène is right. I'm feeling every emotion, every recrimination. Then my worst fear is realized when I hear—

'She's such a pretty child, Mademoiselle D'Artois.'

I spin around. Out of the shadows creeps Herr Geller holding my little girl in his arms, still sleeping. 'It would be a pity if something happened to her.'

He hands her to me and I nearly faint with relief. I touch her cheek to mine. She's breathing softly and her body is warm, drawing heat from the portly Gestapo man.

'You're heartless, Herr Geller.' I glare at him. 'I find what you did despicable.'

'And I find you in a most interesting situation, mademoiselle.' He eyes Arsène, assessing his SS uniform, his good looks, his strength. He grunts his displeasure. The Gestapo man is working solo tonight without backup and is no match for what he might imagine is a seasoned battlefield officer. So he attacks us with words instead of blows with his fists. 'I didn't think you had the nerve to cheat on the major, mademoiselle. But then again, what do I know about women? You creatures are never what you say you are. You can't be trusted.'

The ugly look on his face signals a crack in his armor, that he's speaking from experience, but what are the odds I'll ever know?

Before I can rattle off a smart retort, he turns to the SS officer, clenching and unclenching his fists. So far, Arsène has kept his anger tamped down, knowing a wrong move will make a bad situation worse. The piercing look in his eyes tells me he's ready to take on the Gestapo man, but the sane, cool-headed British agent knows that's a losing proposition. It's more important he keep his identity hidden, not blow his cover.

Herr Geller speaks to him in German. Terse, guttural sounds that grate on my ears, then gives him the Hitler salute. Arsène clicks his heels and in a gritty voice responds.

In German.

Then Arsène returns the Hitler salute. I don't know what chills me more. That appalling 'Heil Hitler' singsong dance, or the sadistic look in Herr Geller's eyes before he turns on his heel and saunters down the narrow street humming a snappy tune.

He's pleased. No doubt he believes he has something incriminating on me. Something he'll use against me when he's ready.

God help me.

# 12

## PARIS, JUNE 12, 1942

*Ève*

'I will never, *never* wear a yellow star.'

That was how it started two weeks ago when Madame de Giocomte stomped her feet, something I'd never seen her do. Hands on her hips, she started pacing, her handmade leather pumps tapping out a hurried rhythm on the marble floor in the foyer. She's always come across to me as elegant, sophisticated, and since the Boches occupied Paris, defiant against Nazi anti-Jewish dictates in her own unique way. I remember when she pulled her shoes out of storage bags, vowing to wear nothing *but* leather. She wanted to give several pairs to Jewish refugees, but I convinced her the Nazis would confiscate them and arrest the Jews wearing them. She refused to sit in the last car in the Métro and she won't give up her furs. *In Russia,* she said, *you'd freeze without them.*

'You have no choice but to wear the star, Madame, the order comes from the German High Command,' Michal insisted. Madame has always liked Michal, how he tried to save Monsieur de Giocomte, but would she listen to him? 'All Jews over the age of six must wear a yellow Star of David stitched onto their clothing over their heart.'

'Another insult,' she spewed. 'As if *they* can rule our hearts. Love rules the heart. You must never forget that, Ève.' Her eyes glowed with tears not yet fallen but sitting upon her dark lashes like iridescent slivers of ice.

'But, Madame, it's the law.'

'I don't care what they call it. Law, edict, regulation. I won't do it. It's degrading and humiliating.' She sucked in a deep breath. 'I am *not* a horse running in a race at Deauville the Nazis can round up and brand its hide. I am a woman. A Jew. Russian born, and now proudly a French citizen.'

'No one is exempt, Madame.'

'No?' she said, indignant. 'I came to Paris more than twenty years ago to escape persecution. "Persecution?" you ask. "But you grew up privileged." Yes, it's true, my family had wealth, but I never took for granted my place in the world. I was proud of my heritage and worked hard as a musician, then I fell in love. I've lost two husbands, but it doesn't stop me from volunteering and using what I hid from the Nazis of the de Giocomte fortune to help those in need. And *this* is how the occupiers treat me? *No*. I shall not be brandished about like a common criminal. It happened to me once and I swore it will *never* happen again.'

She didn't elaborate, but Maman confided in me that her elegant Russian employer—then just a cellist—nearly died in the 1917 Russian revolution after her husband's murder, how she was singled out as Jewish by a jealous conspirator and marked to 'hang until dead' by the radical tribunal. She became stateless, her lands and fortune confiscated.

She swore never again would she allow her fate to be determined by the enemy's whim. She keeps secret bank accounts in

Switzerland, she told Maman, and of course her jewels are 'hidden' where no one will find them.

But I have that square piece of yellow cloth the size of my palm to thank for changing her mind. Because it made Maman and Madame de Giocomte agree to leave Paris. After weeks of pleading, the order coming for every Jewish person to wear a Star of David on their clothing was what did the trick.

Madame de Giocomte was even more upset when she discovered she had to *pay* for the 'privilege' of wearing the star by relinquishing a point from her clothing ration card. *The final insult*, she said. She dashed off to her rooms and packed her bags.

Next came the details. Michal has arranged for Maman and Madame de Giocomte to leave on the train going south to Toulouse to meet his contact. The Basque guide will then escort them over the mountain range into neutral Spain, with four days of hiking over dangerous terrain through thick forests. Word is the German patrols are increasing daily, so they may have to take the trail higher up to the mountaintop. Snow? Maybe. I worry about Maman and Madame de Giocomte making the trek, but with the Gestapo breathing down our necks, we have little choice.

So far, we're on schedule.

We won't be if our contact with the hidden printing press can't finish their forged identity cards in time. Their typesetter was detained at Gestapo headquarters last week and never returned. A new worker joined them, but from what I heard arrests have been on the increase, causing a slowdown in not only forged identity cards, but printing pamphlets. I was surprised at Michal's reaction when he heard that. He left hours ago to see what's holding them up, but not before he ranted on about how they should 'give up printing those damned political tracts or we'll all be twiddling our thumbs in La Santé prison.'

He doesn't understand the power of the pen, how the right words can change the moment, the day... *the war*? That remains to be seen. In his mind, words don't kill Nazis.

Bullets do.

But that's an argument for another day.

Michal is a strong man, a proud man, and knowing the unspeakable horror he's witnessed, I kept my teeth clamped tight together so I didn't blurt out something I'll regret later. I've never told him how certain writings move me, give me courage not to give up, like the pamphlets distributed by the brave souls at le Musée de l'Homme before they were betrayed by an informant, arrested, and then executed. I yearn to write inspiring work as they did, tell other women what I've seen, felt, that they're not alone, but I've yet to extract the essence in the boiling pot of words bubbling in my head. I want to let off steam, but the damn lid is stuck. Someday it will fly off when I can't take the pressure of Nazi bullying and Gestapo cruelty anymore and will come gushing out of me.

I won't be able to write fast enough.

Until then, I hold it in. It festers in me.

For now, saving Maman and Madame is the main thing driving me.

Maman wrings her hands, anxious as she goes upstairs to pack a small suitcase. Maman and Madame need heavy coats, jackets and scarves. Gloves. Here in Paris it's hot, but they're headed deep into the forest, trudging through the cold, thick woods where German patrols won't look.

Madame is ever efficient, her suitcase closed up, ready to go, then she orders Cook to pack us dry biscuits and cheese she got from her black-market connection in Rue des Rosiers where she does her charity work, and two bottles of wine. Sniffling, Albertine wraps up the last two oranges for their trip, while Cook promises, 'Albertine and I will be here when you return, Madame.'

The two women will stay on at Maison Bleue, keep the household going with the funds Madame left for them and, in her most charming manner, she assures the two servants they should not hesitate to make use of the black market to sell the silverware so they don't starve. The paintings, save for a few mundane 'ancestor portraits', are gone, looted that day by the SS major who took Justine. I'm still not used to the empty walls.

I tell them the Allies won't let us down, but no one knows when the invasion is coming.

We smile, tear up, hold hands, praying that will come to be.

A heavy moment descends upon us when we say our good-byes, our hearts sad, but the spirit of freedom lives in all of us. We're set to leave before dawn. Michal and I will take Maman and Madame to the train station, then from there, we'll leave them and continue on our mission to Jonzac to secure guns and ammunition, before returning to Maison Bleue.

*Without Maman, without Madame.*

I'm already dreading it. I've never known life without Maman.

*Is there no greater fear... loss than that?* I don't think so.

'Ève, have you seen my black hat with the lacy veil?' Madame asks. I can hear the strain in her voice when she pulls out her hatbox. It holds a blue silk hat and cockatoo feather. No black hat. She curses in Russian, something she rarely does. Her nerves are taut like the fine strings on her cello. Maman is also in panic mode, racing down the stairs with her small case packed with her threads in a hundred different shades. She stuffed them into her suitcase but it's so full the clasp breaks and her sewing basket falls out and spools of thread fly everywhere. She falls to her knees, her lower lip trembling, mumbling to herself: how she will sew new dresses for Madame without her threads? She gathers up as many as she can, lamenting she can't find her strawberry-red spool of thread or her yellow-peach.

'I'll pick them up, Maman,' I tell her softly, 'go assist Madame.'

She nods. I helped Madame tear apart her boudoir drawers earlier and grab clothes off hangers in the *garderoben,* but no black hat. She settled for a deep maroon cloche that highlights the graying wisps of hair she pulls behind her ears. I think for a moment how pretty she looks, her cheeks tinted with the pink powder and crimson rouge lipstick she favors and hasn't changed since we met her. I'm glad she hasn't let the Nazis take that away from her like so many women her age who gave up and abandoned their toilette. It's a rape of another kind, I decide, not physical but mental, when the Boches take a woman's femininity away from her.

I touch my short hair... My neck is bare... Then maybe I'm a victim, too.

Why didn't I see that until now?

Pensive, I gather up the spools of thread and stuff them into the wide pocket of an apron Maman tossed onto a chair. I pack the apron into her suitcase and push down on the lid to make it close. I have to. Maman without her threads is like Cook without her pots and pans. It's who she is and I'd never take that away from her.

An hour later and we're ready. Darkness outside still hides the denizens of the night-defying curfew, including Michal. He isn't here yet with the forged identity cards. We can't wait any longer or they'll miss the train to Toulouse. I leave a note with Cook telling Michal that we'll meet him at the Gare d'Austerlitz train station.

We're nearly out the door when—

'My birdcage, Ève.' Madame drops her suitcase in the foyer, her frustration getting the best of her, and she bites down on the tip of her beige kid leather glove. 'I *must* have it.'

I don't ask why, but I see by the panic in her eyes there's more at play here than she's letting on. I've always suspected Madame harbors more than a romantic nostalgia about that birdcage. I remember the stories she told Justine and me when we were little girls about escaping from Russia with jeweled eggs and rubies and sapphires and how she refers to the cage as her 'treasure box'. Is she looking for those jewels to take with her? With that thought dancing in my mind, I grab the cage with two chirping birds and hand it to her when—

We hear a loud, insistent knock on the front door.

The 4 a.m. knock every soul in Paris dreads.

* * *

'Open up, Madame de Giocomte, *now*!'

I look at Maman, she looks at Madame, who looks me square in the eye. We're all thinking the same thing. They'll be no train this morning, no trek over the mountains in the snow, no feasting on rich butter and crunchy toast as they'd planned once they got to London.

It's the Gestapo.

*Do we run? Where to?*

The hidden entrance through the root cellar.

It's our only chance.

I grab Maman's hand. Her palm is moist; her face, too. The sweat of fear claims this gentle soul and it makes me sick to my stomach to see her like this. The lines around her mouth have deepened in recent months, her jaw tight. She never speaks of her fears, but they've taken a toll on her since the SS major kidnapped Justine. Unlike Madame who bears a regal deportment that flows like liquid silk, Maman is spun from sturdy cotton. Its edges frayed. Never more so than this moment when the enemy is standing outside her door, a step away from destroying her world.

*First, my daughter and now this?* I imagine playing in her mind.

'Quick, Maman, Madame,' I say in a loud whisper, 'follow me!'

Again, the knock on the door. Louder. More insistent, the interloper threatening to shoot through the elegant wood with a blast of firepower if Madame doesn't open up. No one moves. Madame looks at me, then Maman, her eyes fierce but sad. I know what she's thinking. She's reminded of the day the French police and German soldiers came for Monsieur de Giocomte. A day that still resides in her heart, her love for her husband as bright as ever in her eyes. She will not give up hope Monsieur de Giocomte is alive.

'Forgive me, *mes chéries.*' She wets her lips, glancing at Maman and me, getting ready to play a part she knows well. *Stall them, admit nothing*. 'I won't jeopardize your safety again.'

'Please, Madame, *no*, we can escape!'

'And then what, Ève? Cower in doorways? Steal bread to survive?' She raises her arched brows. 'I know what it's like to sleep on the cold ground with one eye open, to fear every footstep in the dark, your heart racing so fast it becomes a constant pounding in your ears that drives you mad.' She shakes her head. 'No, I shan't put you and your *maman* through that misery because of me.' She turns to Maman. 'Claire, wake up Albertine and go to the kitchen and stay there with Cook. Ève, wrap yourself in the long, damask draperies. You won't be the first spy to hide between the heavy folds of old curtains while I deal with our Nazi friends.' She spits on the floor. 'The bastards.'

I cock a brow, surprised at her candor, then do as she says. A wrinkle in Madame's silken personality I've never seen. She isn't as romantic as I believed, her logic outweighing the grand notions I had of her raging through the horror of the Russian Revolution floating on air and untouched. She isn't. And did she just call Maman by her first name? A sign of affection she rarely shows. She's setting the scene for what she knows will be an unpleasant encounter.

We all do.

*I'm Jewish*, I see written on her face as clearly as if she wears the yellow star over her heart. *They've come for me.*

Head high, she unbolts the door.

'I am Madame de Giocomte. And you are, monsieur?'

'Herr Avicus Geller, Madame... Gestapo.'

He doesn't wait for her to react, but pushes his way inside *la maison*, looking everywhere, smelling the tart orange scent of dried peels that Madame favors, running his gloved fingers over the gilt mirrors, noting the vintage draperies (I don't dare move), a screen from the court of Versailles with original silk damask panels, then squeezing the tasseled velvet pillows on the hard-back chairs in the foyer before looking up to admire the crystal chandelier overhead. His head is on a swivel, taking in the *grand maison* like an auctioneer, his eyes appraising each item. The thought chills me, watching him raking through Madame's possessions. Hasn't she been through enough already?

'Do you know *why* I'm here, Madame?'

Her eyes draw a blank, giving him an indignant stare that says, *Should I?*

I do.

He's not here to take Madame de Giocomte away. He's here for me.

Hiding in the cascading draperies, I'm safe. For the moment. I have a good view of him when I peek through the drapes. It's the same man from the Hôtel Drouot. Black trench coat with wide lapels, Fedora. How could I forget? He was working a crossword puzzle when my sister bade me to follow her. I also remember seeing him hustling Justine at the American Hospital of Paris.

Madame, birdcage in hand, ignores him and shushes the unhappy creatures. 'Hush, my darlings,' she coos, 'or the big rat will eat you.'

I hear a distinct quiver in her voice and her lower lip trembles. She grips the birdcage so tight, the veins on her hand bulge. Madame is very much afraid and trying desperately not to show it.

As expected, a snicker from Herr Geller. He relishes his ability to create chaos. And fear.

'Quit stalling, Madame. I'm here on official Nazi business.'

She raises a brow. 'You have news of my husband, monsieur?'

Simple. Direct.

I smile. *Bon*. She turned the tables on him. He steps back, not expecting her to question *him*. Except for a slight twitch around her mouth, Madame maintains her calm demeanor. I'm in awe of this woman.

'You forget who's in charge, Madame.'

'I didn't forget. *You* did. This is *my* home. Now unless you have news about Monsieur de Giocomte, I must ask you to leave.'

She attempts to shoo him toward the front door, the ornate birdcage swinging back and forth in his face, but she's awakened the ugly beast in the fat Gestapo man. And he shows it. It's one thing to react in a compromising manner to his authority. It's quite another to usurp him. He kicks the suitcase Maman dropped on the marble floor with the toe of his sturdy shoe. Then stomps on the case with his heel. Hard.

'Going somewhere, Madame?' he gloats.

Madame de Giocomte takes in a long breath but retains her composure, keeping her voice steady. 'To visit my sister-in-law, the baroness. Her daughter is ill and needs my assistance to care for her grandchildren.'

'I regret I shall have to detain you.'

'You mean arrest me.' Madame purses her lips in a continued attempt not to show him fear. Beads of sweat break out on her brow, strands of her lovely dark hair escaping from her hat and drooping around her face. She's held up well until now, but the moment of truth is here when all jibes and sarcasm flow like water from the snout of a flowerpot. And are absorbed by the earth.

Like Madame.

She's holding the birdcage against her chest like a shield, but her hand is shaking. She's aware like I am when the Boches have a mind to take away your freedom, you're helpless to change what happens next. It's how I felt when the SS major took Justine. My sister spoke so bravely against him, her courage saving me, but in the end she was no match for the enemy's cunning.

My fear heightens when I hear footsteps outside and my eyes dart to the open door. I see a French policeman enter and hover behind the secret policeman, his eyes lowered as if he's embarrassed to witness this tense confrontation.

Herr Geller, however, is in his element. He walks around Madame de Giocomte in a slow circle, noting her hat, coat. Shoes.

'I shall not arrest you today, Madame, though your impertinence *will* get you into trouble if you disobey my orders.'

'Do I have a choice, monsieur?'

'No.'

'I see.' She gives him a slight nod.

'Contrary to what you may believe, Madame, I need your cooperation.'

She stands straighter, pulls her shoulders back in defiance. 'I am *not* a collaborator.'

She averts looking in my direction, but we're both thinking the same thing. *He expects Madame de Giocomte to inform on me.*

'Everyone has their price.'

'I don't.'

'We'll see, Madame.' He snickers, then plops down in a damask Louis XV armchair no one ever sits on. The royal silk is over two hundred years old and threadbare. I swear I heard the fabric rip under his weight. He ignores his destruction of the precious piece of furniture and rambles on.

'I have orders from a prominent SS general that concern you *and* your staff.' He checks his notes written—where else?—on the same newspaper bearing a crossword puzzle. 'I see here you employ a seamstress, a cook, and a maid.'

He doesn't mention me. *Should I be insulted?*

'And if I deny it?' Madame de Giocomte challenges.

'There's no point in playing games, Madame. I don't ask questions if I don't know the answer. Now where is your staff?'

'Is that a Nazi order?' she cuts through the *merde* Herr Geller is spewing.

'Yes.'

'I employ no one. I am alone.'

Herr Geller shakes his head in frustration. 'When will you Jews learn that lying to the Gestapo will only get you deported to a concentration camp?' He quickly dismisses her denial and orders the French policeman to search the house.

Madame freezes, aware that I'm hiding within the folds of the long draperies, my nails clawing at the heavy fabric. I taste the salt of sweat on my lips. Hot, stuffy in here. I feel light-headed, but I can't let myself faint. I force myself to keep standing, gulping in fresh breaths through an opening in the draperies while Madame sweeps around the room like a grand duchess, diverting Herr Geller's attention from where I'm hiding then volleys with, '*Pardon,* monsieur, I will summon them. I wish no harm to come to my servants.'

Her voice troubled and empathetic, she fires off in rapid French to the policeman that she ordered the servants to the kitchen.

Herr Geller smiles, then nods. He's playing a game and enjoying himself. Like an executioner sharpening his axe.

I shudder.

Moments later I hear hushed whispers in the grand hallway then Maman, Cook, and Albertine peek into the foyer. Madame bade them enter, insisting the Gestapo man has important news that affects *everyone* at Maison Bleue.

Maman keeps looking in my direction, catching Herr Geller's eye for a brief moment, but Madame de Giocomte distracts him. 'I'm curious, monsieur, why you failed to mention my dressmaker's daughter, Justine Beaufort.'

'*Who*, Madame?' The man is so sadistic he taunts her, pretending to have no knowledge of my sister when I know I saw them together at the American Hospital. *What's his game?*

I'm tempted to show myself, demand he tell the truth about Justine, but Maman can't take the tension pulling her nerves taut a moment longer. She faces the Gestapo man head on, shaking her fists at him. 'Justine is my daughter, monsieur, and if you know *anything* about her, I'm begging you to tell me.' She sighs heavily. '*Please.*'

'I have no knowledge of this Justine Beaufort.' He reveals nothing more, chuckling to himself.

I see tears in Maman's eyes.

I know what she's thinking: that she had hopes this secret policeman would deny Justine was working for the Boches. That if she's dead, she'd have a closing, a settling down of the despair she carries around day and night. He didn't, confusing her more than ever. In her heart, she can't... *won't* believe her daughter is a collaborator.

'But I *am* curious about Ève Beaufort.' He drills her. 'Where is she? I demand you tell me.'

She turns away from him and her eyes meet mine. I see that familiar look when I do something she doesn't approve of, but the deep furrow between her eyes tells me that she believes what I told her about the Gestapo list.

'I haven't seen Ève since she ran off with that no-good chauffeur,' Maman says to protect me, and I know she's thinking about Michal and how we hid him in the garage for a time. '*Good riddance,* I say.'

'If she contacts you—'

'She won't, monsieur. She's no longer my daughter.'

I doubt if Herr Geller buys her story, but if he puts out an alert it will be for Ève Beaufort, not Luc Dumont. Before he can continue with his game, the two birds begin squawking again like he'd plucked their feathers and scattered them like rose petals.

'And get rid of that *damned* birdcage,' he yells, annoyed. 'General von Klum will *not* put up with a pair of sick birds.'

'*Lovebirds*, monsieur.' She smiles, then drapes a cover over the cage. I have no doubt Madame has hidden jewels in the cage. She one-upped the Gestapo, but for how long?

Who is this general, I wonder, and what does he have to do with Madame de Giocomte?

Herr Geller continues with his merriment, ordering everyone to remain in the home, pushing himself out of the armchair with a buoyancy that surprises me, then places two stoic German soldiers as sentries at both the front and back entrances. They waited outside—we couldn't have escaped if we tried.

'You and your staff, Madame de Giocomte, will clean and maintain the running of the *maison* for the new owner.'

'Owner?' Madame is livid. 'You can't do this.'

'Oh, but I can, Madame. As a Jew, you're stripped of your rights to own property, giving the commanding officer of the Wehrmacht the right to requisition this abode for the purpose of housing a high-ranking official of the German army.' He takes a beat to allow this information to sink in, then: 'The new owner will arrive in two weeks.' He is clearly refusing to say anything more about this mysterious interloper right away.

Another sadistic play on his part.

*Why would I expect anything less?*

'You would *dare* bring a Nazi into my home, monsieur?' Madame can't hide her anger. 'To sleep in *my* bed? I won't have it.'

'May I remind you, Madame de Giocomte, you are a Jew and no longer owner of this *maison* or anything contained in it. You and your servants belong to the Reich.'

Cook and Albertine cling to each other, eyes wide. Maman turns away, her shoulders slumped. Madame de Giocomte puts her arm around her to comfort her. 'And who do *you* belong to, Herr Geller?' Madame asks.

'I am intensely loyal to our Führer, Madame. I do his bidding without question.'

*I would have said 'the devil'.*

He flings away Madame's hope of retaining a say in the matter of what happens at Maison Bleue with a flick of his wrist and terse, threatening words. 'I have full authority to eliminate *anyone* who defies his orders... *Anyone*.'

She sniffs around him, complaining, 'So be it. You leave me no recourse, but I cannot obey your orders if we have no soap. And what about coal for the winter? Our cupboard is bare, no milk, no eggs. You Nazis have confiscated everything and you expect me to entertain this general of yours? Why choose *ma maison*?'

'The general became aware of your residence from Major Saxe-Müllenheim and requested to requisition your home as a private venue to entertain members of the Wehrmacht and the SS. He will also maintain his suite at the Hôtel Meurice.' Herr Geller plops down again in the armchair with the torn upholstery, delighting in claiming it as his own, then taps his fingers on the gilt golden armrests. 'You will scrub and clean and serve the new mistress breakfast in bed if she requests it, is that clear?'

*'Mistress?'* Madame's hand goes to her throat. 'You intend to bring a *German* woman into *my* house?'

His eyes beam. 'I assure you, Madame, she's an exquisite creature with, what is it you French say, that *je ne sais quoi?* Mademoiselle Rachelle D'Artois will have full control of running this *maison*.'

'A *Frenchwoman*?' she gasps, disbelieving.

I lean in closer. Did he say *Rachelle D'Artois?*

*Why does that name sound so familiar?*

'Yes, you will obey her orders or you *and* your staff will find yourselves locked up in a cattle railcar going east.'

'No, *no*. I won't allow a Nazi collaborator to run my home.'

'In case you've forgotten, Madame, I could have you shot for your actions but fortunately for you, good help is impossible to find in Paris.'

'You *damn* Boche, how *dare* you insult me.'

I swear the woman is forged from Russian iron when Madame de Giocomte grabs a fringed velvet pillow and tosses it at the Gestapo man. He catches it. Do I detect a *slight* admiration in his eyes for her courage?

'You won't act so foolish after three days in a cell with no food, no water, at Cherche-Midi with the vermin crawling up your spine.'

'It can't be worse than the vermin standing in front of me.'

*Slap.*

Herr Geller strikes Madame de Giocomte across the face. Hard. So hard, her hat falls off and her hairpins jar loose and her long, graying hair tumbles down upon her shoulders. I gape at her, my mouth open. I've never seen her like this. Her elegant, swirled, pinned-up hairstyle undone. I always thought of her as an Italian Renaissance masterpiece, her hair painted on her head with tiny, perfect brushstrokes.

She *is* human after all.

The Gestapo man strains hard to keep control, snorting like a bulldog in heat. '*You stupid woman.* You're a Jew and if you can't keep your mouth shut, I will make you disappear to a place where your hide will end up stretched out as a lampshade, is that clear?'

Her chest heaving, she says in a clear voice, 'You may silence my words, monsieur, but not the truth in my heart.'

'I know your type, Madame, Jewish literati with fancy vocabulary and golden tongues, but in the end, they cry for their mothers just like anyone else when their flesh is burning.'

'Don't underestimate me, monsieur. I lived through the Russian Revolution and I intend to survive you Nazis.' She sniffs him. '*Whatever* I have to do. Now if I'm to receive "guests", I shall need strong industrial-strength soap to get the foul smell out of here.'

The Gestapo man rises from his chair like *he* was once the king, itching to sound off, but to my surprise, the secret policeman accepts the fact this woman is more useful to him alive.

If he can turn her, Madame de Giocomte would be a feather in his Fedora.

Only he doesn't know Madame like I do. I can't ever imagine her defenseless, only strong and ready to fight.

'Play your cards right, Madame, and you shall be rewarded.'

'My reward shall be ridding my house of you and your Nazi friends. Now though, I must get to work.'

She turns her back on him and hustles Maman, Cook, and Albertine to the library, mumbling about *cleaning, washing, polishing...* while I see the Gestapo man snicker, then order the sentries to remain at the front and back while he enjoys a 'grand tour of the *maison*' with the French policeman following. I get it. He and Madame each believe they've won the battle.

But the war between them has just begun.

And me? Watching Madame at her best, I'm at my worst, wrapped up in the long, damask hangings, waiting for the right moment to escape when the Gestapo man isn't lurking behind the front door, while asking myself, *where is Michal? Arrested by the secret police?*

I can't stop worrying about him. The man is my anchor and I've come to respect him even if I *wasn't* in love with him. I've always considered myself independent, that I don't need a man, but that was in a laboratory when all I had to fight was bacteria and pathogens. The Nazis are more unpredictable and Michal has experience dealing with them in Poland. He's as smart as any military officer in coming up with saboteur tactics.

I wonder... *who is he really?*

I curl into a ball and beg my lungs to forgive me for not breathing while I mull over everything the Gestapo man said, from requisitioning the house because a general wants it for his entertainment headquarters, to installing the traitorous Parisienne, this Rachelle D'Artois, as the new mistress, to him denying he'd ever heard of my sister—

Oh. God. No.

I choke on dust and nearly gag.

Can it be? *It is.*

*Justine is Mademoiselle D'Artois?*

I *knew* the name sounded familiar. When I asked the nurse at the American Hospital of Paris, *Who's the blonde with the Gestapo?* she told me her name was Rachelle D'Artois.

I feel a bubble of laughter rising up in my throat, the irony hitting me like a moldy grapefruit. *My sister,* the Nazi collaborator, is the new mistress of Maison Bleue.

Maman is going to faint.

* * *

*'Ève!'*

I hear a loud whisper behind me when I slip out of the mansion the way I came in, through the hidden door in the kitchen cellar, the smell of morning dew fragrant as dawn breaks. Michal grabs me around the waist and I warm to the strength of his hands holding me tight.

But his voice is cold.

'I saw the Gestapo officer barge in through the front door.' He touches my cheek, pulls wisps of short hair behind my ear. A loving gesture that entices me to lift my chin, part my lips, hoping for a kiss. Of course, I don't do it. I'd embarrass him *and* myself. Two peas in a pod we're not, though I'd like to be. Instead I shake my head when he asks, 'He didn't hurt you, did he? Or your *maman*, Madame?'

'No, it seems he prefers to wind up his victims with innuendos, then stab them with vicious threats.'

I told him about the Gestapo man denying he knew anything about Justine, then ordering Madame and her staff to prepare for guests. Nazi guests. Including a general.

'*Who*, Ève?'

'General von Klum.'

'I've heard the name. He's from Hitler's old guard, an aristocrat, and known like other Prussian officers for leaning farther to the left than other members of the dictator's staff. Some say *too* far.'

'I can't believe a Nazi general will sit at Monsieur de Giocomte's table,' I begin, wondering how I'm going to spill the news about Justine's part in this, 'but that's not the worst of it. The general is installing a woman in Maison Bleue to act as hostess for his drunken parties.' I pause. 'She calls herself Rachelle D'Artois.'

'A Frenchwoman?' He spits on the ground.

'Yes, but not *any* Frenchwoman.' I want to bite my tongue, but I force the words out. 'I believe it will be my sister, Justine.'

'*What?*'

'The name is an alias, but I'm sure it's her.' I tell him about the incident at the American Hospital of Paris, his mind absorbing this new intelligence, his dark eyes questioning, *What is the play here?*

'The Gestapo never does anything without a reason, Ève. We must be careful.'

'I've got to go back and warn Maman, Madame.' I hadn't dared follow them to the library with Herr Geller on the loose in Maison Bleue. 'Tell them our beautiful Justine is the Nazi mistress coming to rule over Maison Bleue.'

'No, Ève. That's exactly what the Gestapo man wants.'

'He knew I was hiding?' I consider myself fortunate to have evaded him when he strutted like Mussolini through the long gallery where the Impressionist paintings once hung, ordering the French policeman to remove the portraits of the de Giocomtes' ancestors and 'burn the dirty Jews'.

'No, but those sentries aren't going anywhere.'

'I can come back later tonight. They won't see me if I use the hidden entrance.'

'What if Herr Geller stations a guard *inside* the house?' he protests. 'You'll be caught.'

'I can't stand by and let this happen.'

'*Think*, Ève, what you're suggesting doing. You'll be arrested and then deported to a concentration camp.'

'What are you saying?'

'You cannot see this place as home again.'

'Oh...' I sink down into the grass, the pungent smell of earth sticking in my nostrils. That hits me hard. Since I joined the Resistance, I've hidden in empty buildings, slept on the cold ground, lived in an old hunting lodge with pigeons, holed up in an empty apartment in Montmartre with roaches, but I always found my way back here, home.

Until this moment. That's done, finished.

I'm in the crosshairs of the Gestapo.

I can't stay at Maison Bleue, but Michal convinces me that

perhaps with Justine back, Maman and Madame de Giocomte will be safer here now than trying to leave and make their way along the Comet Line, the escape line from Paris to Spain and Gibraltar then London. If they're captured, he says, they'll be shot immediately.

I have no choice but to agree with him. It seems that the Nazi general billeted here wants Maman and Madame to run the household, clean up the mess after their drunken parties. In addition, I have no doubt Michal is right, that Herr Geller will arrest Ève Beaufort if she shows up. I hate leaving Madame de Giocomte and Maman, and what I wouldn't give to try again to convince Justine to fight *with* us, not against us.

I'll not give up; she *is* my sister.

But if I'm arrested, I can't help them.

I take a last look at Maison Bleue, standing strong at dawn under the weight of the Nazi swastika, the lights in the library burning hot with tension. Passion. Female chatter. No tears between them. Instead I imagine Maman and Madame are making plans how to outwit this Nazi interloper, their blood running hot. But they have no idea what surprise awaits them with Justine's return along with a Nazi general and his staff invading the place I've called home since childhood. A rise of anger then despair makes my heart pound, my nerves taut. *It's unjust*, but we're at war. I bury my past life as Ève and wrap my new identity around me like a magician's cape. I'm off on a mission with Michal. I wish I could watch this game play out. See who wins.

The Russian feline.

Or the Gestapo rat.

My money is on *le chat*.

# 13

## PARIS, JULY 6, 1942

### *Justine*

'Return to your apartment, Justine, and pack your things. The game has changed.'

'*Game?*' I protest, pushing the pram along Avenue Matignon, the smell of an unwelcome change in the humid air. The major wastes no time in making his play, falling into step beside me on my morning walk with Ninette, his SS uniform pressed and perfect even in this heat. *Is that what he calls this charade?*

'You will do as you're told or I shall make other arrangements for the child.'

The major said *the* child.

I take a step back even if my heart skips the melody and goes straight to the chorus. I know what I heard. Again. He never refers to Ninette any other way. I don't know why that worries me, but it does, reminding me how precarious my life is. And hers. It hangs on a thread easily snipped.

I put on my sweetest smile. 'Where are we going, monsieur?'

'In due time, Justine.' The smirk that I hate follows.

*To Avenue Foch?* I wonder. Did Herr Geller mention my indiscretion? My 'rendezvous' with a mysterious SS officer?

Arsène in disguise.

The Gestapo man believes I have taken the SS officer as my lover, putting me on guard. That evening when he surprised us still haunts me. Arsène and I barely spoke when he drove me back to my apartment. Ninette's small body shook after the Gestapo had clutched her like a hawk, its hooked claws gripping its prey. She lay fitful in my arms all night.

And what about the terse exchange in German between Arsène and the secret policeman? He assured me Herr Geller gave no indication he suspected anything other than he was a Nazi officer on leave in Paris looking for a little fun. Then Arsène gave me a quick Hitler salute before leaving, for anyone watching my apartment.

That unnerved me.

I continue pushing the pram, aware of the major breathing hard, anxious to finish his business with me. I bite my tongue to say what I thought about him taking away my afternoon fun with Ninette. It's a hot day with a noon sun draining the moisture out of the air. I'm perspiring in my lightweight white linen dress and so is Ninette. My poor baby has a slight rash. I applied cotton soaked with apple cider vinegar on her skin—thanks to Madame Péroline's excellent black-market connection. It's working. My little girl isn't scratching her face today. I want so much to see her smile.

I'd planned to take her to the puppet show in a quiet, wooded area off the Champs-Élysées when the noisy engine of the major's Mercedes motorcar filled my lungs with hot smoke and my heart with fear. He was following me again.

He has a habit of sneaking up on me in that smelly German monstrosity just to show me I'm never free from him. And just when I thought the major couldn't turn my life upside down again, he shows me how wrong I am. The man is not only dangerous, but also unpredictable. He makes me so angry I can't speak when he lays out his latest plan to push his own agenda.

'You're returning to the home of the de Giocomtes, Justine. *Immediately*.'

I squeeze my eyes shut and exhale. He's joking, *n'est-ce pas*? *Home*. I never thought I'd see Maman and Madame again, but wait... no, I can't. What about the major's number one rule about his 'conquests' returning home? Why make me the exception? Even more upsetting, I fear the shock will be too much for Maman and Madame. They'll never let me through the front door if Ève told them I'm working for the Nazis.

'I can't go home to Maison Bleue, Major. Maman and Madame de Giocomte won't understand.'

'Nonsense. Your orders are clear: you're to take over as the new mistress.'

*A pause.*

'As Mademoiselle Rachelle D'Artois.'

'What?'

'You have two weeks to prepare the *maison* to receive important visitors from Berlin.' He sees the shock on my face, then laughs. 'No, mademoiselle, not the Führer... not yet. But who knows? Perhaps I shall meet him someday.' He lets the thought dangle in the air like a frosty breath. I feel the chill up and down my spine in spite of the humidity sucking the breath out of me.

He will resort to whatever trickery it takes to secure a post here in Paris. He admitted his dream of being permanently assigned as an attaché to Reichsmarschall Goering's staff and art curate fueled his newest scheme to secure that position. What angers me is that also means exposing Ninette to his Nazi cohorts, along with Maman and Madame de Giocomte.

*And where is Ève?*

The major makes no mention of her arrest, thank God. She's still free. Yet this entire operation could be an elaborate trap to arrest my sister. I pray I can glean the intelligence from him to warn her—maybe she'll listen to me this time—but his plan took me by surprise.

'I can't go back to Maison Bleue. *I can't.*'

He eyes me with a quizzical look. 'You question my orders?'

'Yes. You're asking me to return to the scene of your crime and you expect me to smile and forget how you assaulted me in that very home?'

He grabs my wrist, squeezes it. 'I'm not asking you. I'm *ordering* you. From what I hear from Herr Geller, your insolence toward him makes him question your commitment to the Party. Now you can *prove* your loyalty.' He leans over so close his musky scent makes me hold my breath. 'I shall enjoy watching you squirm, mademoiselle, entertaining my fellow SS officers.'

'And I'm telling you, I won't do it.'

He raises his hand to slap me, but thinks better of it. We're not alone on the busy avenue. 'Someday your brashness will get you into trouble, mademoiselle, and I won't be able to get you out of it.'

He means Herr Geller.

I stand down. I know when to hold my tongue. I'm reminded of that when Ninette thrashes about in the carriage, her tiny ears burning from so many things she doesn't understand. The truth strikes me hard: I'm a prisoner *and* a mother. I have no right to jeopardize my baby's life. I don't know what came over me. Foolish talk that endangers my child. The Gestapo grows more powerful each day, with more arrests and stories about the 'kitchen', whispers of indescribable torture that slice through my defenses like a sharp blade skinning my flesh from the bone.

They say women suffer more than men. I don't intend to find out why.

Instead, I keep pushing the pram with determination, willing myself not to show my emotions to this man who obviously enjoys making me uncomfortable. When I protest again about his scheme, he cuts me off before we have another argument. I sense he's frustrated with me... or does he have a conscience about me going back home? Is that it? No, his next move proves that isn't what's bothering him. He tickles me under the chin. The gesture is demeaning, but when has he ever shown me anything else?

'You'll make a beautiful hostess, Justine. Quite an impressive step up for a servant working for a Jewish family, *n'est-ce pas*?'

'I was *never* a servant, monsieur. I'm an *artiste*. I designed dresses and gowns for Madame de Giocomte.'

He laughs. 'I can't wait to see the expression on the Jewess's face when you strut thought the front door and demand she vacate her suite so you can move in.'

I hear myself gasp with horror. 'No, I can't do that to Madame de Giocomte. She's always treated me like her own. She's a *grand-mère* in my eyes. I can't ask her to take orders from me.'

'It's either via you or she takes them at Gestapo headquarters. I assure you that won't be pleasant.'

'Your threats don't work, Major. You need me for your game.' I glance at him. 'More treasures to loot from the de Giocomtes?'

I can't help but refer to the esteemed Jewish couple as still together. I've yet to inquire about the welfare of Monsieur de Giocomte after the major promised me nothing would happen to them. Ève's news that monsieur was deported stunned me, making me realize no one in Paris is safe from the Boches.

Including me.

'General von Klum has requested the use of a private venue,' the major says, 'a luxurious residence where he can entertain important visitors from Berlin without the formalities of a hotel. Or unwanted guests.'

*He means spies.*

'You mean where *you* can plan your dirty deeds to make life miserable for Jews, using the general as your foil.'

He says nothing, confirming my suspicions.

'The general requested *you* to act as his hostess.'

'Me? I'm flattered.'

I'll never forget the night I collapsed at Bal Tabarin, an erotic nightclub, when I told the major about the baby. And how, when the major slapped me so hard I ended up at the American Hospital of Paris, it was General von Klum who tried to help me. He seems an old man who's more interested in Paris nightlife than winning the war. He's often critical of the Führer, and has been unfailingly kind to me since then, as well as generous with information.

But it was the tall, handsome waiter who carried me to safety that night. Arsène once again.

'I thought you'd be pleased by the offer, Justine.'

'Should I be? One cage for another.'

He ignores me. 'The general has also requested you put on fashion shows for his invited guests.'

I chuckle. 'What he knows about *la mode* went out with the corset.'

'I assure you, any Parisienne would be honored for this opportunity to be a part of making Paris the center of fashion once again.'

I raise a brow. Not really. The Nazis have stifled the art of design with their boxlike mentality, their fixed quota for cloth, and their marketing approach to the ateliers, including the

House of Péroline, to make haute couture in Paris then run it through Berlin for resale to occupied countries.

And what about Parisians? Are we to starve not only our bellies but our love of silks and lace and fine wools? Dress in rags so the Frauen of Berlin can strut down the Champs? The Nazi approach is an embarrassment to every Parisian designer from gowns to hats, and that includes me. Instead of the hum of sewing machines, the loud pounding of goose-stepping reigns in fashion houses.

I want no part of it.

I can't say that. So, instead I quip, 'The general must be getting soft.'

'Getting?' He shrugs. 'He spends too much time on women and drinking. And cavorting with his aristocrat friends.' He looks off into space, unusual for him, then mumbles, 'Including certain generals.'

I let that pass.

'And does the Führer approve of the general's foray into the world of fashion?' That would surprise me since Hitler hates makeup, especially red lipstick.

'The general is known for his brilliant military strategies.' He explains that General von Klum was among those officers encouraging Hitler to rethink their initial plans and attack the French Army from behind through the Ardennes. He snickers. 'He also convinced the Führer to reopen the nightclubs to boost German officers' morale.'

'I see.'

So requisitioning Maison Bleue for his little 'parties' shouldn't come as a surprise, but I *am* suspicious. *Am I a pawn in a game I'm not aware of?*

We continue walking side by side, each with our thoughts. The major ignores me as if I'm a speck of dirt on his boot. He isn't finished with me, letting the news sink in. General von Klum is an enigma to me. Since the impending invasion of Russia, I sense he's having second thoughts about the Führer's plans, something I heard in his voice when he mentioned his nephew was reassigned to Stalingrad.

An SS officer with a heart beating under that hated uniform?

I wonder—as I turn down the Carrè Marigny toward the puppet theater, the forest-green wooden shack with a small stage and hand-held puppets blending in with the Judas trees—if the general has had second thoughts about this war. I've seen his double chin droop down to his chest of medals when he invites me to dine at the Hôtel Ritz. He's certainly not happy about how the invasion in Russia is going and he disapproves of the Gestapo's methods, commenting how a bottle of good cognac is just as good to loosen a man's tongue. He once told me he worries about the people of Berlin if RAF bombers find their mark. Yet he's never mentioned a wife or family, merely his nephew, making me curious.

I'll do some digging, ask Arsène. I can't help but wonder if the general intends to use Maison Bleue to conduct meetings that have nothing to do with fashion shows.

A dangerous game, if I'm right.

But who am I to question a general's motives?

'*Two weeks*, Justine. I expect the *maison* to be ready for your first soiree.'

'What about my job designing hats at the House of Péroline?'

'Once the general approves the arrangements, you may return to the hat shop... on a part-time basis.'

I nod. I have to be satisfied with that.

Then the major bids me au revoir without even a nod or tickle to Ninette's pudgy pink toes. Not that I encourage him to get anywhere my baby, but it saddens me this adorable little girl has no papa to spoil her.

I pick her up out of the carriage and hug her. A trembling in me awakens Ninette and she waves her arms about and starts to fret, crying, as if she knows a new threat challenges our safe little world in the ninth arrondissement, that the lovely routine we enjoy each morning of tea and milk, bread with sweet butter for me—I let her lick the butter off my fingers—and my baby's gruel thick with country oats and flavored with cinnamon. Food I wouldn't have without the major. It's then I feel like a traitor to every mother in France. Guilt riddles my mind, that I have food and milk because an SS officer fancied my long legs, golden hair, slender hips. No matter how hard I convince myself my work as a double agent makes up for any indulgence I enjoy—for my baby, *n'est-ce pas*?—I know it's not enough. I must do more. Help Arsène gather intelligence.

And that does mean going home to Maison Bleue.

Yet I won't let the major dictate to me. I know how the game is played, how the intricate world of Nazi politics isn't as black and white as I'd thought. If I'm to survive, I have to embrace this opportunity, be strong, become a fabulous hostess who doesn't cower before the Nazis, but weave a web so intricate, they can't get out.

*I* shall be in control.

I see now how much the major needs me. Yes, I suffered a life-altering experience when he sexually assaulted me, but I shall no longer be a victim of his sadistic nature. Instead, I will raise my own battle flag of freedom. I'm a woman hurt, humiliated, but that doesn't mean I can't let those scars heal and fight harder. I will never forget how he viciously raped me, but I won't do myself any good by not letting my wounds heal. Yes, I have scars, but they've become a fabric of who I am, my strength, my power not to let this SS major keep me down.

So, if I am to be a grand hostess, I welcome it.

I will have every Nazi eating out of my hand.

You can bet on it.

* * *

*And how does Arsène figure into this new development?*

That thought races through my mind as I pack my things and Ninette's, remembering the times he's visited me here in my apartment on Rue des Martyrs under some ruse, like delivering precious coal to keep us warm. Meeting me in a house filled with Nazi bigwigs will be a challenge. I wonder if he'll infiltrate the ranks in his disguise as an SS officer. Am I so selfish to hope I'll see him more often? I miss him, his comforting presence that turns dangerous for both of us when I get too close to him. Strange, warm feelings that burn hot when he touches my hand or puts his arm around my waist.

At first, I was afraid of these feelings, lighter than sheer silk.

Then the flutter of that silk covered my body, ravished and scarred. Wrapped me in a tenderness I never thought I'd know again. The searing, ripping pain that tore me apart when the major raped me oozed like an open wound, raw and painful. So devastating, I couldn't even touch myself down *there* when I washed. I never looked below my bellybutton, afraid I'd see my womanhood mangled and not repairable. Then Arsène found me and—

*Yes, things are happening.*

I'm healing.

Feeling pleasant shivers when we're together.

Damn, but I want more than hot glances from him, burning

skin when he touches me... I want *him.* I can't forget how he kissed me. Hard. Delicious moments in his arms that should have satisfied me. I have no right to ask for more. We're at war, Frenchmen and women are dying, Jewish people deported to God knows where, and I keep telling myself, *I have no right to want more in this crazy world.*

But I do. Oh, how I do.

God help me, I want Arsène to hold me tight in his arms. I know he will understand my emotions are still fragile from the rape, that my body healed but—like a scar that tingles long after the flesh is cut—the memory is still there. I want him to slowly lift my skirts, touch me between my trembling thighs with hands that caress me, want me, desire me. Make me feel not afraid. Make me feel like a woman again.

I want him to make love to me.

And *anything* getting in my way be damned.

# 14

## JONZAC, SOUTHWESTERN FRANCE, JULY 1942

*Ève*

I need to confess what's on my mind, what this female saboteur is guilty of that's making me ache so bad I'm losing focus on the mission. It's him. Michal. I tasted the sweetness of what I'm missing, the pleasure of his touch, and I want more. It happened yesterday when we were piling up boxes of ammunition in this munitions depot operated by the Nazis in a massive limestone quarry. It was an accidental touch, nothing planned, but I could feel a sudden heat spark between us in the cold, damp underground cave. A magnetic pull to him that I've denied for too long.

Now he's on my mind all the time, making me lose focus. The increasing hunger I have for this man, in spite of my refusal to accept the fact we can only be partners, resistance fighters, and nothing more, overwhelms me. What's worse is, this annoying ache in the pit of my stomach could get me—and Michal—killed.

We're working undercover in enemy territory outside the city of Jonzac, twenty meters deep beneath the earth in this old quarry where the sublime scent of mushrooms once filled the air. Now I smell the sweat of the men working here and wafts of sulfur drift into my nostrils depending on where they send me to work. Humid. Dark. Ceilings six, seven meters high, I'm guessing.

Outside, the huge quarry gates are guarded by sentries and defended by more than twenty machine guns manned by German soldiers. More guns that I can't identify are positioned to pick off anyone who gets too close, while a steady stream of French workers stockpile guns and ammunition for the German offensive. I can't keep track of the truckloads of guns and ammo, marine shells and torpedoes being deposited in this seemingly endless series of caves and tunnels.

It's easy to get lost, but Michal scouted it out before he brought me here for the job. Our plan: to grab as many rifles, handguns, grenades and as much ammunition as we can hoard in a nearby farmer's outhouse before we steal a truck and hightail it back to Paris. It is actually easier than I thought it would be. With over two hundred men working here, the Germans have abandoned searching the workers and their bags, making it possible to smuggle out small arms and grenades, even rifles. Every night guns and boxes of ammunition disappear and are spirited away by foot in satchels, on bicycles, horse-drawn carts, and then hidden under hay in outhouses on nearby farms. The Nazis haven't figured it out yet; no telling how long that will last.

Dressed in dark overalls, boots, faded muslin shirts and cotton work jackets, and me with a brown felt cap to hide my face, we had no trouble getting jobs in this small spa town. The surly German sergeant in charge glanced at our forged identity cards, then looked us over, giving Michal a nod, his muscular body an asset the Nazis will make good use of to haul weapons. I stretched as tall as I could, hoping my height would overcome my slender build while Michal insisted he wouldn't take the job if his younger brother wasn't hired, too. The sergeant grunted, then stamped our cards and put us to work. The Germans need laborers and from what small talk I've heard, forced labor sending Frenchmen to work in factories in Germany is imminent.

Michal and I blend in with the other locals. Men with country accents and suspicious minds. Looking at us cross-eyed, wondering who we are. I see them whispering whenever we walk by, make crude remarks, especially a burly man with thick scars on his neck and wrists. Gossip is the Nazis tried to hang him, but the rope broke. Instead of shooting him, they put him to work in the caves... No doubt he's a Gestapo informant sent to keep the workers in line.

Michal didn't take the bait when he blocked his way several times. A play for dominance. Michal knew better than to show his hand. No one knows we're here to secure weapons for our network. Michal happened upon the intelligence when he got a tip from a local farmer named Adrien Bodin.

He warned us the work is hard.

I've never ached so much in my life from bending, lifting, and squatting to count handguns and rifles stored in piles of wooden crates. The repetitive motions inflamed my muscles, the long hours making my head woozy, the humidity dehydrating me and making me unsteady. I stumbled against a large box I'd just packed containing a British STEN machine gun the Nazis confiscated from a dead Resistance fighter. I handled the weapon with reverence in memory of its owner, her name *Sara* etched on the handle. A heroic woman lost, but not forgotten. When I raised my head to send a prayer upward, I got lightheaded and turned my ankle. Before I could stop myself, I brushed up against Michal, his hard chest pressing into my breasts bound with muslin strips. Oh, Lord, my nipples tingled and I nearly died. Caught up in this delicious feeling, I moaned, catching us both by surprise. His eyes widened and he grinned so big I knew he liked it.

I looked away. I was so embarrassed I didn't speak to him for the rest of the shift.

Now I can't look him in the eye.

I shudder when I think about how my female needs could jeopardize the mission. I have no doubt I let my defenses wear down around Michal on the more than five-hour jaunt from Paris, relaxing around him, laughing at his jokes, telling him about the numerous times my chemistry experiments blew up in the school lab in the days before the occupiers came, wishing I'd known him then. Impossible. He was back home in Poland with his father, sister... and the girl he had loved. Now he was here with me and that made me feel guilty, laughing with him, bouncing up and down in the beat-up German truck, feeling the way I do about him.

Falling in love with him.

I'll never forget that old truck. Bullet holes in the doors, cracked front window, gears sticking; every kilometer we covered became a small miracle. We prayed the oil gauge didn't lie as they often did. We'd discovered on a previous mission how French mechanics at the factory rig the dipstick to give a false reading to ruin the Boches' trucks and slow them down.

They didn't count on two needy Resistance fighters 'borrowing' one.

I stare down at my smooth hands, clay caked under my broken nails, my scuffed boots. I can't ignore the unpleasant smell bleeding out of my armpits. I've never felt so dirty. My job is not only to gather intelligence about the Germans' operation, but also to discreetly 'eliminate' guns and rounds of ammunition from the inventory stored here at the depot. Greasy, filthy. Weapons piled up in a series of caves that stretch on for two kilometers. So far we've put together a tidy cache of weapons and hidden them at the Bodin farm about ten kilometers from the depot.

We take turns sneaking out the guns and ammo in a large saddlebag when the German guard goes on his rounds.

It's Michal's turn.

After the guard leaves, he appears out of the shadows, his leather saddlebag stuffed with two pistols, ammo, three grenades, then nudges me toward the corner, his dark eyes giving me a silent message. *Look busy. I'll meet you at the rendezvous point.*

I nod. I lift a small case of ammo rounds onto my shoulder and walk with a casual stride over to the French supervisor checking off the stockpile of boxes. It's the end of the work day; laborers are heading toward the exit, so I keep him busy chatting about the heat down here while out of the corner of my eye I see Michal disappear with the other workers. He'll blend in then, once he clears the big gates and the sentries, he'll veer off in another direction toward the small lake. There he'll hand over the guns and ammo to the farmer waiting for him with his horse and cart, hiding the precious weapons under the hay.

I keep a low profile, finish up my job loading several rifles confiscated from the local villagers before I leave to meet him, my head still swimming with that unforgettable moment when our bodies touched and—

'How come I never seen you in the village before?' comes a raspy whisper in my ear, making me shiver. 'You working for the Boches?'

The brute with the jagged, ugly scars. I don't turn around.

*He hasn't left. Why?*

I try to play down the fear creeping along my spine, but I'm no fool. The man has been watching us. Me, in particular. I get the feeling he's a bully who preys on the weak just for the fun of it.

Today it's my turn to spin around on his wheel. 'Me and my brother couldn't get work,' I say, attempting to imitate his dialect. 'The Nazis closed down the marble quarries.'

'Yeah? Where?'

'Montmartre.' Not really. They closed years ago, but it sounds good for this local asking too many questions.

He laughs. 'Paris, huh?' His gaze narrows as he continues questioning me. 'I figured you wasn't from around here, but you're lying. You ain't never worked a day in your life under the hot sun with that smooth skin.'

He tries to touch my cheek, but I pull away. God help me if he discovers I'm a woman.

'So I lied. So what?'

'I get it. You on a Gestapo list?'

'And if I am?'

'What for?'

I see a dangerous light in his eye that tells me I have to come up with something. 'I got kicked out of the Sorbonne for talking against the Vichy government.' I lower my voice. 'Satisfied?'

'Damn Communist, that's what you are. We don't want your kind here, understood?'

'Leave me alone, *please*.' I turn my back and, acting on impulse, I walk away, inciting the man's anger. He knocks off my cap and it flutters to the ground. Instinctively I put my hands up to my face, my hair. It's short and curls around my ears.

Wrong move.

'I'll show you not to turn your back on me.'

He grabs me and slams my head against the hard stone wall, pinning my arm behind me. My ears ring, my vision blurs. *'Let me go, you brute!'*

'Ah, so the boy has some spunk after all. Let's see how much.'

He tosses me into what they call 'the circle'. An open space where the French workers congregate to gamble, throw the die, but we're alone now. They've left for the day. I'm on my own. I hit the hard ground with a thud, don't move. Can't. He knocked the breath out of me. Chalky dust rises around me, making me cough. For the longest moment of my life, I wait for his next move, hoping I can kick him in the groin when he gets close enough, then race through the tunnel, knowing I'm done here.

To my surprise, he circles me, studying me from all angles, a faint recognition in his eyes puzzling him as he appears to search for a truth he can't quite grab onto—does he suspect I'm a woman but can't believe it?—then he shakes his head. *Bon*. I stand a better chance with him as a young man than a girl—the SS aren't the only ones who see females as spoils of war. The moment drags on and I'm still alive. I think about Michal, how I don't want to die here, that I'll never thrill to his touch again. I lie on my stomach, keeping my head lowered, eyes down. I can't give in to him, I've got to talk him out of beating me up. Escape.

We *need* those guns.

He makes a move to grab me, but I kick out my left foot, hit him in the kneecap, but it doesn't stop him. It *does* give me enough time to roll over and out of his way. 'The guard will be back soon,' I shout. 'You want a sharp bayonet in your back?'

'Smart aleck, huh? You little twerp—'

The man grabs me by my jacket collar then pulls me along the ground while I dig in my heels and drag my feet. 'I'll show you I'm no easy mark!' I yell, scraping the stone-hard ground with my bare hands when I hear a deep baritone voice behind me.

'Why don't you pick on someone your own size?'

I look up. The tall, broad-shouldered fighter I've come to know so well seems to materialize out of the chalky dust. *Michal.*

He must have sensed something was wrong.

My heart lights up like a firefly turning on its light. I've never been so happy to see anyone. *He came back for me.*

The brute lets me go and spins around. 'Well, well, if it ain't your big brother—'

Before the man knows what literally hit him, Michal throws a right hook then a left cross. The brute stumbles, works his jaw with his hand, the piercing stare in his eyes telling me he's one angry bastard and wants a taste of his attacker.

Michal doesn't wait for his next move. He steps aside when the brute lunges toward him then socks the big man again on the jaw, throwing punches at him before he can counterattack. I've never seen anyone move so fast. Like a blur. The man wobbles on his feet but he recovers and strikes back. Michal ducks and continues his attack, pummeling the man about the head and shoulders until he hits the ground with a bloodied nose, black bruises on his cheeks, around his eyes, landing flat on his back. Groaning like the sick animal he is.

Michal drags him into a dark corner. 'He'll live,' is all he says, then wipes his hands on his overalls.

At the same time, I grab my cap off the ground and dust it off while I assess if there's any possibility of us getting out of here before the guard returns, sees the brute and raises the alarm. No doubt we're headed for a Nazi prison. They'll be watching for us at the shaft elevator. We have to hide, but where? The depot is a series of caverns and tunnels zigzagging in various directions, giving us a fair chance to disappear until morning.

*If* we don't get lost. The old limestone quarry covers ten thousand square meters.

*'Run, Ève!'*

'Where?'

He grins. 'When will you just do what I say?'

I put on my cap. 'What if we get separated?'

Listen to me. I sound desperate, like I can't take care of myself. *A pitiful female*, is what he's thinking. I bite my lip. No, we're a team and it makes us both better fighters, but I don't *want* to know what it's like without him. I care for him too much.

*'Go!'*

We take off running, jumping over chunks of fallen rocks, skirting around piles of large square stones, twisting around a stockpile of machine guns and boxes of ammunition, heading deeper into the cavern through a series of passages tunneled through the soft chalk-like limestone until—

'Over here, Ève.'

I can't believe my eyes when I see Michal get down on his knees, his arm muscles bulging when he removes a large, square stone from the limestone wall and then hustles me into a small cave and closes up the entrance from inside with a large rock.

Oh, Lord. I underestimated him.

The walls glisten with a crystalline sheen, giving us a glowy light... *Quartz*. I glance around the cave and see blankets, a torch, a saddlebag, handguns, a box of ammo, and a jug of water.

Why do I get the feeling he kept this place a secret until we needed it?

* * *

I've got one big headache.

Tearing off a piece of the cotton blanket, I dip it into the jug of water and hold the wet compress to my head. I'm a sorry sight. Bruised face, stinging lower lip, sprained right arm, my short hair fluffed out and thick with sticky, chalky-white powder like a court jester from Versailles. I've never felt more foolish letting that brute get the drop on me. I take the blame for getting us into this predicament, damning myself for not being more careful and daydreaming about Michal. Of course, I'd never tell him *that*.

'You handled yourself well, Ève. I'm proud of you.'

*Proud of me? Is that all he can say?*

*Like I got a gold star in class today?*

Frustration and pent-up anger make me pace up and down. 'It's my fault we're in this mess, Michal. I should have kept my nose clean.'

'We were set up.'

'How, why?' I sit down next to him, wanting to rest my throbbing head against his shoulder, but I keep my distance. Michal, of course, has no idea of the delicious turmoil rushing through my veins. I'm grateful the brute didn't kill me and Michal came back for me. That means more than anything and I want to believe it's about more than us being partners.

He continues, trying to calm me down. 'I picked up chatter before I got to the quarry gates that someone tipped off the Nazis about political dissidents infiltrating the labor force. And since we're strangers—'

'We're the prime suspects.'

He nods. 'The man who attacked you was a petty thief who'd once been arrested for killing a guard.' He then confirms the chatter we heard, how the man had secured his freedom after the rope around his neck broke by turning Nazi informant in charge of weeding out dissidents among the workers. When I said I was a student, he found his mark and attacked me, knowing the guard would show up and arrest me. And Michal.

'And he calls himself a Frenchman?' I clench my fists, angry. 'How could he betray a fellow countryman? Has it come to this? We're fighting each other in this war?'

'Freedom means different things to different people, Ève.' Michal puts his arms around me, holding me while I calm down. *If* I calm down. How can I with him moving his hands all over me, his fingers massaging my throbbing temples with a gentle touch. He eases me down onto the blanket and rocks me back and forth in a steady rhythm, his voice low and soothing. 'That man cared only for his own freedom, while you and I fight to free our countries from tyranny.'

'But we're just two little people in this war.'

'There are many like us, Ève. Students, teachers, shop girls, factory workers risking our lives for that freedom. Each handgun, each box of ammunition we take from the Nazis gives a man a chance to fight another day.'

'Or a woman,' I add with a smirk.

He smiles. 'Or a woman.' He moves in closer, tangling his fingers in my hair silky with white chalk, pulling my head back in a way so that he can look at me, my lips parted, my whole being hungry for this man. I don't hold back when his mouth claims mine in a long, searching kiss. 'I can't fight how I feel about you, Ève. I want you.'

'Oh, Michal, *mon amour...*'

I'm hurting like hell from being tossed around like a rag doll, but I don't care. I press my aching head against his chest and I hear the pounding of his heart... a steady rhythm that picks up the beat when I fold my body into his. What I believed would never happen is that he wants me, too. Something's changed between us. I saw the way he looked when he found me at the mercy of that madman, not because I'm his partner, because I'm a woman. A deep and abiding need in his eyes to protect me competing with a red-hot anger to take down that monster.

He did both.

Saved my life. And every part of my being went crazy with that freedom you get when you dream that nothing can hurt you, that if you think about it hard enough, hang on a little longer, it will come true in this play of your own making.

That's how it is with me. That deep below the earth, I'm floating in a surrealistic dream and if my emotions were running hot back there with that brute, now they're burning up with this increasingly kinetic situation. Me, him. Alone down here with the musky scent of mushrooms somehow lingering in the hidden cave like a soft perfume that's stimulating my senses and making me ache for him so bad I don't want to be careful anymore. I want to feel his hands all over me, wrap me up in a passion I've longed for. I'm giddy with joy. I almost died out there in that chalk pit and I want to yell and shout *'I'm alive!'*

And in love.

I know now that no one else can ever make me feel this way.

I swear it's the scent of a man that fills my nostrils when I turn over and his arm tightens around me, his hands sliding down the straps on my overalls and finding the thick round buttons on my shirt, unbuttoning one, then two, then reaching under the coarse muslin and finding the swell of my breasts—

'Michal, I...'

'Breathe deeply, Ève, try to relax. I'll stop if you want.'

'No, please don't. I—I need you.'

'I don't want to hurt you.'

'You never could. I want you to—'

'Want me to do what, Ève? Tell me.'

'Make me a woman. *Your* woman.'

'Are you sure?' he asks, his voice tender. 'I know you're frightened after what happened to your sister.'

I tighten my groin and waves of pleasure overtake my fears. 'The Nazi major took Justine against her will. But I want you more than anything in this world.' I heave out a heavy sigh. 'I—I love you.'

He stiffens. 'Oh, Ève, my precious girl, I was wrong to kiss you. You're not like the other Frenchwomen I've known.'

'You mean like Coralie?' *Why is that woman always between us?*

He doesn't answer me on that; instead, he continues. 'You *think* you're in love with me, Ève, but...'

Silence. We're bathed in a dreamy glow, but that dream is gone. I know what's on his mind... what he can't say, so I say it for him. 'You're not in love with me.'

He pulls away. 'I no longer have a heart to give, Ève. I'm sorry. Truly sorry. You deserve a far better man than I am, who can love you as you deserve to be loved.'

'But I want *you*.'

'I'm all wrong for you, Ève.' He folds a blanket around my legs. Kisses me on the forehead. 'Get some rest. That informant will have raised the alarm by now and they'll be looking for us.'

'What if they find us?'

'We're safe here. They'll be roaming the nearby orchard and the forest looking for us. We'll sneak through the quarry gates in the morning during the changing of the guard. They'll be too busy goose-stepping and giving each other Hitler salutes to notice us.'

He wraps me up in his jacket and holds me tight in a warm embrace.

But inside I'm crying.

Not for me. For him. This war has burned the soul out of him with the horrors he's seen. Losing his father, sister. The girl he loved. The flames consuming him, then nothing left but cold embers. He wants me, but he doesn't love me. I should be angry, turn away from him in protest of him leading me on. But I can't. How can I blame him for coming at me strong and hot? I *threw* myself at him. But he forced himself to back away. Quell the passion between us because he—he… Do I dare hope?

*Believe what you want. He said his piece. Now you have to learn to accept it.*

I can't.

*Damn this war, damn the Nazis for hurting this man so deep he's lost the will to love.*

I hear his gentle snoring not long after. The poor man is exhausted. He's asleep. I can't stop the tears staining my cheeks, then I place his hand over my breasts for this one night. His touch tender and warm. A night I'll never forget.

But I swear, I'll never fall in love again.

# 15

## PARIS, JULY 1942

*Justine*

The red roses are dead.

And so are the daisies. *Our* daisies. Ève's and mine. Most likely trodden under Nazi jackboots spying on the occupants.

July in Paris means the daisies *should* be in bloom. *Marguerites.* Morning suns with their pretty white petals and golden crowns. I choke up inside but I refuse to let a tear fall, show weakness when the Mercedes touring car pulls up into the winding driveway on my return to Maison Bleue. The top on the motorcar is down, but the breeze blowing in my face bears no fruity, floral scent to welcome me home. Merely the oil burning from the engine and a faint smell of rubber when the vehicle squeals to a halt.

My driver—the one with the snappy Hitler salute—enjoys racing the powerful engine of the German-made motorcar while glaring at me in the rearview mirror. I see it as a repressed sexual move on his part. Another Nazi with big ideas and a small mind when it comes to women. Fortunately, he only plays the virile

Aryan behind the wheel and doesn't take his fantasy a step further. The major has a temper and the young soldier would find himself shipped off to the Eastern Front if he stepped over the line.

Also in my favor, the major has another meeting with Himmler this morning and can't accompany me to begin my assignment as hostess of Maison Bleue. I shall at all times act in a refined manner, the major preached to me, socializing with the Nazi higher-ups, giving them 'an atmosphere of French luxury and comfort, and appease their war-weary souls' with fine food and liquor and, of course, outrageous flirtation. I'm to create fun parties where the guests—mostly SS and Wehrmacht—can feel free to sing beer drinking songs, indulge in rich entrees, and drink Schnapps and champagne with no rules.

Enter Rachelle D'Artois.

I have to smile. *What will Maman say when she sees me?*

Summer pink silk suit, white lace blouse edged with the tiniest petit-point design, matching soft leather pumps with ankle straps, silk stockings. Pink gloves. And a wide-brim pink straw hat with a band of silk braided ribbons. No veil, but the brim covers my face like the big picture hats of *la belle époque.*

I order the driver in an authoritative voice—I've been practicing—not to park the Mercedes touring car, but to drop me off then pick up a special package waiting for me at the House of Péroline on Rue de Rivoli. I approach the stately home on foot, knowing Maman will peek through the window. I've yet to set the stage for this drama. Every important thing in my life has revolved around Maison Bleue. Our escape from poverty because of our glorious *maman*, designing for Madame de Giocomte, growing up with Ève, and the dark moment I'd like to draw a perpetual curtain over: the major's assault. Even though I'm publicly identified as his mistress, a woman he named

Rachelle D'Artois, we have no relationship other than that. Which is why I'm of a certain mind that Maman and Madame have no idea I'm coming home today. They're on the lookout for Mademoiselle D'Artois, collaborator *horizontale,* not the prodigal daughter returning to the nest. I ask God for courage. It's one thing to lie to Ève.

Lying to Maman and Madame de Giocomte is a trickier venture.

Should I apologize for what I've become? Ask them to understand? After all, that would be so lovely to have them on my side. Also, deadly for all of us. No, I can't unlock the past and pick up where I left off. I also can't ask them to accept me as a collabo. It's against everything they taught me. So I shall re-enter their world as snotty and self-serving Rachelle. It's the only way to save us all.

My chest instinctively tightens, my throat closes off as if I'm a little girl again and I got caught trying on Madame's hat. I was eleven and awash in long ribbons attached to a summer straw chapeau and tried to convince her I needed a new hat for school. She smiled and tied the ribbons under my chin, giving her blessing. It worked then. Sort of. God knows if I can pull off *this* charade. I have to. All our lives are at stake. Ninette, Arsène... Maman, Madame de Giocomte, Cook, Albertine. Ève. And me.

I have a few minutes to prepare myself, giving me time to take a longer look at this wonderful *maison* I've loved since I used to tie daisy chains around my head and pretend I was a dancing princess from the fairy tale. It's lost none of its glamour, but painful to me besides the dead roses is the row after row of daisies, droopy and sad like a line of can-can dancers doing the splits. Did the red blooms also give up the fight and wither away? I don't know why, but that bothers me. A warning that even the strongest flower with its protector-thorns is no match for the

Boches. I've seen what they can do, these demons swathed in earthy green. First, the Nazis stole *The Daisy Sisters* painting of Ève and me along with the de Giocomtes' Impressionist paintings.

Now they've sucked the life out of the red rose bushes.

I'm dismayed to see how Maison Bleue has changed since the Occupation, like a coquette wearing too much rouge and baggy silk stockings, her garter belt loose, her belly empty. Subtle changes. Like how the heavy damask hangings in the foyer sag, and the tall, elegant windows are stained with grime and don't reflect the sun anymore. I see several missing blue tiles on the sloping roof. Patches of dying brown grass. I shake my head. Monsieur de Giocomte would never have allowed that. The man had a head for numbers, but he also loved his garden. I still grieve for him, my anger over the thoughtless answer I received from the major when I got up the courage to ask him about Monsieur de Giocomte haunting me. I can't let go of his casual dismissal of what he calls an 'unfortunate error' on the part of the Gestapo sending a good, kind man to a concentration camp.

A place the major calls Auschwitz.

I attempt to carry on in spite of the sadness filling me, silently thanking Madame Péroline for watching Ninette; I didn't want to spring both of us on my unsuspecting *maman* and Madame de Giocomte at the same time as they first saw me. I press the button on the front door, but the bell doesn't work. I bang on the door knocker until I see movement behind the thick plum curtains, the late afternoon twilight blue shadows that gave the *grande maison* its name hiding someone.

Maman? *Did she see me?*

*Did Ève tell her about me? Is that why she won't let me in?*

I bang again on the door and—

*Crash!*

A red clay flowerpot filled with moist dirt and wilted daisies lands at my feet, spraying my pink shoes with dirt. My heart races; a different emotion washes over me. I have no doubt someone tossed it from the second floor, aiming close enough to scare me.

*Maman, really?*

I bang again on the door and—

*Splash!*

Cool water tossed from the upper floor catches me off guard like a spring rain, my lovely hat filled with water in the brim, making it droop like a soggy flower.

*Do they hate me that much?*

Yes. To them, the woman standing outside their door is Rachelle D'Artois, a Nazi collaborator intent on invading their home. Of course, they don't know it's me. This ring of domestic *résistants* is trying to frighten me away. They have no idea I've come home. I take in a deep breath, eager to get this over with, settle in and somehow convince these two women I'm *not* the enemy without giving away my double life as an Allied agent. A task forged in deception where this devil in pink is really a messenger of hope.

'Open up, Madame de Giocomte, *now*!' I call out, shaking the water off my hat. 'Or I shall return with the Gestapo—'

I wouldn't, of course. I avoid Herr Geller like a rabid dog. But they don't know that. I made it clear to him I had a better chance of getting their help if I returned home alone. For once he agreed with me. From what he said, Madame put on quite a show when he told them the news and, in his words, 'Nothing could top that, mademoiselle.'

Finally, the thick oak portal opens and—

I see a tall figure standing in the deep shadows behind the grand entrance, silent. A smaller one behind her. Waiting.

Madame de Giocomte and Maman. I sigh when the smell of dried lavender and vanilla soap hits my nostrils. A clean, fresh smell. And with that I'm rooted back in that world I've missed. Like a child with a peppermint stick dipped in sugar crystals, my world is right again.

Until I remove my large-brimmed hat.

'It's me, Maman, Madame de Giocomte. Justine.'

Maman's hands go to her chest. Her jaw drops.

'*Justine! Mon enfant*, I can't believe you're *here*... You've come home. You had us so frightened. We thought you were that awful Rachelle D'Artois woman.'

She hugs me. Her cheeks are gaunt; her dress hangs on her, but it's clean and pressed, a summer blueberry print I recognize from before the war.

'Ève told us you were alive,' she continues before I can get a word in. 'I couldn't believe it. My dear sweet daughter, I'm so happy to see you.'

'Me, too, Maman.'

'Where have you been? No, it doesn't matter. You're home now.'

'We heard stories, Justine,' Madame de Giocomte says, concerned. She's wearing a smart blue and tan shirtwaist Maman made for her, but no platinum bracelets or watch on her wrists. Just her plain, thick gold wedding band. Which makes me surmise her bracelets ended up on the black market, telling me that's how they're eking out their daily existence since the Nazis closed Jewish bank accounts. 'We knew they weren't true,' she continues. 'They couldn't be.'

'Of course not, Madame,' Maman chimes in. 'Our Justine just got a job and she couldn't come home sooner because they needed her, *n'est-ce pas*?'

'Well, yes, Maman, but it's not what you think—'

'It doesn't matter. Let me take your wet jacket.'

And so it goes with the two excited women, back and forth we go with excuses, asking why I didn't come home sooner, harsh words about the woman the Gestapo is forcing on them who's due to arrive today, more tears, apologies for their stupid antics with the flowerpot and the bucket of water, and *What if we'd hurt our precious Justine*? And then curious looks, envy at my suit, Maman noting the double seams of my jacket, fine stitches, Madame running her fingers over the soft silk.

I have to stop this. *Now.*

'I have something to tell you Maman, Madame,' I begin, my smile forced. I'm about to break their hearts.

'Yes, Justine?' Maman blinks. Madame smiles at me.

'I pray you'll understand my situation and embrace me no matter what I tell you.'

They nod their heads. I keep stalling, wanting to keep these lovely feelings between us for a moment longer. Then—

'You're right. I *did* get a job designing hats and it's how I survived, but it doesn't come without a price—'

'Yes, child?' Maman asks, not understanding.

'I also have a new name. I am Rachelle D'Artois.'

An hour later and I'm still explaining to these two women I adore that nothing will change with me coming back to Maison Bleue.

'Except *I* am now in charge and you will do as I tell you. Cook, clean, serve my guests. And make certain I *always* have a clean pair of silk stockings.'

'Justine,' Maman says with concern, 'silk stockings when our POWs barely have clean socks?'

I keep my lips tight so I don't smile, keep my eyes lowered so she doesn't see the hot tears welling up at her goodness, the softness she holds in her heart for her 'boys'. I can't tell them I'm a double agent without putting them at risk.

'*My* needs are all that concern you, Maman. And the general's. General von Klum will be staying here from time to time and will occupy the guest suite. You will treat him with the same respect as you did Monsieur.'

It is at that moment I know I've hit a nerve so raw in both women, my usually serene Maman grabs Madame by the shoulders and holds her back from coming for me. Madame mutters a few words in Russian, but her meaning is clear.

*No one takes the place of Monsieur, especially a Nazi.*

'*Please*, Justine,' Maman begs, 'no more. I can't take seeing you like this. It's horrible.'

Madame speaks her mind. 'If that despicable Gestapo man hadn't threatened your dear *maman* and Cook and Albertine, I'd drag you out of my home by your bleached blonde hair. Now let us be. We have nothing more to say to you.'

'I'm not finished, Madame.' Oh, is that me? My voice is harsh like a cold wind biting at your cheeks. 'We are still Parisiennes and you will continue to act as Frenchwomen. Be feminine, kind. Show exquisite taste and good manners. And never forget that our Nazi friends now run Paris. I can only protect you if you behave yourselves. Am I making myself clear?'

'*Very*, Justine.' Madame plops down in the Louis XV chair, holding her head in her hands, murmuring about a fat Gestapo man who will *never* enter her house again if she can help it. I noticed the silk on the seat is torn, but she doesn't explain why.

Herr Geller, of course.

I get on with my agenda.

'I realize the idea of serving SS officers won't be easy for you, but once you accept your new position at Maison Bleue, things will go better for you.' I cringe inside. 'Who knows? Perhaps I can secure more food rations for the household. General von Klum is an aristocrat like you, Madame, and you will find him an eager listener.'

She turns up her nose and moves her mouth like she wants to spit at me. I smile. Madame's spirit is a thing to watch, but I have to break her a little to keep her safe. 'In spite of what you think about him, Madame, the general has helped me adjust to these new times.' I forego any mention of the major. That discussion will be for another day. 'I insist you accept your place and do your job until—'

*Until the Allies invade France?*

No, I can't say anything that indicates I'm not the collaborator I appear to be.

'I shall give elegant dinner parties with wine, beef, sugar pastries Cook will prepare and you, Madame, will serve to our guests. Understood?'

Silence.

My words fall on deaf ears; the two women ignore what I've just told them, wriggling their noses in distaste, asking me where I got pink silk in this war. No self-respecting Parisian would wear such a frivolous color. Maman tosses my wet hat on the marble floor. They're no longer sorry they doused me, since now they know I *am* the woman the Nazis sent to set up house. I want so much to dispense with the formalities and talk to Maman and Madame like I used to do, with girlish excitement in my voice, grand gestures, trying to make them see how important it is to me, to them, Cook and Albertine.

Of course, I don't. But the pain on my *maman*'s face lures me to soften toward her. I take my mother's hand in mine, squeezing it. 'It will be so wonderful being home again, Maman, having parties like we did before the war.'

'You call this coming home, Justine?' Her eyes widen. 'I don't know you anymore, working for them Boches after what that Nazi did to you.' She pulls her hand away from mine and tucks it in her apron pocket.

I was wrong to reach out to her; I've confused her, not made things better between us. And Madame? She'll never forgive me for my remark about Monsieur. But this is how things must be. I can't break down again. I breathe out, 'You must call me Rachelle now.'

'I can't do that,' Maman says, innocent-like, not understanding this is an order from the Gestapo. I let it go for now.

'The general and his guests have never heard of Justine Beaufort. You will not reveal to *anyone* we are related.'

'Oh, I see. You're ashamed of your *maman* because I'm a seamstress. Well, not any more than I'm ashamed of you, Justine. My daughter is dead.'

She starts to leave. I call her back.

'I'm not finished, Maman. You will have to work too. I shall require new gowns, wonderful designs I've already drawn up for you, along with beautiful fabrics, lamé, silk, taffeta, and when the season grows chilly, velvet, fur. No girlish rose point lace collars and cuffs. I shall need sophisticated gowns to create excitement, fun.'

Maman coughs. Madame glares at me.

I clear my throat, try again to get them on my side. 'I designed a black lace dress with a low neckline and black lace bolero jacket. It will be perfect for the hot summer nights. It won't wilt or crush and I shall be the epitome of French womanhood to show our Nazi friends we're still the leaders in fashion.'

'What you ask for is impossible, *Justine*,' she emphasizes. 'I can no longer buy sewing supplies. Wertmann's Needles & Threads shop is boarded up. Do you remember the beautiful display of silky threads? It was smashed to bits.'

I note she emphasized the name of the Jewish shop. Her sarcasm isn't lost on me.

'Paris is changing, Maman, and we must change with it. Old businesses like Wertmann's are out of step with the New Order.'

Maman smirks.

We're both thinking the same thing. *Goose-stepping*. A play on words I never intended, but it has the ability to take us back to the days before the Nazis marched up and down the grand boulevards, rode on horses, leaving their mark on our clean streets. On our souls.

Madame sees no humor in my words, her eyes simmering with a deep sadness. She's thinking of Monsieur, of course. I can't forgive myself for not paying closer attention to the major's 'promise' to keep the de Giocomtes safe. I made inquiries about the camp in Poland where the Nazis sent the 'intellectual Jews' as they were classified on that March morning, but no word yet.

'You *must* follow my direction, do what I ask, Maman, Madame. We have no choice if we want to survive.'

'Your sister Ève isn't a collaborator,' Maman says, 'and she's surviving.'

I sigh. 'Yes, about Ève...' I hadn't intended to bring her up so as not to create a bigger rift between us. 'Where *is* my dear sister?'

'We don't know.'

'You mean you won't tell me.'

'*No*,' Maman emphasizes, 'we don't know where she is, Justine.'

Madame speaks up. 'Ève reminds me of myself when I was her age. Fierce, independent, brave.' She's been mostly silent during this conversation. 'I assure you she's out there fighting for France, Justine, not throwing smart dinner parties for the Nazis.'

'You *will* address me as Mademoiselle D'Artois and wear the yellow star, Madame, or...' I emphasize what I say next, 'I shall have you both detained at Gestapo headquarters.'

The woman glares at me, then turns her back and ascends the stairs like a royal queen, posture straight, her chin up.

In her mind, I stabbed her in the back.

Maman gives me the most sorrowful look, her eyes pleading. 'Why, *why* did you come back?'

'I was told to,' I say, almost too numb to answer her, feeling my own pain at this horrible homecoming. I can't go on like this with them hating me. Everything good about me came from these two women. My strength, resilience, even how to be a good mother. It came from *them*, what they taught me with their deeds and actions. *Listen to your child, praise her, make her bumps and bruises go away with a kiss. Tell her you love her.* What also eats me up inside is that the life I knew at Maison Bleue will be lost forever if we don't oust the Germans from Paris. That means I *must* do my job for the Allies... and to do that, there *must* be peace between us. And I know exactly how to bring it about. 'But also, Maman, Madame, *please*, listen to me. I know this has been a great shock to you both, but I haven't been completely honest with you...'

Madame turns on the stairs, her eyes misty.

'What is it, Justine?' Maman asks, hopeful.

'I have to do what they tell me. Because it's not just me who will be living here. The truth is... I had a child. A little girl, who I've named Ekaterina Ninette.'

'*Oh*,' both women say at once, and I don't know if they're going to laugh or cry. And, as if this scenario is straight out of a

Sylvie Martone film, we hear a loud knock on the front door. I grin. My package has arrived.

I open the grand portal and find Madame Péroline standing there holding my little daughter. With blonde curls framing her round face, pink cheeks, and those big doll-like blue eyes, she's irresistible in her pink pinafore with a big, lace collar.

'*Maman!*' Ninette cries, holding out her chubby arms to me when she sees me.

I've never seen a more surprised look on my own *maman*'s face or Madame's. Like heaven just dropped the sweetest angel into their waiting arms.

I take my child from the milliner, her eyes taking in the impressive *maison*, my wet suit, drenched hat, but she says nothing. I'll explain later. 'My sweet *bébé,* meet your *grand-mère* and your great-*grand-mére*.'

Ninette laughs, claps her hands together and whatever harsh words were said, whatever feelings were dashed and stomped upon, they all disappeared in that warm, wonderful moment when Ninette came into their lives.

What worries me is, *how long will it last when Nazi SS officers show up for tea?*

# 16

## JONZAC, SOUTHWESTERN FRANCE, JULY 1942

*Ève*

With the blush of his touch tinting my cheeks, I grab the box of ammunition and stuff it under my jacket, toss my cap on my head then follow Michal through the cavern, hugging the walls. A hushed morning—I think it's morning; it's difficult to tell. Dim lights. No workers yet. No one's looking for us down here. The old quarry is quiet except for the whisper of the thick, chalky dust sifting beneath our boots.

We don't speak about last night, how I made a fool out of myself declaring my love for him, then Michal's admission that his heart is already broken, and then me asking myself, *Am I woman enough to fix it*? Maybe we females believe we can fix anything when it comes to the man we love. I can't let that persistent thought rule my head as we make our escape after leaving the small natural cave and closing up the entrance with a large square piece of limestone, then racing through the old quarry to the loading area where the weapons are brought up to the top for transportation in trucks. We climbed up the thick rope to the utility lift, the heavy guns and ammo weighing me down, but I'm surprisingly strong and agile in spite of my sprained arm, tougher than I was before the war started. I've learned to ignore pain in my body, but my head still hurts and my right cheek feels swollen. Michal is behind me, not even drawing a breath when we reach the top and hide behind several crates of machine guns. I swear the man is toned like a god. He's certainly in better shape than any German soldier I've encountered. Within minutes the utility lift moves on an automatic iron-rung pulley and we ride to the top.

We jump off the lift before the morning crew sees us and hide in the deep shadows until it's safe to mingle with the incoming flow of workers.

Walking backward.

We make our way to the end of the line.

Then duck down and sneak around the huge quarry running alongside arriving trucks filled with mortar shells. We keep to our own thoughts once we're in the clear, walking the ten kilometers in silence to the nearby farm to retrieve the other weapons and ammo we stored there. I'm aching to hear his voice, a guilty pleasure on my part, but it's better if we don't speak, let down our guard, because God knows I'd probably beg Michal to make love to me. The timing is awful but if we're caught, I can't die not knowing this man in the most intimate way.

We reach the crossroads. The farmhouse to the right. Outbuilding to the left.

I head over to the farmhouse while he goes off in search of the farmer to pick up the cache of weapons and ammo we left in the outbuilding. I'm relieved we're heading back to Paris and looking forward to another jaunty ride beside him. I pull up my collar to hide the smile on my face while I simmer with anticipation that bumping against him brings about again that lovely wave of pleasure—

*'Ève, wait!'*

I spin around. Michal is running back to me, his eyes wild and fierce. 'The Nazis have arrested the farmer.'

'What? Are you sure?' I drop the bag. My heart sinks. A dear, sweet man with a funny mustache that wiggles when he speaks.

'I found his cart with the horse still attached and tire tracks surrounding it. Empty. Blood on the seat. Hay tossed everywhere.'

'The Nazis have been here, looking for us?'

'Yes, but clearly the farmer didn't give us up, because I found the weapons safe in the outbuilding. They must have followed him here from the quarry and confiscated what I gave him earlier. I'll see what I can find out in the village. Stay here, Ève.'

'I'm coming with you.' I pick up the saddlebag, sling it over my shoulder.

'No, go and check on his wife and daughter.'

I nod. I remember the kind-faced woman with the sturdy hands, her callused palms kneading bread on her kitchen table, her shy daughter lurking behind her mother. She can't be more than fourteen.

Michal smiles at me, different than before, but I don't dare read anything into it. 'I'll be back, Ève. I promise.' He squeezes my hand and for a moment I swear he's going to kiss me, but instead he clenches his teeth and takes off. He doesn't look back, but I sense a struggle within him that tears me apart. He can't let me in. Not yet.

I pray he will someday.

I watch him disappear into the deep forest, the vibrant green mist swallowing him up like a thick fog and taking him from me. I struggle to keep my mind on the mission, take long strides to cover the distance as fast as I can to the farmhouse. It's as I remembered it. Flower bushes in bloom. Ivy entwined around a white trellis over near the horizon, the gray dawn settling down on its sloping roof with a shimmer of sunlight. Reminding me of the glowing quartz in the cave and that lovely moment in his arms. All through the night, I kept reaching over to cup his hand over my breasts, thrilling to his warmth and sinking deeper into a well of emotion I can't climb out of—

*Damn*, this isn't me... acting like a lovesick dairy cow.

*Shake it off, Ève, now.*

Shifting the heavy saddlebag to the other shoulder, I keep mumbling to myself it won't do any good to fantasize about what I *want* to happen between Michal and me—

I come to a dead halt.

I can't believe my eyes when I see a young girl in a long nightdress sneaking out through a window on the second floor of the farmhouse, then climbing down the trellis thick with ivy before landing on the soft flowerbed. The farmer's young daughter. *What, why?* A million questions hurl through my mind.

Before I can call out to her, she hobbles to her feet and runs.

I cut her off, grab her, her thin body which is shivering and shaking like I've never seen. She's terrified. She clings to me, holding in her sobs, her deep blue eyes wide, her lips moving though she can't speak, only guttural sounds coming from her throat.

'What's wrong, mademoiselle? What are you running away from?' I look around, see no one. 'Where's your mother?' I whisper, taking her hand. It's cold. Her long gray nightdress is woven from thin cotton with a blue ribbon lacing around the collar, her hair in braids. I fear she's in shock, but she doesn't appear hurt. No cuts, bruises.

She points to the farmhouse, spitting out one word, '*Boche*!' then I hear a woman scream from inside the house.

I tell her to stay here, then grab my saddlebag and make my way to the house standing on a knoll. I dare to peek through a window. Checkered red-and-white curtains in the kitchen, a kettle on the stove blowing steam, and a German soldier pointing his rifle and bayonet at the farmer's wife and yelling in broken French, 'Pull up your skirts, madame, and get down on your knees.'

The girl's *maman*. He intends to rape her.

I stifle a pained cry. Oh, God, not again, *please*. The nightmare returns, the horror of seeing my sister sexually assaulted, brutalized by an inhuman enemy begins all over again when I see the poor woman do as he asks, her lips pursed together, refusing to whimper when he pulls down her underwear, *anything* so that he can be done with the ugly deed and go, to leave her alone. *Leave her daughter alone.*

Of course. The *maman* has led him to believe she's alone; the girl heard the commotion upstairs and escaped. The woman's face cordons into knots of wrinkles, anticipating the pain, her humiliation. I know what she's thinking: that no sacrifice is too great to save her child from Nazi brutality.

Grunting his pleasure at the sight of the woman's bare flesh, the soldier rests his rifle against the stove, then unbuttons his trousers—

Oh, no. Not this time... *This time* I won't let it happen.

*I've got two handguns in my saddlebag. Ammo.* I load the guns, close my eyes and pray, then give it everything I have. Shouting like a banshee riding over the hills on the back of a demon, I run around to the front, firing the two pistols into the air, creating a ruckus so loud my ears hurt, aiming to scare the living daylights out of this pitiful soldier—possibly a deserter?—and stop him raping this brave woman. And mother.

*Oh, my God, what if it was my* maman*?*

A sharp, shooting pain to my heart pushes me on and fuels my courage, giving me the power and strength I need to do the impossible. I kick in the door.

The soldier's jaw drops, his trousers falling down around his ankles when I burst through the door, guns blazing. Seeing his pale torso positioned behind the quivering woman, his hands on her naked buttocks, I feel sick.

'Let her go, monsieur, *now*!'

He curses at me in German, then he goes for his rifle resting against the stove—

*Not today you don't, you sick Boche.*

Without missing a beat, I fire off a shot, then two, grazing the pimple-faced German's hand. He tries again to grab the rifle. I shoot again. He curses and drops the weapon.

Before he goes for it a third time, I slide the rifle now lying on the floor out of his range with my foot. 'I won't miss the next time, *sale Boche*, you dirty Boche.' I raise the handgun, aim at his heart. 'Now, *get out of here*!'

More cursing in German, then the coward trips on his trousers and falls to his knees. I can hardly restrain myself from taking a shot at his naked behind as he scrambles to his feet and races out the open front door.

Running as fast as he can away from the farmhouse.

'You're safe, madame.' I turn away from the poor woman, give her some privacy so she can compose her emotions, wipe herself, then she pulls down her skirts, attempting to hold her dignity together, but her scream will echo for a long time in my head. I pick up the rapist's rifle and sling it over my shoulder.

One woman saved from further humiliation. And one more rifle for the Resistance.

'Don't tell my daughter, mademoiselle, *please*! I'm so ashamed.' I turn and see her bury her face in her hands, shivering.

*'Ashamed?'* I put my arms around her shoulders. 'I promise you, madame, it's not your fault. You were so brave, so filled with courage. *You* saved your daughter from that monster.'

I keep talking, trying to rebuild her self-esteem, but she keeps repeating her shame over and over. I'm not getting through to her; her emotions are too raw, feelings running high, no logic in her thinking, strictly anger and disbelief that it could happen to *her*, but maybe someday when this war is over, she'll accept that it wasn't her fault.

Maybe. But it will take a lot of healing.

I respect her wishes and say nothing to her daughter before the farmer's wife takes the horse and cart and they head for her cousin's farm. She needs the girl's comforting hand in hers, not her contempt.

I raise a brow, thinking. I gave my sister nothing *but* contempt when she cornered me at the Hôtel Drouot. Accusing her of working for the Nazis, being a collaborator, betraying France. I didn't comfort her. I acted like a spoiled brat. I saw only the woman who abandoned Maman and me and Madame de Giocomte. I was hurt, angry. I hadn't gotten over that when she confronted me. I thought she was dead, a martyr in my eyes. I saw only a woman who thrived during the Occupation with pretty clothes, a string of pearls, the freedom to come and go at will, not the frightened girl who survived a horrific sexual attack. Alone. No one to comfort her.

What an awful sister I am.

I put the handguns down on the kitchen table and wait for

Michal to return. What if the Nazi comes back with reinforcements? I pray I scared the hell out of him and he keeps his mouth shut and his trousers buttoned. If Michal doesn't get here in a few minutes, I'll go hide in the barn. Till then, I sit quietly but I'm shaking so hard I'm chilled to the bone. I grab my own shoulders, try to stop this trembling, but I can't. I'm still not over that day when I watched that SS officer drag my sister away. Her dress ripped. Her eyes big and wide, wondering *when, how*, he intended to rape her.

On her knees? Flat on her back? Against the wall?

What's changed is, I never saw what that SS officer *did* to her. The emotional turmoil that hit me hard written on the woman's face, her puffy eyes, trembling mouth, the awkward way she moved afterward because she hurt so, the drooping of her head, her shoulders because she was so ashamed.

I have now.

And I'd give *anything* for Justine to forgive me.

# 17

## PARIS, JULY 1942

*Justine*

My life as hostess at Maison Bleue revolves around keeping my Nazi 'friends' as happy as pigs in a poke at feeding time. A house filled with drunken SS officers enjoying Monsieur de Giocomte's liqueurs, slouched over Madame's elegant brocade divans, the soldiers soused with wine and burping like stuffed crickets, and me wearing eye-popping gowns Maman sews for me that scream —what's the word they use in the cinema?—'bombshell'.

My God, it's exhausting.

Smiling, flirting, lifting my skirt and straightening my seams at opportune moments to keep the guests occupied when Cook burns a precious roast—the poor woman is all thumbs which is so unlike her, but she's never cooked for the Boches before—and listening to their war stories. I have no time for *anything* but these unwelcome officers, but I experienced a surge of hope earlier when I scanned the list and found the name of an SS Captain Dietmar Stolz, who'd recently been posted in Algiers. It got me thinking. Arsène served in the Foreign Legion in Algeria; could that be a code word to tell me it'll be him?

My libido stirs. I hope so. I miss him terribly.

I feel so alone at my own parties. I'm surrounded by the enemy. What saddens the mother in me is that I had to miss my walks in the Bois with Ninette these past two weeks, pushing her in the pram then letting her stretch her cute little legs, watching her waddle up and down the winding stone pathways, giggling with delight when a butterfly touches down on her shoulder. Feeling young, innocent. Picking summer daisies with her and making a 'daisy chain'. Ninette loves the garden here at Maison Bleue, but I find she takes really good naps when she goes for walks in the Bois.

I've been so busy with the general's parties, Maman has mostly taken over looking after her for me. Though I can't deny the joy I get seeing my mother's eyes shine as bright as her granddaughter's when the two of them head out in the morning. My little girl is the adventurous type and the steadier she gets on her feet, the more likely she is to wander off to explore this *grande maison*. I found her yesterday under the piano in the drawing room playing with a ball of Maman's blue yarn. No one knows how she got there, which troubles me.

I vow to get less sleep.

I'm a night flower now, hiding under dark satin petals since I returned home to Maison Bleue. Living under an icy moon. Cold sophistication. Precise, calculating moves with one outward goal: *show General von Klum's guests a good time.*

On the other hand, my emotional life has gone numb. Maman said nothing to me about how I came to have a child, no questions—I think she's embarrassed and doesn't know what *to* say or ask. The time will come when we can have 'that talk', but not now. Everything between us feels strained, like God is waiting to see who will break the silence first. He gave us a push when Ninette twisted her mouth trying to say a new word that sounded like *'Gra-man'*, sending tears to Maman's eyes. The child is magic in this house, her every step, her precious laugh, every new word she says is a celebration of life in a home dark too long with the travails of war.

She's softening up Madame de Giocomte as well. She embraced me and told me that although she welcomed me and my baby home, she could never accept me working for the Nazis. Never. She looked me straight in the eye, as if challenging me to tell her otherwise.

I looked away, afraid she'd see the truth on my face that would instantly put her life in danger. That I'm not the collaborator she thinks I am.

Instead, I adapt to my role as hostess with as much authority as I think decent without Maman and Madame hating me more than they do as we set about making Maison Bleue ready for the occupiers. Cleaning, cooking. Rearranging furniture. These Nazis eager to drink in the city the Boches call 'sophisticated' and 'spiritually uplifting' demand excellent table service, French wine, and pretty girls. I prepared a list of meat and milky cheeses and fresh vegetables for the general's aide to procure for me. I requested the wine merchants supplying Maxim's and La Tour d'Argent to deliver champagne and vintage wines to Maison Bleue—it didn't hurt to have two SS soldiers flanking them with rifles and bayonets when I made my pitch. Beer. And fresh flowers.

Girls are easy.

Madame Mimi has an endless supply of mesdemoiselles eager to offer weary SS officers a respite from the stresses of the

Eastern Front. The irascible madam showed up last week, laying down strict rules. She'll supply three girls for each party to flirt, dance, drink, and show some skin. But any 'transactions' between her girls and SS men *must* take place at Chez Mimi. No exceptions.

I happily agreed, because the last thing I want is to sully the reputation of Maison Bleue as a brothel. I owe Madame de Giocomte that much.

All this just when I had gotten used to the hell of living with the major and his threats and his black hobnail boots. Each party brings a new hell I'll never get used to—never-ending Hitler salutes, drunken men who smell of whiskey and conquest, top Nazi officials who eat stolen beef and get fat on creamy butter and fine cheeses and tell dirty jokes about Jews and French prostitutes.

I bite my lip every time to keep from speaking out and telling them what I think of their disgusting behavior. Because I have too much to lose.

* * *

'I'm pleased you exercised good judgment and spoke to the servants, emphasizing that we Nazis have taken control of this *maison* for the entertainment of SS officers of the Reich.'

My heart stops when the familiar sound of black hobnail boots hits the parquet floor, hammering like a death knell to the joy I saw earlier on Maman's and Madame's faces when they took Ninette on a walk.

The major has returned. Shooting up out of nowhere like a bothersome gopher.

'My *maman* and Madame de Giocomte are *not* servants.' I rearrange the hibiscus, pink and fluffy, in a vase in the dining room. I can't believe he just stormed into Maison Bleue. General von Klum keeps a suite at the Hôtel Meurice but he's a frequent overnight guest and *he* rings the doorbell—I had it fixed—and shows respect, kissing my hand and asking about my little girl with the golden hair and big smile.

The major cares only about me carrying out his orders. 'Call them what you like, but they are to perform their duties and adhere to the general's wishes, obey and do what they're told with no dissident talk or Communist activities like poisoning the soup, is that clear?'

I can't tell if he's joking or serious. His back is to me. He's looking out the window at my little family playing tag. Maman, Madame, and Ninette.

I shudder. What is he thinking? 'You dare question my loyalty?' I take a flower from the vase and walk over under the pretense of adding it to a buttonhole in his uniform, but really to block his view of the garden. I never know what devious plans he has next. He doesn't disappoint.

'No. But Herr Geller is not so trusting.' He yanks out the flower, spraying the air with pink petals, then tosses it on the floor. 'I'd watch your back. I'd hate to see you in Gestapo hands. They've been known to take a woman's soul with their dirty tactics.'

I laugh. 'Who says I still have a soul? I sold it to survive, Major. You've nothing to worry about. Maman and Madame de Giocomte will do as I ask them. They adore Ninette. They'd never do anything to jeopardize her safety. They have accepted me and what I do for the Reich.'

'Have they?' Then he sneers. 'I pray they don't act foolishly. That wouldn't be good for their health. Or the child's.'

I feel a familiar shiver travel through me, that sly and mysterious look in his eye when we discuss Ninette, telling me to be wary, as if he's keeping something from me.

'I promise you, Major, I have everything under control,' I tell him in a heated voice. 'We at Maison Bleue are at your service... and that of your Nazi friends.'

'They're your friends, too, Rachelle. Remember that.' He's taken to calling me by my cover name. 'As for your position at the milliner's, I terminated your employment there.'

'*What?* How could you? I love my job and you promised me I'd return to the shop on a part-time basis once the general settled into a routine.'

'Since when do I keep my promises?' He grins, the deliberate irony of his words reminding me of his failure to keep Monsieur de Giocomte safe from deportation.

I'm reeling, my nerves pulled taut and ready to break. I never intended to quit the hat shop; I love designing hats. I also value the friendship of Madame Péroline. I look out for her, too. The major's influence has been helpful in getting special ribbons and netting from Spain and lace from Belgium. I will never forget her loyalty to Ninette and know it will break her heart not to see the child.

But more importantly, what about the work I do at the shop for the Allies? Or is this a gift in disguise? Imagine the idle talk I can pick up from Wehrmacht and SS officers eager for a flash of skin or a quick kiss?

I'll have to give up that source and so far, I've struck out getting close to my 'guests' to gain their confidence with the major hovering around me.

'With your job as hostess for the general, you have no time for hats.'

He works his mouth into a snarl, and I wonder if he's jealous of the senior officer. The elder Nazi is portly, his jaw sags, and his eyebrows are too bushy, but he's intelligent and a favorite with Mimi's girls with his wry sense of humor. Quite the opposite of the major who, in spite of his Aryan good looks, is not capable of feelings. Still, he doesn't like his toys being taken away.

Me.

Or is it because I won't be working for him spying on unsuspecting Parisiennes at the hat shop? He's never mentioned it, but I fear his ego is suffering from losing his 'spoils of war' to a superior officer who doesn't have the Aryan trademark looks. But the general *is* an aristocrat and I know that sticks in the major's craw.

'Will you be attending tonight's party?' I ask sweetly.

'No. The general will have you all to himself. I have another engagement with a tall blonde dancer from Bal Tabarin.'

I'm not listening to him as he goes on to extol the girl's attributes in colorful terms, most likely to make *me* jealous. I'm already planning the evening with a new objective. With the major not present, I can be more daring in my plans to make this hostess job pay off, gather even better intelligence than I could at the hat shop. I can flutter about freely in the nest of hornets wearing black swastika armbands without the major observing me, questioning me.

And I know how to get them to talk. I learned a lot at Chez Mimi watching the girls at work.

It's all about the tease.

* * *

It's difficult to put into words how I feel when I make my rounds at the party later that evening. I'm keeping my eyes open for Arsène, while pumped up with curiosity as to how many victims have suffered at the hands of these Nazi officers. How can they sleep at night knowing how they've hurt so many with their lies and interrogations?

One thing that brings a smile to my lips—if one is allowed to smile these days—is how the stiff correctness I've come to expect of German officers disappears at my parties. They slouch on sofas, sink into plush wing-back chairs and put their feet up on the ottomans like they own the place. Of course, they think they do, but Madame de Giocomte tosses a shawl over her shoulders to hide her yellow star and then goes around dusting end tables and lamps every time an officer gets up as if to erase their presence from her elegant furniture. The only time I see the SS officers sit at attention is at the long table where Madame and Monsieur de Giocomte once dined every evening. I'm still not accustomed to this new seating arrangement and it takes every bit of amateur acting on my part not to cry, especially since the general ordered a portrait of Hitler to be put in the dining room. The Nazi officers sit up straight and slurp their soup like prep school boys beneath it. The Führer's presence, even on canvas, is apparently enough to keep them in line.

I tried to take down the picture, but when the major popped in unannounced, he reminded me to go check on Ninette. He couldn't have made it any clearer. *Do as you're told or you shall lose your child.* I wonder what Maman and Madame would say if they knew about his constant threats to take Ninette away from me. From us. Luckily, Maman and Madame have agreed to a truce with me. They do as I ask cleaning up and helping Cook in the kitchen and keeping the liquor flowing. They refuse to serve the Nazi officers though. Cook initially balked at preparing meals for the Boches and threatened to leave for her cousin's place in the country. I appealed to her love for Madame de Giocomte, promising her that by cooking for the Germans she's helping keep Madame safe from deportation, which calmed her down and brought her back on my side.

Albertine is a different story. She has seemingly jumped at the opportunity to serve the SS officers. I suspect that's because she has an eye for a young German lieutenant. He's here again tonight, talking to a tall captain over by the bust of Voltaire that Monsieur de Giocomte so loved. I catch him sneaking glances at the girl. The captain also notices the young man's wandering eye and turns around—oh, my God, it's Arsène. *He's here.* I wet my lips and smooth down my silky dress. Just the excuse I need to make my way over to him, to tell him to keep an eye on the lieutenant.

*If* I can get my heart out of my throat.

I can't wait to sidle up next to him with a big smile on my face. Flirt. Isn't that what I'm here for? First, I have to untangle myself from a fascinating conversation with General von Klum and a Wehrmacht officer about a Courbet painting. The German Army officer is boasting how they arrested its Jewish owner when—

I catch Albertine craning her neck to see if anyone is watching her, wiping perspiration from her face, her lower lip trembling. Nervous, unsteady. That's not the look of a young girl flushed with romance. Then I notice her right hand stuffed into her apron pocket. She's holding something—

Wait.

My gut tells me I'm not seeing something in this picture. *What is it?* I know Albertine is lonely since the Jewish boy she'd once liked disappeared. She was smitten with the son of a business associate of Monsieur de Giocomte's. I don't know if the boy ever gave her a tumble, but she was heartbroken when the French police arrested him and his family and sent them to Drancy. After we got the news, her eyes were red for days. I was surprised she didn't rebuff the young Nazi when he flirted with her at the last party. When I chastised her for being too friendly with the Boches, she said, 'If it's good for you, *Mademoiselle D'Artois*, why not me, too?'

*Oh, Lord, what have I created?*

I see Albertine smiling at the young SS officer, wiggling her shoulders, her eyes inviting him to follow her outside to the garden. Arsène sees it, too, and looks in my direction. I see his brows cross. His eyes ask me, *What foolish trick is the girl up to?*

I look closer and see the obvious point of a knife protruding through her white apron. *Good God, what is the girl thinking? We'll all be shot.*

'*Pardonnez-moi, messieurs*,' I say, smiling at the Nazi officers, 'but I must check with the server to see what's keeping the hors d'oeuvres.'

'I shall count the minutes, mademoiselle.' The general kisses my hand while eyeing my cleavage. The tight gold lamé dress is cut low in front and lower in the back down below my waist. I know he's watching me as I walk toward Albertine, who's headed for the double glass-paned doors leading to the garden.

I cut her off.

'I need to talk to you, Albertine, *now*!'

'But, mademoiselle, I have work to do.'

'No excuses. Come with me.' I take her by the arm and drag her toward the kitchen, making a sharp turn down the hallway where Impressionist paintings once graced the walls. And where Ève confronted the major that August morning. I give a quick nod to Maman whizzing by me, carrying a bottle of brandy to the dining room, her eyes questioning. *Nothing* gets by my *maman*, but I don't want her involved. I give her a cold shoulder look and a terse remark. 'Don't stand there dawdling, Maman, the general is waiting. *Now go!*' She says nothing, but all too often I see that hurt look clouding her eyes. She rushes off and I turn back to Albertine, shaking. 'What are you up to?'

'Me, mademoiselle?' Her eyes go wide.

'Yes, *you*. What's in your hand?'

'Nothing, I promise.'

'Don't lie to me. Give me the knife.'

She flutters her eyes. 'Mademoiselle?'

*'Give me the knife before I turn you over to the Nazis.'*

'I wasn't going to do anything, honest.' She hands me the kitchen knife and I pick up the tail of my gown and hide it in the folds of the soft material. 'You wouldn't really give me to the Boches, would you?'

I breathe out, relieved to have the weapon safe in my hand. 'No, but if anyone saw you even attempt to—' I hustle her to the back of the house into a dark corner. 'Why do it, risk torture, even death at the hands of the Gestapo?'

'I *had* to, mademoiselle, after I heard at the boulangerie that Jacob and his family were put on a train and sent to that place they call Auschwitz.' She lets tears fall I imagine she's been holding in all day. 'I wanted the Nazis to pay, *any* Nazi. It seemed so easy. Lure him outside and—' She looks up at me, puzzled. 'You could turn me over to your Nazi friends, but you won't. Why?'

'They're not really my friends.'

'Then who are you?'

'We *all* have secrets, Albertine. I can't say any more. Please trust me.'

'Everybody knows you work for the Boches, mademoiselle. I don't understand.'

I sigh. 'Do you remember when the three of us went to the cinema? You, Ève, and me, and we saw that old Sylvie Martone silent film where she was a singer in a cabaret during the Great War?'

'Of course. Everybody thought she worked for the Germans, but she—' Her hand flies to her mouth. 'Oh, mademoiselle, you're a spy.'

'We all fight this war in our own way, Albertine.' I squeeze her hand, making plans in my head as I speak, knowing she can't stay here at Maison Bleue. I'll send her to Cook's cousin in the country, then ask Arsène to help find a way to get her to Switzerland. I can't take the chance of her slipping up and revealing what she knows about me.

I hustle her upstairs to the servants' quarters and order her to pack her things because I want her to be safe. I shouldn't have given her any inkling about me.

Because Maman also heard us. She didn't go to the dining room, she listened to every word, then followed me, the bottle of brandy still clutched in her hand. 'Justine, is it true? Are you—?'

'*Don't ask me*, Maman, *please*! Your safety, Madame's, and Ninette's all depend on you acting as if *nothing* has changed. And don't tell Ève either—I know you're in contact with her when you disappear on Thursdays for the bread queue. It will put her in jeopardy, too.'

'How did you know I meet Ève?' she asks, surprised.

'The lovely, contented smile on your face, Maman. No one comes home empty-handed from the boulangerie and smiles *that* big.'

'My dear, sweet girl,' she gushes, her eyes shining like the day I saved Madame's hat from an angry swan and simultaneously rescued us from poverty, such is the joy I see on her face that it makes me tremble with relief. 'I *never* believed you were one of them. *Not for a moment*. Not my Justine.' She embraces me and can't let me go.

I hug my *maman* close to me, her thin body trembling in my arms, her sobs of relief a musical chorus for her soul. *She knows.* And for better or worse, my secret is out. I'm working for the Allies.

I pray we don't all pay the ultimate price for my rash decision.

* * *

'I *have* to see you, Arsène, tonight.' I give him a big smile, tease him with a wiggle to keep up my act. 'Albertine knows what I am.'

'I suspected she was up to no good when I overheard her soliciting that young lieutenant.' He lights a cigarette, then hands it to me. I don't smoke, but it gives us a moment to talk without raising suspicion. Around us, the party is loud, raucous, Nazi officers whistling, clapping their hands and stomping their feet when Mimi's girls strike up an impromptu can-can. 'She was shaking like a wet kitten tossed into a well.'

'She had a kitchen knife and God knows if she would have gone through with her plan. She wants revenge and she targeted him.' I take a puff and my throat burns. 'Albertine isn't a bad sort, but the Nazis have sent the boy she loves to a concentration camp, so she acted with her heart, not her head.'

'War takes even the most innocent to a black place in the soul when the pain becomes personal.' Dark, daring eyes bore into mine. 'You're in danger, Justine. I'll set a plan into motion to get the girl out of France to Switzerland where she'll be safe. And so will you.' He attempts a smile. 'Where can we talk?'

'Meet me at my old apartment on Rue des Martyrs,' I say. 'It's empty, but I still have a key.'

'No, it's too dangerous. I've observed the Gestapo snooping around your old place at the oddest hours.'

*Why am I not surprised?* Herr Geller won't be satisfied until he finds enough dirt on me to hang me.

'Meet me at Chez Mimi later,' he says. 'Pretend you're taking one of the girls home, or that you have to book girls in for the next soiree, or something. I'll give you the details for the mission, where to pick up a train ticket and where to secure a new identity card for the girl.'

'Won't Mimi suspect us if I show up tonight?'

Smiling at me with the deep, dark eyes I adore, he takes the cigarette from my fingers and whispers heated words in my ear that ignite a slow burn in me. 'Not if you tell her you've actually come to the brothel to meet your lover.'

Anticipation simmering, I take no more than five minutes to commandeer the general's black Mercedes sedan with a story the soft-hearted official can't resist, taking his weathered hand in mine and stroking his palm while telling him one of Mimi's girls is ill. *Too much caviar.* I'll escort her back to the brothel.

His eyes twinkle. 'I am happy to accompany you, mademoiselle.'

'No need, General,' I say with determination in my smile to keep the mood light. 'I shall be in good hands.'

He heaves out a long, lonely sigh. 'Ah, I envy him, mademoiselle, whoever he is. *Alors*, you may keep the motorcar for as long as you need it.'

*He knows.*

The Nazi proposes a toast, pouring two glasses of the best champagne from Maxim's. And with a subtle raising of his brow and a clinking of glasses to our friendship, General von Klum, a high-ranking SS Nazi official in Hitler's inner circle, becomes my co-conspirator in a plot I suspect goes far beyond aiding me in a love affair.

Which makes me wonder once again, *what is the general really about*?

* * *

'I've been expecting you, Mademoiselle D'Artois. The captain is waiting for you in the Blue Marquis Room.'

Stepping aside for me to go upstairs, Madame Mimi can't resist giving me the once-over in my silver lamé evening dress with a matching capelet covering my shoulders on this warm summer night.

'*Who*, Madame Mimi?'

'Don't be coy, mademoiselle. Your tall, good-looking SS officer has been pacing the floor for twenty minutes. If I may be so bold, he's ripe for sex.'

I can't hide anything from her. She's been at the keyhole. The nosy madam enjoys peeping privileges with her Nazi clients, listening at keyholes. *Keeps my girls safe*, she's wont to say.

'He *is* good-looking, *n'est-ce pas*?' I say with a wicked grin on my face. *Keep up the act.* Don't let her suspect your secret rendezvous is anything but an indiscretion on the part of a lonely woman. A rape victim. A woman healed physically, but not emotionally. A woman wishing this gorgeous, caring man might hold me tonight not out of pity but desire. I know he's the only man for me. The only man who will ever own my heart. Even if I can't tell him that.

She leans in closer. 'Clever of you to keep him waiting. You'll have him eating out of your hand. Though I was surprised it was *you* he asked for. Does the major know?'

'*Madame*, how could you?' I pretend to be shocked.

She grabs my hand, her long red nails sharp as her tongue digging into me. 'Your secret is safe with me, mademoiselle. I never did like that SS bastard. He never follows the rules of the house, but he pays well.'

I smile. Ah, yes, the rules. Nazi officers wishing an evening's entertainment with Madame Mimi's mamselles must show up at the brothel in a clean, pressed uniform and not smelling of gunpowder, boots polished, sidearm stored in the Chinese cabinet in the parlor, and they can only go upstairs with one girl at a time. Unless they pay double the rate up front.

'*Merci,* Madame,' I mutter, eager to wrap up this night of strange events. Albertine... The general... Maman.

Madame Mimi lays her hand on my arm. 'You're a beautiful woman, mademoiselle, and stronger than most that come through here. You impressed me with your grit, fortitude. Not letting a man ruin you. I like that. If you ever wish to moonlight, you know where to find me. Now, go up quickly before someone sees you. And don't forget to change the sheets before you leave, *n'est-ce pas*?'

Then she laughs and plops down into her favorite chair and pours another brandy. I don't waste another second and scurry towards the stairs. But even the breathlessness I'm experiencing about what happened with Albertine can't take over the electric charge making my feet go faster. I should be shocked at Madame Mimi's proposition. I'm not. So many girls raped by SS men end up either dead by their own hand, or under the knife of an illegal abortion practitioner to undo the result of the rape, or living on the streets. Madame might have believed she was giving me a break with her offer. I will thank her later, but I have in my life what others don't. My Ninette. She's my anchor and gives me great comfort. I wish Ève could meet her. My little sister is out there somewhere, fighting the Boches, hating me. Maman knows what I am. *When can I tell my sister? Ever*? I pray she doesn't go to her death in this terrible war never knowing. That makes me sad.

For now, keeping the household safe at Maison Bleue is what's important, and even if I feel strong enough to walk into the sun again with this fascinating man, ready to come alive under his touch, I shall hold back that thought, hold it inside me, like a butterfly fluttering its wings inside a glass heart.

I climb the steps faster. *First floor... second...* yet I can't help but nourish this intense desire I have to make love to him like it's an itch I want to scratch. What if Arsène and I were meeting as lovers?

*Third floor.*

I smile before I knock on the door to the Blue Marquis Room.

*What if?*

* * *

'You told her *what*, Arsène?'

'That you and I met at your party earlier tonight and couldn't keep our hands off each other, and this is the only safe place we can meet.'

'*Très bien*,' I joke. 'What if the major hears about it?'

'He won't. I paid Madame Mimi three times the going rate to rent a room to keep our secret.'

I think a moment. 'And she didn't recognize you?'

'Madame Mimi sees only what she wants to see, especially if it lines her pockets. Besides, under that heavy face powder, she's soft-hearted and would never stand in the way of a good romance.'

I grin. 'Oh… I see.' *Could my loneliness be coming to an end?*

'Besides, it's a good cover since Maison Bleue is filled with Nazis every night. With the madam in our pocket, I can see you here on a steady basis so we can discuss business without arousing suspicion.'

'Oh.'

I struggle not to show my disappointment twisting about inside my mind, like I'm tied up in invisible rope that keeps me from reaching out to touch him and make a fool out of myself. I'm alone with him because we're comrades, nothing more.

I push aside my spiraling emotions and listen intently when he gives me the instructions I need to get Albertine safely away from Maison Bleue. I memorize the address of the print shop where a forged identity card and railway ticket will be waiting, only being given first names of the contacts, and even those are probably false. I also learn the time frame to put the mission into play when—

I hear a shuffle out in the hallway, then a slight cough. Arsène does, too.

'Madame Mimi is at the keyhole again,' I whisper in his ear. 'Do you think she heard us?'

He shakes his head. 'No. She's more interested in looking… so why don't we give her something to look at?' He pulls me closer and holds me still as he captures my lips in a kiss both demanding and tender, then pulls back, his dark eyes questioning if he went too far.

'No, don't stop, please.' I press my body against his when he deepens the kiss and a low, ragged moan escapes from the back of my throat. I can't hold back; I've waited so long for this moment. I lean back and enjoy him kissing my neck, my face, even the tip of my nose. Playful, fun. Not painful, humiliating, degrading, like the raw, jagged pain that I suffered with the major. No, the complete opposite. A torrent of giggles erupts from me, so joyous is my excitement at knowing a man for the pure enjoyment when I throw my arms around his neck.

I hug him and mutter, 'I don't care if the madam is watching.'

'I do,' Arsène whispers. 'I want you all to myself.'

He picks me up in his strong arms and carries me over to the sumptuous four poster draped in blue velvet with its long velvet fringe cords hanging from the canopy. Then before I can protest —as if I would?—he lays me down on the bed and draws the drapes to give us complete privacy. In the dark.

'Clever, monsieur.'

'Not as clever as finally getting you alone, Justine.'

I laugh. The thrill I feel hearing him say my name makes me giddy, then my laughter turns to a wild passion that surprises me when I offer no resistance and surrender to him, moaning when he slips down the flimsy silk over my shoulders and squeezes my breasts, then his hands work their way down over my ribcage and pull up my gown. And still I hold on, kissing him with such heat, my tongue diving deep into his mouth, my nails ripping at the fine wool of his SS uniform. And did he just nip my lower lip with his teeth?

I don't see the hated uniform in the dark.

And for the first time, I don't see the uniform in my mind.

This is Arsène pressed up against me. I trust him not to hurt me, his words no longer teasing but melancholy.

'You're not like any woman I've known, Justine, your strength, your innocent yet provocative moves that torture me, the crying look in your eyes because you believe you have no one to share your feelings with. The violation of your womanhood—that tortures me as well. You have me, *ma chérie*, and I want you, but only if you're ready to have me make love to you.'

How can I not let him? Every night I suffer in silence when I lay my head down, so still I ache for even a ghost to brush my cheek just to shiver from the touch of someone, but there's no one there.

Now, there is.

'Yes, *mon chéri, yes.*'

His warm, soft lips devour me, and I moan, embracing a deeply satisfying pleasure from being kissed by a man who respects me, needs me.

Then he undresses me and gives me that precious gift so long denied me.

Himself.

# 18

## PARIS, JULY 1942

*Ève*

Blood. On her underwear. I see her walking away from me.

The farmer's wife. The girl's mother.

Her skirt is still pulled up around her waist, the blood splattered about in a big circle. Not from her monthlies, but from that miserable coward of a German soldier pushing into her.

I know I'm dreaming, that I didn't really see the blood, but my imagination has conjured up the most awful details I know must be true. I can't get the sight of the woman's struggle out of my mind. Her keen resolve not to cry out while he raped her. In my dream, she turns and stares at me. I can't turn away from the mother's eyes, wide and round, her lips red and swollen from biting on them hard when the Nazi got his hands on her and sexually assaulted her. Then came her silence to keep her daughter from knowing the utter helplessness she felt. Yet I saw in her a brief glimmer of triumph when she embraced her child knowing she'd saved her from a similar fate. Then a powerful look in my direction, nodding her head and thanking me. Something strikes deep in me then. That I *can* reach out and do something to help women suffering like her.

I just don't know how to do it.

I fight hard to push out the horror invading my dream, reliving the moment. I can't. I'm angry with myself because I can't shake it. My dreams are the only place where I find peace, where I'm at home with Maman and watching her knit, listening to Madame play the cello... and I'm sitting with my head tucked into Michal's shoulder—

'Wake up, Ève.'

I rub my eyes. *Michal.* His voice is laced with worry.

'Did I yell out? Sorry. I can't get that woman's face out of my mind.'

I don't elaborate. I didn't tell him what I witnessed, the horrible rape of that mother. It's difficult enough to speak about it to another woman, but I could never talk about it with a man.

He paces up and down. 'We've got a problem.'

'What is it?' I'm instantly awake, sliding my feet into my boots and lacing them up.

'The road back to Paris is blocked with ten, fifteen Nazi trucks. We can't get through with the weapons.'

We're about eighty kilometers south of Paris, an hour and half drive to the city, our truck parked under an overhanging willow, the sun at our back, meaning we're not easily visible to oncoming vehicles with the blazing morning steam heat rising up off the asphalt. We borrowed a small truck from another farmer in the Charente region in exchange for weapons we retrieved from our cache stored in the outbuilding. Turned out he was the cousin of the woman I saved and when he found out how I ran that 'rat's ass Nazi' off the farm, he insisted we take his truck. There is still no word about the woman's husband, but sadly he wouldn't be the first local sent to the prison in Royan for aiding the Resistance.

From Jonzac, we headed north toward Paris, stopping only to rest and refill the petrol from gas cans Michal filled during a night visit to the munitions depot. He siphoned fuel from trucks waiting for the morning pickup of guns and ammunition.

But so far it's not the jaunty ride bumping up and down with my thigh touching his I'd silently hoped for.

It's nothing. Nothing at all.

We barely speak, don't look at each other. We've resumed our relationship as partners, no more passionate moments when I get close to him. No more longing for something I know he's incapable of, and I hurt for him. And me, too. In a moment of girlish pride, I struck out to prove how tough I am and tried to trim my hair shorter with a hunting knife. I ended up making a deep cut in my left thumb. I wanted to sever my romantic ties to him by making my hair so short Michal will forget I'm a woman, like I have.

It's too painful being a female. Silly, but I'm desperate for excuses why he's not interested in me for more than physical satisfaction. I don't want it to be like that. I want the warmth and the fluttery feelings in my stomach, the wiggle in my groin when he touches me. I want 'us' together to be more than a quick release. I want *him*.

And that weak excuse about him not knowing how to love? A stock answer when a girl gets too close and talks about it. I bet Coralie never mentioned 'love' and enjoyed the ride until she got tired of him distancing her and never opening up and took off to join another network. Now *we're* on the run and survival is more important than sex. Like so many Resistance fighters, we spend more time in makeshift encampments, whether it's in the outskirts of Paris or our latest mission in Jonzac. No time to indulge in romantic fantasies. We stay off the streets to keep from attracting attention, but the Nazis are catching on to our tricks, sending Frenchmen who are arrested to work in German factories. So far, they're asking for volunteers, but talk is the 'service obligation' may soon become mandatory, forcing many partisans like us running into the hills, the woods, to hide.

Coming in contact with other *résistants*, we heard talk about forming official encampments and bringing various networks under one umbrella. For now, we're on our own. We must get back to Paris and disperse the weapons to our network, then we'll head for the thick forest north of the city. Our money's nearly gone and Michal hasn't been able to make contact with Remi. For all we know, he's dead or has been arrested. And I can't go home to Maison Bleue to ask Maman for help.

Now this roadblock.

'Are the trucks empty?' I ask. Whatever their cargo, we're in big trouble if we can't sneak around them on a side lane or slip through a break in the long line of lorries.

'See for yourself, Ève.'

I follow him to the edge of the woods and crouch behind a thick tree, peering at the parade of open trucks coming our way, sluicing through the mud, heavy tires weighed down by their cargo. The first truck passes by and I see—

'Oh, my God. *Jews.*'

Twenty, maybe more in each truck. We're close enough to see the yellow stars sewn on their clothing, the confusion on their faces, the hope dying in their eyes with every kilometer. Every roar of the engine. Every tire spinning. Men, women, and...

'*Children*,' I mutter, disbelieving the Boches have arrested these innocent people, just because they're Jewish. 'Why take the little ones? They can't hurt anyone, they're babies.'

'Why do vultures feed on the defenseless? Because they're

cowards.' Michal curses under his breath. 'Damn Nazis. They want to eradicate every European Jew and that includes *every* Jew. Children grow up, problem not solved.' He pauses for a moment, then takes a drink from the flask the grateful farmer gave us along with some cheese and stale bread.

'I can't believe it, Michal. I just can't.' He hands me the flask, and I take a drink. It burns my throat.

'After I escaped from Poland, I saw similar convoys as I made my way to Paris, thousands of innocent people, their suitcases in their hands. Their souls if not already lost to despair soon will be when they reach Auschwitz.'

'*Auschwitz*,' I repeat in a low whisper. 'Is that where they sent Monsieur de Giocomte?'

He nods, his silence giving me the answer I never wanted to hear. I know what he's thinking. If the rumors are true about that place, Monsieur is never coming back. '*Allons*, let's move out.'

We jump into the truck and Michal turns on the engine, then puts the vehicle into gear.

I grab his sleeve. 'We'll never outrun them, Michal.'

'If we can't lose them, we'll join them.' He jams on the gas pedal and we take off through the hanging low branches of the willow tree, tires squealing, gears sticking, but he keeps his eyes on the road up ahead. In the back of the truck, several wooden boxes of firearms, rounds of ammunition, and grenades rattle about under a heavy pile of hay.

'Where are we?' I ask Michal, trying to make sense of the pencil-drawn map he put together with information he gleaned from other fighters before we left Paris. Towns and Nazi outposts clearly marked. Neat handwriting, perfectly shaped numbers, clean lines for the roads. It took a trained observer to put this together with such precision, someone with skills in reconnaissance missions that go beyond blowing up railway tracks, making me even more curious about his past.

'We're a few kilometers from Pithiviers.'

'Cook used to rave about the almond cream puff pastry that town's famous for.'

'*And*,' he tells me, 'there's a Nazi internment camp there.'

* * *

It's a sad, horrible marker in my life when I realize I'm more used to seeing my fellow countrymen and women in pain and suffering by now. The Jewish women in Pithiviers internment camp I come upon are no exception.

We bring up the tail of the solemn line of trucks of Jews bound for Drancy before being deported to Poland. No one questions us. It's not uncommon for the farmers of the Charente region to traverse across the fields from one farm to another with supplies, the post, even gossip. We bring up the rear for a few clicks before arriving at the transit camp. It will take hours for them to unload the frightened people, some running for freedom but not getting far before they're shot at. Whistles, dogs barking. It's horrible.

Michal parks the truck outside the camp. 'Looks like we're staying a while until things calm down.'

What I find strange is that the Nazi patrolmen pushing people off the truck with their bayonets ignore us, like they don't see us. Their goal is Jew-hunting and two curious country farmers aren't worth bothering with.

'We'll wait here until dark, stay low-key, then take off before the moon rises,' he says. 'I need some shut-eye, so I can get us to Paris.'

'You're not asking me to drive?' I tease.

'After that last time? There weren't any gears left on that piece of junk by the time we got to the hospital.'

True. He got shot by a German patrol outside the city, but my wild impromptu driving saved his life. I know he hasn't forgotten that when he gives me a wistful look, then a big grin. I *could* think it was an invitation to come sit close to him, then he slumps down in the driver's seat, his eyes half-closed. I get the message. I mumble that I've got to find a friendly tree and wander off to quiet my nerves. I'm still haunted by my dream. I have a nagging urge to find out what's going on here. I *need* to know. Then someday I can tell the world what I saw.

My heart sticks in my throat when I sneak around to the front entrance of the camp and it isn't Boche soldiers I see heading up the groups of Jewish detainees, but French police. While one group is being processed, others are lined up in a rigid formation, ready to leave camp. I see at least fifty, maybe seventy, Jewish men, women, and children huddled together, ready to get on an empty truck. Men's heads have been shaved, mothers are crying, their children being torn from their arms, while the Gestapo seizes anything that captures their attention from their opened suitcases. Coats are turned inside out, tossing precious photos of loved ones into the heavy mud. Then mud and more mud. And I can do nothing. After the trucks leave, only small children remain with armbands sewn onto their clothes, their names and ages written in black ink, the only identity they have left until the order comes to rip them off. And then load *them* on a truck. Alone. Confused.

*Why? What's to become of these innocents?*

I will myself to find strength to do *something*. The wire fence doesn't look that hard to penetrate, and is that a hole in the wire? A plan forms in my head to grab a child, two, three... when I hear the rustle of a tree, the shifting of ground beneath my feet. I can't move.

*A German patrol?*

'What the hell are you doing, Ève? Trying to get yourself killed?'

I turn. '*Michal*... the children, can't we help them?'

'No.' His answer is firm.

'How can you be so cruel?'

'I wish we could, but we have a job to do. Remi is depending on us to bring back these weapons.'

'Look, there's a hole in the fence and with the ground being so muddy, I can dig underneath and slip through the wire. I'm tall, but thin. I could save three, maybe four children!'

'No, Ève, we can't.'

'Why not?'

'You wouldn't get three meters inside that camp before the German patrol found you with their dogs. I won't see you murdered by those barbaric animals.'

'I have to try.'

'I *order* you to stand down.' His eyes blaze with anger.

'I don't take orders from you, Michal. I'm not letting those children be deported to that place—'

'Auschwitz.'

'I *won't*.'

'Please, Ève, listen to reason. If the dogs don't get you, then the SS will. You know what they'll do to you.'

I stiffen. 'I do.'

'It won't be one soldier who rips off your clothes and leaves you shivering on the cold ground while the others hold you down, but two, three Boches, then they'll each have their turn with you.'

'Why should you care?' I come back with a hurtful retort and regret it as soon as I say it. Before I can take it back, Michal grips me hard by the shoulders.

'I do care, Ève. *I do.*' He heaves out a sigh. 'Now let's get out of here before we overstay our welcome.'

We don't say another word, but sneak back to the truck and sit in silence until it's safe to escape under the cover of darkness. I close my eyes tight. I feel so helpless... Why is it I couldn't save these children from certain death? Because I'm afraid of being raped? Murdered? I was willing to take that chance. I think about that mother who sacrificed herself so her young daughter could be spared. And of course, Justine. She survived, and I will, too. Yet I know Michal is right. My guilty conscience was making me reckless. I had little chance of saving those children.

We head out on the road to Paris, my heart still racing like tumbling thunder. I shall remember *all* the children of Pithiviers, but especially two little sisters about six and eight holding hands when the Nazi guards shoved them into the open truck, their fate sealed by that yellow star. With their hands clasped tight, the two girls never let go of each other.

That could have been Justine and me.

Maybe then, not now.

That unbreakable bond those two girls shared is lost to me.

My sister is a traitor. She let go of *my* hand long ago. I can never forget that, but I will *never* stop trying to get her back, that in spite of her 'walk on the dark side', I will show her she doesn't have to be this way, that a sister's love can conquer all.

Even the Boches.

# 19

## PARIS, JULY 15, 1942

*Justine*

Another *rafle*, or roundup of Jews, is coming in the morning and I can't do a damn thing about it.

I hold my head in my hands, the raging pain of drinking too much brandy clouding my brain, but I *know* what I heard from that fat SS colonel. The Nazis are organizing a *massive* roundup of Jewish people leading to deportation. *Thousands* of Jews will be picked up, their names gleaned from the lists these innocent citizens so dutifully filled out last year. I feel like I'm going to pass out, but first I must confirm this intelligence then pass it on to Arsène.

Oh, Lord, what was I thinking, challenging the old dog to a drinking game? Yes, I hoped it would loosen his tongue, especially when the other officers left early and I had him alone as midnight struck in the library and mine for the taking. I never expected a running flow of expletives flowing from his lips, boasting that they're rounding up the biggest number yet, this time including Jewish women and children for deportation.

*Whores and their brats,* he called them. Then he pinched my cheek—why do Nazi officers like to act like schoolmasters?—and called for his driver to take him back to the Hôtel Raphael. I have no doubt he'll pass out in the lobby and never recall our conversation.

Before I go to Arsène, I have to confirm the intelligence, so I seek out my favorite source. General von Klum.

The soldierly aristocrat arrived late to tonight's dinner party, flushed and anxious. He didn't say why and I didn't ask. I'm more interested in bringing him around to confiding in me the information I need. I ordered Cook to heat up the oyster soup from earlier in the evening to calm the general and satisfy his taste buds. She did so without grumbling, which makes me believe she listens at keyholes like Madame Mimi and knows my secret. She didn't protest Albertine leaving us. *For the girl's safety*, she agreed. I decided not to hire a new maid. It's too precarious to have a stranger judging me. For now, my focus is on the Nazi general. I satisfy his weary old eyes—his words, not mine—wearing a soft green silk gown with a flowing scarf that trails behind me like wings.

I look like an absinthe fairy, he says.

I smile and join General von Klum in the dining room, just the two of us. Maman served the soup and left a bottle of red wine, two glasses, then retired for the evening but not without a secret smile. She now understands what I do, my job. I think she enjoys me being a 'spy', and I pray I never have to see her regret it.

The general reaches over his cooling oyster soup to take my hand and squeezes it, explaining he was late because there were 'complications' that needed fixing, and asking what is so important it can't wait until after dessert. He's looking forward to indulging in a mixed fruit tarte.

'*Jews*, General von Klum. Thousands of them to be rounded up hours from now from the poorer sections of Paris.' I've learned a straightforward approach works best with him. 'Is it true? Are they deporting women and children to the labor camps?'

He nods. 'Yes, Rachelle, unfortunately the colonel is correct. My old friend Horst has the ear of the Nazi officer in charge of the operation and no doubt he received the update while cavorting with him at Bal Tabarin. All he can talk about is making his quotas for the Jews.'

I know he feels comfortable sharing with me obscure details about the war, much of it Nazi propaganda, but every once in a while he leaks intelligence I can share, so I press him further. 'Do you know *exactly* which arrondissement, General?'

I run my fingertips over the medals on his chest, toying with them like they're souvenirs for the taking.

He smiles wide, not answering my question. He's more interested in grabbing my hand and stroking the inside of my palm. 'Shall I request a second bowl of oyster soup for you?'

'You don't need to feed me oysters to make me smile, General,' I bait him. 'I find you most interesting... and appealing.'

'I'm no fool, mademoiselle, but you know how to make this old man remember the days when I could last all night.' He grimaces. 'That was before... well, let's just say, I stopped counting my medals years ago.' He slurps his soup.

I indulge in a glass of wine. My head gets worse, but I still need an answer. 'It's so terrible for those poor people, General,' I lament, laying it on a bit thick, but I'm also a bit drunk. 'Thank God, the major has pledged that Madame de Giocomte is safe from such harassment.'

Why not plant the seed? I must do everything I can to keep Madame safe. 'No worries on that count, mademoiselle. I spoke to the head of the Wehrmacht on your behalf. This house is designated as an official Nazi residence and all who live here are exempt from these roundups.' He goes on to remind me several Parisians enjoy that same privilege, including certain Jewish citizens and others who keep rooms at the Hôtel Ritz.

'*Merci*, General. All this talk of arresting people gives me such a headache. I should like to sleep in tomorrow, but I promised Ninette I'd take her to a puppet show.' I lean in closer and this green fairy knows how to show some cleavage. 'I just don't want to get caught with my baby in the *rafle*.'

He nearly drops his spoon into the soup. 'No, mademoiselle, of course not.'

And with his eyes fixed on my breasts, he spills the information I need about what the French police are calling *Opération Vent printanier,* Spring Wind, since the roundups are taking place in spring and summer. The Germans have dubbed it *Grand Rafle* and they have it planned with annoying precision.

4 a.m.: the arrests will begin with a loud knock on the door by French police, backed up by Gestapo. Everyone on the list will be taken, no exceptions. City buses will then take the Jews to the stadium on the Left Bank then transfer them to Drancy then Auschwitz-Birkenau in Poland. Immigrant Jewish neighborhoods are to be targeted. Every... one.

His grey-flecked eyes look away as if he can't face me. In a hushed voice that sounds more like a little boy's than a Nazi general, he admits, 'The quota set for Jews in the occupied zone is twenty thousand.'

*Twenty thousand?* I want to ask if I heard him wrong, but I don't. His brows furrow, the playfulness in his voice gone from a flirty conversation to a solemn silence forged from... guilt? He hints that the roundup will be bad, *very* bad, and I wonder again as I have so many times why this Prussian follows the Führer when he has such doubts.

I don't protest when the general finishes his soup and bids me an abrupt adieu. I have no more time for this game. I've heard enough.

* * *

8 a.m. Panic hits me.

I can't find Maman and Madame de Giocomte anywhere. They've disappeared like grains of salt dumped into a glass of water. I race from room to room in Maison Bleue when I get home after spending last night with Arsène, passing on my intelligence, then finding lovely moments in his arms that neither of us could resist before he rushed off in his SS uniform on his motorcycle eager to meet up with his contacts to relay the information about the roundup.

Since I moved back to Maison Bleue, the German office of Jewish affairs restored telephone service, so I'd called the number at the pawnshop Arsène gave me for emergencies. I then took the chance of meeting him in the house's garage, finding clean bedding and sheets and a single mattress, as if Madame de Giocomte had been hiding someone here. Ève? I don't think so; the lingering scent was musky, but I didn't question it further.

Last night, Arsène assured me I did everything I could to help save many people, kissed me with such warmth I shall never be cold again, but I made one big mistake. I held to the belief my fears were boundless, that the roundup consisted of Jewish refugees and not the elite like Madame de Giocomte, so I didn't think it was imperative to tell Maman and Madame straight away.

I didn't think. *Didn't think.* And now they're gone.

I checked the upstairs room where Maman sleeps, and her paisley shawl was left tossed over a chair. I'm filled with an instinct I've honed all too well in my line of work. She clearly left in a hurry. Madame's room was empty, too.

*Why? Where did they go?* To queue up for bread? Cheese? Or did the French police not get the notice from the head of the Wehrmacht and show up here after all, and pick her up along with Madame de Giocomte? *And I was so drunk I heard nothing? Really?*

'No, mademoiselle,' Cook assures me, her face white with flour except for her red nose. She has a cold again. Or was she crying? 'Your *maman* and Madame left around five this morning and took two parcels of leftover vegetables from last night's dinner party to give to them poor souls in Bellevue.'

What was it the general said? *Immigrant Jewish neighborhoods are to be targeted. Every... one.*

I almost convinced myself I wasn't awake yet, that this was a bad dream, my subconscious punishing me because I made love to Arsène on a day when so many people will suffer. But Cook's loud sneezing jerks me back to an alertness that wipes away my hangover. Yes, of course, I know where they are. Madame's charity work. I'd warned Maman they must give it up, that nothing is as it was. But she insisted people need food and no Nazi was going to stop them from doing God's work. How were we to know it would be the devil's work they'd find on this morning of July 16?

I jump on the old bicycle I find in the garage, pedaling as fast as I can... It should take me around twenty minutes to get to the Jewish quarter in the Marais.

I pray I find them before they disappear into the abyss.

* * *

Standing across the street from a broken-down red brick building ablaze with body heat and the smell of fear, I watch for two women. Two kind-hearted souls who give for the joy of warm hugs from worried mothers, handshakes from grateful fathers. Smiles from little children.

For the past hour, I've ridden up and down these narrow streets but there's no sign of them. I never dreamed that grand goodness they share between them would cause me such pain. And guilt. In spite of my trying to the contrary, they're still caught up in this madness.

I walk my bicycle across the street, ignoring the French policeman blasting his whistle at me. I don't see them. It's a scene straight out of a film except it's happening now. The melee of people melting together in shades of brown and gray, the French police in their black uniforms, capes, white gloves and rows of silver buttons. The morning sun glinting off the round buttons like sparks of electricity. A scene in which I don't belong in my red jacket, blouse, and tan culottes. I keep looking. That Maman and Madame de Giocomte were here I don't doubt. A woman with two little children hanging on to her coat told me she knows the nice mesdames with the baskets of food. They come every week and yes, she saw them this morning giving out food to her and her neighbors while they waited for the next bus. That they could already have been herded onto a bus makes my skin prickle.

Then I see her. Waiting in line. 'Maman, *over here*!'

'Justine?' she cries out, her hand going to her mouth.

I rush over to where she's standing with the poor souls waiting for the next green-and cream-colored bus. I'm shocked to see a yellow star on her plaid coat. 'What's this?'

'I sewed a yellow star on my coat so the immigrants would trust me.'

I feel like crying at her kindhearted gesture, but it will get my *maman* deported. I rip it off, then pull her into my arms. 'Oh, you sweet angel. I love you, Maman.'

She nods, a quiet sobbing making her shake. I have seen my *maman* sew and knit until her fingers bled to help others. I once walked with her down the path of poverty and fear when Papa died. And I have known her strength, in never giving up until there was no fear for her daughters' future. But I have never seen such horror etched onto her face, her smooth skin as pale as a daisy petal and her quivering body just as fragile. She's scared to death.

I hold her close to me, protecting her while I scan the unfortunate people milling around, waiting to be taken away to the winter stadium according to the general, where they'll be held for God knows how long, all holding suitcases and blankets. Even pillows. Then I see a moment of opportunity. The French police rush in and out of the apartment building, obviously having difficulty with the residents on the top floor. I hear screaming, yelling and cursing. I imagine the police dragging the Jews on the list down the stairwell from the fourth floor. That gives me an idea.

'Take your coat off now, and get on the bicycle, *Maman*. And start pedaling. I'll catch up with you.' I look around. 'Where's Madame?'

'She spotted her family, the baroness, her daughter and her granddaughters, at the end of the block and ran to help them.' Maman's voice cracks. 'I tried to follow her, but the police pushed everyone back and I got caught in the crowd.'

'I'll get her. Now go, Maman, *go*. And don't look back!'

'Justine—'

*'Go!'*

I don't know if it's the harshness in my voice or the real fear of arrest grabbing her like nothing she's ever felt before, but she jumps on the bicycle and heads off down a narrow alley and out of reach of the French police. I watch her until she disappears into the gray mist of this endless morning of July 16.

Now to find Madame de Giocomte.

* * *

'Justine, thank God you're here. Can't you do *something* to save the baroness and her family?'

'I will try, Madame... Here, take my jacket.'

Madame de Giocomte, like Maman, is frightened, caught up in a situation she's astute enough to realize she has little control over. She does as I ask and covers up the yellow star on her thin navy sweater with my red jacket. I found her trying to rip it off about half a block away, huddled in a doorway, her eyes fiercely focused on the commotion on the pavements. French police along with Gestapo eager to get in on the action, dragging women and children toward the waiting buses. They pushed Madame aside since she wasn't on the list, ordering her to stay put until they checked a different list.

They don't know Madame. She kept searching the crowd until she found her woebegone relatives, relegated to seeking shelter here in the Marais after the Nazis also requisitioned their house in northern Paris. She was just as shocked as I am seeing the baroness waving her arms about, shouting, 'You've made a mistake, we're French citizens!' when the man in the black trench coat tries to subdue her. Her daughter and her four granddaughters hold strong, the little ones hanging onto Delphine, the oldest. Aged sixteen. Is she wearing my old blue dress with the pretty shiny buttons? Oh, my God, she is. Maman must have fixed it up for her. She looks so young. So scared.

I can't let the Nazi machine take them.

*What's five fewer in their stupid quota?*

I walk over with assurance to the French officer-in-charge, demanding he let the baroness and her family go.

'And who are you, mademoiselle?' he asks, puzzled but curious.

'A good friend of SS General von Klum... and the consort of SS Major Saxe-Müllenheim.'

'So? Even if I *did* believe you—and I don't—why should I release them? They're Jews, they're on the list. They go.'

'Would you send your own mother, your sister to Auschwitz?'

He balks. 'How did you—'

'The General told me in confidence Poland is their final destination.' I lean in closer. 'Now if you'll allow them to leave with me, I won't mention your insubordination to the general. I promise. If you don't...' I leave my thought unsaid and I swear he was about to strike their names off the list when a Gestapo man I don't recognize waltzes up to the French police officer and whispers in his ear.

The secret policeman turns to me. 'The names stay on the list, mademoiselle.'

'On whose authority?' I demand.

'Mine. They're Jews.' He tips his Fedora. 'You'd best be on your way, mademoiselle, before you find yourself on a bus.'

I know when to back off. I'm outnumbered and outgunned. But I can't resist getting the final word. 'You'll be hearing from me, monsieur, *and* the general.'

I take a long look at the baroness, her daughter, and her lovely granddaughters, especially Delphine, who is blossoming into womanhood, and I vow not to give up trying to secure their freedom. Then I turn to Madame who has been silently backing me up with her piercing stare. She, too, knows we're on the losing side in this argument.

I lock arms with her. '*Allons*, Madame, let's get out of here before they take you, too.'

We walk to freedom and no one stops us because I had just loudly confessed to the French police with a smile on my face I'm a friend of an SS general and the mistress of an SS major. Meaning that I have full authorization to go where I please and with *whom* I please, while these women and children await their fate. Including Madame's sister-in-law and her innocent daughter and granddaughters. I know the baroness hates me, must want to spit on me. I don't blame her, but I hold on to the hope in my heart there's a chance to save them... *if* I ask the general for a favor.

I hang my head. *Whatever he asks for in return? Yes, whatever he asks for*. Their lives are more important to this family than saving my virtue.

Again, I swear vengeance when this war is over.

Again, I shall not forget.

# 20

## PARIS, SEPTEMBER 1942

*Ève*

I brace myself to make a quick turn around the corner tottering in wobbly platform heels and onto the Rue de Rivoli. I *swear* I'm being followed. Two, three blocks. *There.* Coming up beside me on a motorcycle, I see the same SS officer I noticed five minutes ago smiling at me, then giving me the once-over. He's extraordinarily handsome, dark hair, piercing eyes that smolder when he takes me in from head to toe. A captain. Then he tips his cap, guns his engine and speeds away.

Strange.

This isn't the first time I swore I was being followed since I returned to Paris. I slip into the shadows behind the red and black banners hanging from the buildings to escape the nagging paranoia that often grips me. I catch my breath, holding to my belief that I've been careful, that my job is not to be noticed, blend in, then get out. Already planning my next move, which may or may not involve my handsome Polish fighter since we haven't seen each other for weeks, I come out of the shadows and reenter the sunshine baking the pavement, walking at a brisk pace. I'm clutching a mahogany leather satchel under my arm filled with leaflets, tracts actually, political messages. I leave them on benches in the Tuileries Gardens near the Louvre and seats on the Métro. I'm proud of what I've done, a poetic rally cry to the women of Paris to remember names, dates, and fight against the Boches with the power of words, because the day we get justice *will* come.

Women of Paris

I speak to you of daisies and flowers and the bloom of womanhood,

Taken from you… or someone you love.

Violated, humiliated

By the enemy

In their jackboots and beetle green.

I say to you, don't forget!

Remember. Names. Dates.

The day will come when your heart,

Your soul, your body,

Will once again be whole.

We will find justice.

And we, the women of Paris, will triumph over the Boches.

I turn onto Rue Saint-Honoré, skip past the dress shops and perfume shops like the House of Doujan. I can't wait to show Michal. He should return any day from the Free Zone. He's gathering intelligence about a rumored takeover of Lyon. The Nazis want to occupy *all* of France, which will greatly inhibit our Underground activities. Not to mention the mandatory work requirement that is now in effect. Frenchmen have been conscripted to labor in German factories. I miss him so, but after we returned from Jonzac, there was a tenseness between us we couldn't ignore. It put us off our game. We were missing cues in the field, chargers didn't go off, too much dynamite, too little. I memorized the wrong coordinates of the target and we blew up an empty railcar. We weren't good together anymore in the field.

In short, we broke up our partnership.

I'm still not over it, but it's for the best.

That doesn't mean I don't miss him.

I lower my eyes, my lashes wet with salty tears that come upon me all at once, my mood altering to a gentle sadness. We had some good times, bantering back and forth, and we had such scary times, running from Nazi guards firing at us. But always together as a team. When I told him I loved him, put it out there that I wanted more than a slap on the back, that he'd won my heart, we lost the magic. And I don't know how to get it back.

The sting of his rejection cut deep.

It haunts me every day.

Then everything in the Underground shifts. The Nazis start catching on we aren't all Communists and starry-eyed students, but true Frenchmen and women, ready to die rather than give up names, addresses. Networks dissolve because of dissidence and frequent raids by the Gestapo; informants are everywhere. It's too dangerous for us to operate out in the open. I give up making explosives—I can't get the materials I need. Even when I do, the Germans are stepping up their patrols and I know, if I'm caught, the Gestapo will have me in their clutches in no time. Besides, the railyards have a new 'cargo' they're transporting east, so precious I'd die if my work had anything to do with derailing those trains.

Jews.

After the roundup at Pithiviers and what I saw when that mother was raped, I want to do more than blow up German depots. I want to record what I've seen, write it down so others will tell *their* stories and spread the word with their tracts now and after the war. I call it a 'daisy chain' with each woman adding her story, and the more stories, the stronger the chain. I needed a symbol for my cause and it took me no more than ten seconds to sketch what's been festering in my soul since the day I lost Justine.

*3 Pétales.*

A daisy flower with three petals missing.

*Liberté, égalité, fraternité.*

I call it this because the Nazis ripped them from the heart of every Frenchwoman.

Hours later and my satchel is nearly empty and my stomach is growling. I must have walked from one end of Paris to the other, up the grand boulevards and down, a slight drizzle earlier making the pavement slick, but I'm back in Montmartre and close to Iris's apartment on Rue Damrémont. On my last stop, I handed out leaflets in front of Sacré-Coeur and would have emptied my bag if a kind priest calling himself Father Armand hadn't warned me the German patrol makes a sweep through here every afternoon. *They'll arrest you*, he said, and off I go to La Santé Prison for speaking my mind. I thanked him and moved on, humming a tune. I'm not worried about the Nazis recognizing me as Ève Beaufort, since I've dyed my short hair blonde.

Curling at the nape of my neck, it took more than two hours to get this color, sitting in the storage room in Iris's apartment. Her stylist set up a makeshift salon with hard-to-get dyes for any resistant needing a new identity. I only have to worry about dark roots, but who doesn't have dark roots in Paris these days?

I left Luc Dumont back at Jonzac.

He's still a wanted 'man' along with his 'brother' for stealing weapons and beating up a Nazi informant. My new identity is a blonde. Meet Viviane Longré. Typist. Teacher. Still, I can't take chances. Instead of staying at Iris's apartment, I move from one hiding place to the next, thanks to Claude. The reserved fixer and bomb-maker speaks little and always wears a black leather right glove to hide the jagged, red scars from an explosion, but he's a genius at putting together detonators and mixing the right chemicals. He taught me how to use my skills with making bombs. When I told him I needed a duplicating machine to make copies of my *3 Pétales* tracts, he set me up with a printer who once ran a dry-cleaning shop on the ground floor of a building in the Marais district. The printer then set me up with his cousin and then his wife's cousin and so on. Everywhere I go, I drag my small typewriter with me. I paid a visit to the pawnshop on Rue Saint-Jacques at Claude's suggestion and when I told the man there what I wanted it for, he insisted I take the typewriter and 'write the Nazis out of history'. The printer somehow supplies the paper and ink. I print up two, three hundred leaflets, distribute them, and then move on to the next shop or apartment. It's too dangerous for me to stay in one place for too long.

At times, I forget where I am when I wake up in the morning. The only thing I recognize is the ink stains on my fingers.

But my heart is full, my writing giving me what I need right now.

I'm in the fight.

I walk faster and my platform heel catches on a broken cobblestone. *Uh-oh!* I spin around in a circle, slipping on the wet pavement and taking a tumble, hitting my backside on the hard stone.

*Ouch... that hurt.*

I got so used to wearing trousers, I find it strange wearing skirts and sweaters and flared wool coats. And platform heels. I could try my hand at cutting up a skirt and making culottes, but I'm terrible at sewing. I'd love to ask Maman for help, but the time I steal with her is so precious, I don't want to waste it or put her in danger. Every other Thursday, I queue up for bread when Maman shows up with her empty basket at the boulangerie near the great market of Les Halles wearing a roses-and-daisies head-scarf tied under her chin. Dark glasses. If I don't see her, I keep walking.

I notice on our short visits Maman smiles a lot, which surprises me as she chats with the person behind her loud enough for me to hear. We don't speak directly to each other lest she's being watched. She spouts snippets of life at Maison Bleue to keep me up to date. Like Madame de Giocomte is playing the cello again and Cook has a cold, and oh, guess what? Their house guest has an adorable little girl named Ninette.

I smile big. So I was right about the child. A bright spot in Maman's life and Madame de Giocomte's.

And now mine, too.

I'm overwhelmed by a sisterly memory that brings a tear to my eye. Justine loved those old *Ninette* serials. I'm not surprised she named her little girl after the cinema heroine. I hum to myself, thinking about Justine's child as I get on my knees and start gathering up the leaflets. I bet she's the image of her *maman* with golden curls and—

'Need a hand?' a sweet voice asks.

I look up, suspicious, and I see Coralie grinning down at me. Like a run in your stocking, she ruins your day. She always did make me feel awkward and plain, even when I first met her at Iris's apartment when I joined the Resistance. Was she following me? And if so, why?

'You're in love with Michal, *mais non*?' Coralie asks, helping me gather the leaflets that spilled out of my satchel.

'Where do you get such crazy ideas?' I get to my feet, dust myself off.

'Iris. She said you were all glowy-eyed when you returned from your job at the munitions depot in Jonzac.' Her eyes widen. 'I heard you two had to make a run for it.'

I get right up into her face. 'We got the weapons and the grenades, didn't we?'

'Who was your contact?'

'A farmer. I don't remember his name.'

'The great Ève Beaufort forgets a name? You *are* slipping... or in love.'

She laughs, tosses her braids over her shoulders, looks around... for what? Something strange is going on. I don't like her questioning me. I keep what I know close to me. She's never asked me before about my contacts, or what missions I've pulled off. I don't trust her. Something's up. She's changed. She's more serious, deeper lines around her eyes, her mouth. That sweet innocence she always liked to project is gone. At first, I thought she was just jealous of Michal always choosing me for missions, and maybe that's all it still is, but my gut tells me not to trust her.

'Well, I'm off to the cinema,' she says, changing the subject. 'They're running a Sylvie Martone double feature of her old Ninette films at the Gaumont. You want to come?'

Why did she mention the name Ninette? Is it a trick? Does she know about Justine's child?

I whiz by her with a smirk on my face, giving nothing away. I need to get back to the safe house where I'm staying for a few days. I can't help but feel good about my work writing and distributing tracts. Last week I tossed a hundred leaflets from the balcony of the Gaumont then made my escape.

'No, I can't. I—I have to get more ink.'

'Too bad...' Her voice trails off as she scans the leaflet. '*Women of Paris, unite!* Really, Ève? Who reads this stuff?'

I grab the paper out of her hand. 'Lay off, Coralie, I don't need your help.'

'Suits me.' She winces. 'You honestly think women will join you on your stupid crusade?'

'Why not? The Boches don't care who they hurt. It's not just Jews being persecuted, but brave Frenchmen and women risking their lives to join the fight and suffering at the hands of these monsters. I know. I've seen it with my own eyes.'

'Have you?' She gets huffy. 'You're lying. I doubt you know what the Nazis are capable of.'

'Do you?' I ask.

She pulls back. 'No, of course not, but I heard the stories. The sexual intimidation. The cigarette burns on your skin.' She pulls on her sweater sleeves until they cover her hands, shivering even on a very warm day. Her next words arouse my curiosity. 'Who knows what a girl would have to do to survive.'

'How can you even *think* that?' I accuse her, not believing what I'm hearing. 'I pray *you* never find yourself in the hands of the Gestapo, Coralie. I'd rather die than give up my comrades.'

'Why, *you bitch*. You'll be sorry you said that. *Real* sorry.'

Without another word, she pedals off on her bicycle, making me wonder why she kept pulling at her sweater sleeves.

What was she hiding? Was she attacked and trying to talk about it and I got huffy? I don't like her, but I won't forgive myself if I let her down... *Like I let Justine down? Will I ever get over it?*

* * *

'Ève, what's this I hear about you scattering leaflets all over Paris?' Michal bursts through the door of the apartment on the second floor, a room the size of a cubby hole. 'What crazy scheme are you up to now?'

When I heard the loud footsteps in the hallway, I shoved the latest batch of leaflets into the small iron stove, my heart racing, thinking it was the *Brigades spéciales.* They've stepped up their arrests in the past weeks.

I breathe out, happy it's Michal, looking more handsome than ever. *When did he get back?* 'It's obvious you don't approve.'

'I don't.'

'I didn't need to ask your permission.' I open the oven door, pull out fifty copies of my latest tract.

'I told you to cool down, get your priorities back on, and this is what you do?'

'And what were *you* doing? Snuggling up with the mamselles in Lyon?'

He snickers. 'My dear Ève, you *do* have a curious mind.'

'Coralie is back.'

I wait for his reaction, maybe a sparkle in his eyes, a sexy smirk. That's not what I see. More like worry lines crossing his brow. 'I know. I heard she showed up at Remi's hungry and crying, saying she had nowhere to go. He's a softie for girls who need help, though Iris wasn't too happy when he let her sleep on the divan. She doesn't like the girl nosing about the apartment so

Iris told her if she wanted to work with us again, she had to help you distribute leaflets.'

That explains how she found me.

He takes a beat, then, 'Coralie always has an agenda. Did she say where she's been?'

'No... and I didn't ask.'

'Did she ask you about me?' he asks. 'Or Remi?'

'*No*,' I lie with emphasis, not wanting to talk about her and how she accused me of being in love with Michal. 'Will you take a look at what I've written? I'd like your opinion.'

Michal picks up a leaflet, scans it, smiles. 'A *daisy*, Ève?'

'Why not? It's a bit like a fleur-de-lis, which is the national flower of France.'

He keeps reading. 'It's not bad, pretty good actually.'

'*Merci*.' I lower my eyes. I won't show him how happy that makes me even if he doesn't mention my new hair color or that I look like a girl again.

'I admire what you're doing, Ève, but leaving leaflets on benches won't win the war.'

I look longingly at this strong, virile man who's seen so much killing. Why does he refuse to accept the power of the pen? I think if he did, he'd know why I must also take my fight to a different level. 'Words are powerful, too, Michal. We need the people of France behind us, not collaborating with the Nazis.'

Why I said that, I don't know. Or do I? Coralie, of course. Her smugness bothered me, like she's more comfortable in her skin because the Nazis are watching her back. The way she acted continues to nag at me, but I keep my thoughts to myself. I don't want to accuse her of something too horrible for me to believe about *any* partisan.

'You sound like my father, Ève. He wrote anti-Nazi leaflets before they arrested him.'

'He sounds like a brave man.'

'He was,' Michal says in a way that suggests he'll say no more on that subject.

'Words are so powerful that even when you *don't* say them, their meaning is clear in a man's eyes.' I pause. 'Like yours.'

'Oh? And what am I thinking?'

'That you want to share what's bothering you, why my writing is upsetting you.'

'I don't know what you're talking about.'

'Michal, what is it? Please. I thought we shared everything.'

'I'm not good with words, Ève, but I'm worried distributing these leaflets will get you killed.'

The pain in his eyes is excruciating, forcing me to press further with my questions. 'Go on, I'm listening.'

'You never do take *no* for an answer, do you?' He shoots me that grin I know so well. And love.

'Not when I see you in such pain.'

'I never intended to tell you this, but that letter I received was from an old family friend in Warsaw.' He takes a moment. 'He claimed the bodies of my father... *and* then recently, my sister.'

'Your sister?'

He nods. 'Tessa took over printing the pamphlets after they arrested my father. She was a smart girl and liked reading books, her funny glasses sliding down her nose. When the Gestapo came for my father, she tried to fight back, but they pushed her down and broke her glasses. Afterward, they followed her for weeks, gleaning names, addresses, but she couldn't see as well and—'

'Yes, Michal?'

'Tessa was arrested... We can't be certain what happened next, but there were rumors about how female prisoners spent days in solitary confinement before being raped and turned into sexual slaves,' Michal says, and I feel a twinge in my heart that makes my chest hurt at hearing this man I love recount his sister's fate, his voice so hoarse each word catches in his throat. 'Then when a girl was no longer useful, they executed her.' He breathes out, hard. 'Tessa was shot in the back of the head.'

'Michal, I'm so sorry…' I reach out to him and for a moment I feel him wanting to let go, to stop being so strong and let me in. But then the Polish fighter puts up the defense I know so well and the moment is gone, lost between us.

Finally, he speaks and it's not what I expect to hear. 'I'd rather die, Ève, than see anything like that happen to you.'

Before I can utter a word, tell him how much that means to me, he leaves as quickly as he came. But not before giving me a quick kiss.

*The man cares about me.* He said so, and I have to be satisfied with that.

And a kiss.

I touch my lips and smile.

# 21

## PARIS, OCTOBER 1942

*Justine*

I'm pregnant. Again.

Meaning I'm in deep trouble with the major... because he *isn't* the father. Arsène is the only man who can be the father of the child growing within me. How will the SS officer react? I don't know and that's what makes my blood run cold. He dropped in without notice this afternoon, informing me with his usual sneer that he has something important to discuss with me.

I have no idea what it is.

I'm more concerned with how to tell him about my condition.

I will never forget how he struck me across the face when he found out I was pregnant with Ninette. My dearest child, with the sixth sense for crying at just the right moment to interrupt the major when he torments me with a new request, determined to wield his power over me. Like ordering a different wine to please his special guest from the ERR, the task force organized to plunder Jewish books and art. And last week he didn't like the velvet rose gown I wore because it wasn't red enough to go with the Nazi flag he'd insisted be hung in the foyer.

Or barking orders at me. 'Herr Geller is among the guests tomorrow,' he yelled. 'Don't sit him next to General von Klum. They hate each other.'

I still marvel how such a sweet child as Ninette was born from such a horrible man, but I'm grateful to the angels for bringing her to me. I'm experiencing different emotions with the baby I now carry, a deep contentment in my heart because this child was created from healing, not only in my body, but my soul. I feel the two babies share an unbreakable bond though, even if they don't share the same father. A provocative question lays down a track in my brain.

I wonder, could this child *also* be a girl?

I sigh. It would be wonderful, like having Ève home again, watching the two little girls growing up together here at Maison Bleue. My own little *Daisy Sisters*. An idyllic thought I must erase from my heart. Having Ève home won't happen.

I wonder if my sister is still involved with the Resistance. I don't know where she is. I haven't seen her since that day at Hôtel Drouot months ago. My heart tugs, a lonely tug I feel often. Unless she reappears, this will be the second time she won't be with me when the baby comes. I have Maman and Madame de Giocomte, of course, but it's not the same.

I didn't mean to get pregnant. We had to forgo protection at times, my hormones raging to take down the impenetrable steel armor I'd wrapped around my heart. Believe in myself as a woman again. That I *can* love a man. And I did. Which leaves me in a *very* dangerous position.

The major hasn't required sex from me for months. Mind

you, he never *made love* to me; his arrogance doesn't permit he put himself on equal footing with a woman. Still, I live in fear of him discovering my secret meetings with Arsène. I adore him, but our times as lovers don't come often enough. I sneak in through the back kitchen entrance at Chez Mimi with my hair covered by a pleated turban, dark glasses, a tight, garish dress and platform heels so I look like the other girls. I crouch down low, my heels in my hand, head bent and go up to the third floor in the dumbwaiter, the smell of garlic and jasmine at war with each other in the confined space, making my nose twitch. Then we cuddle and sigh *and* make love under the sheets in the Blue Marquis Room.

*Clean sheets,* courtesy of Madame Mimi.

That makes me chuckle.

The major notices my moment of mirth and shoots me an odd look. He must be wondering what made me smile since I often have a scowl on my face when he drops in unexpectedly. He bounded through the front door, leaving his cap and gloves on—it chills me, remembering he didn't remove either when he assaulted me—tapping his fingers on his arms.

It was after the purple twilight shadows had melted into the darkness, leaving me feeling vulnerable. I had nowhere to hide from him and no choice but to allow him to follow me around while I rearranged the fresh flowers in the foyer, checked the menu for tonight's soiree, doing my 'every-little-thing-must-be-perfect' tour. He grunted his surprise when he saw a square card table with a green felt top set up in the drawing room with playing cards and red, blue, and yellow chips instead of the buffet dinner of beef and creamed chicken and roasted potatoes the Nazi SS officers gorge on at least once a week.

'What's so amusing, Rachelle?'

'Your expression, Major, when you saw the decks of playing cards,' I come up with an answer to mislead him. 'Like you don't approve of gambling. I would have thought you were a man eager to tempt Lady Luck.'

'I leave nothing to chance, mademoiselle, especially when it comes to women.'

His words make the hair on the back of my neck rise. I'm more leery than ever to tell him my news. I never forgot the Jewish girl he raped then murdered to prevent a chance of her conceiving a child.

A quiet, ugly truth reigns in me. He must never find out the identity of this baby's father.

So I shall forgo telling him about my pregnancy for as long as possible. Since this is my second child, I will most likely develop a rounded tummy earlier though. Before five months. By my calculations, I'm only currently twelve weeks along. I must have conceived two weeks after that horrible day of the roundup when I rescued Maman and Madame de Giocomte. I remember making love with Arsène on a hot night, falling into each other's arms with a joy I don't regret. I'm safe, for now.

'Speaking of which, I told General von Klum he needed more than liquor and women to keep your Nazi friends satisfied,' I coo sweetly in his ear. I had in fact suggested a card party after the general expressed he wanted a change after a night of drinking and gawking at the girls from Chez Mimi running about in the *maison* wearing nothing but purple satin and ivory lace girdles, black stockings and garters, filmy nude peignoirs and pumps. His desire for a change surprised me; in fact, a lot about him surprises me these days. He's not the bon vivant I'd met at Bal Tabarin back in 1941.

'Card party?' asks the major.

'Yes. Bridge, poker. Something to stimulate their minds.'

'It's not their minds I want you to stimulate, Rachelle.'

'Oh, I see… Madame Mimi is cutting you in on the action?'

He doesn't deny it when he kisses my hand. I cringe. Every time I get close to him, I break out into a sweat. 'Did I tell you that you make a lovely hostess?'

I pull my hand away. 'I'd imagined you found other interests to satisfy your appetite.'

'None as beautiful as you, Rachelle. However, it's my work for the ERR that keeps me busy or I'd visit you more often.'

'Stealing paintings… or women?'

'Both,' he whispers in my ear.

'We've nothing left here at Maison Bleue for you to take.' I tread carefully, leading him back to the foyer. I hear the guests arriving with choruses of 'Heil Hitler' off key, though I don't feel the parquet floors shake from the defiant boot stomping and clicking of heels. A quieter group this evening? Am I to be spared endless renditions of brotherhood drinking songs?

*Hmm*… interesting. Something's up. I can feel it… *but what*?

'I don't need to take what I already own.' He squeezes my bare upper arm. Tight. Like a leather band compressing my flesh. A habit I detest. It leaves marks and I dread having to explain the bruises to Arsène. I know he'd welcome the opportunity to go one-on-one with the major. I've stopped him more than once with, *What if they arrest you? I'll lose you… Our child will lose you*. Imagine my relief when Arsène embraced me tight and kissed me all over when he found out we were blessed with conceiving a child. I shall never forget it.

And I can't forget the tightrope I walk.

'Does that include me?' I ask, keeping up the banter. *Don't let him see your happiness; he'll suspect something*.

'Yes. And the child.'

I stiffen. 'You can do what you want to me, but my daughter is off limits.'

'For now, Rachelle. With America in the war, I've altered my plans to take the child to Berlin at this time. I don't want her in harm's way should the Americans send bombers to Germany, though it's not likely.'

'Isn't it?' I raise a brow. 'General von Klum says it *will* happen. It's an open secret the Allies are planning an invasion, landing either here in France or North Africa.'

'General von Klum is a doddering old fool. I sometimes wonder where his loyalties lie.'

*So do I.*

'I can't stay long, Rachelle. I have other business tonight before my train leaves in the morning.'

*Where's he going?*

'Before the evening gets underway—' he begins.

'With a card game,' I remind him. 'Then we'll serve open-faced sandwiches and beer.'

'I need to speak to you about why I'm here.'

'It's not to torment me?'

He grins. 'It's about Ninette actually.'

*He said her name*, and that sends shudders through me.

'Yes?'

'It's too dangerous to travel to Berlin, but I intend to take us to the Berghof near Berchtesgaden next spring for Hitler's birthday party. The Führer loves children.' He smiles wide. 'I intend to bring him a special gift too. *The Daisy Sisters*.'

'No, you *can't*.'

'*Pardon,* mademoiselle?'

He thinks I mean the painting of Justine and me. No, what

worries me is my baby is due in May. I'll be as big as a house. I'll get no mercy from him when he finds out.

'You stole the painting, then kidnapped me,' I protest. 'How can you give the Führer soiled goods?'

'Exactly, Rachelle.' He sneers at me through elegantly shaped nostrils, enjoying the moment. 'The invitation is for me and the child *only*.'

I'm at a loss for words, stunned. *Ninette alone in the Eagle's Nest?* He's hurt me bad, like carving out my heart, and he knows it. Why do I have the feeling this news is not only to upset me but also to keep me on my toes? To remind me that neither I nor my child are safe anywhere, even here at Maison Bleue.

His clear blue eyes glow. The glee of putting me in my place is so evident in those eyes I shudder to think what he'll do when he finds out I'm pregnant again. With another man's baby.

*Can I fool the major into believing it's* his *baby? Why not? Change the delivery date. I doubt the major keeps track of his sexual encounters. What choice do I have?*

I admit my idea has holes, lots of holes. I'm not a trained spy —the world of tradecraft is something I've learned through experience and guidance from Arsène—but I believe even the most articulate agent would struggle to know what to do here. The irony is, I will lose *both* my babies if I don't execute my plan to perfection to keep them safe from this man.

The major smiles. 'We shall discuss the details of the trip to Hitler's mountain retreat after I return from Nice. We're still organizing the paintings purchased at the Hôtel Savoy auction last summer... including *The Daisy Sisters*. Adieu.'

He leaves without another word, barely acknowledging the three SS officers removing their caps and their side arms and placing them on the long table dressed with Mademoiselle de

Giocomte's finest Austrian lace white linen while I digest this strange and worrisome news.

It's moments like these I realize I'm living in a dream world where I choose what to believe or not, that Ninette is *my* baby, no one else's. I have a tendency to soften the edges of my little girl's existence, add a blur to anything in the background that disturbs me. Which is why I keep her upstairs with Madame de Giocomte during these rollicking parties in the back of the house where it's quiet and she can sleep undisturbed, with Maman serving and me as hostess.

The truth is, my little girl isn't safe anywhere.

* * *

'Three kings, two queens.'

'You win, General von Klum. *Again.*' I look at the other three SS officers grunting and bellowing and drinking warm beer, their half-eaten sandwiches littered about, but the mood isn't what I thought it would be. Very contained, restrained. Conversation is mostly in German, which the general is aware I *don't* speak, and that's what sets the stage for what I believe is a story so unbelievable I get goosebumps every time the three SS officers make a call in the poker game, fold their cards, ignore their growing pots of winnings or losses, then say something in German, argue... then ask for a new deck of cards.

The general is winning tonight, but I detect something else is at play here. A secret meeting where they know they won't be overheard. Awkward glances in my direction every time someone raises his voice, looks from these strange Wehrmacht and SS officers that are nothing like the salacious looks I receive from our usual 'guests', looks that remind me of a slimy worm curling up inside a jackboot. Not here. These Nazis smoke too much, drink beer but don't get drunk, and whisper among themselves. I imagine them saying, *Who is she? What does she know? Can we trust her?*

The general is very *hush hush* about the soiree he holds in the library tonight. He was explicit about *who* was coming and absolutely no one but me would attend to them. Then a twinkle and a smile to lighten the mood, only to be replaced by a fierceness in his eyes when he arrived and saw the major on his way out. A quick, imperious Heil Hitler then he hustled his guests into the library, but their voices were *too* loud, *too* filled with laughter. As if they're faking it.

*Why the secrecy?*

When I ask him, he says, 'There are those who think differently now, mademoiselle, but are too old to do anything about it. Then there are those who are not.'

I sense a change in him; he's more cautious, spilling information then taking it back, looking around to see if anyone is listening to our conversations. And most important, he's not as flippant around the major. Like he doesn't trust him.

I don't either.

I have a hunch what the general is about, a seed planted in my brain a while ago from my many conversations with him, a man I saw at first as a typical Nazi, awkward around women, boisterous, full of conceit and Aryan smugness. But over the past year and a half, I've seen a different man. Worried about his troops, writing letters to their families when they're killed in battle, critical of the push for dominance by the Führer and his henchmen.

And he's kind to Ninette. Taking her on his knee and laughing with her. The major never does that.

Now, tonight, I'm more convinced than ever he's conspiring

to do *something*, but I need more evidence before I bring my findings to Arsène.

Bottom line? I know General von Klum is far from happy with how the war is going on the Eastern Front as well as the incessant roundups of Jews, the destruction of the cultural heritage of not only Jews but Roma. He brings up his frustration every time I see him with a sadness coloring his voice that puzzles me, but he doesn't explain. *The ramblings of an old man, mademoiselle.*

I sense it has something to do with his own aristocratic background, banished when Hitler took power, but his mood isn't that of a hardened general. It's more personal. With the British RAF bombing Berlin, I wondered if it has anything to do with his family. He admitted his wife died years ago and he has no children. He only has his nephew in the Luftwaffe. All I know is that it's no secret the German Army didn't achieve the quick victory they planned after they invaded Russia last year, boasting they'd be in Moscow in weeks. The Allies are gaining ground according to Radio Londres reports, causing a subtle shift among Parisians the general is worried about. He hears too often from informants that the citizens of Paris are questioning the presence of the occupiers and that the Allies haven't abandoned them. They *will* liberate Paris, they say, so why not help them?

Which explains the Gestapo push to recruit *more* informants.

The general warns me to be diligent, that the secret police promise rewards to anyone coming forward with information about anything, from hiding Jews to keeping pigs. And the price for the arrest of a political dissident? A thousand francs. A paltry price considering a new pair of shoes costs over two thousand five hundred francs.

I'm also surprised to discover from General von Klum that holiday excursions to Paris are part of the Nazi plan, a means of helping their fighting men regaining strength and spirit after grueling duty in the field. Not for these officers. They left before midnight with tense smiles, curt nods, and no Heil Hitler salutes.

Odd.

Which brings me to my tête-à-tête with this very unusual general at 1 a.m. in the library. Two shots of after-dinner lemon liqueur and frank conversation.

* * *

'It's true, mademoiselle, the Vaterland takes care of the soldier's physical needs,' he says, referring to the Nazi-run brothels, 'but it fails to give their brains a holiday from the prattle from Berlin.'

A strange choice of words. I probe him further. 'Tell me more about this "prattle from Berlin". What is Hitler up to besides adding fish eggs to his diet?' I ask, though I doubt the Führer even knows Russian caviar *is* fish eggs.

He laughs, tickles me under the chin like a precocious child. 'You have a curious mind, mademoiselle, *and* beautiful legs.' He pats me on the knee. 'If I were twenty years younger, I'd seduce you and find out why you ask so many questions.'

'And if you *were* twenty years younger, I'd let you,' I quip, raising my glass. My cheeks tint and I realize my quip gave me the perfect time to bring up that favor I need. 'You remember the roundup in July of Jewish women and children?'

'How can I forget it, mademoiselle?' He downs his liqueur with one gulp. 'I never did go along with that edict we all signed last January. Damn cold weather at Wannsee set off my arthritis.'

'Monsieur?' I ask, confused.

'I can't explain, Rachelle, except to tell you the deportation of Jews is accelerating beyond last summer's stadium roundup. The daily quotas that sadist Dannecker has decreed be met every day try my soul.'

I don't know the name, but it's obvious the general is privy to inside information. He's my only hope to save Madame's sister-in-law, her daughter, and her granddaughters. I was hesitant to ask him before because I wasn't sure I could trust him, seeing how anyone sympathetic to Jews can be arrested and sent to Cherche-Midi prison. I can still see Delphine wearing my blue dress, hugging her little sisters tight. I envied her closeness to them, wondering where my sister Ève is, wishing I could give *her* comfort. Or am I the one needing comfort?

What I'm about to do goes against my code... yet I feel compelled to go forward with it. 'Madame de Giocomte's family, the baroness, her daughter, and her four granddaughters, were caught up in that roundup and sent to Drancy. The last we heard, the children were still there, though we have no information on the baroness and her daughter.' I take a breath, wet my lips. 'I'd be willing to grant your wish, General... if I can save their lives.'

His eyes widen. '*Mademoiselle*... Rachelle, do you know what you're proposing?'

'Yes.' I pull up my gown high enough to show off my legs, trying to look sexy, though my heart isn't in it. I entered this agreement as a Nazi major's mistress and now I carry the child of a Resistance fighter. A man I love. Arsène will *say* he understands, but does he? What man wants such a woman?

I face a blinding fear whatever happens, but I fear more the wrath of God and my unborn child condemning my soul to damnation... and losing the faith in myself I cherish.

I lower my eyes, lashes resting against my cheeks like lacy fans to hide my thoughts. I fold my hands across my belly to protect this child I carry, ashamed I'd even think about doing such a thing, but I'm desperate to do what I can to save the baroness and her family. Yet, I can't shame myself. This time I have a choice. I break down. I can't stop the tears welling up in my eyes. I can't go through with this charade.

'Tears, mademoiselle?' the general says in a calm voice. 'For them... or for you?'

'Both, General. I'm a coward. I can't sleep with you and I can't tell you why. I was wrong to say so. What am I going to do? I can't let them die.'

'I fear from the reports I've read, Madame's family including the children may have already been deported to Auschwitz and died there.' He sighs heavily. 'You're a brave woman, mademoiselle, and I'm flattered by your proposal. But I've seen how this war has turned good women into making bargains with the devil to survive. I won't let that happen to you. We shall not speak of it again. I'll have my aide contact the Kommandant at the transit camp, see what he can do.' He kisses my cheek. 'Enough sadness, mademoiselle. I'd rather talk about how beautiful you look tonight, the glow radiating from you I saw once before when we first met at Bal Tabarin.' He notices my hands lying across my belly. 'Who is the lucky man?'

I pretend to look shocked. 'I'm the major's girl, General, or have you forgotten?'

'I haven't... but maybe you have.'

I panic. I can't tell him the truth but I can't lie to him either, give him any reason to go to the major with his suspicions. That I've been unfaithful to him... *Wait*, unfaithful to what? My rapist? No, I have no regrets about loving Arsène, carrying his child. But the SS officer is too arrogant and self-absorbed and sees only his own distorted logic. I slept with another man. He won't rest until he finds out who the baby's father is and orders him killed to salvage his pride. And God help me if Herr Geller finds out, I'll be arrested, my child taken from me. I shudder to think what will happen to the baby.

'You're right, General,' I admit, 'the major hasn't come to my bed in months. It's not his child.'

'Your secret is safe with me, I promise.' He smiles wide. 'It gives me great joy to see you happy, Rachelle.' He stands up, pours himself another shot of liqueur. 'A toast to your unborn baby.'

'*Merci*, but I fear the major will try to harm my child when he finds out.'

He winks at me. 'Not if you tell him *I'm* the baby's father.'

'Why would you do this, General?'

'Karl, my dear.'

'Karl.' I smile. 'Why take on that responsibility?'

'Whatever you may think of me, I'm not a monster. I was born to privilege and acted accordingly, fighting for my country when called upon, doing things I'm not proud of and for which I shall pay when this war is over but—'

'Yes?'

'I will *not* kill babies.'

'I don't understand...'

'It's simple logistics. If the major and the Gestapo believe you're carrying my child, you won't be deported to Auschwitz for your indiscretion, nor undergo the special cruelty allocated for pregnant political prisoners.'

'What is that?' I ask, curious.

'Those women are allowed to give birth.'

'Why would that be cruel?'

'Because then your child will be taken from you, strangled, then dumped into a suitcase and added to the pile of "luggage" sitting on the train tracks at Auschwitz, to be disposed of as quickly as possible.'

'It can't be true.' I lean over, my stomach turning, nausea hitting me.

He puts his arm around my shoulders to comfort me. 'After the war, you must bring the guilty to justice and tell the world what happened here. I won't be around, not if my plans fail.' He kisses me on the forehead. 'And now, I must placate a very snobby Wehrmacht official waiting for news from the front.'

He leaves and I ponder for a long time afterward our strange conversation.

What is the general about? *Will I ever know?*

# 22

## PARIS, FEBRUARY 1943

*Ève*

Coralie—the girl with the impish braids, flirty lips, squeaky voice, who I remember playing an innocent schoolgirl in white ankle socks and rope-soled shoes—is a Gestapo informant.

My God, it's nightmare I'll never stop seeing in my dreams.

She did the unthinkable. Giving up our names, the address on Rue Damrémont where we meet, telling the French police when we'd all be together on a night black and wet like printer's ink. It was so dark it hid them from the old man on watch in the street below. The trio of *Brigades spéciales* took him down with a sharp blow to the head, leaving him in the gutter, rain washing away the blood but not the deed.

Then the plainclothesmen made their way up the stairwell to the second floor like fallen spirits with no allegiance to good. Only evil. Nazi evil. They broke down the heavy door, yelling, hollering, calling out our names, grabbing Claude and Iris and slamming them against the apartment's flimsy walls so hard the Apache dagger Remi threw into the plaster shook loose and fell to the floor. Remi, Michal, and I were in the back storage room when two Gestapo men rushed in and grabbed the others, new agents I just met—eight of us working on a plan to blow up a German depot outside Paris. My heart bleeds for them. A teacher from Rouen and a young, married couple who'd made their way north from Lyon. A mother with two children she'd left at home with her *maman.*

And now the two men are dead. So is the fixer and bomb-maker Claude.

I rushed back to the parlor to help... Michal grabbed me, but not before I got a quick look at the horror unfolding. The shock of seeing Claude lying face down in his own pool of blood kicked me in the stomach, a single bullet to the back of the head. But first, he'd knocked over the lamp shining over the large map spread out on the round table, sending the room into semi-darkness. Then a shot rang out. I caught a brief glance of his lifeless body before we heard Iris and the *maman* from Lyon screaming, the French policemen grabbing them by the hair and forcing them down on their knees, then handcuffing them. I knew what came next. They pushed the two women into a black van and sent them to La Santé prison for political prisoners, as Drancy was only for Jews awaiting deportation, then on to a concentration camp in Germany or Poland.

Michal gave Remi a hard look because he wanted to stay and take on the French police and Gestapo, but we'd learned it was more important to live and go on fighting.

The three of us escaped through the back window down a thick seaman's rope twisted with steel fibers Michal insisted Iris keep hidden in a box of old clothes. We could have tried going up on the roof and then over to the next building, but with the rain coming down in a steady stream, I didn't hesitate to follow Remi unfurling the makeshift escape line, then lower myself over the side and make a quiet descent with Michal following behind me, then Remi. We wouldn't have had a chance to escape if Michal hadn't called us to the back storage room. I know the pain he suffers with the loss of his father and sister and his fiancée, but for the first time he shared with me how he smuggled Jewish children out of the Warsaw ghetto. That explains his resolve to answer the plea from a priest who needs forged identity cards for Jewish school children holed up in a convent. Twin sisters. He gave me the photos and I had the names on a piece of paper, but I had no time to memorize them.

I stuffed the paper and photos into my jacket pocket.

Our lives were at stake.

Michal locks me in his arms so tight I can hardly breathe, the pelting rain drenching my hair, my clothes, as we race into a dark alleyway, but I'm alive.

*Alive.*

'I knew something was wrong when Coralie shied away from coming to the meeting tonight,' Remi says, pulling up his collar. The rain hits us hard, but it creates a diversion. The *Brigades spéciales* give up looking for us... for now, and the two Gestapo men in their slick black raincoats never come out of the building. Waiting for us to come back. Because of Coralie's betrayal of the Jade network, they know who we are.

The irony is, they don't know who *I* am.

I never showed Coralie my new identity card.

We're on the run, making our way down the hills of Montmartre, headed for the old Jewish quarter. Now if we can make it down the Butte, wind our way through the narrow side streets toward the Seine, we have a fighting chance to find that safe house Remi is muttering about, intelligence he got from his comrade from his old days with the notorious Lafont gang. His boyhood chum refused to join La Milice, the French Gestapo.

Instead, he's been hiding out in an abandoned Jewish dry goods shop in the Marais.

'Can you trust this friend of yours?' Michal asks Remi, suspicion clouding the tone of his voice.

'With my life.'

'Why did Coralie betray us?' I don't like the girl, but selling us out to the Nazis is something I can't wrap my head around. I should have seen through her. Like the way she asked too many questions, not just about Michal and me, but she was too curious about our mission in Jonzac, and that should have aroused my suspicions. But no, I was so self-conscious about my failed attempt at lovemaking with Michal, I didn't see her true colors.

'Money,' Michal says, 'or she was picked up by the Gestapo and promised her freedom if she gave us up.'

Remi smacks his fist into his palm over and over. I've never seen him show so much emotion it's painful to watch. 'Iris was loud and brassy, but she loved me... and Claude was like a brother to me. That *damn bitch* is going to pay.'

'We don't know for sure she betrayed us,' I sputter, raindrops wetting my lips. *Why am I defending her?*

'*If* Coralie is guilty of selling us out to the Gestapo—' Michal says slowly, keeping me wrapped up in his embrace. We catch our breath inside a church, surprised to find the front door unlocked like before the war. *Why is he holding me tight? So I don't run?* I sense he's concerned about my reaction to what he clearly sees as a problem. 'She's a threat to not only us,' he continues, 'but also to every Resistance fighter she has come in contact with. Your safety depends on mine and so on. She must be dealt with, Ève. There's no other way.'

I look from Michal to Remi, our faces shiny and golden under the tall, burning candles on the altar, intense fury in their eyes. They know something they won't tell me, and it terrifies me.

'What will happen to her?' I have to ask.

'We have only one way to deal with traitors.' Remi looks straight at me.

'Yes?' I ask.

'We execute them.'

'What? *No...*' I can't believe I'm hearing this in a church, the house of God, my ears burning, my senses reeling. I never expected *this*; she's a Frenchwoman. I can't believe she'd sell us out. Then it hits me. Didn't Justine? My own sister? *But she was raped,* I protest silently, taken against her will, and yet she tried to *save* me, not have me arrested, then killed.

I turn to look at Michal to refute Remi's words, to confirm that it isn't true. That we're not like *them*, the Nazis, that we don't murder traitors like Coralie without a trial. He doesn't. He says simply—

'We're at war, Ève.'

'Yes, but—'

'Taking a life will tear your guts out, wondering for days, weeks, afterward if God will judge you as a saint or sinner.'

'And which are you?'

'Each man, woman, decides that for himself.'

I groan, the sound coming from deep in my gut. I'm cold and wet and wanting to hit back at the evilness that's taken over my beloved Paris, the shock settling in that what I witnessed back on Rue Damrémont is a brutal reminder that war is a living hell and I'm caught in its deepest depths.

Even God can't get me out of this.

* * *

*Two weeks later...*

I stare at Coralie coming out of Gestapo headquarters where she went to collect her money for turning us in, counting the franc notes and licking her lips. She doesn't spot us observing her from behind a tall willow across the street. A black Gestapo Citroën motorcar is parked at the curb, and a Mercedes with that unnerving swastika flag on the hood is behind it. I can't stop looking at her, trying to understand this woman who dares to believe she's safe because the Nazis paid her to betray us.

*She's a wounded creature... which makes her dangerous.*

*She's also foolish.*

Remi agreed we needed evidence before we carried out the sentence, that she's not the first member of the Resistance to be put on trial before they're shot. Such a sentence is not carried out lightly, whether it's a planned hit where guilt is already established by a committee or a trial held under the judicious eye of a bright moon, the traitor shot, two witnesses present as Underground tradition demands with the commander of the Resistance unit conducting the trial and recording the event in a journal.

What happened here, her foray into Gestapo headquarters to receive money, is witnessed by a member of the Resistance, confirming it. Coralie is guilty of treason.

What's changed is me. Seeing Claude lying face down in his own blood, hearing Iris's terrified screams, a woman I never saw cry, hardened me. Michal helped me through the process as we sat in the safe house after the raid, the smell of stale air sticking in my throat, my clothes still wet, discussing the code every Resistance fighter follows. If you're captured, resist for a week, no matter *what* the torture, giving the cell time to move their location, get new identities, but *never* give up your comrades.

I never had to think about it. That someone *would* give up names. Until now.

My shoulders stiffen, my breath catches. I feel no emotional trauma observing the scene playing out before me. Knowing why Michal and I are here, to make a final decision. There is no doubt Coralie is guilty. She didn't try to hold out, from what we heard from our source inside Gestapo headquarters, a 'cleaning woman' with sharp eyes and ears and fluent in German. So many brave women fighting for France experienced torture, rape, and then death rather than give names, addresses, to the Gestapo.

*So how did Coralie come to this? A twisted sense of her own importance?*

'Remi found out from his source the Gestapo followed Coralie for weeks,' Michal tells me, 'noting her activities followed the same pattern. Pick up a knapsack at the train station, then bicycle to a different station and stash it in a locker.'

'How did she attract their interest in the first place?' I want to know.

'Coralie couldn't resist flirting and struck up a conversation with a young man at a café looking for an escape route out of France so he wouldn't have to report to local police for the mandatory work program in Germany. She told him she had "friends", meaning us, who could help him and—'

'Let me guess, he was a Gestapo informant.'

Michal nods. 'When the secret police confronted her at the train station and found leaflets and pamphlets in her knapsack, they arrested her.'

'Oh, my God, Michal, my *3 Pétales* tracts.' I panic. If the Gestapo knows I printed *3 Pétales*, I have no choice but to discontinue it. Or do I? No, I won't let the Nazis silence me. I'll keep writing.

'Yes, along with other pamphlets and papers she was delivering for Remi. They tortured her and promised her freedom if she gave up names and the address of our operation.'

'I almost feel sorry for her.'

*Don't. Claude is dead... Iris is in prison because of her.*

'She knew the risks we face every day, Ève, but she was always more interested in the game and what she could get for herself. What's more devastating is that Coralie didn't end her terrible deed with betraying us. She's apparently working for the Gestapo now, doing the bidding of an agent in the secret police named Herr Geller.'

I scream inside. 'I know him. The man is obsessed with crossword puzzles... and threatening Jews.' I'll never forget him harassing Madame de Giocomte the day I left Maison Bleue. 'When will she stop?'

'She won't. We have to stop *her*.'

It pains me to agree with him, but Michal is right, the evidence against Coralie is overwhelming. I can't refute his findings. He's dutiful, strong, and fair. I keep watching her, then see her get on a bicycle and put on lipstick, a deep red, then pedal away down Rue des Saussaies toward Avenue de Marigny. A gray Peugeot with a battered fender pulls up to the curb with Remi at the wheel and stops. I jump into the back and Michal slides into the passenger seat. I don't ask where Remi got the vehicle, I never do, or enough petrol to carry out the act. The motorcar moves slowly along the avenue flanked by five-story buildings in the elegant eighth arrondissement.

We're following Coralie. *Easy*. There are fewer bicycles on the boulevards since the Germans started confiscating them for their own use. We remain silent, each with our own thoughts but knowing how this turns out. We'll follow her until she's in an area with little traffic where Remi can slow down. Then Michal and I will get out of the motorcar and secure a hiding place where we'll serve as witnesses. Remi will get closer to her, fire at her with his revolver, then before she knows what happened to her, has time to process *why*, he'll speed away. Job done.

A sudden flash of nausea hits me. I know we're at war, I've accepted that, but I still can't come to grips with taking a girl's life on a cool spring day when she should be picking flowers and inhaling their scent. Instead, she'll breathe in the coppery smell of blood, her own. I want to grab Michal's hand, ask him one more time to convince me this is right, but he's staring straight ahead and taking in slow breaths. Calming his nerves. Remi is driving with one hand, the revolver in his left hand, ready to fire out the window at his target. The surety of how he handles the weapon while driving the motorcar tells me he's done this before. I hunch my shoulders, preparing for what happens next. Coralie will soon find out what happens to traitors. And in spite of the fact I know this is justice, I wonder how God will judge us.

It takes us a slow ten minutes to drive down the avenue then turn right onto the Champs-Élysées. The afternoon sun beams down, glinting off her bicycle rims. The sky is clear, no clouds. The usual traffic of Mercedes motorcars and German Army trucks amble down the boulevard with Coralie easing her way in and out of traffic on her bicycle, smiling and waving at the young Nazi soldiers hanging out of the back of the truck, flirting with them.

*How can she?* They're Boches.

But then, she doesn't care, *n'est-ce pas*? She has francs lining her pockets and I've no doubt she plans to add more. She disgusts me. And it's in that moment I accept what we're doing as right. She'll continue selling out anyone she can, doing the Gestapo's bidding, and others will suffer.

Or die.

We *have* to stop her.

'She's heading toward the Bois.' Michal puts his head out the window to get a better view.

'I'll take care of her,' Remi says. 'You two get out and follow her on foot.'

Remi slows down and we jump out, keeping our eye on the bicyclist heading toward the Bois. We have to stay out of sight but keep her under surveillance before she disappears into the labyrinth of cedars and oaks and winding pathways. She's walking the bicycle, picking up her pace, her head turning left then right. We can't let her see us. Michal takes me in his arms and nuzzles his face into my hair, my pulse racing. The tension we both feel is so strong our bodies press together as one, not moving. We can't. I peer over his shoulder. Her red mouth is set in a grim line, her brow furrowed. Craning her neck to check out the Parisians strolling through the park. Is she here on Gestapo business?

She goes up one path, then turns around and down another. It's obvious she hasn't found her mark.

*Who*, I wonder, is she looking for?

## 23

## PARIS, MARCH 1943

*Justine*

Ninette has the sniffles again so I shouldn't have taken her for a walk in the Bois in her stroller, but my back is aching and I needed to get out of the house. Relieve my frustrations as I toil over my options in a world that has been turned upside down by the major. He has once again sent a tremor of fear through me.

But I won't think about that now.

It's chilly this afternoon and damp, so I put on the heavy, sunny-yellow sweater Maman knitted for me and a matching one for Ninette, who's wearing a cute bonnet with her blonde curls peeking through. I'm seven months pregnant and I look like a big, fat yellow tulip waddling among svelte roses in my two-piece navy jersey dress. White lace collar. Pearl buttons down the front. It's the only maternity outfit I have that still fits me. The low ballet flats with button straps that Madame de Giocomte pulled out of her storage shoes boxes are a bit tight, but they'll do.

I take a final swing around the park, grinning when passers-by smile and wave at Ninette. Parisians yearning for the city they remember before the war when a mother could walk with her baby without the fear of someone stopping you and asking for 'your papers.' I notice one young woman riding a bicycle takes a special interest in Ninette, whizzing by me, then slowing down and smiling at her. I ask her if she has a child of her own and the sadness in her eyes hits me hard. She jerks her head back and forth, then speeds away. How sad for her. I know how lucky I am. My little girl looks adorable sitting up in the stroller and playing with her favorite wooden toy blocks, but my heart tugs when she sneezes with an 'ahchoo'.

'We'll cut our walk short today, *ma petite*, so Maman can get you home for a long nap. Me, too.' I yawn. 'I'm so tired.' I'm suffering from bouts of fatigue which take a toll on my hostess duties. I turn off the pathway and head back toward Avenue de Ternes then home when I get a stone in my shoe. I'll never make the forty-five-minute walk back to Maison Bleue if I don't fix it. I sit down on the bench and wiggle off the ballet flat, thinking. Strange, but my life has taken on a new normalcy since my pregnancy. I'm still adjusting to my new moniker as the 'general's girl.'

Agreed, it doesn't have the same connotation as 'Nazi mistress' since General von Klum stepped in and declared he's the father of my baby. Eyes rolled, but then congratulations came from Maman and Madame de Giocomte, who winked and nodded their approval. Yes, they know I'm in love with the dark-haired, handsome SS captain who shows up on party nights, mingles, then leaves before anyone asks too many questions, but not before we meet in the kitchen and embrace. They don't know Arsène is a British agent, but they suspect he's with the Underground because, as Maman puts it, 'No Nazi could put those stars in your eyes, Justine.'

Madame chimed in with: 'We don't need to know who he is, Justine. We understand it's better for us if we don't.'

The major wasn't as accommodating and offered no congratulations. I'm not sure he bought the general's confession, but he must have found a new paramour because he seemed rather blasé about my 'affair' with his superior officer. I assume I'm not much use to him now that I'm not working in the hat shop. He rarely comes by now, since my role as hostess for the general has taken on a less frivolous tone in my condition.

More card games with the general's cronies and fewer of Mimi's girls, which is fine with me. I admit, I relaxed my hard-nosed Nazi mistress 'cover' around him, but my pregnancy exhausts me. I seem bigger, more tired, and the general notices it. He teases me about my Nazi salute not having the same 'vigor'. What surprises me is the general doesn't object to me sitting in on his poker nights after our conversation over lemon liqueurs. As if he's testing me. Or am I testing *him*?

Last night he dropped hints about Arsène that made me double burp while I sipped a glass of seltzer with him after dinner. The two of us. Then he wandered off to the guest room. To keep up appearances, he stays at Maison Bleue once, twice a week. I look forward to our midnight talks when the house is quiet and steeped in deep, comforting shadows. We settle in on the divan, my tired bones resting among the gold velvet pillows with long fringe and tassels. With our voices hushed, we speak freely to each other.

'I haven't seen Captain Stolz here at Maison Bleue recently.' He downed a shot of whiskey and smacked his lips.

*Arsène's cover as an SS officer.*

'Lover's quarrel, mademoiselle?' he asked. A curious but direct look beaming in his eyes demanded I answer him.

I smiled. '*Mais non,* monsieur. He's away on assignment... Algiers. A charming man and very kind to Ninette.'

'He runs off to North Africa, leaving you at the mercy of the SS?' His bushy brows crossed.

'I can handle myself, General... even around you.'

I remember how he didn't laugh at my joke, something he does even when I'm not funny. I felt a moment of angst hit hard in the pit of my stomach. *What's his game?*

'I inquired about your captain with an old friend of mine, a field commander in the panzer division before he joined General Rommel in Tunisia.'

'Oh?' I sputtered, the word sticking in my throat.

'Yes. He couldn't recall the young SS officer ever serving under him *or* the general mentioning the captain.' He gave me a stern look. 'And General Rommel has a reputation for knowing and caring about his men.'

'Captain Stolz is a translator for the Africa Corps and is embedded with the local tribes,' I blurted out. 'Naturally, their paths wouldn't meet.'

My God, what else could I say? That the handsome captain is a British spy? And I'm helping him gather intelligence? Arsène admitted to me the Allies were grateful for what I gave him about Rommel's push into Tunisia, information I gleaned from Nazi officers at my parties resulting in the British blowing up a train containing petrol for the Luftwaffe.

'I see.' He winked. 'Well, you needn't worry, mademoiselle, what we discuss here stays between us.'

'My lips are sealed, General.'

'As are mine.'

Then he kissed my hand and chuckled. I think he enjoys guessing about my secret life, but this was the first time I had the feeling he didn't believe I'm the Nazi *collabo* I purport to be.

Should I be afraid? Or is he probing to see where my loyalties lie? My gut tells me I may be right, and that frightens me even more. Anyone who crosses the Führer faces uncompromising scrutiny from the Gestapo. I can't afford that horrible Herr Geller sticking himself to me like a pesky shadow. I'd felt a sense of relief when the major stopped coming around, now I'm fearful of the general involving me in his games.

Never was that more evident than when the major took his leave, giving me a hard glare when he said, 'You're General von Klum's problem now, mademoiselle, not mine.'

Or am I the general's cover? Interesting...

Yet my new station in life hasn't changed the major's mind about taking Ninette to Germany with him next month for Hitler's birthday. I begged him not to take her, saying that I need her here with me. She's a great comfort to me.

His answer? 'You would deny our Führer the privilege of meeting my daughter?' he said, smug. 'Even if her mother is a whore?'

That's when I lost any control I had left when I'm around this man. When the years of frustration of dealing with him, tiptoeing around him so as not to anger him, living as the captive of this insufferable Nazi major uncorked like the finest champagne and I tossed every insult I could think of at him.

'How *dare* you call me that... that horrible name. You raped me, hurt me, made me do your bidding and I did what I must to keep my child safe. But Ninette is *our* daughter, though you've done nothing but frighten the child so she cries when she sees you. You will never be her father in the truest sense of the word. And someday, *someday*, when this terrible war is over and we drive you Nazis out of France, you *will* pay for your sins. I promise you.'

He gave me that arrogant smirk he's never lost, but to my

surprise he didn't strike me. He *knew* Germany is in trouble. I heard from General von Klum that the Führer and his generals face great anxiety over the course of the war, Goebbels is worried and Goering said it's either victory or destruction. That didn't change his mind. He just reminded me to have Ninette ready to travel the second week of April.

'A female German auxiliary worker will act as her nurse,' he said. Then he walked over to the grand staircase, sweeping his gloved fingers along the bannister. He wasn't finished with me. 'In spite of the sleepless nights you've caused me, Justine, I shall miss you.' He looked at me with a combination of both desire and disgust. 'Your body pleased me and you always knew what you wanted, but I never thought you'd be foolish enough to have another man's child. And don't tell me it's that fool general's doing. I don't believe you. When I find out who the man is... and I will... he'll be no more than this speck of dust when I'm finished with him.'

He blew the dust off his fingers and then stormed out the front door, but not before he fired off a parting shot. 'Adieu, Justine. You no longer amuse me. Lucky for me, the general has to put up with your arrogance now. You shall never see me again.'

* * *

'Justine... *run*!'

*Ève?* My sister? I swear that's her voice.

I spin around, see a tall blonde girl and a man racing toward me. No, it can't be Ève. She's not blonde. And what would she be doing here in the Bois? The Gestapo might see her, and I know Herr Geller would show her no mercy. When do the Gestapo ever let up? I push the baby's stroller toward her, trying to get a better look at her, but the sun is in my eyes when—

Gunshots ring out. They come out of nowhere.

*One... two... three* shots fired in rapid succession.

*Someone's shooting at me.*

The loud popping is so close it hurts my ears. Ninette cries out, terrified. I want to pick her up, comfort her and hold her tight, but if I'm the target, she's safer in the stroller... Then I hear screaming. The girl on the bicycle races past me—she's been watching me.

*Where did the shots come from? A passing motorcar?*

I flatten myself on the ground. Oh, my God, the bullets stripped the green hedges next to the bench, barely missing me. *Ninette*. She's still crying... I check her. She's not hurt, my poor baby, but she's as frightened as her mother.

'Let's get out of here, *ma petite*.'

I grab on tight to the long handle of the stroller and move as fast as I can, heading back into the Bois to find safety under its canopy of oaks and chestnuts. I grab Ninette out of the stroller, hold her close to my chest and kiss her over and over again.

'Don't cry, *ma petite*, Maman's here, you're safe.'

I wonder, what happened to the blonde who called out my name? Whoever she is, she saved my life... and Ninette's. It surely wasn't Ève. It's all in my head. My brain is so addled with stress and my hormones are out of control like a raging army on a battle march. I know these feelings will pass; it's normal. All the more reason I wish Ève were here. I need her and want to share the birth of my new *bébé* with her.

*Then I hear two more gunshots.*

*Screams.*

I turn my head around and peek through the trees and see a

gray Peugeot speeding around the corner and down the avenue, tires squealing.

*They can't see me. Who are they shooting at?*

My heart is still pounding when the morning sun beams down on the girl on the bicycle lying in the street, blood seeping from her wounds... and calling for her *maman*.

*What's going on? Oh, that poor girl.*

She's crying, bleeding from her shoulder, and her arm is mangled, and I have the nagging sense whoever shot that girl wasn't aiming for me after all. I want to run and help her, ask why she was following me, but I can't get close to her. A small crowd gathers around her and the man I saw earlier puts his jacket over her and... Oh, my God, there's the blonde. I push the baby stroller with urgency closer, trying to see her face, but she's leaning over the girl with her back to me. I move closer. A policeman arrives on the scene blowing his whistle and wrapping up the wounded girl in his cape then dispersing the crowd. I hear the familiar *dee dee... dee dee* siren in the background.

The French police.

I step back. There's nothing I can do for the girl. I have to get out of here.

I push the baby's stroller farther into the wooded area, and I'm just stopping to take a breath when I feel a tap on my shoulder. I turn and my heart stops. The last person I expect to see during this heartbreaking afternoon—or maybe not—is Herr Geller.

* * *

'How did you find me here, Herr Geller?' I ask, sitting Ninette back down into the stroller, though it unnerves me how the secret policeman keeps sneaking looks at my baby.

'Your habits are well known to us, mademoiselle, including that you walk your child here in the Bois. For months I suspected you were meeting that SS captain I once caught you with, but I was wrong. You've made no contact with him here.'

'Naturally your informant told you that. That poor girl. Tell me you didn't order her to be shot.'

'I didn't.'

A simple, direct statement, and I believe him. He prefers a more subtle way of eliminating anyone getting in his way, like making certain they disappear, never to be seen again.

'A most unfortunate incident, mademoiselle,' he continues.

'Don't give me your usual excuses, they don't work anymore. That girl was working for you, wasn't she? And spying on me. Why?'

'It's my job. Unfortunately, she's no longer useful to me. She'll survive her wounds, but she'll be deported to a labor camp to keep her quiet. She knows too much.'

'A death sentence.'

'Is it?' He raises his brows.

I start walking, eager to get back to Maison Bleue and hold my child tight. I need sanctuary right now, not interrogation. 'If you'll excuse me, Ninette and I have had enough excitement—'

The Gestapo man falls in line next to me. 'I would like to speak with you, mademoiselle.'

I stop, turn to face him. 'I was almost killed just now, when someone took potshots at me and my child, and you want to talk?'

'I'm going to ask you a question, mademoiselle. Answer me with the truth and your indiscretion with the SS captain will remain between us.' He takes a beat. 'However, if you lie to me, I will tell the major what I know and he will see it as a betrayal. He will kill you *and* the SS officer. Not a pleasant outcome since I have reason to believe *he* is your baby's father, not General von Klum. Do you understand me?'

'You have no proof.' I don't deny it. I don't want the Gestapo poking into the background of this mysterious SS captain who claims he's been fighting in Algiers and find out he doesn't exist. I know Arsène is mired down in his latest mission to assist in uniting the cells to fight as an armed Resistance with the Allies. He left yesterday for London and I've never seen him so excited, telling me it's vital we work together with England and America before the invasion begins.

'Ah, mademoiselle, you try my patience. I'm not interested in your sordid love affairs, but I have reason to suspect the general is holding subversive meetings at your home that involve, shall we say, sensitive information not friendly to the Reich?'

'You call poker games subversive?' I laugh. I'm not surprised at Herr Geller's accusation. I always suspected the general suffers from guilt and wants to end this war. I'll not give him up.

'And he's shared nothing with you about his plans?'

'No, he's quite charming and romantic but I shall not kiss and tell. What we have between us is a private affair.'

'I assure you, the general is up to something. It's most important you say nothing to him about our little talk. He must not know that we suspect him of, shall we say, plotting against the Führer? If you do, there is nowhere you can hide from the Gestapo. I don't have to remind you we have unpleasant ways of dealing with you... and your family.' He reaches down to pull Ninette out of her stroller.

'Don't you *dare* touch her.'

'Then we have an agreement?' The Gestapo man narrows his eyes. 'Otherwise, things will go badly for not only her and you, but also your *maman* and Madame de Giocomte.'

My defenses shut down. I'm tired, I'm frightened, and I'm pregnant. And he knows it.

'You have me where you want me, Herr Geller, *n'est-ce pas*?'

'I'm pleased you understand my position. Do I have your word?'

'Yes. I will do as you ask. I will say nothing to the general.'

I turn the stroller onto the avenue, careful not to look at him as I pass. One look into my eyes and he'll know I'm lying. Because I owe it to the general to warn him.

# 24

## PARIS, APRIL 1943

*Ève*

I wish I could forget the look on Coralie's face when she saw me standing over her, trying to stop the blood gushing from the jagged wound on her shoulder with direct pressure because I didn't know what else to do.

Remi had fired off five shots.

He'd hit her, but he didn't kill her, and somewhere in the deepest recesses of my mind, I couldn't bury the terrible truth it was my fault the mission went wrong. I inadvertently warned Coralie when I yelled to Justine to get out of the way when I saw Coralie racing on her bike toward my sister and her child snuggled up in the four-wheel stroller.

My sister's also heavily pregnant, *damn it.*

Maman had told me so it's not a surprise, and she also assured me Justine is in love with the baby's father, but she wouldn't say who he is. I panicked. I knew Remi was around the corner, waiting for Coralie. I knew he would fire his weapon out the window of the moving car. I knew there was a damned good chance Justine or her daughter could be killed.

What do you do when God shows you a different way?

You act.

Michal understood my quandary, laid his jacket over Coralie, and then dragged me away when we heard the policeman's whistle.

Her life is now in God's hands. Ours too though, if she talks. I can't dismiss from my mind her whispering to me words I will never forget: 'I'll pay you back for this, Ève. I swear.'

Those words haunt me. She knew we found out she's a Gestapo informant and had no choice but to take her down. She saw me yelling at Justine. I swear she was following my sister, maybe hoping to get a new location on me. That's why I'm at the boulangerie today, looking for Maman to tell her she *must* warn Justine the Gestapo is having her followed. With Coralie out of the picture, they'll assign someone new to tail her to get to me and my fellow *résistants*. They never give up.

But neither do I.

I approach the corner bakery with caution, the familiar smell of bread baking in that massive oven, the golden-brown crust dusted with flour and so crunchy my mouth waters. But I'm not here to fill my belly. I look over the motley group chattering and holding up their coat collars to keep the morning chill off their necks. It's an unseasonably cold morning for April and we had a light rain yesterday, making it seem colder. Women mostly lining up outside the shop in wool coats, cotton stockings, and wearing shoes with wooden soles and tops made from paper. Everyone looks thinner than they did at the beginning of the Occupation. Thinner, but not healthier because of the lack of fresh vegetables.

I keep to the doorways, head down, my blonde hair covered

with a black velvet beret that once belonged to Iris. Remi insisted that I have the soft, pretty beret, that Iris always liked me, admired me. And, he said, grabbing me by the shoulders, he did, too. Then the two men took off for the south to join the Vercors maquis in the Rhone-Alps, armed Resistance fighters living off the grid in small clandestine groups, their name derived from the 'scrub' of the land since they hid out in the hills and wooded areas. Michal will help train the men flocking to join the maquis to avoid the mandatory work program in Germany, and he won't be back for weeks. We decided it's best if we separate to keep the Gestapo off our trail.

I'm staying in Paris, mostly to warn Justine, something Michal agreed to, sending me off with a kiss lasting a lot longer than the first one, a kiss I keep close to my heart. I can't wait for more when I see him again. Until then, I have a job as 'Viviane Longré' teaching French children mathematics at a convent school in Montmartre, again thanks to Iris. I found out from Remi she made quite a tidy sum playing the ponies at Longchamp and she'd been a silent benefactor to the school for years, and the sympathetic nuns were eager to give me shelter. I pray Iris survives the camp and I can return the beret to her personally after the war.

I count the women queuing up in front of the boulangerie. Eight.

I start pacing. Maman should have been here by now. Maybe she's not feeling well. Maison Bleue is a big house to heat. I doubt the Nazis deliver coal by the bucket. I put my cold hands in my pockets, telling myself I'll give her five more minutes when I see a woman in a long navy coat walking at a brisk pace down the side alley, pushing a stroller and—

She's wearing a roses-and-daisies headscarf tied under her chin. Dark glasses.

I smile big at her. It's Maman.

I approach her slowly, wondering, *Why did she bring Justine's child with her*? It's too cold for the little girl to be out so early in the morning, though my heart warms at the thought of seeing the child, holding her, and smelling that sweet scent I pray someday will fill my hours.

My fear for the little girl is exchanged for a lovely anticipation at properly seeing my niece for the first time when I hear—

'Ève, oh, thank God you came.'

I blink. '*Justine?*' My voice catches in my throat. 'What are you doing here?'

She looks like she's about to collapse. This isn't the sophisticated Nazi collaborator I saw a year ago at Hôtel Drouot. Her long navy coat hides her condition, but her coloring is dull ivory instead of pink, her hair drooping around her face. And she's not wearing a hat which is *not* my Justine.

'Maman told me she meets you here every other Thursday. I prayed you'd come. I need your help.'

'That's why I'm here, Justine. You're in danger… That girl you saw shot—'

'She was an informant for Herr Geller.'

'The Gestapo man?' I ask. 'So you *knew* the girl was tailing you?'

'Yes.'

'Why would the Gestapo follow you, Justine? It doesn't add up. Is it to try to get to me? Or are you in trouble with the Nazis? I thought they believed you to be a collaborator? Tell me what's going on, *please*. I'm your sister. I need to know. I'm having a hard time understanding with everything that's happened… the assault, that major, your new baby, coming back to Maison Bleue. I get it, you're working for the Boches to protect your daughter. But we can fight them *together*, if you'll just listen to me...'

'I didn't come here to talk about me, Ève. It's Ninette.'

I feel her soften toward me when she mentions her child, brushes my hand, then stops herself from grabbing it. She wants to reach out, but can't. What has changed her?

'Can I hold her, please?' I beg, hoping to draw her out.

'*Hold her?* My dear sister, I'm begging you to *take* her... to keep her safe from the major and the Gestapo.'

* * *

But the minute I take the little girl in my arms I know something's wrong. She's coughing, her cheeks are hot... her skin pale with a slight bluish tint. I don't say anything to Justine. Not yet. I want to be sure first.

I rock the little girl back and forth in my arms humming a lullaby, the vanilla smell wafting through the bakery as good as any sleeping potion. The owner opened up and we brought the stroller inside, and we sit huddled in a corner next to the baking oven to get warm. Ninette has calmed down, but her breathing is labored. I saw similar cases when I volunteered at the Rothschild Hospital for a paper I was writing about germs and infection. I'm surprised Justine didn't see the signs. Her hair wet with perspiration, the child is shaking and crying like she has chest pain, but my sister's nerves are so on edge she's about to burst. I worry about her, too.

'What's going on, Justine? Why are you so frightened?'

'The major has gotten it into his head to take Ninette to Germany, to mingle with Hitler and his close circle, and introduce his daughter to them.' Her piercing stare locks with mine, the haunted look of a mother faced with losing her child. 'I'll never see her again, Ève.'

'No, I won't let that happen, Justine, I promise.'

'Can you hide her with your Resistance friends?'

I shake my head, my heart heavy. 'My friends are dead, betrayed. Our network destroyed. Only two others survived and they've left Paris to join the maquis.'

'That girl on the bike,' Justine whispers. '*She* betrayed you?'

I nod. 'I *want* to take Ninette but—'

Justine looks horrified. '*But what*, Ève? I know we've had our differences, but this is my baby, your niece, and I've got to keep her out of the hands of the Nazis. Help me, *please!*'

'Your little girl is very sick, Justine. She needs to go to a hospital.'

'She has the sniffles, that's all.'

'Justine, *listen to me*—'

'You don't understand, Ève. The major will find her *wherever* we take her. He'll have the Gestapo and French police check every child admitted to a hospital within the past twenty-four hours.' She shakes her head back and forth. 'No, there must be another way. Please.'

While I'm confident about my skills in chemistry and biology, my medical knowledge has limitations. I *have* observed the steps necessary in cases like this at the Jewish hospital. Do I dare attempt to save the child's life?

Do I have a choice?

I blow out a heavy breath. 'It's a gamble, Justine, but if we return to Maison Bleue—'

'Yes...'

'I'll do my best to get her through the crisis.'

'Crisis?' She winces. 'What are you talking about?'

'I think there's a chance your daughter has pneumonia.'

# 25

## PARIS, APRIL 1943

*Justine*

'Pneumonia kills one out of four of its victims, Justine, especially *les petites.*' Ève tucks the coverlet around my sweet child, then turns to me. 'All we can do is wait.'

We made our way back to Maison Bleue several hours ago and Ève is doing everything she can, but I wonder if I made the wrong decision about not going to the hospital. Yet I have no doubt if the major gets wind of her illness, he'll let Ninette die if she's no longer of use to him.

'Isn't there *anything* I can do?' My response to her candid words is to collapse into the round-back, white silk chair next to my baby. 'I had no idea she was so sick. You must let me help. I can't watch her suffer.'

'It's important we keep an accurate record of her fluid intake and output. Did you get the paper and pen I need?'

'Yes.' I hand them to her. 'Monsieur de Giocomte always kept his stationery in the mahogany desk in the library.'

I watch Ève fumble with the pen. Dipping it into the ink,

then trying to write on the rich linen paper Monsieur de Giocomte favored. She becomes frustrated when words don't glide from its scratchy point, but she doesn't give up, making notes. I know my sister. Like Maman, she's cut from sturdy cotton that doesn't tear easily in a time of crisis. She looks up at me, gives me a serious look. She's clearly in charge of the situation. Like she's the older sister now.

Maman and Madame de Giocomte were beside themselves when we returned to Maison Bleue, with tears and hugs at seeing Ève, then they set to preparing a room for Ninette. Thick, plush pearl-grey carpet covers the floor, muting our footsteps so as not to wake her. A fireplace, white daybed, Empire furniture. Maman replaces the white china vases and silver and pewter objects with clean, white linen towels and a pitcher of water. Cook is steaming fresh tea for the night ahead.

'Bed rest is of primary importance.' I follow my sister's soothing voice, listening to her intently. 'We want to help the child's body combat the infection and prevent unnecessary strain on her lungs.'

'What are my baby's chances?' I ask.

She lays a hand on my shoulder. The pressure of her warm touch reminds me how much I've missed her.

'Pneumococcus pneumonia strikes suddenly,' Ève says. 'It's often bacterial. Without an X-ray, I can't tell if *both* her lungs are infected. If so—'

'*What*, Ève?'

'It doesn't look good, Justine, but I swear I'll do everything humanly possible to get the child through this.'

'Oh.' I bury my face in my hands and the baby in my belly kicks wildly, as if they know their sister is dying. The deep, heavy breathing of my little girl lying beneath the white brocade coverlet tears me apart.

*Ève will save her. She has to.*

'If only we had the right drugs to kill the infection. We'd have penicillin by now if it wasn't for these damn Nazis.'

I can see my sister shaking with anger, rambling on about 'penicillin', her frustration with not having it, but I know she's doing everything she can.

The afternoon is giving way to evening.

I brace myself for the night ahead, the heaviness of fatigue clouding my eyesight with a gray gauze. I can't stop trembling; the thought of my little girl wasting away in the darkness is too much to bear. She's unconscious, breathing heavily, and perspiring. The thought of losing a child is a pain that runs deeper, strikes harder, and lasts longer than any other wound nature could inflict upon mothers.

I'd rather die than see anything happen to *mon bébé.* Ève's going to pull her through, *I know she will.*

I lose my tiredness, ready to begin my vigil.

'We need to keep out any draft,' Ève insists, wiping the child's brow with a soft, white towel.

I go to the tall, aristocratic window and take a long, hard look outside. Out there the world is cold and unfeeling. I want to keep it out, protect my child. I won't let that world in again until the crisis has passed.

I start to close the drapes when I see a black Mercedes touring car pull up into the winding driveway. *The major.* I wipe my eyes with my fingers. I can't believe I'm seeing this. Why is he here *two days early*? Of course. To surprise me so I don't have the chance to take Ninette away.

Moments later, Maman bangs on the bedroom door.

'*Justine*,' she calls out, panicky. 'There's a German woman here to pick up Ninette.'

* * *

The German auxiliary worker's accented voice sounds shrill and unnerving when I confront her at the front door, rising to a crescendo of guttural French that grates on my ears. 'I am here for the child of Major Saxe-Müllenheim. Please, you will bring her to me. I wait.'

I make every effort to remain calm, but the words come out in a whisper. 'I regret, Fräulein, I can't do as you wish.'

'Why not?' She makes a face, as if she can't believe I would disobey a direct order from the major.

'She's sleeping quietly and I would not wake her up to put her on a train even if the Führer himself were standing here in your shoes.'

She looks puzzled, trying to translate what I said. 'The major is waiting. We must go.'

'She's *not* leaving this house, is that clear?'

'Mademoiselle, I have my orders.'

'You tell the major my daughter has pneumonia and *may die* if I don't go back upstairs and take care of her.'

The young woman's stern features soften and I have the feeling she's as petrified of the major as I was. 'This is true?'

'Yes. See for yourself so you can report to the major.'

The young German woman nods, follows me up to my baby's room. Her eyes widen when she sees Ninette fretting and Ève placing cool cloths on her head, then tossing linen stained with pus and vomit into a straw basket. My sister keeps her face turned away so the German can't see her, her voice in whispers as she comforts the child. There's the smell of fear and sickness here, a rotting smell we're praying will become fresh and new by morning, but for now, it makes the German girl gag.

She coughs, puts her hand over her mouth.

'If the major takes my child from me and she dies,' I emphasize, 'it will be his fault *and* yours, do you understand?'

She nods. 'I shall inform the major the child is gravely ill and cannot travel.'

With a deep groan in her throat, she races down the staircase and out the front door. I stand on the landing, breathing so hard I swear I'm going to faint. I wait. Five minutes later I hear the Mercedes motorcar race away.

I close my eyes, relieved.

My baby is safe. *If* she survives this terrifying illness.

# 26

## PARIS APRIL 8, 1943

### *Ève*

The pure silver point scratches and scribbles the royal blue ink across the soft linen paper as I write. I'm sitting at Monsieur de Giocomte's desk with my fingers pressing against my brain, putting my thoughts to paper.

> April 8, 1943, 5.37 p.m. *and the child is running a high fever, although her sputum is brown-colored now instead of that awful blood-streaked red. Her pulse and respiration are almost twice their normal rate. I check her pulse again and she has a tight grip on my fingers, which surprises me, then slides her small hand down and lets go. She's half-conscious. Opens her eyes. I stare into their pure blueness, hoping she'll understand how much her* maman *yearns to hold her in her arms and sing to her. It's more than I can bear, talking to her, whispering how everything's going to be all right, when I know her life depends on what happens in this room tonight.*

April 9, 1943, 12.01 a.m. *Every four hours I record her pulse. It's more than 110 beats per minute and she's breathing heavily. Dyspnea or shortness of breath. Her fever must be around 39 degrees Celsius, down somewhat from earlier. I know from experience I must be ready when the temperature falls with frequent changes of her gown and bed linens. Justine went to check with Maman to get more linens. Madame de Giocomte peeked in, her lovely eyes worried. She and Maman are standing by, ready to grab whatever we need from the armoire with its neatly folded piles of linens, white sheets, pillowcases, coverlets, and towels. Madame prides herself with a well-stocked linen chest, a symbol of domestic order. A comforting sign we'll get through this.*

April 9, 1943, 8.05 a.m. *Justine brought hot tea and leftover bread. She sits beside me in the child's bedroom, asking me if I want to rest, but I shake my head. She nods off, holding her belly, and I let her sleep. Meanwhile, the pain in my fingers throbs from writing, but if I don't put my thoughts down, I fear I will lose whatever sanity still resides in my mind. I can't let my sister down. I must save her child.*

April 9, 1943, 2.07 p.m. *I'm worried about the child's high fever. I know children can run high fevers without being in danger, but what if she needs an oxygen tent? I pray that won't happen. I can prevent dehydration by giving her lots of fluids, so I wet her lips often with fresh water from the pitcher Cook refills every hour. Justine woke up and took over, insisting I let her do something, that she's ready to lose her mind. I see lingering questions in her eyes. Like, how can she live with herself if something happens to Ninette? I tell her it's not her fault, that God will help us. She hugs me, settles down.*

*I have the same fear. Fear of what will happen if the child doesn't survive. I shall blame myself for the rest of my life. I think about Michal and his strength to survive, strength he's given me to tackle whatever comes at me. He gives me the strength now to keep my stomach from purging itself, my eyes from turning away from the soiled mess on the sheets I must carefully record for fluid loss. The smell of the sick room is indescribable, not because of bodily functions, but because it pulls me back to the reality that death hovers over Maison Bleue, teasing, taunting us with a whisper.*

*A whisper that grows louder with each passing minute.*

*What if the child doesn't survive? I'm compelled by a force deep within me to keep fighting.*

April 9, 1943, 6.22 p.m. *I checked the child's TPR and loss of bodily fluids. I'm more fearful than ever. Tonight will bring the apex of the crisis. The moment of life or death.*

April 9, 1943, 11.15 p.m. *Ninette's mouth is open. Lips cracked from the fever. Blue eyes crying. Sweating and shuddering with chills. She's frightened. I can see it in the way her little mouth quivers, how her body shakes when she coughs. I lie her on her affected side, the side that hurts the most, so it's splinted during her coughing episodes. Justine is helping me hold her, wiping her brow with the softest linen, so soft you'd swear it was made from the hem of an angel's gown.*

*Justine looks at her child and struggles to keep from bursting into tears.*

April 10, 1943, 3.52 a.m. *Why does everything always seem to happen in the pale, sleepy light before the dawn? The sight of the sick child writhing on the bed is unendurable. Yet I'm compelled to look, to touch, to hold, to soothe, and God help me, to pray, as I frantically change her perspiration-soaked gown again for the third time in minutes. She's going through delirium, thrashing about, calling out for her* maman, *and trying to scratch her face, her body.*

*Her tortured expression is so poignant that her pain is my pain, her heavy breaths my breaths, and her violent coughs rack my own throat. I feel her fear, yet she is so young, so childlike, but she knows she's on the brink of death and horribly alone in her struggle to survive. Justine, her sweater sleeves rolled up above her elbows, holds her, wiping her brow, speaking to her in a soothing voice I scarcely recognize as hers. It's the most beautiful melody of a mother's love with every word a whisper but crisp as a bell. I will never forget how wonderful it is for us to be together again, her hand reaching for me when my step falters from fatigue, her courage fueling mine to save her child.*

*Together we're re-forming our sisterly bond of strength over the child's shivering, perspiring body, and somehow infusing that strength into her. Slowly, hour by hour, the coughing subsides, the fever plunges, the sweating slows down, and the baby's pulse is close to normal. When I see her blue eyes close, I jump, grabbing Justine's hand in fear, but then I see a sweet pinkness return to the child's lips and I hear a sigh escape from her small chest. A sigh of peace after a long, hard fight. A peace won, not lost.*

*The crisis is over.*

April 10, 1943, 7.12 a.m. *I believe Ninette will recover quickly now. As she sleeps, I shiver as a feeling of well-being descends upon the room, as if the spirit of life is again entering this domain. I'm shivering, not from fear, but from joy, relief, and a furtive promise not to give up on Justine. Keep talking to her until she believes she doesn't have to work for the Boches, that I can and will protect her and her babies.*

On April 10, 1943, 7.35 a.m. I finish my notes and Justine brings me hot tea. We yank the drapes open wide and watch the sun rise in the sky, sparkling with golden streamers.

It's the most beautiful morning I've ever seen.

* * *

*A week later...*

'Tell me what, Maman?'

I'm surprised to see Justine and Maman in a huddle with Madame de Giocomte when I go into the library to find a book on mathematics. I'm starting my teaching job at the convent school next week and I can't wait. I need something I can hold on to in this crazy war, something normal. I still see Coralie's body lying in the street, the blood, so much blood. I still shiver under a warm duvet at night thinking how close I came to losing my sister even if she's turned into a cold-hearted Nazi collaborator. What's funny is, I haven't seen *that* Justine since I've been here, why I don't know; her pregnancy, perhaps? Still, I'll come back every week to check on Ninette, but the child is recovering well. We decided it's best for me not to stay here at Maison Bleue. Justine warned me about that horrible Gestapo man showing up at odd times.

Or is she making certain I don't eavesdrop on her conversations? I can't forget, even if the major is gone—we hope—she's still working for the Boches. We haven't talked about it and I admit I pushed it to the back of my mind. I don't want to lose my sister again even if I don't understand her. What's strange to me is how Maman and Madame de Giocomte have warmed up to Justine, and then there's the whispering and nudging each other, the unfinished sentences as if they're trying to tell me something but can't.

I feel my heart skipping and I lay my hand over my chest, waiting for what, I don't know, but whatever it is, there's no stopping Maman. She's giggling and holding her hand over her mouth, trying to contain herself.

Finally, she says, 'Justine has something to tell you, Ève.'

'Yes, it's very important,' Madame de Giocomte chimes in. They give each other a look that's so filled with joy it makes me smile, and I have *no* idea what I'm smiling about. Why all this buildup with Maman and Madame? To soften me up? What can the three of them be hiding that brings such smiles I've not seen since the Occupation began?

'I'm listening.'

'I can't thank you enough, Ève, for what you did for Ninette,' Justine says, reaching for my hand. I stiffen. I'm not ready for *that*. 'How you risked your life by coming here, not knowing if I'd call the Gestapo, how you put your soul into saving my little girl even if—'

'She's the daughter of an SS officer?' I stare at her, her face puffy from her condition but still pretty. 'I don't blame the child, and even if I hate what you've become, I'd never abandon you when you needed me,' I say with so much emotion, my voice breaks. I don't know why I said that when I've been so against her. Of course. I get it. I've been looking for an excuse to find common ground between us. Ninette did that, but where do we go from here? Back to how things were between us before the war? Impossible. I'd never join her side, *never*. So why this big speech?

'Ève...' she begins, biting her lower lip. 'I have to tell you something...'

Here it comes, the pitch that we have to accept the 'New Order', that the Nazis are our friends, and so on. No, I'm not buying it.

I set her straight. 'You can cry, plead, threaten me, Justine, but I will not *ever* betray France and work with the Boches.'

'You don't have to, Ève.'

Her words stop me cold. 'I don't understand. What are you talking about?'

'Because I'm not working for them either. Not really. I'm working for the Allies, Ève. I'm a double agent...'

'What?' I can't believe it. I *want* to believe it. *Oh, God, thank you.*

'I have been since I met up with a man who helped me through the worst of times after the major assaulted me,' Justine continues, gushing forth with so much excitement to tell me her news she shivers and rubs her arms to steady herself. 'A man I didn't know then was a British agent... A wonderful man who gives me love and courage every day. He's away now on an assignment, but you'll meet him, I promise you.'

'You're a spy? And you're no longer working for the Nazis?' My mind is spinning in every direction at once. 'My brave Justine. How could I have misjudged you so?'

'I've become very good at fooling people, little sister, even you.' Her eyes grow misty with tears. 'I hope you'll forgive me.'

'Forgive you? I'm so relieved. I never could believe you'd betray France. Not you, my sister. I should have read between the lines when I saw Maman at the bakery, the way her eyes shone and the lilt in her voice when she mentioned you and Ninette. And here she was trying to tell me all along, but I was too hurt and angry to listen. I was a fool. Forgive *me*, Justine.' I hug her tight, the two of us laughing because her big belly keeps getting in the way. 'I have to ask, is the Englishman the baby's father?'

She chuckles. 'Well...'

Of course. But she can't tell me any more than that.

'Oh, Justine, why didn't you tell me before?'

'I couldn't put you in danger, Ève. The Gestapo could interrogate you, hang you by your hands from a rafter and burn the bottoms of your feet to make you give me up. I *couldn't* run the risk, or put you through that horror.'

'I've seen a woman lose her soul because she lacked courage.' I think about Coralie. 'I pray I'd be strong enough.'

Justine smiles. 'You would. You're the strongest woman I know.'

Maman puts her arms around both of us. 'Oh, my darling daughters, I'm so happy I have you both back. And soon I'll have a new grandchild.'

Madame de Giocomte laughs. 'And a great-grandchild for me.'

Justine pats her tummy. 'I wouldn't be surprised if I'm carrying Ninette's little sister.'

'You need rest, Justine.'

'Rest? With a war to be won? No, Ève. We've just begun. With our men away, that leaves liberating Paris in *our* hands, *n'est-ce pas*?'

'I can't believe *we* were at war with each other.'

'Not ever again. The Daisy Sisters are back together.'

I take Justine by the hand and hold it tight. 'When the war is over, we'll have another war to fight. Justice for you, my sister, and *all* the women who suffered at the hands of the Nazis.'

'You mean the major.'

'Yes,' I say.

'I won't rest until we make him pay for what he did, not only to me, but other innocent girls.' She's breathing heavy, holding her belly. I worry about her and the baby, but I'm here now and I'm not leaving her.

'What other girls?' I ask.

She hugs me around the shoulders. 'Girls he raped... and an innocent Jewish girl. He's a murderer, Ève... a girl he sexually assaulted then strangled. I saw her body with my own eyes after she was fished out of the Seine.'

'Oh, my poor Justine. And you carried this burden by yourself?'

She manages a smile. 'Arsène gives me strength. I love him, Ève.'

'Then I like him, too.' I take a moment, reflect on everything my sister said. The Englishman, her love for him. Her double life. Extraordinary. And wonderful. There is a comfortable silence between us as we wrap our heads around this new beginning for The Daisy Sisters. The challenges we face to keep each other safe, and Maman, Madame, and Ninette. We owe it to them to continue the fight as sisters *and* comrades, knowing that danger and arrest by the Gestapo is but a whisper away from now on, *wherever* we are. We *will* and must fight them. Together.

'You're right, Justine. We can't, *we won't*, let the world forget these women.' I grin. 'Now let's go drive those damn Nazis out of Paris.'

## 27

## PARIS OUTSKIRTS, NOVEMBER, 1943

*Ève*

Lying on our bellies in the dirt near a wooded forest, we hold our breaths as I lay down the explosives on the railroad tracks. Plastic explosives courtesy of a drop by the British RAF. Michal is my partner tonight, the two of us staking out a spot near the tall trees and grassy overgrowth running alongside the tracks. He's back in Paris to rev up our acts of sabotage now that we have small arms and explosives being parachuted into France on a regular basis. The heavy scent of oil on the tracks fills my nostrils as the moon breaks through the darkness on cue, giving me the light I need to complete the job. *Stick the long, slender detonator into the explosive, break off the end and the acid will burn through the cord and set off the explosion.* I'm back to my old habits, blowing up trains coming *from* the east... *not* going there. The railcars heading toward us are empty as they race toward Paris and stop at Drancy, the transit camp, where they'll be filled with Jews and anyone else the Nazis deem a dissident unless we stop them. We pray if we stop enough of them, we'll save lives.

I'm sweating under my heavy jacket, my bleached-blonde hair stuffed under my cap, my mind focused on escaping into the woods and back to Paris. I have my teaching job and, most important, Justine and her new baby need me. I ready the detonator, a task I've done so many times it's routine, but Claude taught me never to skip steps and that in the end it comes down to three things: timing, luck, and skill.

*Claude.* I lose focus for a moment, my emotions taking me off my game. I put down the explosive, my fingers trembling remembering seeing him lying on the floor in Iris's apartment. Bleeding out. It hits me hard every time I relive that day and sets my heart racing, my whole body exploding—

'*Careful*, Ève, or you'll blow us both up.' Michal puts his hand on my shoulder to steady me. *Breathe out.* I feel my heart slow, my mind scrambling the pieces back together, my emotions taking on a more pleasurable feeling with his touch. I try not to think about how much it hurts loving him, knowing I can't have him. *I try.* But he's a part of me now and forever. A poignancy that warms me. Like a recurring dream you look forward to revisiting when your heart is lonely.

I nod. 'Sorry... I—I was thinking about Claude and everything he taught me.'

'He'd be proud of you, Ève, for carrying on his work. So am I.'

'*Merci.*' I feel embarrassed hearing his praise after I let my emotions interfere with my assignment. I'm more uneasy on missions than before, not so cocky after everything that's happened. I've seen war at its ugliest, but Michal gives me strength... and keeps me in line. I'm so glad he's back, though I don't know for how long.

Although we hadn't spoken for over an hour, he is every bit on the alert as I am. We hadn't planned on being here, but

Michal received a tip about the extra train coming through tonight. It's not without danger, though. German patrols with their 'gassing' vans canvas this area looking for Jews on the run, along with direction-finding vehicles catching radio operators when they turn on their wireless. Brave souls hidden in barns and attics. We've seen the secret police camped out behind trees, then move in on a house or shed with their torches turned on bright, pistols drawn, and drag out *résistants* and arrest them. We can only watch. Afterward, Michal reports what we've seen to a contact I've never met, telling me it's safer that way. We're doing this mission alone since our cell was compromised. Michal encouraged me to join him in the maquis. I can't. Now that I know Justine is risking her life to fight alongside us, I won't leave her.

But winning the war even *with* my sister is hard. It's one thing for Justine and me to fight the Boches together, it's another to *survive* to fight them. We Parisians struggle every day with a new dilemma, from cases of typhus showing up in the city, to the Nazis threatening to shut off our electricity if we don't respect the blackouts, to a new round of young men scheduled to be shipped off to Germany to work in factories.

What frightens me most are the rumors that Hitler's elite SS guard has arrived in Paris to complete the Aryanization of France. Stricter rules, more arrests, harsher punishments. I shivered when I heard the news from Justine. I don't know if it will affect their lives at Maison Bleue, but I *do* know the Germans take and take and make everyone miserable, even depriving us of bread. The wheat harvest is in short supply with most of the grain going to the *Vaterland*. Olive oil is even scarce. The nuns at the convent where I teach have little more than leeks and cabbages, artichokes, and dandelions from their garden to eat. We'd starve if my sister didn't use the general's influence to procure food supplies for them. The nuns don't ask where the milk comes from and I don't tell them. They raise their eyes to heaven and give thanks.

So do I.

I put my ear to the railway track and listen. The vibration buzzing in my head tells me we haven't much time. Michal taps me on the forearm, our signal to speed away and cut through the darkness and back into the woods, then pray the explosives go off as planned to derail the locomotive and wreck the train.

But the rumble on the track isn't the only enemy heading our way. Before we can make our escape, a square van with that damn signal-finding apparatus on the rooftop roars to life a few meters away and blasts on its headlights aimed in our direction. It was hidden among a cluster of willows and we didn't see it in the darkness. Didn't notice the tire tracks. I blame myself. I was too eager to set the explosives and head back to Paris.

We hunch down, then Michal presses me hard to the ground. '*Lie still.* I'll take care of this, Ève.'

'*Michal...*' I mumble, spitting out the dirt in my mouth.

*'Don't move!'*

'Come out *with your hands up*,' comes the order in French with a Boche accent. The Gestapo, of course. '*Now!* Or we'll send the dogs in after you,' threatens the unseen enemy, the bright headlights from the van hiding them from view.

I freeze up when shots ring out and ricochet off the wide trunk of an oak tree and whiz past my ear. I roll over to my side, hug the ground. I look around. '*Michal...*' I whisper. 'Are you hit?' I can't tell. He's wearing an extra thick jacket. I didn't ask why.

I hear him mutter, '*No*,' before I feel the warmth of his body covering mine.

'We can lose them if we run deep into the woods,' I tell him.

'No, Ève, we'll never outrun the dogs.' I hear him breathing hard. 'When I walk out of the woods, *run*! And don't look back.'

'No, I can't leave you—I won't.'

'It's an order, Ève.'

'*Why*... why are you doing this?'

'If *I* surrender, they won't dare shoot me. If you're caught... just do as I say, Ève, *please*.' He holds me tight, his lips brushing mine. There's something in his voice that sends me reeling, a confidence in his words I don't feel. 'I can't explain now.'

'*Please*, Michal—'

'Sorry, Ève, but I have to do this.'

He catches me off guard when he shoves my face into the dirt. He's dead serious about giving himself up to save me.

*'Hold your fire!'* I hear him yell as I poke my head up and see him standing up slowly, his hands raised up high as he walks toward the bright headlights.

I choke on my tears, dirt in my eyes and mouth, but I stay flat on the ground. My stomach plummets when I see Michal led away by two German soldiers as an unknown Gestapo man walks in front of the headlights. He's holding the leashes of two barking dogs and pointing a pistol at Michal's head.

'Where are your comrades?' the Nazi demands.

Michal stands tall. 'I'm alone... *alone*, do you understand?'

This brave, crazy man is trying to save me, but I can't let the Nazis take him. How to stop them? I crawl on my belly away from the tracks when I hear the loud whistle of the locomotive, the train barreling my way... *fast*. If I don't run, I'll get caught in the explosion, or I can try to help Michal. If I do, I risk capture by the Gestapo.

*It's an order, Ève,* he said.

Since when do I obey orders?

* * *

*Paris*

'*Ève!* My God, are you hurt?'

Justine rushes to wipe the dirt off my face and neck when I collapse on Maman's rocking chair in the kitchen at Maison Bleue. The creaking sound soothes me. I walked for hours, dodging German patrols, hiding in doorways, behind parked motorcars, anywhere I could find shelter to catch my breath. I had to come back here—*had to*. I'm not ready to return to the convent and face the bare walls of my tiny room. Wallow in self-pity while I cry my eyes out.

My man is gone and I have to talk to Justine, make plans and figure out how to get him back. Somehow I made it home and sneaked into the house through the hidden entrance in the root cellar. I startled Cook at this insane early hour with my disheveled appearance. Her eyes widened and she dropped a precious egg onto the floor, splattering it on the hard stone when she took me in, then ran off to get Justine. I'm covered in dirt, my face smudged; even my eyelashes are fringed with earth particles. I lost my cap and my hair hangs like straw, the sleeve on my jacket ripped open at the shoulder and my trousers torn around the knees.

I *have* to go on and I will, but I need my sister first. I need her strength, for I've lost the man I'd *die* for and I'm breaking apart inside. Like my bones are crushed and I'm as useless as a marionette with her strings cut. What am I going to do? It was different before when Michal disappeared and I didn't know where he was, except I *knew* in my heart he was safe. I had hope he'd come back to me. Now I have nothing. I have no close contacts with anyone in the Underground to find out what's happened to him and I don't dare seek out new ones. Coralie taught me that anyone can be an informant. The odd thing is, the woman I thought was the enemy is my best hope.

Justine.

'I'm shaken up,' I tell her, 'but I'm unhurt.'

'Thank God. Tell me what happened while Cook puts on the kettle and I clean you up.' She dabs a warm cloth to my cheeks and I flinch. 'And don't leave *anything* out.'

I settle back into the soft cushion of the rocking chair and let the words flow. 'Michal and I went on a mission tonight to derail a train on the outskirts of Paris when we were caught by surprise by the Gestapo...' I begin, then ramble on while I let my sister take care of me. I need this, but I insist she doesn't tell Maman until I fill her in.

I can't believe I made it back here. A grayish pink dawn winked at me when I carefully made my way around to the back of Maison Bleue. I saw a Mercedes motorcar parked in the long driveway, but I didn't panic. I've learned from Justine that means the general stayed the night. I was surprised to find the high-ranking SS officer insists on keeping up appearances for my sister and spends his time here alone in the upstairs guest room talking on the telephone. He even drives himself.

'I'm alive, Justine, but I couldn't get anywhere close to Michal when the explosives went off and knocked me down,' I tell her. I keep gripping the arms of Maman's rocker tight. 'I saw the locomotive jump the tracks, followed by several rail-cars landing on their sides before I blacked out. When I came to, it was chaos. I heard German soldiers shouting and cursing, the railroad motorman yelling for help, the Gestapo shooting their pistols into the air to maintain order, but the darkness hid me. I waited and waited until I had a clear path. Then I ran.'

'*Damn* those Nazis, Ève, you could have been killed.' She lifts her eyes toward mine; they're big and shiny with tears.

'But I *wasn't* and I'm here, Justine. It doesn't matter about me. The Nazis arrested Michal.' An intense fear as sharp as a knife grabs my chest and rips through me. It hurts when I breathe.

'You're shaking all over, Ève. Here, take my sweater while I get you a blanket.' She pulls off her pretty yellow sweater and wraps it around me, its cozy warmth soothing me.

'Please help me, Justine. I have to find out what happened to Michal.' I crumble in her arms like a daisy drenched by rain. I need her more than ever. 'I have the worst fear I'll never see him again.'

Justine keeps her eyes on me. 'We're working together now, dear sister. Don't ever forget that. I'll ask Arsène to make inquiries. If anyone can find out what happened to your Polish fighter, he can.'

She hugs me tight and I settle down, knowing I have to be content with that. Still, I can't forget Michal's words: *They can't shoot me.*

What did he mean? *Will I ever know?*

# 28

## PARIS, JULY 1944

### *Justine*

I'm harboring a Nazi resistant at Maison Bleue and I have never been more in fear for the lives of those I love. Maman, Madame. And my two little daughters. My new baby is a precious gift of smiles and wonder, such curiosity in her serious dark green eyes with the thickest lashes. She arrived right on time. Claire Marianne came crashing into the world in May of 1943 amid rumors of an Allied landing on the Riviera. It didn't happen. No one knew then when or where the invasion would come, but in anticipation, I named my baby after Maman, whose first name is Claire, but also Marianne, the goddess of liberty of France. Running my fingers through Claire's dark curls atop her head, I give thanks for my two little girls and in a moment of whimsy, I nickname them *Snow-White* and *Rose-Red* after the classic story about sisterhood and loyalty. But my life is no fairy tale.

I shall never forget the horrible scare I had with Ninette. Thank God my little girl regained her health and was giggling and clapping her hands when she met her baby sister for the first time. And for a while, life seemed almost normal... then hopeful when the Allies landed at Normandy last month. Everyone says it's just a matter of time before they reach Paris. Many Parisians dared to mark Bastille Day, taking to the streets wearing tricolor cockades and singing 'La Marseillaise'.

That doesn't mean the Nazis are giving up or abandoning their 'Final Solution'.

Ève discovered that Jews are still being deported on a regular basis from Drancy to Auschwitz on railcars filled with over a thousand poor souls on board at each departure. She's in constant motion these days, teaching mathematics at the convent school, but her heart is still heavy after Michal's arrest. I know without her telling me she's working again for the Resistance, thanks to Arsène. He got eyes on a Gestapo report indicating Michal is a prisoner of war in Germany in a place we've never heard of. Colditz Castle. Odd, but we can't find out any more than that.

That only fueled my sister's resolve to continue her fight against the Nazis. Arsène directed her to his contact in the pawnshop on Rue Saint-Jacques, which made Ève smile. She bought her old typewriter there and admitted she'd always wondered if it was a secret meeting place for the Resistance. We never discuss what she does... As we've all learned, it's safer that way. She's focused and brilliant, Arsène says, and the only time I saw her show any emotion since Michal's arrest was when she teared up telling me about a prostitute at Madame Mimi's named Francie she helped escape to Switzerland—Ève delivered a hat for me—and that she'd paid her debt to the girl. I didn't ask what she meant. Someday I will.

That was before chaos descended upon us.

On July 20, a plot orchestrated by several Nazi generals and officers to kill Hitler failed. Arsène heard the news and told us that after the announcement, Berlin cut off all communication with the outside world until the Führer took to the radio airwaves and assured the German people he was 'unhurt and well'. Suddenly everything that was calm and hopeful at Maison Bleue turned into fear and angst, wondering how long before the Gestapo came knocking on our front door. Again. Not for Ève, but for someone very important to me that I never dreamed I'd risk my life to save.

General von Klum.

'It's only a matter of time, mademoiselle, before the Führer's general staff discovers my part in this recent plot to kill Hitler,' he tells me, adding he was also in on the aborted plot last March which would have eliminated Himmler, Chief of the Gestapo, as well. 'I'm even more distressed to find out the Führer has appointed that butcher Himmler Commander of the German Army. His reign of terror *must* be stopped... This man is the architect of the plan to exterminate the Jewish population.'

He gives me a worried look and starts pacing up and down. I'm still in shock, thinking, *The general is hiding out in my kitchen while we come up with a plan to help him escape. Am I crazy?* We both know all too well the consequences of his involvement in the assassination plot. Dribbles of information have been coming in all day on the secret wireless radios around Paris. So far, we've learned that conspirators in Germany have been hung by the neck with piano wire or shot in the back of the head or committed suicide.

'*Your* part?' I ask, disbelieving. 'But you're a Party member and an SS officer.'

He grins. 'Do you remember our poker games here at Maison Bleue, mademoiselle?'

'Yes. I wondered why the Wehrmacht and SS officers you played cards with never cared if they won or lost.'

'Our sole purpose for meeting here wasn't for a friendly game of poker or to gaze upon our beautiful hostess, though you *did* provide an exquisite diversion.' He kisses my hand and I see that old sparkle ignite in his eyes. 'I requisitioned your home to plot with my fellow officers from the old Prussian school of thinking. We were determined to find a way to secure a future for Germany and stop these crimes against humanity.'

'I'm not surprised at what you're telling me, General.' My heart tugs and my mind tries to absorb all that I'm hearing. 'I've believed for a long time you weren't like the others, that you have a conscience... and a soul.'

He shrugs. 'I'm no hero, mademoiselle. If I were, I never would have joined the National Socialist Party in 1933, listening to a fanatic spewing promises he could never keep in hopes of rebuilding my defeated homeland.'

'Germany will need men like you after the war,' I insist.

He chuckles. 'I'm an old man, mademoiselle, and I have no more to give but to do the right thing for the heritage I honor.' He sighs and the pain in my heart grows when I see the sincerity in his eyes. To my surprise, he kisses me on both cheeks. 'I shall never forget the joys of being in your presence, mademoiselle. Knowing you has been the delight of my life. Now I must go. I have important business to conduct, *if* the Gestapo doesn't arrest me first.' He heaves out a heavy sigh. 'It shall not be pleasant if they do.'

'Why the Gestapo?' I'm curious to know.

'The Gestapo may be a small organization of secret police, but they enjoy complete power in keeping order, and that includes jurisdiction over criminal activities.'

'Including members of the SS?' I ask slowly.

'Yes. Most unfortunate for me.'

'So Herr Geller will come calling.'

'A man I have little respect for, mademoiselle. He has no conscience. Like all Gestapo, he'll use every method of surveillance, blackmail, torture, even murder to get what he wants.'

'And the SS?'

'We operate in the field, act as security, and do the administrative work, including organizing this obsession the Führer has with acquiring art for his museum.' He rubs his forehead to ease the strain. 'And I regret to say, special "death squad" SS units make up the guards in the labor camps. They're a degenerate bunch of sadists.' He sighs. 'I was once proud of the prestige of my rank. Not anymore. The problem is, members of the SS believe they're superior to everyone, but in the end, we're nothing but flesh and bones.' Head in hands, he leaves the rest unsaid.

I know what will happen to the general, and it's breaking my heart. This is a man who saved me from shame and kept us all safe at Maison Bleue during the Occupation. We remained under his protection even if everyone suspected Claire isn't his child, but no one dared to say it. We also have him to thank for keeping Madame de Giocomte with us, granting her amnesty so they couldn't deport her to Auschwitz.

I owe him the courtesy of helping him make his final journey.

I know what I have to do. A call to Arsène and the use of the general's motorcar should do the trick. That way I can help the SS officer and also protect my family. I think of my two little girls sleeping in their beds. I'd die if they took them away to a labor camp and, knowing what I do, they'd never survive the cruelty, not to mention the inhuman living conditions. And it's for those poor children who suffer in such camps I pray this war ends soon. Afterward I will do everything I can for those who make it back home to Paris.

'Stay here, General, until my sister Ève comes to fetch you.'

'Then what, mademoiselle?' He juts out his chin in defiance. 'I will not run from my fate, but I *will* be master of it.'

He doesn't have to spell out his decision, and I respect that.

'Trust me, General, I have a plan.'

* * *

*Ève*

It's not every day I assist a Nazi SS general to escape from the Gestapo. If anyone but Justine asked me to do it, I'd balk and protest and question her loyalty to France. But I have no doubt she has a good reason. My sister's eyes seem to turn a deep cobalt blue when she asks me, telling me she's deadly serious when she explains her plan to get the sad and defeated gentleman secretly back to his suite at the Hôtel Meurice. Yes, *gentleman*. Whatever reservations I had about this assignment, I also fall under his spell. He's not only charming but also respectful, and at one point in our conversation, he apologizes to me for the 'maniacal madness' that has fallen upon Paris. I nod, then smile because I don't know what else to do. We speak very little after that when I escort him through the hidden kitchen entrance in the root cellar. I swear Cook has a moment she'll never forget when she sees the older man in the gray-green Nazi uniform tip his cap to her. Then I watch as a German officer whisks him away in the sidecar attached to his motorcycle.

Arsène, of course.

Then I wait. Justine warned me what would happen next.

That Gestapo man, Herr Geller, will come calling. Right on cue, I hear a loud knock on the front door. I open it.

'I wish to speak to Mademoiselle D'Artois,' he bellows before I can say a word. 'I need to see her *immediately*, do you understand?'

'*Pardon,* monsieur, this is not a good time.'

He regards me with disdain. 'And who the hell are you?'

'I'm the nanny to her little girls.'

He pushes his way inside and circles me, curious. 'You look familiar, mademoiselle. Where have I seen your face?'

He saw me at the Hôtel Drouot, but I wasn't blonde then. I attempt a crooked smile to put him off. 'I imagine all Frenchwomen with blonde hair look familiar, monsieur.'

He shrugs and glares at me and for a moment I think he's going to ask me for my papers, but lucky for me, he's preoccupied with Gestapo business. 'You don't object if I search the house?' he asks with a smirk. 'It doesn't matter. I shall do it anyway.'

'The children are sleeping, monsieur, and Madame de Giocomte and... the maid'—I almost said 'Maman'—'are out.'

'Where did they go?'

'Where else do Frenchwomen go this early in the morning, monsieur?' I say with an attitude I immediately regret, but he lets it pass. 'To queue up for bread, though these days they come home empty-handed.'

He grunts, then groans. Typical Nazi attitude.

I can't let him unnerve me as I show him around the *maison*, not letting on I know this isn't his first visit to Maison Bleue. I get the shivers when he looks behind the long draperies in the foyer, remembering the night I hid there. He pokes his nose everywhere, from the long hallway into the kitchen pantry—I sent

Cook to her room with a hot cup of tea for her nerves—sniffing everywhere like a dog looking for a corner to mark his spot.

'And Mademoiselle D'Artois?' He raises a brow. 'Where is she?'

'She's resting in her room and can't be disturbed,' I lie easily.

'And the general?' he probes further. 'I saw his motorcar parked in the driveway.'

'Do you *really* wish me to answer that question, monsieur?' I shoot him a look that clearly says the general is the reason Mademoiselle D'Artois is not to be disturbed. I don't know if he buys it, but it gives Justine more time to put her plan into action.

'Then I shall wait,' he continues, smirking.

We chat about the cool weather and recent rain while I show him around the library, my pulse going mad waiting for Justine's cue which never seems to come. The Gestapo man makes a rude remark about my sister's 'sloppy housekeeping' when he runs his finger over the torn fabric on the Louis XV chair *he* ruined when—

I hear the roar of the big Mercedes engine come to life. I smile. The Gestapo man scowls then slams his fist into his hand. 'So, you tried to fool me with your flirty talk so the general could escape. Be careful, mademoiselle. I don't forget.'

'Neither do I, monsieur.'

'You haven't seen the last of me. If I don't find the general, you'll be spilling your guts out at Avenue Foch.'

'I assure you, monsieur,' I say with a whisper in my voice, 'you needn't worry. The general knows his duty.'

And with that, the Gestapo man runs out the front door without closing it. He jumps into his big, black Citroën, yells at his driver, and then races off after the general's motorcar while I collapse into Maman's rocking chair.

It's done. I've had my first, and hopefully my *last*, personal encounter with the nefarious Herr Avicus Geller.

* * *

*Justine*

I'm not surprised when we're run off the boulevard by a black Citroën nearly sideswiping the general's Mercedes. I'm jolted about, sitting alone in the back of the motorcar, the passenger curtains half-drawn, when we screech to a stop. With Arsène at the wheel wearing his SS officer's uniform, we were driving down the Champs-Élysées with the Citroën on our tail, giving the general the time he requested to carry out his duty. He wished to be alone. Not at Maison Bleue. I don't want to dwell on it—it makes me so sad, my lips tremble—that even to the end, he insisted that I not be connected to him. *For your protection, mademoiselle.*

I think about how after Claire was born, I'd see the general smile when he observed the handsome SS captain holding my new baby, tickling her under the chin and looking so proud. I will always remember the general like that. For now, I have a more unpleasant duty upon me. I peek through the window curtain and see the passenger door to the Citroën pop open, and Herr Geller jumps out.

I smile. *Perfect.*

'Justine... are you hurt?' Arsène turns around to check on me, his dark eyes grave. He made no attempt to evade the near collision. It's part of our plan. After he escorted the general to the Hôtel Meurice, he returned to find me hunched down in the back of the motorcar, waiting. He jumped into the driver's seat and gunned the engine and we raced away from Maison Bleue with a loud roar to attract the Gestapo man's attention. The second act is in play.

'I'm a bit shaken, but—'

Before I can finish, the Gestapo man yanks the passenger door open and grunts his displeasure at finding me alone. He pays no attention to Arsène. Typical. He considers the driver a lackey and not worth acknowledging his presence.

If he only knew...

The Nazi grabs my wrist hard, but I refuse to show him fear. 'Where is he, mademoiselle?'

'Herr Geller,' I say with sweetness coating my voice, 'what a nice surprise to see you.'

'Don't give me your usual flimsy excuses. I'm not in a pleasant mood.'

'Are you ever?' I dare to say, even if I make him angry. I shouldn't be so bold, but I need to stall him... for the general's sake.

'Where is General von Klum?' he demands, squeezing my wrist. I wince, bite down on my lip. I'm not worried about myself, but if Arsène thinks the Gestapo man goes too far, I'm afraid of what he'll do to protect me.

I back off. 'I'm sorry for my abruptness, Herr Geller, but you caught me off guard. You see, the general left in a huff this morning over something he wouldn't share with me. An officer I didn't recognize picked him up and they sped off. I'm worried about him and I was on my way to his hotel—'

'I'll take care of the situation, mademoiselle,' he says with glee. 'Go home and wait for my orders.'

'But what about the general—'

'General von Klum won't be coming back, mademoiselle, but if you do as I say, you have nothing to worry about.'

Then with a grand flourish, the secret policeman slams the door shut and screams at his driver, 'Hôtel Meurice, and *hurry*!'

I lie back in the comfortable black leather seat and close my eyes. The deed is done. History will report this day as a failed attempt by several Nazi officers to end the madness. And I have no regrets for my part in it.

* * *

Soon after, a small item appears on the back pages of the *Paris-soir* newspaper. It simply says that General Karl von Klum was found dead in his hotel suite at the Hôtel Meurice and hinted that he committed suicide after he learned about the death of his nephew on the Eastern Front. Ève and I know better: that he was not only part of the aborted attempt on Hitler's life in March 1943, but also recently when high-ranking German officers tried and failed with a 'suitcase bomb' to kill the Führer. He was labeled a traitor to the Reich but I don't see it that way. Yes, the general was a Nazi, but he was also a man with dignity who tried to right the wrongs of an evil leader and destroy the Nazi regime that devastated a whole race of people. A regime that shook the world to its core with its cruelty and the murder of more than six million Jews, Roma, and others.

I will remember him as a good man trapped in an evil system, a man who tried to bring it down from within, just as I had in my own way by acting as the major's girl to gather intelligence. I shall never forget the last time I saw him when Ève and I helped him escape the Gestapo. Warm, respectful. And filled with that Prussian sense of duty he was so proud of. He took his own life later in his hotel suite rather than face a trial and defame his heritage.

I shall miss him.

# 29

## PARIS, AUGUST 1944

*Justine*

Ève and I walk arm-in-arm down the Rue de Rivoli on this glorious day of liberation, taking in the awe and wonder of seeing Allied troops everywhere, smoking, gawking at French girls, taking pictures, when I see the man who raped me.

Major Saxe-Müllenheim. I stop cold.

The tall, blond SS officer scowls even now when the German Army has admitted defeat, still arrogant when he's ushered out of a big, black motorcar, a limousine actually, parked at the pavement curb along with several other German officers.

I peek over the rim of my dark glasses to get a better look. 'Ève, it's *him*.'

My sister squeezes my arm. 'What... *Who*?'

'The major. He just got out of that motorcar.'

Ève turns her head, gasps. 'Oh, my God, Justine, I don't believe it. It *is* the bastard.'

We hold each other tight, knowing what we see isn't an illusion, but still not believing it. We're not the only ones gawking at the Nazis. A small crowd of curiosity seekers mulls around, whispering, pointing. I'm just plain stunned. What are the chances of me running into the SS officer who changed me forever? We heard they were rounding up German officers, but to come this close again to that ugly moment in my life makes me queasy and my emotions spark all over the place. I take in deep breaths to tamp down the flame of reliving the horror that will burn me if I get too close. I thought I was done with it.

Obviously I'm not.

Earlier we watched German prisoners in beetle-green uniforms be paraded down the Rue de Rivoli by Allied soldiers with their hands raised above their heads. There were no smiles, only jeers and cries of anguish from the onlookers, and I swear if anyone *had* a rotten tomato they'd toss it at the bunch. Enlisted men with an officer or two, fat and surly, all forced to march together. We were shocked then disgusted, turned around and went in a different direction. I didn't want to see them and get that sickening feeling in my stomach. Not when we were in a lovely mood.

We were enjoying a sisterly stroll to revel in this marvelous new freedom, but our main goal was to check on Madame Péroline at the hat shop. It was closed but I was happy to hear the milliner had left for Lyon to be reunited with her husband and son. Maman didn't need to be asked twice to babysit my two girls —she can't get enough of her *grand-mère* duties. I bade her and the girls to stay at Maison Bleue. The Allied Forces have taken Paris, but the danger isn't over. Reports of German snipers shooting from the rooftops keep us vigilant on our walk while armed Resistance fighters patrol the streets. We've kept to the *maison* until today to stay clear of skirmishes with the occupiers the past few days. Ève took up arms at the barricades around Notre-Dame, but returned home to Maison Bleue when she got wind of a new danger. Angry Parisians out for revenge. *Anyone* who collaborated with the Boches is being arrested, but she's got a plan to keep me safe. Which is why I'm wearing dark glasses, a plain tan skirt, white blouse, and a white turban to cover my hair. No more Rachelle D'Artois with her stylish silk suits and flamboyant hats with long veils.

Justine Beaufort is back.

We were on our way home when I saw the big, black six-seater limousine with the word 'Police' painted in big, crude white letters on the roof parked at the curb not far from where we were standing on the pavements. A Resistance fighter wielding a rifle stood guard and hustled out its occupants. Something I can't explain drew me to look. I observed several German officers in uniform all looking dazed. The major was the last Nazi to exit the vehicle, a French soldier yelling at him to get going.

All at once, the day changed from a day of celebration to a day of reckoning.

What makes me smirk is when I see that the major isn't wearing that stiff Nazi cap. Or his black leather gloves.

He looks as naked as a dead black crow, its feathers plucked.

'You can't hurt anyone now, can you?' I mutter under my breath, more to myself than the major. I'm grateful Arsène isn't here—he's working with British intelligence to clean up the Nazis' mess at the Hôtel Majestic where they tried to burn papers, files, notes, even maps. I wouldn't trust my man not to take a punch to the major's jaw; not that he doesn't deserve it, but this is something I have to do on my own.

I get closer to the prisoners, but Ève lays a hand on my arm. 'Be careful, Justine. That's not a real police vehicle,' she warns me. 'The Resistance has commandeered motorcars and painted the word "Police" on them. They're working with the Allies, but they have their own set of rules.'

I nod. She means they're looking for women like me. *Collabos.*

'We should move on, Justine,' my sister continues. 'Get back to Maison Bleue and get you out of Paris as we planned.'

'Just give me one minute with him, Ève.'

'Justine...'

'I need this, little sister.'

She lets out a heavy sigh, but she understands. '*Bien.*'

I keep my head down, my hands to my sides and move closer to where the prisoners are hustled together. The American and French soldiers milling around give me a cursory glance; I'm just another curious Parisienne. There's no real order to what's going on, Americans chatting with each other, French giving orders, *résistants* keeping an eye on the prisoners, giving me the opportunity to seek out the major waiting impatiently with the others while Ève diverts the attention of the armed fighter with a pretty smile.

I take off my dark glasses and step forward so the major can see me.

I don't have to say a word.

He knows it's me. The look on his face is so twisted, so scornful, it shocks me. Crossed brows. Jaw set firm. Blue eyes razor sharp. Cutting. Hateful. No remorse, no regret on that face. We lock eyes and he glares at me. The SS officer knows he's beaten and he *hates* it. I swear it's too much for his ego. He turns and walks away and I wonder if he intends to make a run for it, though God knows, there's nowhere to hide. I sense this final show of bravado is for my benefit, to show me he's still in charge. He isn't. His freedom doesn't last.

An American soldier shouts at him in English, calling him a

'dirty Kraut...' and shoves the butt of his rifle into his back, forcing the major down on his knees, then he shouts again and the major puts his hands on top of his head.

Right in front of me.

The young American soldier in battle-worn khakis, the strap hanging loose on his hard helmet, regards me with curiosity, but he doesn't order me to go away. I sense he knows I have something on my mind and he's curious to see what happens next. He keeps his rifle pointed at the major, then nods his head, as if to say, *Let him have it.* He has no idea I'm not just an angry woman wanting to give this Boche a piece of my mind. He'll never know he's brought home a personal victory to me today. Time has stopped and I stand so still I feel carved in marble as I look at the major. I inhale a deep breath, filling my lungs with freedom until I feel as powerful as a goddess on the mount judging the fate of this mere, disgusting mortal.

'Do you remember that day at Maison Bleue, Major?' I step closer to him to make sure he hears me. Then I whisper, 'The day you *raped* me?'

'You have mistaken me for someone else, mademoiselle. I never touched you or any French whore.' He gloats at seeing me blush at his use of the pejorative word, then mutters an expletive in German.

'You can't deny what you did, Major; the party's over. You'll pay for what you did to me and other women, I promise you. You've lost. And I've won. The whole world has won because we beat you and your whole damn Nazi regime. *Vive la France!*'

I turn my back to him and take long, confident strides down the boulevard, rounding the corner, knowing Ève is close behind me. I'm shaking all over, but life is good. *Very* good.

Today I saw the man who raped me and I confronted him.

I don't feel revengeful; I don't feel sad.
I feel free.

# 30

## PARIS, MAY 1945

*Justine*

I am coming undone in ways I never imagined. I am suffering from survivor's guilt hearing the stories from the deportees returning from the concentration camps, especially the women released from Ravensbrück. I hear harrowing accounts about the inhuman medical experiments the Nazis conducted on their bodies and how they were forced to work in the camp brothel serving German soldiers. I am shivering, feeling lightheaded, almost fainting reliving my own sexual assault five years ago as I try to help these women. Some refuse to talk; others talk too much. Some just walk the corridors and cry. And I cry with them.

I wear gloves on my hands and my heart on my sleeve as I go from table to table in the reception room in the Hôtel Lutetia, handing out lime-blossom tea in silver cups, crusty bread and butter to the stream of poor souls who never stop coming and have no idea where they're going, but hope to find the smallest piece of normalcy here. And if they're lucky, reconnect with a dear family member.

What tears me apart is how little we knew about what was happening in Germany and Poland. *Will Monsieur de Giocomte show up? Iris?* I ask myself every day. Sadly... no. They don't return from the camps. But the others who do are now the tellers of these stories. They sit at small round tables in their concentration camp uniforms, their emaciated faces with sharp cheekbones lit up under the chandeliers, their heads shorn, their faces dirty, sniffing fresh flowers in a vase, the pleasant scent reminding them *they* survived. They made it home.

If only that's all it takes.

It's not.

We can't completely eliminate the smell of old blood and filth lingering in their nostrils from months, years, of unsanitary conditions. We try. Ève is assisting me this morning with female deportees from Ravensbrück pouring into the reception room from the corridor. My sister and I are among hundreds of volunteers working around the clock with the Red Cross and the help centers established by women like Madame de Giocomte. She recounts often to the deportees how *she* received help when she showed up at the Hôtel Lutetia during the Russian Revolution. She and Maman oversee the bulletin boards that span an entire wall filled with photos, identity cards, passports, handwritten notes, scraps of papers with names on them, giving guidance to the scores of souls haunting the hotel looking for loved ones.

Every morning we tune in on the radio to hear the latest list of deportees who have arrived at the hotel, some on stretchers. Sadly, we never hear the names of the baroness, her daughter, or her four granddaughters. Still, Madame de Giocomte and Maman continue to ask the new deportees for information about her family. They keep hoping and so do we. And Ève is praying Michal was freed after we heard about the liberation of Colditz Castle last month. Still, she admitted to me she's resigned herself to believing her Polish fighter returned to Warsaw, not Paris. I hugged her, trying to give her hope. For now, once the deportees enter through the revolving wooden door at the entrance, our job is to make sure they're deloused, washed, fed, given medical care, a bed to sleep in, and, when they're ready to leave in a few days, a week, two thousand francs and a voucher for a new set of clothes. It still isn't enough.

I've seen confusion, fear, hatred, loneliness—every emotion coloring the rainbow of human feelings since I started helping out here. The Hôtel Lutetia on the Left Bank was once the headquarters for the Abwehr, German military intelligence, but since April it's a center for returning deportees to rally and get a semblance of normalcy where even the simplest thing is a luxury. Earlier I was touched by a woman who survived Auschwitz when she told me the best part about being here was sleeping in a room alone.

By herself. Not in crowded bunks filled to four times their capacity.

Others have similar stories about the unspeakable conditions they lived through, and I listen to every word, how they can't believe they have hot and cold running water to wash with and jam to spread on their bread.

Still others don't talk at all, their jaws clenched and their eyes growing big and glassy when they're asked by shattered and worried families if they knew their mother, father... their sister in the camp. Which makes me suspect they *do* know and the horror is still so real, so *vivid*, they can't talk about it.

I check my watch. Five o'clock. Arsène will be here soon to pick us up. We arrived at 7 a.m. this morning and I'm eager to go home and check on my little girls. But Ève is clearly upset when she rushes to my side, holding the hand of a girl no more than sixteen. She's one of the lucky ones having only spent a few months in the labor camp, but the story she tells grabs my sister and me and doesn't let go.

'Blanche... that's her name, says she was raped over and over by the SS guards at Ravensbrück, Justine,' Ève whispers in my ear. 'I'm afraid she's going to hurt herself if we don't help her.'

My sister found her muttering about 'being unclean, not fit to be here', staring at knives, picking them up, and then putting them back down. As if trying to decide what to do.

'How long has she been here?' I ask.

'She arrived this morning with three other survivors from Ravensbrück from Gare d'Orsay in an open truck.'

I let out a deep breath. 'I'll try to help her, give her hope.' I muster my courage to broach a subject I keep hidden behind my smile: my own rape by the SS. I approach her slowly so as not to frighten her. I've seen deportees drop to the floor and cover their heads when someone talks too loud.

'My sister says we have something in common, Blanche.' I try to smile, show her kindness. 'I was a victim of the SS, too.'

She looks at me odd. I must appear strange to her in a pretty dress with puffed sleeves made from silk printed in a pink and green floral design. My long hair is pinned in round curls on top of my head. Ève stands next to me in her smart suit, her hair reaching over her shoulders.

'You were in the camps, mademoiselle?' Blanche asks.

'No,' I say softly, not certain I'm ready to speak about the rape. 'I was—'

'I'll tell you what she was,' shouts a female voice from the corridor. 'She was a Nazi major's mistress by the name of Rachelle D'Artois. Even had a brat by him.'

I try to get a grip on what I *think* I heard, but my heart is thundering too loud in my chest, and my cheeks flame. Bright and hot. My worst nightmare come true. *Why now?* I escaped the head shaving and shameless treatment of women accused of having liaisons with Nazi officers after the liberation of Paris in August 1944 by Ève taking me and my little girls to an old hunting lodge outside Paris. She told me all about the carrier pigeons she tended to, sending secret messages to England, and a brave pigeon she named after me. Then her face dropped and her eyes got misty when she said it was also where Michal was shot by the Germans. I couldn't get any more out of her than that.

Her ploy to save me worked. Arsène spread the word among the FFI—French Forces of the Interior—sporting armbands and hunting down collaborators to be tried and convicted that Mademoiselle Rachelle D'Artois had fled to Switzerland. It was a dangerous time with justice handed out to anyone accused of being a collaborator anywhere, anytime.

I thought I was safe.

Until today.

Ève squeezes my hand tight and calls out in a firm voice, 'Who said that?'

'*I* did, mademoiselle, and you know it's true.'

A slight figure of a woman walks from the corridor into the reception area, but she's blocked from my view by curious deportees and workers who can't believe their ears. 'Who is she?' they whisper among themselves. Everyone claiming to be freed from the camps is interviewed by the police before they're given shelter to prevent this from happening, but now it has. Only it's not a deportee getting the scowls and dirty looks. It's me.

I fight back. 'You're mistaken, mademoiselle. My name is Justine Beaufort.'

'I don't care what you call yourself now, mademoiselle,' the woman says, coming forward and standing under a chandelier so we can see her. 'I saw you cozying up to Nazis. You were a major's mistress.'

Ève gasps loudly, her hand going to her chest. I've never seen her eyes pop open so wide, like the doll's eyes when the major tossed it on the floor. 'I *know* that voice, Justine. I know who she is.'

*Do I?* I study the young woman in her tattered, striped prisoner gown hanging on her thin skeletal-like body, her hair short, sunken eyes ringed with a bluish cast, her skin as pale as the hotel's stone façade. She can't weigh more than forty kilograms.

I ask, 'Who is she, Ève?'

'I never would have recognized her if I didn't hear her speak. It's Coralie, the Gestapo informant on the bicycle who—'

I nod. 'Yes, I remember. She followed me and then she was shot.' I want to yell back to her, *Yes, you saw me because you were following me under orders from the Gestapo.*

I don't. The woman was a Nazi informant. Everyone is listening, waiting as old prejudices reignite. I remember after the liberation when the thirst for revenge was so high people were falsely accused of collaborating with the enemy and arrested and beaten in the streets. What was even more unnerving was that Resistance fighters had taken over the police headquarters because the French police lost their credibility. No one trusted them, not after they assisted the Germans in the roundups of Jews, guarding government buildings and doing the Nazis' dirty work, whether it was arresting citizens for being out after curfew or street prostitutes. I thought those days were past us when rumors alone could get you arrested, but with so many people from the camps returning to Paris—hundreds a day—the old hatred has flared up again.

And I'm caught in the middle. If I reveal the woman to be an informant, angry survivors will tear her apart before we can stop them. If I say nothing, they'll turn on me. Blanche pulls away from me. 'You *slept* with a Nazi. How could you let him touch you?'

Shouts, crying, wailing from the crowd follows. These survivors I'm trying to help turn on me. I've *got* to defend myself.

'*Please*, listen to me,' I shout, trying to speak over their jeers. 'You don't understand. I'm a victim, too, I was—'

Before I can finish, Coralie rushes at me, denouncing me with vulgar words, pulling at my hair until it comes undone and falls upon my shoulders, grabbing my puffy sleeves and ripping them. Where she gets the strength, I can't imagine, but I won't fight her. She's guilty of being an informant, but she's a concentration camp survivor and suffered the most horrific torture and humiliation at the hands of the SS. From what I've heard from other survivors, servicing five or more men a day in the camp brothel.

I keep pushing her away. She's got to get tired and let go of me, then I can calm her down, but the crowd keeps calling *me* out, in their minds the terror returning, the SS guards shouting, then the dying. The workers try to diffuse the situation, when Ève grabs a tall crystal glass and *bangs* on it with a silver spoon. Several times. *Loud.* The effect is chilling. And sobering. Everyone stops. Even Coralie backs off, her fragile spirit shattered by the noise.

'*Quiet, everyone!*' Ève shouts. 'My sister Justine has the right to speak in her own defense and you're all going to listen.'

# 31

## PARIS, MAY 1945

### *Ève*

*'I'm not a collaborator!'* Justine says in a loud, clear voice. Her eyes are glassy, their blue color so clear it scares me, like she's shut down inside. She can't believe these people have turned on her.

'Go on, Justine, I'm here for you. Tell your story.'

She nods. 'I worked for the Allies in a hat shop gathering intelligence which I passed on to my handler, but before that I was... Oh, how can I explain what happened to me, what it was like to be—'

She stops. Cold. I know Justine; she's reached that moment when she has to talk about the rape to strangers. And she can't. She's brave, wonderful and daring, but to talk about the degrading act in public?

I know what I have to do.

I step in front of her to speak my piece.

'The war is over, the Nazis driven out of Paris,' I begin, 'but there are many among you who fought in the Resistance. You kept secrets, told lies to your families to keep them safe, risked your lives and did whatever you had to do to win the war. So did my sister. She went undercover to get inside the Nazi war machine, uncover important information. And this woman who accuses her, who is she? She's—'

Justine tugs on my arm, shakes her head. I'm so fired up I almost exposed Coralie for what she is. A Gestapo informant. I look at this girl still young in years but old in spirit. She's still wearing the drab, torn prisoner uniform from the concentration camp. I heard what happened at Ravensbrück. Justine is right. She's suffered enough, but I won't let her hurt my sister.

'Justine has never spoken about it, but my sister is also a victim of sexual violence by the SS. She was kidnapped and taken from us in the first weeks after the occupation began,' I continue. 'No woman wants to be raped. The shame, humiliation, the extreme guilt that it's *her* fault, takes years to get over, if she ever does. Her family suffers, too. I was there when Major Saxe-Müllenheim invaded our home and raped my beautiful sister. Afterward I thought she was dead, but then I found out she was working for the Boches. I *hated* her. Refused to speak to her. Even *I* believed she was a Nazi collaborator, and I know her better than anyone. We were so close growing up, sharing secrets, but this was one secret she couldn't share with me without putting my life in danger along with our *maman* and Madame de Giocomte, who's like a *grand-mère* to us.'

'*You're lying!*' a man shouts, tearing off his prisoner cap and waving it in my face. 'She was a Nazi whore.'

'How *dare* you, monsieur. My sister *never* slept willingly with the major, *never*. He raped her more than once while she acted as a double agent for the British working to help the Allies win the war and save your arse.' It pains me to be so harsh with the man knowing what he's endured, but Justine's life is on the line. This will break her if she can't go home to her two beautiful daughters.

'You can't prove it,' someone says.

'I can, and I will.'

*Where is Arsène?* He should be here any minute to pick us up. I look out over the people gathering around Justine and me, some challenging me, others believing me. I've *got* to find him. He'll back me up—my heart stops when I see another man in the crowd watching me, a man so filled with purpose and with that crazy swagger that makes me smile, that cocky attitude that got us through so many missions. A man I'd give my life for. He's here, *oh my dearest God,* he's here, he's safe, he came back to me, thank you.

'Michal...' I whisper, taking in the wonder of him standing tall in a Polish officer's uniform. His jacket is dirty, torn. He looks tired and he's lost weight, *but he's alive*. Now I understand why he surrendered. He must have worn his uniform underneath his jacket and knew he'd be considered a prisoner of war and not a spy. He never looked more handsome: wide, strong shoulders, broad chest. His dark hair mussed and falling over his eyes. He sees me and smiles and I love the wonderful feelings filling me up. I can't wait to rush into his arms, but not before I get my sister out of this mess.

'I want you all to know that what my sister went through was a living hell that haunts her to this day, but she didn't cower before the Nazis. *Ever*. The man who took her beat and violated her, her spirit so damaged she wanted to end her life, but she didn't. She gave it right back to them when she became a double agent for the Allies.'

'Prove it,' I hear someone say.

'She doesn't have to,' echoes a man's strong baritone. 'I can vouch for mademoiselle's sister.'

I hear Justine gasp. She's smiling at the man in the RAF uniform racing to her side.

*Arsène.*

'Justine Beaufort as Rachelle D'Artois gathered intelligence for the Allies since the summer of 1940,' Arsène tells the crowd in a clear, determined voice. 'She was a valuable and protected asset of the SOE F, Special Operations Executive, French Section. The rest is classified, but if anyone here *dares* to accuse her of being a Nazi collaborator, they will have me and the entire British Foreign Office to deal with.'

Then without another word, Arsène scoops Justine up in his arms and carries her out of the reception room and out of the Lutetia Hôtel and into history.

Not a sound comes from anyone.

Even me.

* * *

'I've never been more proud of you, Ève,' Michal says, holding my face in his hands, his eyes joyous, and me not believing he's really here. 'You spoke the truth with so much admiration and feeling for your sister, I wanted to grab you and kiss you.'

'Then why didn't you?' I tease him, not the least embarrassed when he sweeps me up in his arms and nuzzles his face in my hair.

'Here?' he says, his voice hoarse. 'Don't tempt me, Ève.'

The foyer of the Hôtel Lutetia is filled with concentration camp survivors milling about, so many lost and confused. This isn't the place I'd have chosen to reunite with my Polish fighter. Then again, maybe it is. Everyone here has survived the horror of the camps and, like Michal, found their way back to Paris to search for loved ones. What could be more hopeful to them than seeing us reunited?

Or am I a fool?

I couldn't be that lucky Michal came looking just for me, *could I*?

'I dreamed every night, Ève, about holding you in my arms.' He runs his fingers through my hair falling past my shoulders. 'I *have* been gone a long time. Your hair has grown out. I've never seen you look more beautiful.'

'You've been in a Nazi prison for eighteen months and all you can talk about is how much my hair has grown?'

'Well, we could discuss other parts of you that I missed.' He leans over and looks at my backside, reminding me of all the late-night missions we spent in the dirt lying on our bellies crushed together.

'Michal Laska, you're incorrigible.'

He grins. 'Miss me?'

'No, I was too busy doing *your* job blowing up trains since you had to go and get yourself arrested by the Gestapo.'

'I had no choice. I found out the Abwehr was on to me, Ève,' he says with a seriousness in his voice that tugs at me. 'I was on borrowed time until the Nazis picked me up, then arrested me for espionage and executed me.' He tells me he was a commander in the Polish Army and a military strategist before he escaped from Warsaw with a price on his head before he joined the Resistance. 'I never expected to run into a Gestapo van in the middle of the woods. I blamed myself every day in that cold, damp castle prison for putting you in danger.'

'You did?'

'Yes, I did.'

'Then you *do* care... about me.' I'm not holding back my feelings. I can't, even if I lose him again.

Exasperated, he says, 'You haven't changed, Ève, still putting words into my mouth.'

'Because I care about you, Michal. Oh, don't worry, I'm not going to say I love you… I know how you feel about that.'

'Then let me say it.'

'*What*?' Am I hearing my big, brave Polish fighter correctly?

'I love you, Ève. I thought about you every day in that damn place. You got me through the worst when I escaped and the Nazis recaptured me and put me in solitary for a week. I kept thinking, *Ève wouldn't let you give up*. I was planning another go at it when the Americans liberated us.'

'Why didn't you return to Warsaw?' I dare to ask.

He ignores the longing stares and curious onlookers listening to us and says what's on his mind. '*You*, Ève. I'm never going to leave you again.'

'Even if I cut my hair?' I tease.

'Yes, even if you cut your hair.'

His words make my heart sing. The war is over, Paris is free, and I have the feeling life with Michal is just beginning. I can't wait to tell Justine, though I have the feeling she and Arsène have things to talk about after what happened here today.

'Well then, you big, wonderful man,' I say, lifting my chin and standing on my tiptoes, 'what are you waiting for? *Kiss me*.'

# 32

## PARIS, MAY 1945

*Justine*

'I'm not letting you out of my sight again, Justine.' Arsène heads down Rue Raspail toward the Boulevard Saint-Germain, my head on his shoulder as he drives me home in an American jeep with a white star on the hood. I give thanks I no longer have to ride in a Mercedes motorcar with that annoying tiny swastika flag. 'Those poor souls got so fired up,' he continues, 'they would have you tarred and marched through the streets of Paris if it wasn't for Ève.'

'And *you, mon chéri,* looking so handsome in your uniform.' I sound brave, but I'm still shaken up by the ugly confrontation with Coralie at the Hôtel Lutetia. I'll always hold close to my heart the moment when Arsène swept me up into his arms. I felt so protected when he carried me out of the hotel, I didn't want it to end.

We arrive back at Maison Bleue. I kiss my babies on their foreheads, my two little angels asleep in their beds and dreaming wonderful things, having no idea what their *maman* just went through, an awakening within me how fragile life is and how lucky I am to be surrounded by such love. Madame de Giocomte and Maman came rushing back to the *maison* to check on me. We hug and talk, and hold hands. Arsène never leaves my side. And Ève? Maman says she and Michal took everyone's breath away, several survivors expressing both joy and hope watching their reunion. And when they kissed, she said, there wasn't a dry eye in the hotel. I can't wait to hear all the juicy details.

Ève. Where do I begin?

I learned a lot about my sister today. That I hurt her more than I imagined with my 'double life', but she never stopped believing she could bring me home. That she came through for me in spite of her intense hatred for the woman she thought I'd become when I needed her the most with Ninette... and again today at the Hôtel Lutetia. That I'm lucky to have a sister like her.

And a man like Arsène.

We're walking in the garden hand-in-hand among the daisies starting to bloom. I can smell the basil Ève is so fond of tickling my nose with its fragrant scent. It's here where Ève and I forged our strongest bond as The Daisy Sisters, a bond that almost didn't survive the Occupation, but in the end it did.

'We're getting married, Justine,' he says. 'I was a damned fool not to make you my wife after the liberation of Paris.'

'You're still in the RAF. God knows the red tape you'd have to go through to marry me.'

'I don't care if I have to ask General de Gaulle for permission.' He stops; his lips brush my cheek. 'I want to marry you, Justine.'

'Arsène—'

'No more excuses. I won't take no for an answer. I love you.'

'But—'

'We'll get married tomorrow if I can get Father Armand to pull strings for me with the local magistrate.'

The kind-hearted priest has already agreed to help us arrange to name Arsène as the father on Claire's birth certificate. She was born at the American Hospital of Paris like her big sister. A place of comfort and safety for me when it came time to bring both my children into the world. The hospital doesn't register a baby's birth; the office from the Neuilly-sur-Seine *mairie*, city hall, takes care of that. An understanding clerk allowed me to leave the father's name blank, not unusual with so many babies born from the union of Frenchwomen and German soldiers.

'You say you want me to marry you,' I fire back, teasing, 'without letting me get a word in edgewise?'

'Forgive me, Justine, I die inside every time I relive that scene at the hotel.'

'Me, too, but I'm sure I'm not the only Frenchwoman reluctant to speak about her part in the Resistance. I hope others will come forward and get the recognition they deserve.' My eyes grow misty. I can't help it. 'I wouldn't be here without you. You kept me safe during the war.'

'I'd have married you then if I could.'

'You would?'

'Yes, all I ever wanted was to make you my wife since that first day I saw you. You were so hurt and wounded, yet determined not to be a victim, and your spirit was golden like the sun, so strong that even that SS major couldn't burn out your light. I saw a fierce need in you then to survive. You haven't lost it.'

'I never will... as long as I have you.'

He smiles wide. 'Justine Beaufort, will you marry me?'

'Oh, yes...' I stop, think. 'Wait, I don't even know your name.'

Arsène is what he called himself when I first met him at Chez Mimi disguised as an old soldier from the Great War.

Arsène leans in and whispers in my ear.

I blink, my hand going to my throat. I can't believe it.

* * *

Late afternoon the following day in the Church of Saint-Pierre-de-Chaillot where Arsène and I met in the confessional during the war, where I felt safe and secure hearing his voice coming through the grill, then his hand brushing mine when I lit a votive candle, Father Armand joins us together as man and wife. When the priest reads the sacred vows, I can't say 'I do' fast enough. I look at my new husband, beaming. Ève, Maman, and Madame de Giocomte toss daisy petals at us and cry, while my two little girls can't help but giggle helplessly through the informal ceremony. Michal waits patiently for Ève to join him once we get Maman to stop crying. I cry, too, seeing Ève glowing with joy to have her man back in Paris with her. He's a fine match for my little sister and afterward they speak to Father Armand to plan their own wedding.

I give thanks to God for every day we shall all have together in a free France.

'I love you, Justine.' Arsène wraps his arms around me. 'You *are* Paris in my eyes. The elegance of her grand boulevards, the sweet perfume of her flower markets, the hot passion of her cabarets, the holy white purity of Sacré-Coeur; you're everything to me.' He lowers his voice so only I can hear him. 'Shall we take a room at the Hôtel Ritz, milady? I can't wait to make love to you as you should be loved without those damn Nazis hanging around.'

I smile. He called me 'milady'. I could never have imagined

me, a little girl from the slums of northern Paris, a girl who suffered the horror of rape at the hands of the SS and then became a spy and double agent for the Allies, becoming the wife of the son of a British earl. Maman faints when I tell her, Madame de Giocomte congratulates me, and Ève hugs me tight.

I look at this man whom I first met in disguise as an old soldier, a man who saw the best in me when I didn't see it myself, a man who risked his own life to shadow mine and keep me and Ninette safe from the wrath of the Nazis.

A man who blessed me with my second daughter Claire to make our little family complete. Whatever cloth he wore, priest or SS officer, when I lifted my gaze to his and stared into his dark, smoldering eyes, I knew he loved me.

I place my hand in his and the simple gold wedding band on my finger glints off the late afternoon sun blazing through the tall, stained glass church windows. 'I'll always respect our marriage vows,' I tell him, 'but I feel strange calling you "milord".'

'We'll talk about that... later.' He starts kissing my neck, my face, making me laugh. The man is wonderfully unpredictable and why I adore him and always will.

I sigh. He may be next in line to be Earl of Flintridge, but to me, he'll always be Arsène.

# EPILOGUE

## PARIS, 1947

*Justine*

I'm sitting on that threadbare damask Louis XV chair once damaged by the Gestapo man on this spring morning here at Maison Bleue contemplating the irony. I survived the war, he did not. I shed no tears for a man who hated women and destroyed so many lives. I've made my peace with that. What's done, I cannot change, but I did seek justice for those he hurt. I'm bursting with wonderful news this morning when the daisies are in bloom in the garden, their honeybee yellow crowns and fluffy white petals blowing their grassy scent through the open doors leading to the library. Ève sits beside me at the big mahogany desk where Monsieur de Giocomte worked on his accounts and where she made notes on that frightful night when Ninette had pneumonia and almost died.

Today I take up that same blue-ink fountain pen and make a 'V' for Victory on the document.

Ève and I just signed a book deal for *The Daisy Sisters*. Our memoir and personal account of how we survived the Occupation of Paris during the war, our intense, volatile relationship as sisters, the men we love, our dear Maman and Madame de Giocomte, and the birth of my two daughters, Ninette and Claire.

Over the past year, Ève and I have spent months gathering material for the book while we take up our lives again. After the war, life at Maison Bleue returned to the normalcy we all hoped for with Madame de Giocomte mounting a campaign to locate her looted Impressionists and other paintings while helping other Jewish families recover their art. I admit, Maman, Ève, and I were deeply touched when she talked about how important it was to recover the works for future generations, meaning my little girls. With her family and Monsieur's all gone, she legally adopted us so Maison Bleue will thrive for generations to come.

Ève picked up that grant she coveted and worked on her experiments with new drugs like penicillin to save lives while I teamed up again with Madame Péroline designing hats. It's wonderful to create without the shadow of the swastika over us, a freedom that we thank God for every day. I still have bad dreams about the war, the rape and what happened to me afterward, how Ève and I spent years apart before Ninette brought us back together again, then spying for the Resistance until Paris was liberated in August 1944.

I shall never forget that day when I confronted the major on the Rue de Rivoli when he expressed a rare show of emotion and clearly showed his hatred of me. And the Allies. He never accepted the fact the party in Paris was over, that Germany and the Wehrmacht were losing the war after the defeat at Stalingrad in February 1943. He did get his comeuppance in a macabre way. He was set to go on trial in Bordeaux for looting Jewish art, but while he was being transported to a prison in southwest France with another SS officer, the police van was 'mysteriously attacked'. The major and the SS officer were killed. It was speculated in the newspapers it was a revenge killing by Resistance fighters, naming the *other* SS officer as the target—he was responsible for sending Jews to Auschwitz. The major was caught in the crossfire and died from his wounds without confessing what he had done to me and other women during the war. Not the justice I wanted, but it fueled my desire not to let his deeds of sexual violence and rape—and other Nazis—be forgotten.

When Arsène returned from London, my joy at seeing him was overwhelming... He witnessed the birth of our daughter before the British Foreign Office called him back to England where he coordinated 'drops' of weapons and agents into France before rejoining me in the summer after the invasion. I shall relish recounting in our memoir that night the Gestapo man stopped us in the general's Mercedes touring car, expecting to find the high-ranking military officer. He knew the Allies were on their way to Paris, but he wouldn't concede the end was near. He did, however, leave me and my little girls alone after the general took his own life. I think he lost interest in me, knowing the end was near.

It came. August 1944.

His own, as well. Herr Geller's body was found in the Seine, most likely dumped there by a Resistance fighter.

When I heard the news about the Gestapo man, I couldn't wait to tell my sister. We sat in the garden on the white Carrara marble bench where we posed as teenagers for *The Daisy Sisters.* In silence, holding hands. A silent prayer between us that this evil man couldn't hurt us or my babies anymore.

Ève and I are closer than ever. We started talking about getting justice years before, but when we heard about the Nuremberg trials starting in November 1945, we knew it was time to speak out. Even though the SS officer who raped me was dead,

I wanted justice. Not just for me, but for every woman who suffered rape and sexual violence at the hands of the Nazis. We worked for months putting together notes, evidence, and with the help of Father Armand, we gathered up paper links of what we call the 'Daisy Chain', honoring victims of rape and sexual abuse during the war. Women writing down the dates of their rape and sexual violence, the name of the Nazi on a piece of paper and leaving them in a special wooden box near the holy water font of the Church of Saint-Pierre-de-Chaillot.

Then we waited.

We never expected such a response.

The box overflowed with pieces of paper. We emptied it, it overflowed again. Until we had over one hundred fifty pieces of paper with names and dates that we forged into a three-meter-long daisy chain.

Next, we faced our biggest challenge. We took the Daisy Chain to Nuremberg when the trials were getting underway. When we tried to get a hearing, we got nowhere. Ève and I were shocked when we were told by a representative of the tribunal of the trials that rape wasn't on the agenda and wouldn't be prosecuted as a war crime.

*Why?* we asked.

When an official stated they didn't want 'crying women' on the stands, Ève and I were appalled, devastated.

Our daisy chain of names, dates, even places meant nothing to them. These men would never be brought to justice. The vow I made to see Major Saxe-Müllenheim pay for his crimes would never be fulfilled.

Until Ève got the brilliant idea of sneaking past the guards into what they called the 'Witness House'. Located in a villa outside the city, witnesses for both the prosecution and the defense boarded together during the trials. Their stories were 'newsworthy' and that meant the local and foreign press would be there. If we couldn't get the tribunal to listen to us, maybe the press would.

We did one better.

We found an American female reporter staying around for the trials instead of going home. She couldn't take notes fast enough, spending hours with Ève and me recounting every detail we could remember about the Occupation of Paris, my rape by an SS officer and how it affected both of us and the men we love. We talked about Maman, Madame and Monsieur de Giocomte, the Gestapo man with his crossword puzzles, the general, Madame Mimi, Ève's work with the Resistance, and the strong women of France we met along the way. Madame Péroline, Iris, and the farmer's wife.

Sadly, we didn't find out until last year the baroness and her family all died at Auschwitz. The general had in fact tried to intervene, but as he had warned me, it was too late, even for the children. The baroness, her daughter, and her four granddaughters were gassed upon arrival. I shall never forget Delphine wearing my blue dress, her eyes as shiny as her buttons. A poignant reminder we must never forget *every* woman who died in the camps.

The reporter took photographs of us wearing our long 'Daisy Chain' around our necks and held nothing back about the rape and sexual violence women suffered at the hands of the Nazis and the Gestapo during the Occupation of Paris.

Her story ran in every newspaper in the United States, England, *and* France.

And what of the painting of *The Daisy Sisters*?

An American captain with the Third US Army found it among the looted art hidden during the war. When he saw the story about us in the Paris Herald Tribune, he hand-delivered it back to us at Maison Bleue.

*The Daisy Sisters* hangs once again in the library alongside paintings retrieved from the de Giocomte collection.

Which brings me back to this spring day when the ink is drying on our book contract as Ève and I hold hands and hug each other, my little daughters play in the garden, Maman and Madame de Giocomte are having tea and laughing together, and Arsène and Michal, calling themselves the luckiest men in the world, propose a toast to us.

Ève and me. The Daisy Sisters.

We fought.

We loved.

We won. And if there's one thing I learned during those war years, it's that the power of sisterhood endures through the toughest times. I was dealt a harsh blow during the war when I was raped, but I didn't accept what the Nazis did to me and then hide in shame. I kept fighting the Boches even though it meant losing my little sister to keep her safe.

It was the hardest thing I ever had to do.

If my story and Ève's can help another woman find her way back on the winding journey of fear, guilt, and build her life again after suffering rape and sexual assault, then we *have* found justice after all.

*Merci*, Ève, for being my sister.

*I love you.*

## ACKNOWLEDGEMENTS

I never dreamed when I set out to write about the Beaufort Sisters that it would take me on a two-book journey, with twists and turns along the way I never saw coming. Including having my Letter to the Editor about the sexual violence I experienced printed in *The New York Times*.

I can't tell you the validation I felt when I braved the heaviest rainstorm of the year here in California to hunt down print copies of the newspaper. Very exciting day for me.

If you've read *Sisters at War*, you know my personal story about rape and sexual violence. I shan't repeat the details here, but suffice to say, I've been on my own journey of self-awareness writing the story of Justine and Ève Beaufort, while exploring my own feelings and coming to grips with what happened to me. How it shaped my choices in life, led me around in circles at times until I finally reached the point when for the first time, I've been able to talk about it.

If you or someone you know has experienced sexual violence, there are resources to help you. You're not alone. Remember, we get courage from each other.

Bringing the story of Ève and Justine to you, my readers, was the next step. I am so lucky to have the most amazing team at Boldwood Books. I couldn't have made this journey without my fabulous editor, Isobel Akenhead. She became my champion for this story in *Sisters at War* and rallied around me with *Sisters of the Resistance* with dedication and insight into how to bring the story of the Beaufort Sisters to a resounding crescendo in Book Two. She not only brought her editorial knowledge and expertise, but she also put her heart and soul into this story. I shall be forever grateful to her for her belief in me.

I also want to thank Nia Beynon, Publishing/Sales & Marketing Director, who brought me into the Boldwood Books family and is always there for us authors. And CEO and Founder Amanda Ridout, who never fails to astonish me with her energy and innovation in publishing to make Boldwood Books an industry leader and winner of several book awards.

Thank you also to my copyeditor Jennifer Davies and my proofreader Shirley Khan for their help in making the story the best it can be.

And to you, my readers, who undertook this amazing journey of the Beaufort Sisters with me. We've had quite a time of it, haven't we? Exploring rape and sexual violence toward women isn't talked about enough and how it affects the victim and those she loves.

But we did it, and I thank you from the bottom of my heart.

# ABOUT THE AUTHOR

**Jina Bacarr** is a US-based historical romance author of over 10 previous books. She has been a screenwriter, journalist and news reporter, but now writes full-time and lives in LA. Jina's novels have been sold in 9 territories.

Sign up to Jina Bacarr's mailing list here for news, competitions and updates on future books.

Visit Jina's website: www.jinabacarr.wordpress.com

Follow Jina on social media here:

- facebook.com/JinaBacarr.author
- x.com/JinaBacarr
- instagram.com/jinabacarr
- bookbub.com/authors/jina-bacarr
- goodreads.com/jina_bacarr

## ALSO BY JINA BACARR

Her Lost Love

The Runaway Girl

The Resistance Girl

The Lost Girl In Paris

The Orphans of Berlin

**The Wartime Paris Sisters**

Sisters at War

Sisters of the Resistance

Printed in Great Britain
by Amazon

48008244R00215